CRY OF THE MARTYRS TRILOGY
Book Two

What ROUGH Beast

A Novel

Shawn J. Pollett

WHAT ROUGH BEAST

ISBN-13: 978-1-926676-69-2

Printed in Canada.

Published by Word Alive Press
131 Cordite Road, Winnipeg, MB R3W 1S1
www.wordalivepress.ca

WORD ALIVE PRESS
Just Write!

DEDICATION

For my parents, Wally and Eileen Pollett,
        who taught me about honour and respect
        even though I was too "cool"
        to listen . . .

For Donna Lee,
        who taught me how to love
        always and forever . . .

And for my sister Sheila,
who fed me onions . . .

ACKNOWLEDGEMENTS

I could not send this book to press without acknowledging at least *some* of the many people who made it possible. First and foremost I want to thank my friends Pastor Leon and Dana Van Dyke, who lent me an amazing computer on which to write *What Rough Beast*—23-inch monitors rule! Leon, whose historical interests complement my own, was an invaluable reader, whose suggestions and prayers helped keep me focussed and on schedule. Roger Gingras of the Lighthouse Bookstore in North Bay orchestrated my "baptism" into the public eye—many thanks, Roger. My buddy, Terry Terrell, helped me over a few rough patches—I can never thank you enough for that. Never surrender, Terry! Thanks as well to the Bakkers, the Haufes, and the Tuckers, who are good friends and good neighbours, and, of course, to the rest of the gang down at the Corner, who supported me with their prayers.

To everyone at Word Alive Press—Caroline, Jen, Jeremy, Warren, Evan—my editor—and anyone else I might have missed: many thanks for making the process so simple. You guys are the best!

Special thanks to all my readers, who inundated me with cards and e-mails and good wishes, and, of course, the persistent question: "When's the sequel to *Christianus Sum* going to be ready?" Thank you as well for identifying so readily with Damarra and Valens and wanting more of them. Who'd have thought that the third century A.D. had so much in common with our own!

Thank you to my wonderful children, Mackenzie and Faye, for their patience. They gave me the space I needed to write, and yet were always right there the moment Daddy realized he needed a hug! To my eldest child, Katie-Lee, who no longer lives at home but will always live in my heart, thank you for all the Facebook messages and the visits and the prayers. Treat her well, Caleb—living angels are rare indeed.

To my wife, Donna Lee . . . what can I say? You ran life so I could write, you brought me food and coffee and kisses (not always in that order!) when I needed them, and you kept me sane with your prayers and your love. I adore you; I thank God that you are in my life. This book is as much yours as it is mine, because without you it could never have been written . . .

Finally to the Warrior King who reigns over the ages, I humbly pledge fealty, honour, and obedience. I await your summons, My Lord.

The Roman Empire and Frontiers in the Mid-Third Century

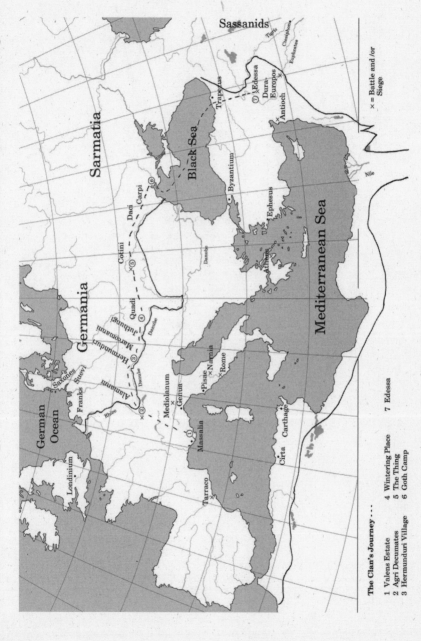

The Clan's Journey - - -

1 Valens Estate
2 Agri Decumates
3 Hermunduri Village

4 Wintering Place
5 The Thing
6 Goth Camp

7 Edessa

x = Battle and /or Siege

PART I
SLOUCHING TOWARD BETHLEHEM

"A bad peace is even worse than war."

TACITUS

"And what rough beast, its hour come round at last,
Slouches toward Bethlehem to be born?"

"THE SECOND COMING"
WILLIAM BUTLER YEATS

"Let us pray for the lapsed, that they may be raised up;
Let us pray for those who stand, that they may not be tempted."

EPISTLE. 30.6
CYPRIAN, BISHOP OF CARTHAGE
[WRITTEN A.D. 251, DURING THE PERSECUTION OF THE
EMPEROR DECIUS]

ONE

NARNIA, CENTRAL ITALY
SEPTEMBER A.D. 253

P erhaps it is his way of celebrating your impending reunion, my lord?" Tribune Marcus offered. The disgust in his voice was almost palpable.

"Perhaps," General Gallienus replied. He raised his fist, signalling a halt. They had been riding all day through the hill country south of Narnia, and as his bodyguard and the officers of his entourage surrounded him, the smell of horse sweat grew thick in his nostrils. But that smell could not mask the other stench stewing in the hot Italian sunshine. One of his officers held a linen handkerchief to his nose, gagging. A murmur ran through the company—incredulity, revulsion, and on every face, in every voice, outrage.

Agitated by the scent of decomposition, Gallienus' horse reared and neighed with fright. Gallienus checked the horse with his knees and stroked its powerful neck to calm it. His features were soft and boyish, with a hint of femininity, a defect for which he had long ago compensated by growing a short, black beard. He was thin, but endowed with a wiry musculature that enabled him to wield sword or javelin with effortless grace. His *lorica*, a breastplate shaped like a human torso, shone in the sunlight, thanks to the ministrations of his slave, but all the polishing in the world could not hide the scrapes and dents that pocked its surface. Still, battle scars looked better on metal than on human flesh.

Removing his red plumed helmet, he studied the source of the stench with his usual efficiency, assessing each detail before moving on to the next. His eyes were brown and had a depth that suggested there was always more going on behind them than he revealed. His mother had once called them 'thoughtful eyes.' "By which I mean you are a thinker," she had clarified. "And that is a good thing; but genuine thoughtfulness lies in putting the needs of others ahead of your own. That is true nobility, my son, and that is the Roman way. Never forget it."

Gallienus shooed away the image of his mother as she had been on that day, so young and beautiful, so full of life.

So sad.

His eyes moistened and he gave a wistful sigh. Here he was at the age of thirty-three, a Roman general, a veteran of three successful campaigns against the barbarians on the Rhine frontier, a man respected by his troops and feared by his enemies, and yet the ghost of a woman who had vanished from his life when he was eight years old could still reduce him to tears.

"I think I might know him, General," Marcus said hesitantly.

"How can you tell, Tribune Marcus? His face is . . . all but gone."

A crow settled on the shoulder of the man nailed to the cross and began to peck at the empty eye sockets. A cry of outrage rose from the company's throat, and an instant later an arrow whizzed over Gallienus' head and pierced the crow through its glossy, black chest. It dropped to the foot of the cross, landing in the pool of blood congealing there with a wet thud.

The man on the cross was stripped to the waist. His bloated torso was a maze of torn and blackened flesh from the scourging he had endured before his crucifixion, a scourging so severe that in places the ribs gleamed white through the deep red of extruded tissue. What remained of his face after his torturer's fists had finished their work had since been obliterated by putrefaction and the predation of the birds. He wore a *cingulum militare*, the Roman military belt from which dangled an apron of leather strips that protected the groin in battle and which marked him as a soldier.

"That is no way for a soldier to die," an angry voice rumbled behind Gallienus.

"And a waste, when we are beset by enemies," another responded.

Gallienus read the placard that hung around the crucified man's neck. The words written in blood on the whitened board were smeared but still legible:

CHRISTIANUS SUM

I am a Christian.

Tribune Marcus pointed at the placard. "It has begun again."

Gallienus glanced sidelong at his friend. Marcus Gaius Fortunatus had stood by his side through many battles, a stalwart comrade who feared neither warrior nor weapon, yet there was fear in his friend's voice now. He grasped Marcus' shoulder and squeezed it. "Not if I have anything to say about it," he promised.

Marcus bowed his head. "May the *Christos* bless you, my lord," he whispered.

THEY LEFT A DETAIL BEHIND to give the crucified soldier a decent burial, then continued northeast along the *Via Flaminia*, the main road between the city of Rome and the Adriatic Sea on Italy's east coast. Over the crest of the next hill they encountered another crucified soldier, and a little further on, another, and Gallienus realized that the burial duty he had assigned his men was pointless, and sent a rider back with orders to rejoin the company. For the next three miles they met a cross every hundred yards, each bearing a corpse in various stages of decomposition.

All of them soldiers.

Gallienus glanced at his companions. They were stiff and tense, their knuckles white as they gripped the reins too hard, faces sombre, eyes furrowed and staring into the distance to avoid looking at the tortured remains of former comrades. Gallienus felt their anger, felt it in himself. Whatever these soldiers had done, they did not deserve such a death. It was unseemly for a Roman soldier to die by crucifixion. Behead them if their crime was so great, and leave it at that.

He scoffed. Their crime was obvious: each corpse wore a placard around the neck, and each placard told the same story: *Christianus Sum*.

I am a Christian.

And was that a crime worthy of death? Sometimes it was and sometimes—he glanced at his friend Marcus riding beside him, his lips moving in silent prayer to his God—sometimes it was not. He had not made up his mind yet, but the man who had ordered these crucifixions, he *had* made up his mind. Many years ago. And he had never wavered in his hatred of the Christians.

And what other reason did Gallienus need to believe the opposite?

He chided himself for being childish. Christianity was illegal—that was official Roman policy. And he could not oppose a policy just because one man favoured it and pursued it with such passion.

"General Gallienus," Marcus called out, rousing Gallienus from his dark broodings. Gallienus reined in his horse and the tribune stopped beside him. He was perhaps three years younger than Gallienus, the descendant of a Roman noble family that traced its lineage back to Aeneas, who, according to legend, had escaped the fall of Troy with his aged father on his shoulders, only to reap vengeance upon the Greeks by founding what was later to become the same Roman Empire that marched into Greece and made her just another Roman province. Gallienus grunted. Every great Roman family traced its lineage back to Aeneas, of course. The joke amongst the common people of Rome was that Aeneas must have been a very busy fellow indeed to have sired so many illustrious descendants. But Marcus did have an aristocratic bearing to support his claim—a strong chin, shortly-cropped brown hair with brown eyes to match, an aquiline nose that reminded Gallienus of his father, although Marcus' nose was not as large or as curved, and an impressive physique, not overlarge, but muscular. Like Gallienus, he wore the officer's *lorica*, attached to back plates by hinges under the arms, and a red military cape affixed to the shoulders. Gallienus looked at Marcus, whose thin, face had blanched whiter than old bones. The tribune flicked his head at the far side of the cobbled road and Gallienus turned. Another cross, another soldier, another Christian—but this man was still alive.

The man on the cross groaned. His breath came in short, hot gasps as he fought to push himself up on the foot piece nailed into the cross and take the pressure off his lungs. Blood bubbled between his lips.

Alive, but not for long.

"Break his legs," Gallienus ordered.

Marcus nodded and wheeled the horse around. A few moments later a large soldier with a club hurried up to the cross. Two mighty swings and both legs were broken. The crucified soldier slumped down, stopped breathing. A minute later his head dropped to his chest. Dead.

No more crosses greeted them as they continued down the *Via Flaminia*. Workers dressed in rough tunics moved amongst the vines that bordered the road, picking ripe grapes for the wine presses. Here and there gnarled, old olive trees drooped in the hot sunlight, bowing their heavy heads like respectful spectators watching a triumphal procession. Another mile and the River Nar, from which the city of Narnia took its name, curved in beside the road running shallow and slow, as silent as the river Styx, before winding off again to water some hidden valley far below. At last they topped the final crest of the road, and Gallienus ordered the company to halt.

Marcus reined in his horse beside him. "Four, maybe five legions," he said, pointing to the valley below them.

Gallienus nodded agreement. "At least," he said.

The sun was westering behind them, and the shadow of its setting was creeping up the valley wall on the far side, reaching for the city of Narnia squatting on the next hilltop, its white marble and granite buildings reflecting the sun's orange fire. The valley below lay in shadow. Cooking fires and watch fires dotted the valley floor, shining like the eyes of a thousand hungry predators waiting in the darkness. A large Roman camp had been erected. Even though it was temporary, it was surrounded by a palisade of tall logs, and beyond, earthen ramparts and a wide moat, all to protect the encampment from enemy attack. But there was no enemy; one army occupied the valley.

Marcus had made the same observation. "Where is Aemilianus?" he asked.

Gallienus shrugged.

"The messenger said Aemilianus had arrived at the head of an army."

"Perhaps he and the governor have worked out their differences," Gallienus suggested. But he did not believe it. Where *was* Aemilianus? "Come," he said, signalling the company forward. He dug his heels into his horse's flanks and the horse trotted on. "We should not keep the governor waiting."

THEY FOLLOWED THE *VIA FLAMINIA* down into the darkness that engulfed the camp. Two men, dressed in the banded armour plates of the common soldier, met them at a makeshift drawbridge, three planks laid side by side across the moat that could be retracted when the enemy appeared. They crossed over and the soldiers passed them through the palisade's gate with a salute. Inside the walls, Gallienus and his company dismounted and their horses were led away to be fed and watered. A young tribune appeared from the row of tents to their left and greeted the company. His face was clean shaven and innocent—he looked untried as a soldier, much too young to be an officer. Another senatorial brat whose father's money had paved his way up the ladder of success, Gallienus thought with distaste. The tribune raised his fist in salute. "Follow me, General Gallienus; the emperor awaits."

Gallienus turned to Marcus. "See that our tents are set up." He glanced around the encampment—there did not seem to be much room. In fact, it was over-full, far surpassing regulations. "Better yet, set up camp above and await further instruction."

With a nod, Marcus withdrew to carry out his orders. Always efficient Marcus—how would Gallienus ever survive without him? "Lead on," Gallienus told the young officer.

They marched down the row of tents to the centre of the camp. Soldiers crouched beside small fires, cooking supper. A group of soldiers, wearing nothing but tunics, kneeled in a circle, playing dice. Every man he passed glanced his way; every eye was upon him. One soldier, sitting on a low stool outside his tent and sharpening his sword, stared at him so long that Gallienus barked, "Mind your business, soldier, or I'll make your business mine!"

The soldier dropped his eyes and attacked his task with renewed vigour.

Finally Gallienus and his escort arrived at a large tent. To one side of the entrance two of the emperor's standards—tall metal rods surmounted by the imperial eagle, with the name "Aemilianus" visible beneath it—were stuck into the earth. They leaned over haphazardly. Sloppy work—the emperor would not be pleased to see his standards displayed with such obvious disregard. Two guards stood on either side of the entrance, hard looking men with dark eyes and darker scowls, holding their javelins straight. Gallienus' gaze fell upon the emblem at the centre of their breastplates—a stylized cobra, coiled to strike, the eyes catching the light of a nearby campfire and glinting red in the gloom. He recognized the symbol—the governor's bodyguard. Perhaps the governor and Emperor Aemilianus had put aside their differences after all?

Inside the tent, the gloom was thicker, despite the coals burning in twin braziers. Grey tendrils of smoke swirled overhead and seeped from a chimney hole at the tent's peak. A large table dominated the room. On its surface was a map, a stack of parchment, and a pyramid of scrolls. The tent was divided into two rooms by thick curtains that ran from side to side. Light gleamed through a split in the curtains that served as the entrance to the second room. This room was empty.

Gallienus approached the table to study the map. Daggers set on its edges kept it unfurled. The map was a detailed depiction of the Roman Empire, divided into provinces and showing geographical features such as rivers, lakes, and mountains. The main ports, capitals, and most important cities of each province were also marked. A long, slender dagger protruded from the middle of the map, dividing the empire into west and east.

The curtain swirled open and a man entered the room. He wore a silk toga with a scarlet stripe along its hem and a circlet of golden olive leaves on his head. He was tall and gaunt, with short black hair salted with grey and a long nose that curved over his top lip like the beak of a bird of prey. Dark brown eyes as hard as slate studied Gallienus in the gloom, and then recognition sparked in them and his sallow face spread into a thin smile. Or was it a sneer? So many years had passed since their last meeting that Gallienus could not decide. But then, this man's expressions—and emotions—had always been inscrutable to him. He was and always would be a familiar stranger.

"General, you have arrived at last." He held out his arms, mockingly, Gallienus thought. They embraced, then Gallienus stepped back. "How long has it been, General?" he asked.

"Twenty years."

"That long?

"Yes, Governor. That long."

"Well, you have never been far from my thoughts. I have followed your career closely."

"And I, yours." And that was pleasantry enough for Gallienus. "You summoned me and I am here; my officers and bodyguard will soon be encamped above. And now I am told that the emperor wishes to see me?"

The man's smile spread, and yes, it was a sneer. "Ah, my boy, do you have no kind words for your father?"

"What would you have me say, my lord? I am pleased to see you? I missed you? We are both military men, who must be about the business of empire—we have no time for lies and half-truths."

He laughed. "Well said, General Gallienus. There will be time later to . . . reminisce. And make plans." He cleared his throat. "You wish to see Aemilianus?"

Gallienus nodded.

"Then come," he said, pulling back the curtain.

The tent's second room was smaller than the first. A single candle guttered in a tall stand, providing the only light. Most of the room lay in flickering shadow. He could distinguish the outline of a dining couch pushed up against one wall and a cot for sleeping against another. In the corner nearest the candle was an elaborate altar of stone and wood, engraved with images of the gods. A dead animal sprawled on its polished surface—a goat, Gallienus thought, or a lamb; there was insufficient light to tell. The coppery smell of blood was strong, but not as pungent as the hot reek of the animal's entrails. Loops of intestines draped from the gaping wound in the animal's belly and spilled out over the altar, onto the ground. Beside the head, the organs were laid out in a neat row—heart, liver, kidneys, lungs. The augurs had attempted to divine the future, then. Or perhaps his father had performed the sacrifice and augury himself? He had always been a passionate student of the divine. At the family estate in Etruria in Central Italy, where Gallienus had grown up, his father had compiled a vast library of esoterica to assist him in his researches, books of spells, curses, and divinations, the rarest and most arcane texts collected from the farthest reaches of the empire and beyond, with one goal in mind: the mastery of the sacred rites and ceremonies that would win the favour of the gods. During the reign of the Emperor Decius, he had served as the empire's high priest. In fact, rumour had it that he was the architect behind Decius' religious policy. Knowing his father as he did, the rumours were likely true.

Emperor Aemilianus was nowhere in sight.

"Where is he?" Gallienus asked.

"Shh . . . perhaps he is sleeping. He has had a most difficult day." He put his hands on either side of his mouth and called in a whisper, "Aemilianus?"

No response.

"Aemilianus . . . my son is here to see the emperor?"

Again, no response. The silence stretched out, entwining with the gloom and thickening it. A spectral hand crawled up Gallienus neck. Something was wrong.

His father grinned. "Let me bring him to you." He stepped into the shadows at the back of the tent, calling Aemilianus' name, then re-emerged carrying an imperial standard like those outside the tent.

Only at the top of this standard was a human head.

Gallienus did not recognize the face—the eyes had been gouged out and the ears sliced off—but he knew who it was and what had happened, as he should have known when he looked down into the valley below Narnia and saw one army encamped there instead of two. His father would never have forgiven Aemilianus for arresting him when Aemilianus had first arrived at Rome on behalf of Emperor Gallus. Gallienus doubted he even

11

had the capacity to forgive.

"Emperor Aemilianus!" Gallienus whispered the name as if it were sacred.

"Emperor no more," his father spat. "As he deserves." He raised the standard high and plunged it into the earth. The head tilted, and Gallienus reached out for it reflexively, but it did not fall. Its mouth hung open in a silent scream. And then the full ramification of Aemilianus' death struck home like a thunderbolt, and Gallienus' mouth fell open in shock.

"Then *you—*"

His father's head bowed in mock humility. "Yes, I am. And once we return to Rome at the head of *our* army, the senate will have no choice but to ratify what my legions have already declared. So begins the glorious reign of Valerianus Augustus," he clasped his son's shoulders, "*and* Gallienus Augustus."

Gallienus touched his breastplate, scarcely able to believe what he was hearing. "Me? Emperor?"

"Yes, you. Like Decius and Herennius three years ago, there shall be two emperors, father and son, ruling together. Except where Decius and his son failed, we shall not." His father's laughter rumbled like thunder in the gloom. "We shall re-create the Roman Empire in our image, and together, when we have earned the favour of the gods by crushing all who oppose us, the emperors Valerianus and Gallienus shall usher in a new golden age, and forge a dynasty of iron that shall last ten thousand years."

TWO

"More have come, my lady."

Damarra Valensia set her spindle down on the stone bench beside her with a sigh. "How many?" she asked and shivered. A cool breeze was riding down from the north, where the first snows of winter would soon cover the land. But not here at their villa in Gallia Narbonensis near the city of Massalia. Here, where the warm Mediterranean whispered that the cold lands of the north were just a myth, the only thing that *remotely* resembled snow was Damarra's hair. She touched the light blond locks which tumbled down to the middle of her back in long ringlets, remembering how two years ago she had cut it and dyed it black. Again she shivered, but not from the cool this time. She hated thinking about those days, when the world had descended into madness and she and her husband had almost died, but the pilgrims kept coming, driven here by their needs and their fears, and so she could never forget. And Valens said they never *should* forget. That it would be madness to forget.

"Just fifteen this time, my lady. But I think you should rest."

Damarra smiled up at the slave, a recent addition that Valens had made to the household staff. She was in her forties, plump with dimpled elbows and dimpled cheeks, and a bow mouth that made her look like she was frowning, even when she was not, but it was for her skills, not her appearance, that Valens had purchased her. "She must stay near you at all times. At *all* times—do you understand?" he had told her last week, when he had brought the new slave home from the slave market in Massalia.

"Oh, don't fret so, Prisca," she said. She held her hand up. Prisca hesitated, then took the offered hand and helped Damarra to her feet. Steadying herself, she nodded at Prisca who released her slowly, as if she thought Damarra might topple over without her assistance. Damarra caressed her swollen abdomen and the excitement made her shiver again. Soon, no more than a month from now, she and Valens would have their first baby. She prayed for Valens' sake that it was a boy, to carry on the family name, but in her heart of hearts she wanted a little girl. She patted her abdomen, which seemed impossibly large, even for a woman eight months pregnant, because her frame was otherwise so petite. Of course, she would love the child no matter *what* it was. And so would Valens. If he managed to survive the pregnancy.

"The master will not be pleased," Prisca said.

"You're right." Damarra smiled up at the taller woman. Her face was delicate, like a fine piece of glass shaped by some ethereal craftsman, and it glowed with health and vitality and a beauty that one local sculptor had copied for a statue of the goddess of love, Aphrodite, which now stood in the Temple of Aphrodite in nearby Massalia, much to Damarra's chagrin. "Which is why we will not tell him," she added.

Prisca looked horrified. "But, my lady," she protested. "I cannot keep anything from the master. My task is to—"

"Yes, yes. Very well. I shall make a bargain with you, dear Prisca: if you accompany me to the gate, I promise to return and rest."

The smile returned to Prisca's plump face. "Really? You promise?"

"You have my solemn word."

"And you will come when I say it is time?"

"Yes."

Prisca sighed, then offered Damarra her arm. "On your honour, my lady."

Damarra walked down the laneway, listening to Prisca's happy chatter and enjoying the warm sunshine as the sun dipped into an evening sky that was a cloudless blue. The north wind had changed into a gentle breeze from the south, and Damarra inhaled the salt scent the breeze carried up from the sea. In the distance, not half a mile away, the Mediterranean glimmered a light blue that matched Damarra's eyes. Gulls played in the surf and over the fields of golden wheat that rolled down to the shore, their calls so familiar now that she scarcely heard them anymore. On either side of the laneway, rows of vines laden with deep purple grapes stretched away into the horizon. Slaves and local freedmen hired by Valens for the harvest were already at work, under the watchful eyes of Valens' foreman, Sukuta, a huge Ethiopian with coal black skin that glistened in the sunlight. Sukuta spotted the mistress and handed his tablet to a nearby slave, then jogged over to the laneway. "Good evening, my lady."

"Good evening, Sukuta."

"Is there something my lady needs? Something that brings you from the cool of the villa today?"

Damarra frowned. "Et tu, Sukuta?"

The big man laughed, and several of the slaves working amongst the vines paused to look. People always stopped to look when Sukuta laughed. It was such a big laugh, almost as big as the man himself. Damarra loved to hear it. "'You too, Sukuta.' Very good, my lady," he was finally able to say. "I believe the last person who said those words was Julius Caesar on the Ides of March. But he was talking to Brutus, who held a knife in his hand." Sukuta bowed. "I hold no knife, my lady; simply the sharp edge of my concern for your welfare."

Now it was Damarra's turn to laugh. Sukuta was Valens' right hand man for the Massalia estates, five other vineyards surrounding the city like a necklace of green and purple aside from this one, where they lived. Valens' father had purchased Sukuta as a boy and groomed him for the position he now held, which included a basic education—reading, writing, and numbers. But even after he had completed his training, he had continued to read anything he could get his hands on, which, in the house of Valens, whose library rivalled the libraries of many a city, was an impressive accomplishment. "Did Valens tell even you to keep an eye on me?"

Sukuta grinned. His teeth were very white. "I believe every worker on the estate has been given those instructions, my lady. And the surrounding estates. And the stevedores down at port and the gladiators in the arena and every fishwife, barmaid, and hawker."

Damarra laughed again. Even Prisca tittered into her plump hand. "I'm simply walking to the front gate to meet with some visitors, and then I shall return to the villa," she glanced at Prisca, "for a rest."

Sukuta turned toward the gate, one large hand shading his eyes. He shook his head. "I do not understand these Christians," he muttered. He glanced down at Damarra. "Forgive me, my lady."

Damarra smiled at him. "Not to worry, Sukuta. We Christians have very thick skin."

Damarra said farewell and continued along the gravelled laneway. Here, closer to the road, the lane was bordered on both sides by olive trees. Up ahead, she saw a group of men and women milling about on the green swatch beside the road. One of them, a young man in his early twenties with brown hair and beard, spotted her and pointed. "The confessor comes," he exclaimed. By the time she arrived at the wooden gate, the pilgrims were standing in a tight knot on the road. All but one, a tall man with long blond hair that had been tied into a knot at the top of his head. His shoulders were broad and heavily muscled, and he wore chainmail and breeches instead of a tunic. He stood apart from the others, chewing on a piece of grass, a bemused expression on his bearded face.

Prisca opened the gate and Damarra walked through. Her back was aching now; the baby was sitting so low that her walk was really a waddle. She loved being pregnant, but sometimes—

The pilgrims swarmed her, tears on every face, calling her name, touching her *stola*, begging for her blessing. A large, oval-faced woman dressed in a rough, brown tunic dropped to her knees before Damarra and began kissing her feet. "Please," Damarra said, trying to bend over and help the woman up, but her swollen abdomen got in the way. She nodded at Prisca, who grabbed the woman under her arms and dragged her up.

"Please," Damarra said again, only louder. "I will speak to each of you."

The faces surrounding her transfigured from anguish to joy. As one the group stepped back, allowing Damarra to breath and compose herself. In the sudden quiet she heard the distant sound of hoof beats and glanced down the road. A cloud of dust billowed on the horizon. Time was short.

"You have come a long way?" she asked the group.

The young bearded man shouted out. "Antoninus from Rome, Most Holy Confessor."

"Londinium," the oval-faced woman said.

And the others responded in turn: Athens, Arelatum, Edessa. Only the tall, blond warrior standing apart from the others said nothing. They had come from all over the empire and beyond to see her; yet it was not she they really wanted to see and touch. But she would do.

"Do you have food and drink?" Damarra asked.

"We care not for sustenance, unless it be sustenance for the soul," said a tall, gangly man in his late fifties. His grey eyes were wet with tears.

"And forgiveness," another added.

Damarra smiled at the man's eloquence; he sounded well-educated. A tutor perhaps, from his bearing. She glanced down the road. The horseman was closer, visible as a sharp, vertical line on the horizon. The others began their clamour again, moving in toward her, but she raised her hands and they retreated.

The gangly man in his fifties pulled a piece of parchment from his cloak and held it up. "My name is Cleon, Most Holy Confessor. I have written a Certificate of Peace already; all you need do is sign it."

"I cannot simply sign your certificate, Cleon," Damarra said. "You must tell me your story first." She turned to the others. "You must all tell me your stories."

Cleon returned the parchment to his cloak, nodding.

The young bearded man stepped forward. "I was weak, Most Holy Confessor," he blurted out, and his tears were a swollen river on his cheeks. "I admit it before you all. I was weak, but when I went to Novatianus, he turned me away."

Damarra's sea-blue eyes closed. Novatianus. Of course, it would be him. The young man had said he was from Rome. But now the horseman was merely a few hundred yards away, and she heard her name drift through the clear air, and she knew that time had run out. The group turned and gasped as one.

"It's him," the bearded man whispered, awe in his voice.

The others began to clamour, and as the horse, a proud, chestnut mare named Lucia, pulled to a stop beside Damarra, they fell to their knees and began to weep and throw road dust on their heads. Even the young warrior bowed his head in reverence. A hand shot up to touch the rider's foot, but he nudged it aside. "Damarra," he said, and in that single word was a world of exasperation. "Why are you not *resting*?"

He furrowed his eyebrows at Prisca, who dropped her head and began to babble about evening walks and naps until the rider raised a finger, silencing her.

Damarra smiled up at her husband. "It's such a beautiful day, Valens. The perfect day for a walk. And exercise is good for pregnant women, isn't that right, Prisca?"

Prisca nodded. Damarra could see the terror in her eyes and touched her hand to calm her. Damarra held the smile on her shining face until Valens began to laugh. She loved to hear him laugh. When they had first met, when he was a senator and she was just a frightened slave girl, he had rarely laughed. After the death of his wife and child, he had forgotten how. Sometimes in the night, when they lay together in their bed before sleep claimed them, he whispered that learning how to laugh again was one of the greatest gifts she had given him. But these days, as her stomach swelled and the day she would deliver grew closer, he laughed less, frowned more.

Valens jumped down from the horse, and the pilgrims began to crawl forward on their knees. He ignored them as he took Damarra into his arms. He was a handsome man, with a sculpted jaw and jet black hair above light brown eyes. Now that he had retired from public life he wore his curly hair over his ears, and there was a hint of a beard on his strong chin. But aside from Damarra, whose heart still trembled every time she looked into his brown eyes, people rarely noticed his looks anymore. Their attention most often focussed on the puckered scars at the top of both wrists, just beneath the flat of the hand. Especially when those people were Christians, like she and Valens were. He lifted her up onto the horse, then jumped up behind her. Cleon got up off his knees and approached the horse, staring at the scar with reverence shining in his eyes and murmuring, "Mark of the *Christos*," over and over. With trembling hands, he swept up Valens' hand and he kissed it, then held the mark to his forehead.

After a moment, Valens pulled his hand from Cleon's grasp and turned to Prisca. "You follow on foot, Prisca; I'm taking Damarra back to the house."

Prisca nodded.

"But Valens," Damarra exclaimed. "They have come from such a long way."

Valens eyes lighted on the German warrior, who nodded in response, then swept over the kneeling group. Even Cleon was on his knees again. He kissed Damarra's cheek. "Do not worry, my love. I will deal with them for you later," he said and nudged the horse forward.

THE HORSE MOVED UP THE LANE at a gentle walk, slow enough for Prisca to follow without falling behind. Valens didn't think riding a horse was a good idea for a woman in Damarra's condition, but it was better than walking all the way back to the villa. She had walked enough for today. More than enough.

They came to a cluster of workmen carrying bags of ripe grapes to a wagon for transportation to the wine presses in one of the villa's outbuildings, finishing work for another day. Valens caught Sukuta's eye and pointed at Damarra. Sukuta shrugged and grinned.

"I'm not an invalid, Valens," Damarra complained. "I'm just pregnant."

Valens drew her closer and kissed the top of her head. "You shouldn't wear yourself out with unnecessary exercise," Valens replied, and glared at Prisca.

Damarra caught the look and slapped her husband's hand. "And don't take it out on Prisca. It's not her fault. She tried to talk me out of going."

"Then why didn't you listen to her?" Valens sighed. "According to the merchant from whom I purchased her, Prisca is perhaps the finest midwife north of the Alps." Valens turned to Prisca. "How many babies have you delivered, Prisca?"

"One hundred and seven, my lord."

"You see," he said to Damarra. He touched her abdomen. "And in here is one hundred and eight, if you will just listen to her."

Damarra nestled into his shoulder, and he felt a surge of love for her that brought tears to his eyes. "And some day, one hundred and nine," Damarra said. "And one hundred and ten, and one hundred and eleven. I want to take Prisca's tally all the way to one hundred twenty."

Valens laughed at that. "Thirteen children? The name of Valens will conquer the world with that many children to carry it forward."

They arrived back at the front of the villa, to the stone bench where Damarra had been sitting with her spindle and wool. They passed through the open front gate into a large courtyard paved with cobblestones. In the courtyard's centre was a fountain that sprayed a gentle arc of water into a round pool. To the left were the stables, to the right a row of workshops, most of which were already closed up for the day. In front of one open doorway, a young woman in a white tunic sat before a loom, humming as her fingers shot the shuttle back and forth. Valens dismounted and carefully lifted his wife from the horse's back. A groom arrived and took the reins from Valens' hand. "The leg still seems weak, Cecht," he said to the groom, a young blond boy of ten. His father, Conall, was Valens' *Magister Equitum*, his Master of Horses. The horses bred in this estate, and on several of the other estates around Massalia, were considered some of the best in Gaul, if not the entire empire.

"I shall tend to it, my lord."

"And prepare another horse for me; I shall ride out again once I have seen to my wife."

The boy bowed and led the horse off to the stables.

Valens turned to take Damarra's hand, but she was gone. His

eyes flicked about the courtyard until he spotted her over by the loom. The young woman working there was laughing, sharing some joke with her mistress. And where else would his wife be? Damarra had once been a slave herself, and had spent many happy years at the loom before her master, Valerianus, saw how beautiful she was. He shivered at the thought of Valerianus, feeling once again the familiar throb in his wrists. Lifting his hands, he studied the scars, "the marks of the *Christos*," the *lapsi* had called them. Even now, two years after that fateful day, when Valerianus had attempted to crucify him like their Lord had been crucified, his wrists still ached at times. It was the *Christos* who had saved him, given him this blessed reprieve, by permitting Aemilianus to arrive at just the right moment and put an end to Valerianus' wickedness.

But it seemed the wickedness had not ended after all.

Valens had risen early that morning, leaving Damarra sleeping peacefully in their bed, and taken Lucia for a ride. He had told Cecht it was to check Lucia's leg, but that had been only part of the truth. He had ridden to the forum in Massalia for the news, as he did several mornings each week. The news from Italy had been bad lately, but this morning it was even worse—plague had broken out again in Rome, civil war and unrest, and on every tongue one name kept rising like a Phoenix from the ashes.

Valerianus.

He had been surprised when that name resurfaced a year and a half ago, especially after seeing Valerianus' bodyguard cut to pieces and Valerianus himself placed under house arrest. Surprised, but not worried. Not with Emperor Gallus on the throne. But now he felt the ethereal fingers of fear stroking his gut. Somehow Valerianus had not just survived, he had *prospered*, and now that name hung over their household like a storm cloud, and the only question remaining was, would that storm blow over, or would it crash upon them and drag them down into the maelstrom once again?

He glanced at his wife. She was still talking to the young woman at the loom, Persephone was her name. As he watched, Damarra lifted Persephone's hand and placed it on her abdomen. Persephone's eyes widened and she laughed. "He is strong, my lady. What a kicker!"

"Or she is strong," Damarra corrected.

Persephone laughed again. She was very pretty, especially when she laughed. Her hair was brown, as were her eyes, and her complexion was olive and flawless. She was Damarra's handmaid, both slave and friend to his wife. Her duties had lightened now that Prisca was here to watch over Damarra, but the two of them still spent time together daily; both women were in their early twenties and they enjoyed one another's company.

Valens smiled, in spite of the worry nibbling at his heart. Damarra looked so happy, so radiant. He decided then and there that he would not ruin the day by mentioning the bad news from Italy. Besides, nothing was certain yet. Nothing ever seemed certain these days. If there were one god other than the *Christos* that Valens thought it reasonable to believe in, it was Chaos. Sometimes it seemed that Chaos was the true god of this world. The only god.

Forgive me, Christos.

He went to his wife's side and took her hand. She smiled up at him. "Persephone says there is a meeting tonight at the Manlius estate." Damarra looked at him hopefully.

Marcus Manlius was a local landowner and amateur philosopher who indulged his wife's devotion to the *Christos*. "Persephone, please take our greetings to the brothers and sisters. Damarra will be resting tonight."

"Yes, my lord."

"But, Valens!" Damarra exclaimed.

Valens raised a finger, and Damarra rolled her eyes. She turned to Persephone. "Damarra will be resting tonight," she said.

Persephone's brown eyes twinkled. "Yes, my lady."

Damarra took her husband's hand. "Come," she said, and began tugging him toward the pillared porch that fronted the villa. "Damarra needs to rest."

Valens followed, smirking at the way his wife waddled up the steps into the portico's cool shade. "Damarra, my dear, you walk like a duck."

She spun on him, mouth hanging open in disbelief. "Julius Valens Licinianus!" she exclaimed. "How dare you say that!"

Laughing, he swept Damarra into his arms. She struggled against him for a moment, then gave up and rested her head on his shoulder. He lifted her chin and kissed the tip of her nose. "Like a very beautiful duck," he added.

She draped her arms around his neck and pulled his lips towards hers. At the last moment she nipped his nose with her teeth. Valens jumped back, startled. "Quack, quack," she said, and raced into the villa as fast as she could go—which was not very fast at all—giggling as she ran.

Laughing again, he counted to three, then darted after her.

HALF AN HOUR LATER, as the long, slow Mediterranean dusk was filling the sky with strokes of orange and red and yellow, Valens exited the villa. Cecht was waiting with a new horse. He told the boy to wait for him (he did not expect to be gone long), then mounted the grey stallion and rode out of the courtyard. The trip to the front gate took a few moments. They were still waiting for him there, still on their knees, and as he came to a stop and dismounted they all looked up at him expectantly. "What is it you want?" he asked the group.

A tall, thin, grey-haired man spoke. "Most Holy Confessor," he began. "I am Cleon, and I speak for all of us."

"My wife cannot be disturbed; she is, as you saw, very pregnant and needs her rest."

"But we came to see you, Confessor. We seek absolution—"

"You will get none from me," Valens snapped. "I have no absolution for you; there *is* no absolution for you. You are *lapsi*, and I want you gone from my home."

The men and women kneeling before him got up slowly, dejectedly. They gazed at one another, every face showing the same fear, then looked at Valens. "But Holy Confessor," Cleon said. He pointed at the scars on Valens' wrists. "You have the marks of the *Christos*?"

"Earned," Valens said. "But what did you earn, Cleon?" He looked at the others. "What did any of you *lapsi* earn?"

"We seek—"

"Begone!" Valens demanded, and in his voice was a firmness

that would brook no defiance.

As one the crowd drew back a step.

"Seek forgiveness elsewhere. Try the *episcopus* down in Arelatum—I hear he is in the forgiving mood. But do not bother stopping in Massalia; the *episcopus* there is in agreement with me and Novatianus in Rome."

With that they turned and began to trudge down the road into the gathering dusk. "And tell your brothers and sisters to stay away, *lapsi*," he called after them. Many of them had sought them out in the last few weeks, once news got out that they had settled in the area. It was his fault rather than Damarra's. He was the one who went so often into Massalia, and it was the Christians there who had spotted the marks on his wrists and found out who he was. But this was too much. Walking out here in her condition, just to talk to this rabble, these *lapsi*. No more! He would see to that. Starting tomorrow he would post a guard at the gate and shoo them away before Damarra even knew that they were here.

"What is *lapsi*?" a voice in the gathering gloom asked.

Valens turned. The German he had nodded at earlier was still there. "And what do you want?" Valens asked.

The German stepped toward him and bowed his head. "What is *lapsi*?" he asked again. His Latin was broken and slurred. The German was obviously uncomfortable with the language.

"The *lapsi* are cowards. They were Christians who sacrificed to the gods during the persecution, or bought a forged *libellus*, a certificate of sacrifice, so that they could pretend they sacrificed to avoid punishment and death. They feared to stand for the *Christos*. They are beyond forgiveness." Valens looked the German up and down. "And are you one of the *lapsi*?"

The German struck his mailed chest. "I no *lapsi*," he said proudly. "I Gundabar of the Suevi and I no *lapsi*."

"Then what do you want?" he asked again.

Gundabar bowed his blond head. "I join you *sippe*."

"My *sippe*?"

The German warrior grinned at Valens' butchered pronunciation of the word. "Yes . . . uh . . . clan . . ."

"My family, you mean?"

The German smiled again. He was very handsome when he

smiled, despite the road grime smeared on his face. "You Chief; we make war band; we gather; we go," he struggled for the right words, "*witan* . . . uh . . . *thing* . . . *mot*."

Valens had not heard the word *thing* before, but *witan* and *mot* were familiar terms. "A *witan* is an assembly of warriors under a chief. You want me to form a . . . council?"

The German shook his blond head. "No, we go *thing, witan*, err . . . *a-zem-bly*." This time it was Valens' turn to smile over Gundabar's pronunciation, but the German did not seem to mind. He continued: "We make war band, we go *a-zem-bly*. You Chief."

Valens paused for a moment. It was odd enough that a Suevi warrior had left his homeland in the north to journey to Southern Gaul in the first place, but that he had come to make Julius Valens his chief? A proud German warrior offering to serve a Roman? "Why me?" he asked.

"God," he replied.

"Your god sent you . . . to me?"

The German nodded. "*Christos*," he exclaimed and smiled.

Valerianus started in surprise. The man was a Christian! He glanced up at the clouds rolling in from the Mediterranean in the twilight sky, extinguishing the stars one by one, then turned his horse back toward the villa. "Well then, you'd best come with me, Warrior," he said.

THREE

Gallienus and Valerianus sat in silence on either side of the map table. Slaves had brought food and wine and torches to chase back the gloom. Valerianus held a golden chalice as his gaze roamed over the map, but Gallienus' cup remained untouched. He needed to think, to sort out the amazing and convoluted chain of events that had brought his father—and him—to the imperial throne. And Valerianus seemed to recognize that necessity; he had not said a word since ordering Dionysius, the hulking commander of Valerianus' personal bodyguard, to give Aemilianus' head to the soldiers, "for their amusement." The sound of their taunts and jeers burned in his ears.

At last he sighed and looked at his father. "So, I arrived too late for the battle?"

"There *was* no battle." He selected an olive from the platter on the table and popped it into his mouth.

"No battle. But how?"

"I fear he suffered the same fate as Emperor Gallus."

Gallienus nodded. Kniva, the King of the Goths, had invaded the empire again last spring, asserting that Gallus had failed to pay the annual tribute promised him in the agreement he and Gallus had struck after the death of Decius at the Battle of Abrittus. But this time the God-With-The-Blood-In-His-Fists, the God Kniva claimed had secured his victory at Abrittus, had not favoured the

Goths. Kniva had suffered a major defeat at the hands of Aemilianus and scurried home with his tail between his legs, and the
Moesian legions, still smarting from the dishonourable treaty Gallus had concluded with Kniva, a treaty which in addition to the
tribute had permitted the Goths to return to their homeland beyond the Danube *with* the booty they had pillaged from the empire, had declared their victorious general, Aemilianus, emperor.
Aemilianus and his legions had then marched on Italy and, despite inferior numbers, defeated Gallus at Interamna Nahars in
Central Italy. Hoping to meet up with Valerianus, who was hurrying to Italy to reinforce Gallus, Gallus had fled north, only to be
cut down by his own bodyguard, who then delivered his remains
to their new emperor, Aemilianus, a betrayal for which they had
been handsomely rewarded.

Gallienus' sigh was weary. "So Aemilianus was murdered by
his own men, as Gallus was?"

"Yes. When I arrived, his soldiers brought Aemilianus' head
to me on one of his own standards. They opened up the gates and
let us in." Valerianus grinned. "And now Aemilianus' legions belong to me."

For now, Gallienus thought, and a strange sense of foreboding
suddenly left him feeling hollow inside. Three months before,
some of the soldiers who were now spitting curses at the head of
Aemilianus in the darkness outside had declared him emperor;
and two years before that some of those same men had stood by
the bloodied waters of Abrittus and raised Trebonianus Gallus to
the imperial purple. Now they had declared his father emperor,
and would soon do the same for him, if Valerianus had his way.

And who would be next? What general awaited his turn,
ready to offer an extra acre of land, a few more sesterces, a larger
share of the booty, ready to purchase the hearts of a mercenary
soldiery at any cost and win the honour of desecrating the severed
heads of the great emperors Valerianus and Gallienus?

No. There must be a way to stop the cycle, once and for always. The power to choose emperors *must* be removed from the
legions and their senatorial commanders. But who should choose?
The senate? The people? The gods? Certainly not the gods. They
were even more capricious than the soldiers.

As if his father had read his thoughts, he continued: "And that is why I need *you*, my son—so that if something untoward should happen to me, there would still be a Valerian on the throne. My name—our family name—must live on; we must ensure a stable succession."

"I am a soldier and a general, not a politician. You have another son—weave him into your plans and let me serve empire and emperor in my own way."

"What, your brother Gaius?" His father laughed. "Yes, he may yet serve a purpose, but he has neither your abilities as an administrator nor your reputation as a general and a leader of men. Nor does he have any offspring, while you, I believe, have sired two sons? Sons who may one day succeed us and carry on our dynasty."

A brief smile flickered on Gallienus' lips at the mention of his sons. Emperor Gallus had sent him to the province of Germania Inferior on the northern reaches of the Rhine River, charged with keeping the barbarians on their own side of the river and patrolling the German Ocean to the north, which separated the mainland from the province of Britannia. He had not seen his wife, Salonina, nor their sons in over a year. In fact, he had been on the way home to the family estate in Etruria when he had received Valerianus' summons.

"Three sons," Gallienus corrected. "I have three sons."

Valerianus waved the error away as of no consequence. "All the better. The greatest lesson that recent events have taught us is that the empire is too vast for one man to rule effectively. But two men bound by blood and blessed by the gods can succeed where one has failed."

"Bound by blood."

Valerianus raised his chalice to his son. "My blood runs through your veins, Gallienus."

"As it runs through your daughter's veins."

A shadow passed through Valerianus' hard, brown eyes. He drained his cup and set it down on the table.

"Let me see if I can remember her name." Gallienus paused for effect, then snapped his fingers. "Damarra, that was it!"

"What of her?"

"What will be the lady Damarra's role in our new empire?

"I will deal with her, you need not worry."

"Must I remind you what happened the last time you tried to kill Damarra and her husband?"

"A minor setback."

"A minor setback? Aemilianus butchers your bodyguard and places you under house arrest, and you call it a minor setback?

"Perhaps we should inquire of Aemilianus?" Valerianus turned and spoke into the darkness: "My son thinks your interference in my plans was somehow significant. What do you think, Aemilianus?" Valerianus cocked his head, as if listening, then turned back to his son. "Aemilianus says he is beneath contempt."

Gallienus picked up his cup and drank to stifle a sarcastic laugh. He remembered enough of his father's methods to know that his theatrics were a ploy to redirect their discussion. But he was no longer the little boy who stood in awe of the tall, thin man who had ruled his household as he was about to rule the empire— with an unforgiving iron fist. Still, he decided to allow the redirection for the present. "I was in Numidia visiting Festus Macrinus when I learned of your arrest. I expected news of your execution to follow, but Festus laughed at the idea. 'Mark my words,' he said. 'My old friend Valerianus is much too cagey a campaigner to end his life with his head riding the executioner's block.' And he was right. Instead of news of your death, I received orders from Emperor Gallus charging me with the defence of the Rhine frontier in the far north."

"A command with excellent prospects."

"Indeed! And imagine my surprise when I learned that the new governor of Rhaetia and Noricum had nominated me for the command, and that the new governor was *you*."

Valerianus laughed. "A nice touch: father and son charged with defending the Rhine frontier—you in the north and me in the south—with all those seasoned legionaries at our command."

Gallienus shook his head in amazement. "I thought history was about to swallow you whole. Instead, you not only extract your head from the lion's jaws, you end up wielding his claws? How did you do it?"

"The gods favour me."

Gallienus snorted contemptuously.

"You don't believe me?"

"I believe the gods help those who help themselves."

Valerianus thought for a moment, then nodded. "That is true."

"And how did you help yourself?"

"By allowing the gods to favour me."

Unable to help himself, Gallienus laughed.

Valerianus continued with a snicker. "Each man brought his own doom with him. Take Aemilianus, for example. He was a man of extremes; that was his undoing. He saw the world as black or white, and was incapable of differentiating the myriad shades of grey in between. To him, Kniva and I were monsters and deserved a monster's fate. But Gallus was a different sort—his mind was at home in the grey areas."

"How so?"

"Well, for one, he understood the necessity of compromise, as he demonstrated when he allowed Kniva to return to Germania with his plunder."

"A compromise for which he was reviled."

"True, but what choice did he have? Risk his army to defeat Kniva? Or return to Rome and, with the support of his legions, press his claim to the imperial throne on the senate?"

Gallienus lifted his eyebrows, to say he understood but did not approve.

"Gallus let Kniva go, vowing to return later and crush the Goths and their king. But 'later' was not good enough for Aemilianus. When he learned of Gallus' treaty with Kniva, he flew into a rage and insisted that Roman honour demanded nothing less than the immediate and utter extermination of the Goths. In fact, Aemilianus was so adamant in his demands that some of the senate began to support him openly. So Gallus compromised again. He ordered Aemilianus to return to Moesia and prepare an invasion of Germania, 'to avenge the divine Decius and the honour of Rome.' The next day Aemilianus left the city in triumph, vowing to return to Rome with the head of Kniva on a plate and place it on the altar in the Temple of Mars as a holy offering.

"With Aemilianus out of the way, it was an easy thing for Gallus to quell any opposition in the senate and set his imperial house in order. He planned to march north the next spring to deal with Kniva—and Aemilianus, if necessary—before Aemilianus had time to gather sufficient troops to deal with Kniva on his own. But before he left Italy, he wanted to make sure he had someone he could trust to cover his back. And that was when he made his compromise with me."

Gallienus choked on a mouthful of wine. "*You*," he sputtered. He set the cup down on the table and coughed into his hand. "Why would he trust *you*?" *Of all people*, he almost added, but left the thought unspoken.

"And why not me? I served Decius and the empire well. Do not forget that Gallus was friends with Decius' son Herennius, and thus knew that Decius had entrusted me with the care of his retarded son Hostilian, not to mention the reins of empire, while the three of them chased Kniva to their ill-fated meeting at Abrittus. Because of that he was inclined to look favourably upon me, despite Aemilianus' rather . . . inopportune interruption of my dinner party and my subsequent arrest. And when Gallus found out that I still had the support of Gaul and Spain, he remembered my great service to the empire and compromised a third time. He recalled me and bought my good will by making me the governor of Rhaetia and Noricum and granting me control of their combined legions. He even banished Cornelius, the new *episcopus* of Rome, and his successor, Lucius, from the city as a sign of good faith."

Gallienus' eyebrows rose. "But I understood that he opposed the persecution of Christians?"

Valerianus chuckled again. "Another compromise. He knew my position and was willing to meet me halfway—exile rather than death. I fear he never truly believed that the Christians are the source of the empire's problems."

"As you do."

"As I *did*."

"Are you saying you no longer believe it to be true?" Gallienus could not keep the incredulity from his voice.

"Yes, I am saying that: the Christians no longer concern me. My sources tell me that the persecution initiated by Decius has left the cult in a shambles, completely divided. They are too busy fighting amongst themselves to trouble us."

Gallienus stared at his father, dumbstruck. He had, of course, heard the rumours about the Christians from his friend Marcus . . . but that his father had changed his mind so radically? Could that be true? His father's rabid hatred of the Christians had not changed in twenty-five years, and if anyone were to ask Gallienus, he would say that once Valerianus made up his mind on an issue he never changed, never backed down. And yet . . .

"And yet how many crucified Christian soldiers did I pass along the *Via Flaminia*?"

Valerianus spread his hands. "Not my doing, I assure you. After slaughtering Aemilianus, his soldiers purged the Christians from their ranks, thinking, I suppose, to please me. But enough of the Christians. We were speaking of the reason for Emperor Gallus' failure."

"And what was that reason?"

"His inability to decide on a single course and follow it through—his penchant for compromise."

"But you insinuated that the ability to compromise is a good quality."

"It is . . . to a point. But it can also be a weakness. Aemilianus had once been Gallus' most staunch supporter, but Gallus' compromise with Kniva earned Aemilianus' enmity. Aemilianus refused to compromise on any issue; Gallus compromised on every issue. The results were the same: alienation. Both men ended up pleasing no one . . . with the possible exception of me. And you, if you are wise."

Gallienus set his cup down on the table and stood up. He hovered over the map, his gaze following the curves and contours of the empire, until it came to rest on the knife which protruded from the province of Thrace, where Kniva had sacked the city of Philippopolis two years before. Thanks to Aemilianus, Kniva would not be a problem again, not for a few years anyway, but tribes other than the Goths roamed the vast forests of Germania, and they all had one thing in common with the Goths: they coveted Rome's wealth and her lands. He touched the hilt of the knife. "This is where you would divide the empire?" he asked.

Valerianus stood up and swept his hands over the map. "Yes, my son. East and West, two worlds welded together by our forebears into one empire, but they are very different worlds with very different problems. Each of them requires the iron fist of an emperor who will do more than sit in luxury in far-off Rome and watch impotently as his dominions fall prey to the predations of barbarians." Valerianus paused and stroked his chin, his eyes shifting from east to west, north to south. At last he looked up at his son and grinned, and his hard eyes gleamed with what was either ecstasy or anticipation, he could not tell which. "Two worlds, two emperors," he said again. "But one accord."

"One accord," Gallienus echoed. He sat back down, picked up his cup and gazed into its depths. "That remains to be seen."

"What do you mean by that, General?"

Gallienus looked at his father. For the first time since Gallienus had entered the tent, the sound of victory that lifted every word Valerianus spoke had faltered. There was doubt there now, just a hint of it, and the first staccato tones of anger.

Gallienus drained his cup and set it down on the table. "And which of these two worlds is to be mine?" he asked.

"What did you mean?" he pressed again. He loomed over the table, fists pressed against the map, and the anger in his words was sharper.

Gallienus stood up and leaned over the table, imitating his father's stance. "I mean I have three conditions."

Valerianus smiled, but the smile was false, a mask that could not hide the flush that crept up his face. "What conditions?"

"First, I will take the West; you will take the East."

"Why?"

Gallienus knew he had to tread carefully here. His father had done an adequate job in Noricum and Rhaetia, repelling barbarian incursions from across the Rhine and Danube, but that had been his first military command since the reign of Maximinus Thrax, almost fifteen years ago, and the reports that he had received about his father's activities—his father was not the only one who kept a watchful eye on his relatives—showed that he had devolved many of his military duties onto his officers, while he remained in Noricum's capital, Virunum, wiling away his days at the theatre and the games, or feasting at one senator's estate after another. Gallienus did not doubt his father's abilities—he had proven himself an able general time and again in his thirties—but he was in his fifties now, and the Rhine and Danube frontiers required more . . . vigorous leadership. The East, on the other hand, was threatened by only one enemy of consequence, Sassanid Persia. Certainly, Persia's self-titled King of kings, Shapur, was not an enemy to be underestimated, but he was only one and the West's enemies were many. Better to let Valerianus re-sharpen his military skills on a single whetstone. Besides, the West had the city of Rome, and Rome was still the mistress of the empire. If she must invite just one man into her bed, it should be him. It *must* be him.

"If I recall, you served in the East under Alexander Severus. You know the territory." Gallienus bowed his head. "I therefore defer to your superior geographical knowledge and strategic abilities."

"Oh, you are my son indeed," Valerianus said with a chuckle. "And your desire to rule the West has nothing to do with the location of Rome, I suppose?"

Gallienus smirked. "How could you think such a thing?"

Valerianus laughed harder, then nodded his head. "The fact is, I had already mobilized the Rhine armies in preparation for a campaign against Shapur, at Gallus' behest. Gallus ordered us into Italy in response to Aemilianus' threat, but now that both men are dead, I intend to continue to the East. The gods wish it."

"The gods? And how do you know this?"

He pointed to the gap in the curtains, to the tent's second room and the altar on which the recently sacrificed animal cooled in the night air. "The augury says so; *every* augury has said so. And more." He stroked his chin, studying Gallienus' face as if looking for something, and then came around the table and stood beside his son. "Many years ago, I visited the Oracle at Delphi, and the priest prophesied that I would be emperor." He held out his hands. "And so I am."

Gallienus shook his head. "And what does that have to do with Shapur?"

"The priest also prophesied that one day I would stand in glory in the very throne room of the Persian King of Kings." He struck his chest. "My destiny lies in the East, so I will take the East and leave the West to you."

"Very well."

"Then this is settled?"

Again Gallienus shook his head. "Two more conditions."

"Name them then."

"Condition number two: I will be emperor in more than just name. I will not be your puppet; I will be your equal."

Valerianus relaxed noticeably. "Of course. When we return to Rome, the senate will ratify my ascension to the imperial throne. *And* yours. I thought I made that clear."

Gallienus held up his hand. "Which means I have full control over all policies in the West, even if they are not in agreement with the policies you implement in the East."

Valerianus studied him, his grey eyes expressionless.

Gallienus continued. "With you campaigning on the Eastern Frontier and me dealing with the Germans, we must be able to act independently of each other. Is that not correct?"

At last, Valerianus nodded. "Agreed," he said. "And your final condition?"

Gallienus smiled. "I will deal with Damarra and Valens."

Valerianus blinked. "Excuse me?"

"Earlier you said that you would deal with Damarra and her husband. But as emperor of the West, Damarra and Valens are my subjects and thus under my jurisdiction, so I will deal with them, not you."

Gallienus waited for his father's response. Like everyone else in the empire, he had heard all the stories about Damarra and Julius Valens and his father. Had it not been for Aemilianus' fortuitous arrival, Damarra and Valens would be dead and Valerianus' vengeance complete. If his father still wanted vengeance— and he had already insinuated as much—then there could be no better test of Valerianus' promise to allow Gallienus complete autonomy in the West than to prevent that vengeance and study his response. Besides, Damarra was his half-sister, and he wanted to meet her at least once and determine if all the reports about her beauty were true.

Valerianus grinned. "I understand and agree." He stuck out

his hand. "Are we in accord, then?"

Gallienus looked at the proffered hand. He had been thirteen the last time his father had offered him his hand, thirteen and eager to get underway. His father had arranged for him to continue his education in Numidia, under the tutelage of one of the empire's most beloved and respected generals, Festus Macrinus. Festus was to teach him the art of war, the use of sword and javelin, how to ride and fight on horseback, tactics and strategy, all he would need, his father had explained, to one day achieve his destiny as a great general . . . and perhaps something more. Yes, he had been eager to get away, desperate to get away, but it was not because he was anticipating what was to come. It was because of what he was leaving behind.

His father.

Twenty years ago they had shaken hands and he had fled his father's hard eyes and the hard heart and the hard memories that the mere sight of him invoked. Forever, he had thought. Now he was back, and those hard eyes were staring at him again, waiting for him to respond, and the hard heart he could never understand was still there, beating in his father's chest, and the hard memories were flooding him again, threatening to swamp him with emotions unbefitting a general. Or an emperor.

He could refuse his father's hand, turn away, and leave the empire to his father's machinations. Or he could take his hand and temper his father's reign.

For the good of the empire.

"Agreed," Gallienus said, and grasped his father's hand.

FOUR

Night had settled over the city of Rome, but at the praetorian barracks set beneath the vast imperial palace on the Palatine Hill, the office of the commander of the Praetorian Guard was awash with light. Paulus Antoninus Quaerellus sat at his desk, writing hastily on a piece of parchment. Normally, his sense of duty and decorum would have demanded full dress uniform in his office, but tonight he wore a simple tunic and cloak. He folded the parchment and drizzled wax along its edge, then pressed his signet ring into the hot wax, sealing the document. And his destiny.

He sat back in his chair and stared out the window. In the darkness, he could just make out the serpentine course of the Tiber far below, and the first tendrils of mist arising from the water like ghostly hands. His face was handsome, chiselled like his body, which was muscular from a lifetime of soldiering and exercise. His hazel eyes turned to the document again, and he took up his reed pen and signed his name and a few final instructions above the seal. There. It was finished. He grunted. If he believed in the God Valens and Damarra worshipped, now would be the time to pray. But that he would never do. He could honour no God who would allow a lunatic like Valerianus to pound spikes into the wrists of his best friend, let alone a God who would permit his own son to be crucified.

There was a knock at the door.

"Come," Paulus said.

A man entered the office, shutting the door behind him. Like Paulus, he was not in uniform, but it was obvious from his bearing that he was also a soldier. He stopped in front of the desk and snapped to attention. "You summoned me, Commander Paulus."

"Yes, Centurion, I did. And I thank you for coming."

"You are still my commander," the centurion said.

Paulus felt a moment of affection for the man. Centurion Petronius Crispus had served him faithfully for many years, first in Britannia and now as a trusted member of the elite Praetorian Guard. But what he was about to ask of this man would strain the bond between them; in fact, circumstances being what they were, Petronius would have every right to refuse the request.

"You have heard the news, Centurion?"

Petronius nodded. "We have a new emperor. Even now he marches on Rome."

"Then you know what will happen when he arrives?"

For the first time, Petronius looked away. He nodded his head.

"You have served me well. Served the empire well."

"Thank you, Commander."

"There is one more duty I wish you to perform."

"Anything, Commander."

Paulus held up his hand. "Do not be so quick to agree. Consider this a favour, not an order." Paulus smirked. "I think I am no longer in a position to hand out orders, Petronius."

Anger flashed in Petronius' eyes, but he said nothing.

Paulus picked up the document and showed it to Petronius. "I need you to deliver this," he said.

Petronius took the folded parchment and glanced at the message scribbled over the seal. His olive skin paled. "You cannot be serious, Commander Paulus!"

"Deadly serious."

Petronius examined the document again. "I will not betray my homeland," he said stiffly.

"Nor would I ask you to. This will harm neither Rome nor her people."

Petronius tapped the document against his fingers. "It is a long journey."

Paulus dropped a leather purse full of gold coins on the desk. "That will more than suffice. And here," he said, pulling another piece of parchment from his cloak and setting it on the desk beside the purse. "When your mission is complete, seek out the lawyer Alcibiades at the forum in Athens and give him that. He will make arrangements to turn over a vast sum of money to you—your retirement fund, let us call it. Buy an estate somewhere, find a wife, and live the rest of your life in luxury."

For a long moment Petronius stared at his commander, then he said in a whisper, "And what of your retirement?"

"I begin that tonight."

Tears swelled in Petronius' eyes. Paulus looked away, not wanting to embarrass the man by acknowledging them, or exacerbate the moment with tears of his own. "This is the end of your career, then," Petronius was finally able to say.

"So it would seem." He did not add that Petronius was doomed himself if he remained in Rome. Valerianus was not the kind of man who would allow Paulus' most dedicated officers to continue as praetorians. Quite the opposite—he was the kind of man who would put them to death. Several of his other officers had already deserted their posts and fled the city, wanting to put as much distance between themselves and Valerianus as they could. But not faithful Petronius. The imminent danger to his life had not occurred to him; but it *was* obvious to him whom Paulus was really trying to protect.

"For Valens and Damarra?" he asked, but it was a statement rather than a question.

"Yes."

Petronius swept up the purse and the parchment and dropped them and the document into a fold in his cloak. "I would consider it an honour, Commander."

Paulus stood up and shook Petronius' hand, and they bid each other farewell. A few moments later he heard the clip-clop of Petronius' horse as it headed out of the courtyard into the empty night.

Paulus tied his military belt around his waist, then dropped his sword and two daggers into their sheaths. He took a quick look around his office—the silver-tipped spears mounted on the wall behind his desk, the legion standards, the gold spears displayed in a tall wooden barrel in the corner, the scorpion crest of the Praetorian Guard above the door, the trophies of a soldier, of a man of honour and devotion to duty, who had served his empire and his emperor well.

All meaningless now. Valerianus had stripped him of his honour as deftly as a butcher skins cattle.

Paulus touched the purse secreted in the folds of his cloak and nodded. That was all he really needed now. Travelling light was essential. If any of Paulus' devoted officers were still in Rome when Valerianus arrived, he would have them put to death, but if they escaped Rome now, they would be safe—Valerianus would not bother to cast his net for such small fish. But Paulus was a different matter. Paulus had betrayed Valerianus, he had embarrassed him, and most importantly, he had denied him the vengeance he craved against Valens. No matter where Paulus ran, Valerianus would track him down; Germania, Hibernia, even distant China would not be far enough. But maybe, if he travelled quick and light, he could slip through Valerianus' net before he pulled it in. And maybe he could stay ahead of him just long enough to make a difference.

After one final glance at the bits and pieces of his life, he exited his office for the last time and closed the door.

The darkness was heavy outside the barracks, the courtyard silent and empty. Paulus hurried to the stables and readied his horse, Asclepus, a black stallion given to him by his friend Valens last year. Once outside the stables, he mounted Asclepus, exited the main gate, and began the slow descent down the Palatine. The city streets were quiet. Here and there a lamp flickered in the darkness. Ahead, he saw a man lying in the street beside an open doorway, a flickering torch clutched in one hand. At first he thought the man had imbibed one too many cups of wine at the tavern and passed out on his way home, but as he drew near, he saw the telltale ring of black bruises on the man's neck and knew the man was not drunk, and that he would never drink wine again. Another victim of the plague. It had started several years ago, during the final days of Emperor Decius—the emperor's surviving son, Hostilian, had been one of its earliest victims, but it had pretty much burned itself out by the time Aemilianus took the throne last spring, a body here, a body there, quite normal for a city the size of Rome. Nothing to worry about. But last week the fire had flared again, and the corpses had begun to appear in greater numbers. "An even better reason to leave the city," he muttered to himself as he passed the corpse, giving it a wide berth.

He followed a winding course through the city, bearing north, favouring side streets and alleyways instead of the main thoroughfares. He passed a row of brightly-lit shops, the shopkeepers already up and working in the pre-morning darkness. The warm aroma of baking bread wafting from one doorway was soon overpowered by the astringent stench of uric acid from the tanner's next door. A man unloading an amphora of wine from the back of a wagon nodded at him and commented on the excellence of his horse, to which Paulus grunted his agreement. Had he been dressed in full uniform, the man would not have dared to look at him—one did not purposefully draw the attention of the commander of the Praetorian Guard to oneself, after all—and that realization gave him some hope. He was, along with the current emperor, the Praefect of the City, and a few other important officials, one of the most recognizable figures in Rome, in the whole Roman world. His bearing might give his military background away, but out of uniform, he might just pass as a simple off-duty soldier, no one of consequence.

Three roads led due north out of Rome, the *Via Flaminia*, the *Via Cassia*, and the *Via Aurelia*. At this very moment, Valerianus and his army were proceeding south from Narnia along the eastern route, the *Via Flaminia*, so Paulus could take either the *Via Cassia*, the middle road, or the *Via Aurelia*, the coastal route. He decided he would take the western route, along the coast—better to put as much distance between him and Valerianus as possible. He turned west and accessed the *Via Aurelia*, crossed the Tiber by means of the Aemilian Bridge, and came, just as the sun was beginning to brighten the eastern sky, to the *Porta Aurelia*, the Aurelian Gate. Three soldiers were standing guard, just finishing the last night watch. Torches flickered in sconces on either side of the gate As soon as they saw him, the guards began to argue amongst themselves. Paulus sighed. So much for slipping away unnoticed.

As he approached the gate, the two younger soldiers crossed their javelins in front of him, barring the exit, while the third, a tall, thin legionary with blue eyes and a face into which years of service had carved many scars, ordered him to halt.

Paulus tugged on the reins and Asclepus stopped, side-stepping nervously. "What do you want?" Paulus asked.

The veteran saluted. "Commander, forgive me, but I cannot allow you to leave the city."

Paulus dropped the reins and leapt down from his horse. "And why is that?"

"We received word from Emperor Valerianus not an hour ago, ordering you placed under arrest."

"Let me see these orders."

The veteran pulled a scroll from his belt and handed it to Paulus. He opened it and scanned the document quickly. It amounted to a proscription list, the new emperor clearing his house of undesirables as he began his reign, not an unusual tactic in times such as these, when an emperor had so many enemies that he often measured his lifespan in days rather than years. The last emperor, Aemilianus, whose three month reign had just come to an end, was a perfect case in point.

There were three pages of names on the list, many of which he recognized. Some of the names he was surprised to see, a few harmless senators and officials, some shrewd businessmen who were living in wealthy retirement on nearby estates. Probably they had crossed Valerianus at some point in the past and were now about to pay for that indignity, whether real or imagined, with their lives. Even more of a surprise was that he could find neither Valens' nor Damarra's names. Perhaps the document applied only to Valerianus' enemies in the vicinity of Rome? Whatever the case, one thing was certain: the name Paulus Antoninus Quaerellus, former commander of the Praetorian Guard, occupied the place of honour at the top of the list.

Nodding, he handed the scroll back to the veteran. "It appears you are correct," he said.

The veteran saluted. "If you would be so good as to come with me, Commander."

"What is your name, soldier?" Paulus asked.

"Quintus."

Paulus looked him over. "You look familiar to me, Quintus. Did you serve with me in Britannia?"

Quintus stuck out his chest. "Yes, Commander. With the sixth legion at Eboracum, under Tribune Valens." Quintus grinned. "You caught me drunk on duty once . . ."

". . . and sent you to the stockade for the night to dry up," Paulus finished.

Both men laughed at the memory. "You could have had me executed," Quintus said. Suddenly the grin melted from his scarred face. "I never thanked you for that."

Paulus waved the remark aside. "Thanked me? Please, I did it for my own benefit. If I remember correctly, I was in charge of execution detail that week, and I simply wanted to avoid all the paperwork. Britannia is dreary enough with all that rain; why add insult to injury by following procedure, when it is less tiresome to turn a blind eye?"

Quintus hesitated, his eyes searching the eyes of his former commander, then he gave the slightest hint of a nod and tucked the orders back into his belt. "What about these young ones?" he asked.

Paulus glanced over Quintus' shoulder. The two soldiers were watching them, their javelins still crossed. He reached into his cloak and revealed the purse hidden there. Quintus grinned his agreement. "You," he said, pointing at the two soldiers, "come here."

Paulus dipped into the leather purse and withdrew four gold *aurei*. When the two young men stepped up beside Quintus, Paulus opened his hand. The golden coins glittered in the light of the torches; the grim face of the emperor Caracalla looked more glorious than it ever had in life. In an instant, the two soldiers snatched up their bribes and vanished into the guardhouse by the gate. Paulus turned to Quintus. "And for you," he said, opening the purse again.

Quintus shook his head. "May the gods be between you and all harm in the places you must walk," he whispered. With one final salute he spun around and marched toward the guard house.

Paulus was about to mount Asclepus when a voice shouted: "You! Stop!"

He and Quintus turned around. A unit of soldiers, most of them low-ranking praetorians, led by a centurion that Paulus did not recognize, had just crossed the Aemilian Bridge and was hurrying toward the gate. Paulus knew immediately what had happened. These praetorians had decided to salvage their careers— and their lives—by capturing their former commander and turning him over to the new emperor.

"Guard! Stop that man," the centurion bellowed.

Quintus drew his sword and began to run . . . then tripped over an imaginary obstacle and sprawled to the pavement. He glanced up at Paulus with a grim smile. "Go," he mouthed.

Paulus leapt on his horse and dug his heels into Asclepus' flanks. An arrow whizzed past Paulus' ear and struck the stone lintel above the gate.

"Stop him," the centurion yelled.

As Asclepus jumped forward, Paulus felt a burst of white hot pain in his shoulder and gasped. He listed to the left and would have tumbled from the horse were it not for Asclepus compensating for the shifting of his weight. Asclepus' hooves echoed off the pavement as he raced down the *Via Aurelia*, past the sun-bleached tombs that lined either side of the road, through the first pilgrims making their way into the city in anticipation of the arrival of the new emperor. His left arm fell lifeless to his side, and, as the first thrum of shock began ticking in his head, he clutched the reins of his consciousness with all his remaining will and urged Asclepus into a full out gallop.

FIVE

Valerianus and Gallienus entered the city of Rome on the *Via Flaminia* two hours after dawn. Gallienus had wanted to slip into the city with their bodyguards and officers unannounced, with none of the pageantry that had accompanied Decius' triumphal entry almost four years before. Valerianus had agreed—it was a small concession to make to guarantee his son's continued support. Valerianus glanced sidelong at his son, the slightest of scowls on his gaunt face. There had been a number of concessions in the last few days as they journeyed down the *Via Flaminia* to Rome, a necessary evil, until he was able to fully assess the timbre of Gallienus' character. Unlike his brother Gaius, Gallienus was no fool—he had demanded an equal share of the power before accepting Valerianus' offer, setting his terms upfront like any shrewd businessman. Of course, he had already known that his son was no fool. Telling Gallienus he had watched his career "closely" had been an outrageous understatement. Since the age of thirteen, when Gallienus had gone to Numidia to be trained in the art of war by Valerianus' friend Festus Macrinus, Valerianus had received weekly reports on his son's activities from agents specially hired for that duty. It was an edge that he had already used to manipulate his son, and now that he was emperor he would sharpen that edge even further by using the *Agentes in Rebus*, the imperial secret service, through whom he could continue surveillance of his sons activities even from the Eastern Frontier. And beyond.

Valerianus glanced at his son again, and his heart beat faster for a moment. With the morning light shining on Gallienus' features, there was a slight resemblance to the boy's mother. A faint smile crossed his face. Mariniana. He had tried not to dwell much on the memory of his wife since her death, twenty-five years ago. She had been an exquisite flower, her beauty almost as legendary then, during the reign of Severus Alexander, as was the beauty of Valerianus' daughter Damarra today.

A sudden cry of "Hail the Divine Valerianus" drew Valerianus from his musings. Gallienus' plan to enter the city unannounced had failed. Cheering crowds lined either side of the *Via Flaminia*, and from the look of the crowds, this celebration was planned, not spontaneous. Women who looked like temple prostitutes hired for the occasion were throwing flowers and gifts in their paths, and up ahead, as their route narrowed down to the entrance to the *Via Sacra*, banners had been stretched between buildings from one side of the street to the other, commemorating the "Glorious Reign of Valerianus the Divine." Gallienus shrugged at Valerianus and Valerianus laughed. "Best get used to this kind of display, *Emperor* Gallienus," he said.

Gallienus sighed, then drew himself up straight and began to wave to the spectators. Immediately the volume of their cheers increased.

Good.

At last they came to the *Via Sacra* and proceeded up the pillared avenue to the Arch of Titus and the Roman Forum beyond. Now the crowds were immense, the cheering thunderous, and the sound of Rome's jubilation was so great that Valerianus could not hear his horse's hoofs striking the pavement. The emperor's party passed by the Rostra, where four years before the Emperor Decius had made his first speech to the Roman people, the temples of Saturn and Concord, the law courts and the imperial archive, finally halting in front of the *Curia Julia*, the senate house, where the senators of Rome waited to greet their new master. Senators in white togas dotted the senate steps, eyeing the procession nervously.

Valerianus and his son dismounted and headed up the steps. They were greeted near the top by a stout man in his early sixties, whom Valerianus recognized as Senator Sextus. "Hail, Augustus!" Sextus exclaimed, and the other senators in his entourage, seventy or eighty men in total, took up the chorus. Valerianus let them strain their voices for a full minute before lifting his hand. The senators fell silent.

"Greetings, Senator Sextus. You are responsible for this most exuberant welcome, we suppose?"

Sextus bowed with a flourish. "The least I could do, Your Excellency. Please consider me your humble servant."

Valerianus' gaze swept over the assembled senators. "We are surprised that Senator Severus is not here to greet us. Is he unwell?"

"Alas, Severus . . . died during the night." Sextus cleared his throat. "Perhaps the excitement of your advent was too great for his aged heart?"

Valerianus gave Sextus a wry smile. Severus had led the senate for many years, but he was better known for the role he played behind the scenes than in the hallowed halls of the *Curia Julia*. The infamous Severus had skulked behind every scheme and conspiracy fomented in the city for more than thirty years. But no proof. Never any proof. Valerianus suspected that Severus had also instigated the Rebellion of Julius Valens, his daughter's husband, against Decius. Which is why the erstwhile Severus had been the second name on his proscription list, immediately after Paulus Antoninus Quaerellus, the now *former* commander of the Praetorian Guard. Even Gallienus, who had spent little time in the capital, had heard of Severus' machinations and had agreed that his continued existence would be a threat to their reign. Severus had most likely committed suicide in the night rather than face execution. A pity. Valerianus would have enjoyed spending time with the ugly old fool in the imperial dungeon, ferreting out his secrets.

"Perhaps, Senator Sextus." Valerianus swept his hand toward his son. "May we present to you Augustus Gallienus."

A murmur arose amongst the senators and swept down the steps and through the crowds like fire through a forest. Before the imperial party finished climbing the steps to enter the senate house, cheers of Hail the Divine Valerianus *and* the Divine Gallienus erupted behind them.

THE *CURIA JULIA* HAD BEEN THE SEAT of the Roman senate since the days of the Roman Republic. Over the years it had had several incarnations. The current one had been restored by the Emperor Domitian, almost two hundred years before, after suffering severe damage in the conflagration that had destroyed much of Rome during the reign of the Emperor Nero. It was, for the most part, an unimpressive structure, a great rectangular building fronted with marble slabs and stucco that sat like a huge, immovable block at one end of the Forum. Beyond the bronze doors, in the meeting hall itself, the austerity continued. Three shelves of stone provided seats for three hundred senators, although there were twice that many senators now. A marble veneer covered the walls; an alternating pattern of rosettes and cornucopias created with bits of porphyry covered the floor. The most striking feature of the senate house was the Altar of Victory at the far end, a gift to the senate from the Emperor Augustus, in commemoration of his victory over Marc Antony at Actium. Even now, covered in the blood and gore from the bull just sacrificed in honour of Emperor Valerianus, the huge altar, surmounted by a statue of Victoria, the goddess of Victory, was an impressive sight.

A single throne occupied the floor before the rows of senators now waiting for Valerianus' first official speech. Instead of sitting himself, Valerianus directed his son to sit, which started the senators murmuring again. Gallienus drew his cloak about him as he took the throne. He sat with his back straight, his plumed helmet clutched in one hand, his other resting on the hilt of his sword, his eyes locked on his father. Like everyone else in the *curia*, he was anxious to hear what Valerianus would say.

The last few days had afforded Gallienus new insight into Valerianus' character. To say that he now trusted his father was an overstatement—he doubted he would ever fully trust this man, whose blood flowed in his veins—but he had developed a grudging respect for his abilities both as an administrator and as a student of human nature. He had donned armour to project the proper image for his entry into Rome, but it was nothing like the armour a Roman general would wear, not even the dress armour that his friend, Tribune Marcus, had insisted that Gallienus wear for the occasion. The *lorica* Valerianus wore over a tunic of purple silk was a breathtaking mosaic of beaten gold and silver, inlaid with precious stones. The hilt of the sword at his side was encrusted with jewels, as was the gold band that encircled his head. His cloak was imperial purple, to match the tunic. Gallienus had never seen anything so splendid in his life. Valerianus stood in the sunlight that streamed through the windows cut high in the curia's walls, shining in his glorious raiment, and Gallienus could almost believe he *was* the god that the senate was about to make him.

"Senate and People of Rome," Valerianus began. His voice was silky, a resonant baritone that was pleasing to the ears, even when he was projecting as he was now. He had obviously studied the art of rhetoric. "We are beset by dogs."

"Yes," a senator shouted.

"Curs!"

"Yes," shouted several more.

"Mongrels!"

"Yes!"

Valerianus paused. His piercing brown eyes swept about the room. "The empire stands on the edge of a sword. On the one side the Germans swarm our northern frontiers: Marcomanni, Franks, Alamanni, Saxons, Jutes, Suevi, a boiling mass of barbarians poised along the Rhine and the Danube like packs of ravening wolves, waiting for the first opportunity to pounce and devour our land, our people, and our wealth."

Shouts of "Here! Here!" arose from the assembled senators.

"Even that dog Kniva and his Gothic rabble, defeated by one of the generals of my glorious predecessor, Emperor Gallus, is simply licking his wounds, biding his time."

Gallienus kept a smirk from his face. Of course, Aemilianus was the unnamed general who had defeated Kniva and his Goths, and was Valerianus' *actual* predecessor. Valerianus' refusal to mention Aemilianus' name suggested he intended to issue the *damnatio memoriae* against him. If so, Aemilianus' name would be erased from all public records and his statues would be destroyed. It would be as if he had never existed.

"On the other side of the sword is Shapur, who calls himself the Great Lion of Persia. Some say he roars at the west. Some say his claws are sharp and sure and will rip the empire's eastern provinces to shreds. So some say."

Valerianus paused, then stepped closer to the senators, who were leaning forward as one, spellbound by their new emperor's words. He raised his fist and struck his armoured chest. "But we say that Shapur is a mongrel who has yipped at our heels for more than ten years. And that is long enough!"

"Yes!"

"He speaks true!"

"Hail, Valerianus!"

He waited until the clamour died down, then continued. "Shapur's hatred for the name of Rome, for the people of Rome, knows no bounds. How many times has he invaded Mesopotamia and Syria, only to flee like the dog he is when a Roman army advanced to meet him? And now, in this time of crisis, when he knows that we are fighting for our lives against the German mongrels of the north, he slinks into Armenia like a fox into a chicken coop and makes himself at home. He creeps into Syria looking for treasure like a hyena sniffing out rotting flesh. He howls on the edge of Mesopotamia, thinking himself a mighty wolf. But I say that Rome is the mighty wolf; and I say again that we tire of that mongrel Shapur yipping at our heels."

The senators jumped to their feet in thunderous applause. Valerianus stood before them with his chin up, his hands fisted on his hips, allowing the applause to break upon him like waves upon a sea wall. Finally he raised his hands, signalling them to stop, and they sat again. "Two sides to the sword, most honourable senators. Two sides, but only one hand on the hilt; two enemies pressing so close that a single hand finds the sword immovable." He swept his hand towards his son, who stood up. "Ah! But *two* hands on the hilt . . ."

The applause began, low and soft.

"Two hands working together as one, but with two heads like the god Janus, each facing in a different direction."

The senators in the back stood up again. The applause crescendoed.

"One facing East. The other facing West."

All the senators were on their feet now, and the applause was more thunderous than ever.

"One emperor to drown the Germans in the Rhine and the Danube forever. One emperor to drive Shapur back to his hole in Ctesiphon, to drown him in the Tigris river that flows by its high walls, and stand in glory in Shapur's throne room for all the world to see. An emperor for the West," he cried, drawing Gallienus up beside him. Grabbing his son's wrist, he raised it up above their heads. "And an emperor for the East. What say you, senators of Rome?"

"We will have two emperors!" Sextus cried.

"Augustus Gallienus and Augustus Valerianus," the others began to chant, and Gallienus could not help but wonder if their acclamation was even now ringing like a death knell in the ears of Shapur and every warrior mustering on the edge of Germania.

AFTER RECEIVING DIVINE HONOURS from the senate, the new emperors and their entourage processed through the jubilant crowds up the *Clivus Palatinus*, the gently sloping road that connected the forum to the imperial palace. After another quick speech, this time by the Emperor Gallienus, who promised ten days of celebratory games and an increase in the wine and bread doles—promises which met with raucous cheers from the poor, who predominated in the crowd, they entered the palace and proceeded to the imperial living quarters. The suite of rooms was opulence incarnate. The entrance opened into a sizable hall, where the emperor could conduct private meetings. Tapestries draped the walls, depicting battle scenes and various gods and their antics. The entire ceiling was a painting of the gods sitting on stone benches, as if they were a divine senate participating in the affairs of state conducted in this room. To the left of the audience hall was the emperor's personal *triclinium*, where he could dine with family and friends in groups as large as a hundred. More expansive banquet halls elsewhere in the imperial complex could seat hundreds more. To the right was the *tablinum*, a large office equipped with a massive desk hewn in a single slab from the trunk of some huge northern oak. The chair behind the desk was draped with silks and skins. Small writing tables stood in one corner, ready for the imperial scribes whenever he summoned them. A bed chamber opened off the far end of the hall, complete with the emperor's personal toilet.

Gallienus ordered food and drink for their entourage, then led his companions into the dining hall. Valerianus begged off—a slight headache from all the excitement, he had told his son—then sent a slave to fetch Dionysius, the commander of his personal bodyguard, and retired to the *tablinum*. He dropped into the chair behind the desk and glanced out the office's solitary window. The view was spectacular. The city of Rome stepped down to the Tiber in rows of gleaming marble. Sunlight shimmered on the river's sluggish waters. *Mine*, Valerianus thought. *At last, all mine.*

The voices of Gallienus and his comrades rising in laughter in the dining hall reminded him that Rome was not his alone. But no matter. Gallienus was a definite asset. He had handled the adoration of the crowds well, and it was obvious from his impromptu speech outside the palace that Festus Macrinus had not neglected his education in rhetoric. Nor in politics. Games, wine, and bread, the three ingredients that equalled a Rome free of civil unrest and strife, and Gallienus had promised them all. Despite his protestations, he did have the makings of a politician and a leader of men; add to that his abilities as a general and a strategist, and he was almost perfect for the role of Emperor of the West.

Almost.

That the empire required two emperors at this time was beyond dispute. He had realized that many years ago, watching Philip the Arab dart from one end of the empire to the other and failing in both places. Once they had pacified the frontiers, however, one emperor would suffice. At that point, his son Gaius' little character flaws—his devotion to wine and women in particular—would make him an asset as emperor of the West. Gaius would be happy to pass the mantle of power over to his father and spend the rest of his life at play. Not so Gallienus. Once the West's frontiers were safe again, he would continue to exercise power; certainly he would not simply hand it over to his father. Not without a fight. And that was out of the question. He needed Gallienus; he needed Gallienus' sons—the Valerian Dynasty must not fail, not if history was to remember its glorious founder.

Which left subterfuge.

A slave entered the room, an exquisite young Egyptian girl with black hair and eyes, dressed in red silks. "Commander Dionysius to see you, Your Excellency," she announced.

Valerianus stared at her hungrily. "Send him in. And when he leaves return with wine and entertain me." With a coy smile she bowed and left the room.

Commander Dionysius marched into the office. He was an imposing figure, both in height and breadth, an inch below seven feet and almost three hundred fifty pounds of compact muscle. Thick black eyebrows joined over his nose and a scar jagged down his left cheek. His hair was black, his eyes a piercing blue. Rumour had it that he could drink wine in greater quantities than the god after whom he was named. If it were true, it had never affected his duties. He wore the cobra crest that signified Valerianus' personal bodyguard on his *lorica*. He saluted and stood at attention before the desk. "Your Excellency, you wished to see me?" His voice was very deep.

"Have you an update on our proscription list?"

"Yes, Your Excellency. All have been dispatched but three: two senators, who are out of the city, and Paulus Antoninus Quaerellus."

"Ah, Paulus. Where is he?"

"I received a report from a centurion of the Praetorian Guard who tried to apprehend Paulus at the Aurelian Gate this morning. Apparently he escaped, but he is wounded. He will not get far."

"Good. We want you to direct the search for Paulus, Dionysius. We want him eliminated as quickly as possible."

"Yes, Your Excellency. I have also located the head of the *Agentes in Rebus*, as you requested."

Valerianus smiled. "Excellent. We wish to see him."

"He is waiting outside, Your Excellency."

"Show him in, but stay."

Dionysius saluted and exited the *tablinum*. A moment later he ushered in a second man, who came up to Dionysius' shoulders.

His brown hair was straight and short. Hazel eyes sparkled in a face that was good looking, but not remarkably so. His smile was pleasant, unobtrusive. He looked like the kind of man you might nod at as you passed in the street and then forget you'd ever seen. It occurred to Valerianus that the man's looks were an asset in his line of work. "Your Excellency," he said, with a bow. "You wished to see me?"

"Yes. You are Publius Cornelius Tacitus?"

"At your service, Your Excellency."

"Any relation to the historian?"

"Indeed. He was my great, great, great grandsire. It is a source of pride in our family."

"As it should be." Valerianus grinned. "You do not intend to write a history of recent emperors when you retire, do you, Tacitus?"

"No, Your Excellency. Unlike my forbear, I do not reveal imperial secrets; I keep them."

Valerianus laughed. "How very judicious of you. How is it that we have never met?"

"Few of your predecessors reigned long enough to make use of the *Agentes*, Your Excellency."

"True. A fact we intend to change." He pointed to a chair in front of the desk. "Please, have a seat."

Tacitus sat down and crossed his legs. He wore a toga and sandals and a single ring on his left hand. The sheath at his side was empty. "Dionysius, return Tacitus' dagger, please; we believe we can trust him." Dionysius took a dagger from his belt and handed it to Tacitus, who slipped it back into its sheath. "Forgive Dionysius' enthusiasm when it comes to our protection. He is very devoted and quite formidable."

Tacitus glanced up at Dionysius, who towered over him. "He looks it."

"We understand you are quite formidable as well?"

Tacitus shrugged. "Modesty prevents me, Your Excellency."

"And are you devoted?"

"I place empire and emperor above all things."

"That is what we wanted to hear. Unlike our predecessors, we understand the potential of the *Agentes in Rebus*, and we intend to make full use of your organization. The *Agentes* will be our ears and our eyes throughout the empire; and you, Tacitus, will be *my* ears and *my* eyes in the West, and especially here in Rome." Valerianus dropped a leather bag on the desk and pushed it toward Tacitus. "This is but a small fraction of the imperial monies that we plan to divert to the *Agentes in Rebus* for its development. Do we make ourselves clear?"

Tacitus picked up the bag, hefted it with his hand. When he glanced inside, his lips tipped in a delicate smile. "Consider the *Agentes in Rebus* at your disposal, Emperor Valerianus," he said, tucking the bag into his belt.

"Excellent, Tacitus. Then let us begin with this." Valerianus leaned forward and folded his hands on the desk. "We wish you to deliver a message."

"I WISH YOU TO DELIVER A MESSAGE," Gallienus said.

Several officers lying on a nearby dining couch were singing drunkenly, and Marcus had to lean closer to his friend so he could hear over the noise. "A message?"

Gallienus pointed at the exit and they rose from their couch and headed back out into the audience hall. As soon as the thick silk curtains dropped behind them, the noise eased. "A message?" Marcus repeated.

"Actually, two messages." Gallienus removed a leather folder from his belt. "The first is to my wife, Salonina. She probably knows about Valerianus, but the news of my accession will not have reached her yet. Tell the Empress Nina I wish her and the children to join me in Rome. We must introduce my subjects to the fair Nina."

Marcus grinned. "The Empress Nina. I like the sound of that."

Gallienus smiled at his friend. "The second letter is to Damarra Valensia."

Marcus' eyebrows shot up. "Damarra the confessor?"

"Confessor?" Gallienus asked.

"A Christian who endures persecution. They are revered and have great power. I have heard that some have been healed by touching a confessor's robes."

"And I have heard some have been healed by drinking noisome potions made by Greek physicians."

Marcus pursed his lips and said nothing.

Gallienus slapped his back. "Marcus, I jest. Must you always take your beliefs so seriously?"

"Civil War is a serious thing, Your Excellency."

"Civil War?"

"Those who survived the persecution of Decius are divided." He paused for a moment and studied the thick curtain that separated them from the banquet hall, where the drunken trio had just launched into a bawdy song about an innkeeper's daughter. "I witnessed it myself when I was visiting Carthage in the province of North Africa. *Episcopus* Cyprian, a good and worthy man, is trying to negotiate between the two sides, smooth over the conflict. But now," Marcus sighed, "Valerianus sits on the throne and his hatred of all things Christian is legendary."

"I assure you that Valerianus does not intend to persecute the Christians at this time. He told me he planned to leave you to your squabbles."

"And you believed him?"

"Of course not," Gallienus laughed. "But you are safe either way, friend Marcus."

"I cannot be safe while my people suffer. Not again. The *Christos* says . . ."

Gallienus held up his hand. "I have no desire to hear what the *Christos* says. You keep your faith and I will keep mine—let us agree not to inflict them on each other."

"As you wish, Your Excellency."

Gallienus squeezed his friend's shoulder. "Now, go fetch the Empress Nina, Marcus. And then seek out the lady Damarra and see if she can heal that wart you have on your shoulder."

SIX

My lady."

Damarra bolted upright in bed, her eyes blinking like an owl's in the darkness, trying to place the voice that had just woken her. It couldn't be Valens. Valens had left an hour ago for another meeting with *Episcopus* Pius down in Massalia. The curtains covering her window fluttered in the night breeze. "Is someone there?" she whispered.

"My lady, please do not be afraid. I must talk to you."

She sensed a hint of fear in the man's voice, a voice that was somehow familiar. "What do you want?"

"May I light the lamp?"

"Yes."

A shadow moved through the darkness toward the fireplace. A few red coals still burned there. It must be almost morning. She glanced out the window. The eastern horizon was a thin red line. The man picked up a coal with tongs and touched it to the wick of the little lamp that sat on the night table beside the bed. As he tossed the coal back into the fireplace, the lamp light swelled. She could see his tunic, the dagger sheathed in his belt, a pair of sandals grey with road dust and wet with morning dew. He picked up the lamp, held it closer to his face, and she knew him. "You were here last week at the gate with the others."

A look of relief washed over his bearded face. "Yes, my lady."

"My husband said he dealt with you."

"He sent us away, Confessor."

"Sent you *away*?"

He set the lamp down on the table. "Yes."

There was a blur of motion in the darkness and the bearded man—Antoninus, she remembered now—let out a yelp and was jerked back out of the light. A war cry split the silence of the room. Immediately Prisca appeared at the door, holding a lamp. "My lady," she cried, then shrieked and backed up. A moment later she could distinguish Gundabar with his muscular arm around Antoninus' shoulder and the man's own dagger pressed into his neck.

"Stop, Gundabar!" Damarra cried.

His green eyes found hers, but he did not release his prisoner.

Damarra fumbled for her robe and swung it over her shoulders. "Prisca, come help me." The slave hurried over, put down her lamp, and arranged Damarra's clothing, then helped her up. "Gundabar, please release him."

Gundabar's eyes narrowed. "I protect you."

The German had appeared a week ago and had become part of the household. Now she knew why he was always nearby when she was outside—Valens had ordered him to be her bodyguard. "He's not here to hurt me, Gundabar."

Gundabar glanced at his prisoner's face and recognition lit in his eyes. "He is—" he searched for the word and found it, "*lapsi*."

Antoninus' eyes closed. There was pain on his face.

"Yes, Gundabar, but that doesn't mean—"

"*Sankt* say no *lapsi*."

Sankt. It was what the German called her husband. As near as they could figure, it had something to do with the scars on Valens' wrists, the marks of the *Christos*. Gundabar claimed that the *Christos* had sent him all the way from distant Suevia, in the northern reaches of Germania. Conall, their Master of Horses, knew some of the German dialects, but he had gone to one of the estates in Aquitania to procure new breeding stock and would not return for a few more days. Until then, everyone was trying their best to understand the young Suevi warrior. But it was rarely an easy task. "No *lapsi*?" she repeated.

He shook his blond head. "No *lapsi*."

Damarra sighed. She was beginning to see what the problem was now. They had spent the last year and a half on an extended honeymoon—the grand tour of their estates, through Italy and Greece, North Africa, Hispania, even to Britannia, which was Damarra's homeland. How wonderful it had been, seeing the world in a way Damarra could never have imagined in her former life as a slave, sharing their days and nights together, just the two of them. They had settled here on Valens' family estate a few months ago, when her pregnancy became very obvious and Valens began to fret about it. In all that time, wrapped up in themselves as they were, she could not remember hearing anything about the controversy that had rocked the Church. But once they settled down, once they reconnected with the world they had so blissfully ignored during their travels, everything changed. She had visited Massalia only once—the physicians had ordered her to stay off her feet as much as possible, an order which Valens strictly enforced—but even living the sheltered life her condition necessitated, she had heard the rumours. And when the first of the *lapsi* found her here, a few weeks ago, she had heard the whole story. And she was appalled by it.

She and her husband had never discussed it—he steered away from anything that might cause her anxiety, again because of her pregnancy—but she had just assumed his feelings on the matter were the same as hers. Apparently they were not.

"Release him, Gundabar," she ordered.

Slowly he withdrew the knife from Antoninus' throat and released him. "I keep," he snarled and tucked Antoninus' dagger into his own belt.

Antoninus stared at the German with wide eyes, nodding. He rubbed his throat with his hands. There was a small desk in the room, close to the fireplace. Damarra went to it and eased herself down into the chair. "Come here," she said to Antoninus.

He went to the desk. So did Gundabar. "You seek forgiveness, Antoninus?"

"Oh, *yes*, Confessor, more than anything."

"I don't know if I can forgive you, Antoninus."

Tears welled in his eyes.

Damarra took his hand. "No, no, you misunderstand me. I know you sacrificed; I understand the fear you faced only too well, and *I* can and do forgive you for that, but I am not convinced that will make a difference to the Holy God."

"But my lady Confessor, you are one of the holy ones, *Amicula Christi,* dear friend of the *Christos,* you stood with Him and . . . I did not." He choked on his words, then forced himself to continue. "Because of that the *Christos* will listen to you—He will forgive me through you."

"Antoninus, you know the *Christos* will forgive your sins if you ask Him."

He shook his head. "Not for this. There is no forgiveness for the sin of apostasy. So says Novatianus; so say those in communion with him."

"Well, I do not believe that." She sighed, then took a piece of parchment from the desk. "But I can see you do. I see also that you are contrite and sorry, so let me ask you this: if persecution comes again, if you are forced to choose between death or the *Christos,* what will you choose?"

"The *Christos,* Most Holy Confessor. I shall never deny Him again."

"I believe you." She picked up a reed pen, inked it, and began to write on the parchment. When she had finished the document that she had already written many times in the last few weeks, she signed it at the bottom, then passed it to Antoninus. "There is your Certificate of Peace. You are forgiven."

Antoninus dropped to his knees, tears streaming down his cheeks. He took her hand and kissed it and thanked her again and again and again. She kissed the top of his head and told him to stand up. A bright smile burned on his face. The fear she had seen was gone. It was as if she had lifted the weight of eternity from his shoulders with the simple stroke of a pen. "I am happy for you, Antoninus. But you understand this will not change the hearts of men like Novatianus?"

"Yes, Confessor. One *episcopus* says yes, we can be forgiven, the next says no, we cannot be forgiven, and so the battle rages on. But this," he shook the Certificate of Peace, "this says 'yes' from a confessor; this says 'yes' from the *Christos.*"

She sighed. She was not sure about the legitimacy of his argument, but what she did know is that in addition to being forgiven by God, he needed to forgive *himself*. And if a Certificate of Peace would help him do that, then what harm could it do? "Do not stand on this alone, Antoninus. Seek the will of the *Christos* for your life."

"Yes, Holy Confessor."

He turned to leave and Gundabar fell in beside. As he was heading out the door to the terrace, by which he had gained access to her bedroom, Damarra called his name one more time. "And Antoninus?"

He glanced over his shoulder, his eyebrows raised.

"Please do not sneak into a woman's bedroom ever again."

With a laugh, he allowed Gundabar to take his arm and lead him out into the dawn.

PAULUS OPENED HIS EYES TO DARKNESS. Almost darkness. To his left was a thin rectangle of light which he recognized as a draped window. Across the room, a low fire burned in a hearth. The smell of cooking stew tantalized his nostrils. He tried to sit up, and groaned at the pain in his shoulder.

"You are awake at last," said a voice from beside the fire. The drape was drawn back and the light of morning streamed into the room. Paulus squinted his eyes against it.

"Where am I?" he asked.

"In my home," the woman said. She was pretty. Her long brown hair was pulled into a tail at the back, tied with a bit of string. She wore a brown tunic of a very coarse material cinched at the waist with a piece of rope. She was a poor woman, then. "My name is Diana."

"How did I get here, Diana?"

"I found you and your horse in the back field. You were lying under a tree; your horse was eating my oats."

"I'm sorry."

She laughed. It was a very high, sweet sound. "Do not trouble yourself. I have plenty of oats. The Lord has provided well for me."

"You are . . . a Christian?" he asked.

She bowed her head. "I serve the *Christos*, yes. And who are you?"

"I am Paulus. A Roman soldier. Where is your husband?"

"My husband died in the arena two years ago. Decius fed him to the lions."

"And you survived?"

"I was not a Christian then. But seeing him die like that," she sighed, "I suddenly knew he was right. I came back to our little farm and pledged my troth to the *Christos* and have served him ever since."

"And you have lived here alone all this time?"

"Me and my son Philemon."

"You work this farm by yourselves?"

"Yes. Philemon is eight. He is very strong. We do all right and there are neighbours to help us if we need it."

"How long have I been here?"

"Three days. I have tended to your wound."

He glanced at his shoulder. The arrow had been removed. She had spread some kind of paste over the wound, front and back. It no longer hurt, but it smelled hideous. "I must leave at once," he said, and tried to sit up again.

"You must stay still," she corrected and pushed him back down. "At least two more days. If you ride too soon, the wound will open again and you will lose even more blood."

"And where exactly is it that I am staying still?"

She went to the hearth and began to fill a small wooden bowl with stew. "You are ten miles south of Pisae."

Pisae was some two hundred miles north of Rome, not quite halfway to his destination. He could remember three days on the road, running as fast as Asclepus could with only brief stops to rest the horse. There might have been one more day—things had gotten scattered in his feverish brain toward the end—so fifty miles per day. Not every horse was capable of such stamina. He felt a surge of pride in the horse, and gratitude to the man who had gifted it to him.

Julius Valens.

"I must go," he told her.

She rushed back from the hearth with the bowl of stew, but he was already on his feet . . . and then he was falling, back onto the bed and she was leaning over him, laughing. "Diana knows best, you see?"

"Diana knows best."

And so he stayed, gnawing on the pieces of his broken life and fretting about what was happening while he lay on this bed. In a few days his shoulder had knit, and Diana said there was no more need for the rank poultice she had smeared on the wound twice daily. When she scraped it away and washed the residue off the front and back of his shoulder, he had to admit the poultice had done its work. A puckered scar, front and back on his left shoulder, was all that remained of the damage caused by the arrow. Something to tell his grandchildren about.

He spent a third day sitting by the fire with Diana and her son, Philemon. Despite their circumstances he was a happy child, tall for an eight-year old, with red hair and a smattering of freckles across his nose and cheeks. He told Paulus stories about the fish he caught in one of the nearby streams, about his friend, Primus, and their adventures in the caves at the back of their farm. There were stories about the *Christos* as well, how He had changed water to wine, how He had raised people from the dead, his love for publicans and sinners and outcasts. Paulus listened politely, but he had heard many of these stories before. Once, during a visit with Valens and Damarra on their sweep through their Italian estates, the three of them had spent an entire night sitting by the fire and discussing the *Christos*. Valens and Paulus had argued; Damarra had kept the peace. At dawn, Valens threw up his hands in exasperation and exclaimed, "My dear Paulus, you are the Wayside Seed."

"Not so," Damarra said. She patted Paulus' hand. "He just needs time to reflect, to think about the truths we have spoken here."

Paulus got up, stretched. "My lady, there will never be enough time for that." He turned to Valens. "What is this Wayside Seed you speak of?"

"A parable from Matthew's history of the *Christos*. We have told you about the *Christos*, that is the seed; but in you it falls by the wayside and never grows because you will not understand it." Valens stood up and embraced him. "And yet, my friend, I shall continue to pray for you."

They had slapped each other's backs. "Then pray also that I have a good sleep," Paulus had replied with a yawn.

That had been the last time they were all together.

As dusk fell, Paulus asked young Philemon to ready his horse, which they had stabled in the small barn attached to the house. "You are leaving then?" Diana asked.

"Yes. It is safer that I travel at night."

She gave him his cloak, his weapons, and his leather purse. He opened the purse and took out ten gold *aurei*. "For you," he said and offered her the coins.

Her brown eyes widened. "So much money," she breathed. She looked up at him. "You do not need to pay me, especially not a fortune such as that."

He shook his head and dropped the gold coins into her hands. "I am not paying you; I am saying thank you."

She handed them back. "I cannot accept this."

He turned and placed them on the small table. "They are yours. Do with them what you will."

Diana bowed her head in thanks, then helped him with his cloak. His left arm still ached, but he could move it again. Once he was ready, she led him to the doorway. Philemon was outside with Asclepus, petting the proud stallion's flanks.

"He is a beautiful horse, my lord," the little boy said.

Paulus ruffled the boy's red hair. "And you are a fine young man. You take good care of your mother now."

"Yes, my lord."

He turned to Diana. She kissed his cheek, and for a fleeting moment he pretended that the woman and the boy were his wife and son, and he was simply going on a short trip into Pisae to buy supplies and catch up on the news at the forum. And then the fantasy whisked away and he was Paulus again, once commander of the Praetorian Guard, now a fugitive. And fugitives must ever flee. "Goodbye, Diana. Thank you again; you saved my life."

She kissed his other cheek. "I will pray for you. May God speed you on your journey."

He winked at her. "I will allow Asclepus here to do that."

She smiled at him, and they waved goodbye as he mounted his horse and trotted out of their lives.

He found the *Via Aurelia* a mile away just as full night fell, and headed north, toward Pisae. As the lights of the city appeared on the horizon, he left the main road and began working his way northeast along a system of smaller roads and cart tracks that sometimes narrowed down to no more than a few feet in width. Asclepus, always sure-footed, found his way through the darkness until at last, several hours before dawn, he had circumvented the city and rejoined the *Via Aurelia*. Then he pressed on, urging Asclepus to run faster and faster, pushing the horse to its limits while night remained. When the eastern horizon began to redden, he once more left the road. He found an abandoned hovel behind a copse of aromatic Bay Laurel trees where he could hide Asclepus and sleep until darkness fell again. And when he finally fell asleep in the hovel's cool shadows, he dreamed of a farmer sowing his fields, while the seeds that fell by the wayside burned in the hot Italian sunshine.

WHEN VALENS RETURNED TO THE VILLA later that morning, he found Damarra sitting at the loom in the outer courtyard, while her handmaiden stood by studying her technique. Cecht came and led his horse away. Gundabar was over by the blacksmith's workshop, watching him pound out shoes for the horses. When he saw Valens, he trotted over. "Sankt," he said. "We talk."

Damarra's eyes flashed at him and Valens felt his heart sink in his chest. She had only once been angry at him. He had gone on a boar hunt with friends at the estate near Londinium in Britannia and had neglected to tell her he wouldn't be home that night. By the next afternoon when he did return, she had been frantic with worry; and when he had told her he had forgotten to mention it, her worry instantly became anger. He had seen it in her eyes, as he was seeing it now. "Yes, Gundabar, we talk."

In his broken, slurred Latin, Gundabar told him what had happened after he had left in the morning darkness. By the time he finished, Valens was as angry as Damarra was. He marched over to his wife. "Come with me," he said.

She did not speak. Her fingers continued to shoot the shuttle between the brightly coloured threads of the cloth she was weaving. Persephone looked from Damarra to Valens and back again, then backed away until she was standing beside Gundabar. She looked at him and grimaced. He nodded agreement, then flicked his head toward the blacksmith's stall. Together they drifted over to watch the sweating slave pound away on the red hot metal, out of earshot of the lord and lady of the villa.

"I said come with me, Damarra," Valens ordered.

"I do not wish to speak to you," she replied. "I am too angry right now."

"You *will* speak to me," he demanded.

"I will not."

With a growl of exasperation, he swept her up into his arms, oblivious to her protestations, and carried her inside, through the atrium, and down into the *peristylium*, the inner garden courtyard about which the villa was built. There was a bench there, nestled in a copse of small craggy apple trees where they often came for morning prayer. But Valens did not have prayer on his mind at this moment. Nor did Damarra.

He set her down gently, then towered over her with hands on his hips. "He was a trespasser, Damarra—you should have let Gundabar kill him."

Her mouth dropped open. "Kill him! He was seeking *peace*."

"Let the *lapsi* seek it elsewhere and leave us alone."

"You say *lapsi* like it is a piece of rotten meat."

"It *is* rotten; it leaves a foul taste in my mouth."

"Have you forgotten the grace that saved you?"

He shoved his wrists into her face and showed her the puckered scars that marked them. "Can I ever forget it?"

As she stared at the wounds, he could see her anger deflating. "I'm sorry, my love, but can you not see that all they want is love and forgiveness?" She laughed. "In truth it is not me they come to see—it is *you*. I am a confessor because I confessed the *Christos* and faced death rather than deny Him. But to them you are *the* Confessor. You have the marks of the *Christos*; he is the Emperor of Heaven and you have his ear."

He let his hands drop to his sides. "I do not feel I have his ear." He paused, thinking, then: "It does not matter. Clearly there is no forgiveness for the sin of apostasy. So says Pius of Massalia and Novatianus of Rome, and so say I."

"But Novatianus is not the true *episcopus* of Rome, is he?"

Valens frowned.

"Novatianus wanted to be *episcopus* of Rome after our dear friend Fabian was martyred, but Rome chose Cornelius instead. Novatianus was so angry that he deceived a few good men into declaring him *episcopus* of Rome as well. But Rome can have only one *episcopus*, and that was the first man elected: Cornelius. And now that Cornelius is dead, Lucius is his legitimate successor, not Novatianus. Novatianus' claims are false."

"Where did you hear all that?"

"From the pilgrims who have come to stand at our gates and beg forgiveness."

Valens waved her argument aside. "Just because Novatianus is not the true *episcopus* of Rome does not make his arguments about the *lapsi* wrong," he said. "You sound like Cyprianus—he also argues that Novatianus is wrong because he is not the legitimate *episcopus* of Rome."

Damarra sat up straight on the bench. "Cyprianus? Of Carthage?"

Valens nodded.

"Cyprianus is a great man, a leader in the church."

"And being a great man does not make one right about the *lapsi* either," Valens said. He gave a sarcastic laugh. "Novatianus claims Cyprianus ran away during the persecution."

Now Damarra laughed. "He went into hiding, Valens. That is not running away; that is wisdom. I went into hiding during the persecution as well, remember?"

Valens grunted.

"I met Cyprianus before I left North Africa. I heard him speak in Carthage. He has the gift. God speaks through him."

"If that is true, then your own words convict you. Cyprianus of Carthage argues that the *lapsi* must first undertake a long period of penance before they can be forgiven. Neither Cyprianus nor Novatianus permit confessors to issue Certificates of Peace. So you must stop handing them out."

"If it means granting solace to the poor wretches who come here looking for hope, then I shall issue them."

"I forbid you."

She glared up at him. "I shall issue them."

"I will not allow the *lapsi* into our home."

"Then I shall meet them at the gate."

"You will do no such thing. You are to stay off your feet, as the physicians prescribed." Suddenly reminded of her condition, he dropped to his knees and took her hands. "I am sorry, Damarra. We should not be arguing. I do not want anything to happen to you or the baby."

She smiled at him, touched his cheek. "I am fine, my love." She laid his hand on her swollen belly. "Your child is healthy and safe. We are both safe. The *Christos* will watch over us."

As he watched over Julia, he wanted to say, but he didn't. When his first wife, Julia, had died in childbirth, along with their still-born son, Valens had thought his heart would never mend. But the *Christos* had sent Damarra into his life and every time he looked at her, his mended heart soared. *Don't let it happen again, Christos*, he prayed. *Please, not again.*

He stood up and lifted his wife in his arms. Even pregnant she was as light as the breeze that flitted in over the courtyard's high walls and played in her bright hair. "Time to rest," he told her and carried her into the cool of the house, to their bedroom, where the breeze coming in off the terrace carried the smell of the sea on its back. He set her down on the bed, then laid down beside her, holding her in his arms until she fell into a gentle slumber.

He rose, watched her as she slept. Her skin was smooth, flawless, and peaceful. But the issue still burned between them, hot and unresolved. It had been their first real argument, and he suspected as he slipped from the room that it would not be their last.

SEVEN

Tacitus rode along the *Via Iulia* outside the small coastal town of Veluma, two days west of Genua. What a beautiful city Genua had been, the glimmering waters of the Mediterranean set against a backdrop of blue-green hills and the distant Alps. If he had had the time, he would have stopped for a few days to sample the local cuisine and take in the sights. Alas, the emperor's orders permitted no such frivolities.

They had travelled north as far as Pisae with Commander Dionysius and his unit of praetorians, but there the commander had heard rumours of Paulus and their paths had diverged. Some of his men had raced on ahead, some had detoured into the countryside, while Tacitus and his two aides had continued on by themselves at a more leisurely pace. He was convinced from the few days he had spent in Commander Dionysius' company that the huge Greek knew his business and would eventually catch Paulus and finish him off.

Such a pity. Tacitus had observed Paulus during his tenure as commander of the Praetorian Guard, and knew that he was an honourable man, a faithful and valiant soldier and servant of Rome. The only mistake he made during his entire career was crossing Praefect of the City Valerianus by siding with Aemilianus, and thus saving the lives of his friends, Julius Valens and Damarra. Now Praefect Valerianus was Emperor Valerianus, and it was well within his rights to dispatch Paulus for his perfidy. Yet it was still a waste. He hated to see a good man or a good opportunity fall by the wayside.

Behind him his aides were whispering about the pretty barmaids that made Genua such a favourite with the sailors. He scowled at their vulgarities. They were young, in their mid-twenties, about ten years his junior, but even in the bloom of his youth Tacitus would never have talked in such a manner. He could not countenance rudeness or crudities. He turned to his aides. "If you wish to dwell in the gutter, I will place your heads there permanently," he barked.

Both his aides paled. "Yes, my lord," they said in unison.

He glared at them a moment longer to be sure that they were sufficiently cowed, then turned back to his musings. The black-haired one with the little moustache, Martial was his name, was adequate at his job. He followed orders without question and had a talent for gathering intelligence. But the other one, Plautus, was a buffoon, little more than a thug dressed up in a rich man's clothes. He was balding and beardless and had dull eyes that made him look stupider than he was; still, he was large and frightening to those who did not perceive his poverty stricken intellect, and he was good with his fists and fair with a knife, although from the scars on his arms you would never know it. Both men had their uses, and as far as the *Agentes* in the vicinity of Rome went, they were the best of a bad lot. With an emperor like the Divine Valerianus on the throne, however, that would change. His excellency grasped the value of the *Agentes* better than any of his predecessors. He had offered imperial funding, as much as Tacitus needed, and with that financial support in place, Tacitus planned to expand the *Agentes in Rebus* into a first class organization and make it an indispensible part of the imperial machinery.

"Plautus," Tacitus called over his shoulder.

The big man hurried up beside him. "Yes, my lord?"

"There is an inn about ten miles from here. Go ahead and reserve food and rooms for tonight."

"Yes, my lord," and with that, he slapped his horse into a gallop and headed off into the late afternoon sunshine.

Martial trotted up beside him. "How much further, Commander Tacitus?"

"From the inn, perhaps sixty miles. We shall sleep tonight and tomorrow quicken our pace. I wish to arrive at our destination by the *Dies Solis*, the Day of the Sun."

"Two days from now? Why the hurry?"

"The Day of the Sun is significant to the Christians."

"Why is that?"

"It is the day their god rose from the dead. They celebrate that resurrection weekly."

"You sure know a lot about the Christians."

"I know a lot about many things, Martial. Knowledge is my business."

"So we arrive by the Day of the Sun. What then?"

"And then," he smiled at Martial, "we shall deliver the emperor's message."

Martial laughed. "I think you're looking forward to this."

"A job well done? Yes, that is worth looking forward to."

Martial laughed again. "You know what I mean."

Tacitus smirked. "Yes, my friend, I know what you mean. Emperor Valerianus had heard of my flair for such tasks and left it to me to decide how best to deliver the message."

"An honour."

"I think so."

"So, have you decided?"

Tacitus shook his head. "No, but I have two days to come up with something special. So I suggest we enjoy this lovely scenery in silence and allow me to think."

Martial grinned and bowed his head. "Yes, my lord."

"PITY THE HORSE THAT HAS to carry that man," the praetorian whispered to his companion.

They watched their commander ride through Veluma's western gate. The horse he rode, a grey stallion called Pegasus, was the biggest available at the praetorian barracks, but Dionysius made the horse look like a little pony. He stopped beside them and hitched his thumb behind him. "Paulus has been here. He was seen entering the town by the eastern gate just before dawn. The guard recognized him, but did not know there was a price on his head."

"What do we do, Commander?" asked the man to his left. His name was Licander, and he was the centurion who had attempted to apprehend Paulus as he left the city of Rome. The other praetorian, named Ulf, was a red-haired Saxon who had joined the legion in the province of Germania Superior fifteen years before and was now a common guardsman in the praetorian ranks. Both of them had seen many years of service and Dionysius had come to respect them as they travelled north in search of their fugitive.

Dionysius removed his helmet and passed his huge paw through his black hair. He glanced back at the city, then to the junction ahead, where the road split in two. The northern route was a narrow cart track that led into a forest half a mile away, and from there, who knew? The other route, the *Via Iulia*, continued west along the coast. "He is obviously travelling at night. If he spent the day in Veluma, then he must exit this gate." He gazed about, until he spotted a pale white mausoleum a hundred yards up the road. "There," he said. "We will take the horses in behind that tomb."

The tomb turned out to be little more than three walls. The roof had collapsed and taken the fourth wall with it, leaving them the perfect blind from which to watch the traffic proceeding from the city gates. There were no bones amongst the rubble. Wolves had dragged them away long before any of the men who now hid in the crumbling edifice had been born. They waited as the sun set, talking amongst themselves while they chewed on their daily grain ration, for lack of anything more interesting to eat. When the talk turned to the new emperor, Centurion Licander asked Dionysius, "Will you be the new commander of the Praetorian Guard?"

Dionysius spit some chaff from his mouth and grinned. "Me? No. The emperor—the *emperors*—have selected another to command the guard. He will arrive in Rome soon, if I'm not mistaken." He glanced at the city gate again. The torches had been lit. A horse and cart was trundling out of the city, laden with barrels of wine. He turned back to Licander. "But I could use men like you in the emperor's personal bodyguard. What do you say to double your pay as praetorians?"

Ulf slapped Licander on the back. "What do you say, Centurion? Feel like getting rich?"

Licander scratched his chin. "How do you Saxons say yes?"

Both Ulf and the commander laughed. "*Gyse*," Ulf said. He turned to Dionysius. "We say *gyse*."

Suddenly Licander stiffened, dropped into a crouch. "There," he whispered. His hand fell to the hilt of his sword. "Just outside the gate. I think that's him."

The others dropped down beside him. "Are you sure?" Dionysius said. He had Paulus' description, but he had never met the man, and the light was failing, almost gone.

"I saw him only from a distance at the gate in Rome," Licander said. "Ulf, come here."

The German crept up beside him.

"You have met him, seen him up close."

"Once."

"Is it him?"

Ulf peered out over a marble block. A smile spread across his narrow face. "*Gyse*," he whispered.

The three of them backed out of the tomb, careful not to disturb the debris and signal their presence. Dionysius ordered them to mount up, and they waited in the twilight. The moment seemed to stretch out into eternity, but at last the sound of hoof beats drew nearer, and a horse and rider appeared on the road, moving slowly in the gathering dusk.

"Take him!" Dionysius ordered.

Ulf and Licander spurred their horses and leapt forward onto the road, cutting off their quarry's path. "It is him," Ulf yelled and slashed at Paulus with his sword, but at the last possible moment, Paulus got his horse turned and Ulf sliced only the meat of his arm. Licander's thrust did more damage, piercing Paulus' side, and then Paulus was away, pounding up the northern route that would take him into the forest, with Ulf and Licander following hard on his tail.

Dionysius urged his horse into a steady gallop. He could not keep the pace of the others. His horse was larger, but Dionysius' weight combined with the weight of his equipment meant his horse was carrying close to four hundred fifty pounds, while their horses carried no more than two hundred fifty. But he had seen damage done, to what extent he could not say, and they would catch him quickly if he did not elude them in the darkness.

Ahead the eaves of the forest loomed, and already Paulus, Ulf, and Licander had vanished into its deeper gloom. Just inside the forest, Dionysius halted Pegasus to listen. From up ahead came the sound of clashing metal, and then an ululating war cry, probably Ulf, and another voice, definitely Licander, yelling: "Don't let him get away!"

Dionysius spurred Pegasus onward again. Tonight, if the gods allowed it, Paulus Antoninus Quaerellus would breathe his last, and Dionysius and his men would spend tomorrow evening drinking the health of the new emperor in one of Veluma's little seaside taverns.

THE THIRD DAY AFTER THE KALENDS of October was long remembered in the city of Rome for the confluence of three important events. First and foremost in the minds of most Romans, it marked the inauguration of ten days of games to celebrate the ascension of the emperors Valerianus and Gallienus. Second, it was day that the Empress Nina arrived in Rome with her three children, just in time to stand beside her husband as he opened the games. While the crowd looked on, cheering, Emperor Valerianus greeted his daughter-in-law with a kiss, spoke briefly to each of the two older boys, then took the three-year-old Egnatius Marinianus into his arms and went to the second throne set up in the imperial box where he sat down with his grandson dangling on his knee, for all the Roman world to see.

Third, and perhaps most significant for each member of the imperial party, although no one present would have guessed it at the time, it was the day that the new commander of the Praetorian Guard entered Rome. After the two emperors had agreed on their choice—not Gallienus' first choice, but when Valerianus suggested him, Gallienus wondered why *he* hadn't thought of his old mentor in the first place—a *liburna*, a smaller, faster version of the *trireme* with two rows of oars instead of three, was dispatched to the African province of Numidia and returned with Festus Macrinus before a week had elapsed. Festus landed at Ostia, where he was met by a delegation who accompanied him to the imperial box at the Circus Maximus, the largest of Rome's entertainment venues. The Circus Maximus held seating for over two hundred thousand people, with standing room for at least that many more on the hillside above. Down on the long elliptical track, a race was already underway. Twelve chariots sped into the first turn around the *spina*, the raised central median on which statues of the gods and a tall Egyptian obelisk had been erected. At each end of the spina was a turning post, called a *meta*, around which the chariots careened at dangerous speeds. Before the pack had navigated the first turn, three chariots were down, and one of the drivers had been crushed under the wheels of his opponents. The spectators leapt to their feet, screaming out the names of their favourite drivers, their fists pumping up and down in time to the beat of the horses' hooves.

Festus entered the imperial box behind Gallienus. Empress Nina saw him first, and her beautiful face opened in a bright smile. Festus shushed her, then stepped around from behind the emperor, who was talking to his oldest son, the twelve-year-old Valerianus. Empress Nina, always the optimist, had insisted on naming their first child after his grandfather. Although she had never met the elder Valerianus before this day, she had hoped all her married life that Gallienus and his father would one day put aside their differences and reunite. And so they had, for the good of the empire.

"Does a young man not rise in the presence of his elders?" Festus boomed with his deep bass voice.

Gallienus looked over his son's shaggy brown hair and saw Festus standing there in full military uniform. The praetorian scorpion raised its vicious stinger at the centre of his *lorica*. "Not when that young man is emperor," Gallienus replied. He lifted his second son, Saloninus, off his lap and stood up. "But for you, old man, I'll make an exception."

They embraced and then Gallienus stepped back to look at him. Festus' silver hair was cut short and balding at the rear; it was the only sign of his age, which was fifty-five, about the same age as Emperor Valerianus. Otherwise he was fit and muscular and could easily have passed for a man ten years younger. Gallienus had met few men in his life who could equal Festus on a horse or with a sword. In their heyday, he and Valerianus fought side by side under Emperor Alexander Severus in the East, checking the nascent Sassanid Empire in its first bid to conquer Rome's easternmost provinces. He had gone on to serve as governor of Numidia no less than three times. Soldier, general, administrator, and lifelong friend of both emperors, he was the perfect choice to take command of the Praetorian Guard.

"Thank you for agreeing to come out of your retirement, Festus."

"When my emperor calls, I can do nothing else," Festus replied. They embraced again, then Festus skipped around Gallienus and approached his father, who handed off his grandson to a slave and stood up. "Emperor Valerianus at last," Festus said.

Valerianus stepped toward him. "The gods have smiled upon us."

"Well, the gods help those who help themselves, don't they?"

They laughed, then embraced. "Now," Festus said as Valerianus led him to a chair beside his throne, "why don't you tell an old comrade all about how you will soon be making that fool Shapur wish he had stayed in Ctesiphon."

PAULUS CRASHED THROUGH THE WOODS on Asclepus, working his way west, always west, while the sounds of his pursuers grew fainter behind him. His left arm was cut, but not badly. As he rode, he had ripped a length from his cloak and tied it around the wound to staunch the flow. He dropped his hand to his side and it came away slick with blood. That was the wound that really needed attention. From its position he judged that it wasn't fatal. It had passed through his side back to front without striking any organs. But the blood flow there was quick. As Asclepus picked a path through the trees, he tugged off his cloak and tied it about his waist, then clutched the wound with his left hand. The pain made him gasp, but if he held it tight, it would slow the blood loss.

The trees suddenly thinned, then vanished. He was in a field, a meadow; somewhere to his right he heard sheep and saw the distant twinkle of a campfire. The sound of pipes drifted toward him on the night air. Turning to the left, he headed back toward the road. The sounds of pursuit had ceased; he had lost them in the woods. Now was the time for speed, while they attempted to pick up his trail in the darkness. If he was lucky, he could gain an hour on them, even two, then find a place where he could hole up and tend his wounds.

At last he came to the drainage ditch beside the road and climbed back up onto the pavement. The *Via Iulia* was empty in both directions. Paulus turned west and continued his journey. Far below the road, waves crashed upon the rocks and the strong, clean smell of salt filled his nostrils. Close now. Another day, two at the most, and he could stop running. For a little while.

For just a moment, the enormity of what had happened to his life overwhelmed him, and the thought of leaping from Asclepus' back and hurling himself over the cliff into the sea seemed not only comforting, but imperative. Then anger erupted in his heart, and he kicked Asclepus' flanks until the horse was galloping at full speed again. Valerianus' smug face egged him on, and in his mind he heard the madman's pompous laughter as the citizens of Rome screamed his name and worshipped him as a god. There was only one way to hurt a man like that, one way to bring him to his knees. Paulus might not live long enough to see that day, but while he drew breath he would do everything in his power to ensure that bitter end for his enemy. And if the gods decreed he must die before avenging himself, so be it. One day he would stand on the banks of the River Styx in Hades and laugh at the fall of the great Valerianus. And when that day came and Valerianus crossed the river, the first face he saw would be the face of Paulus Antoninus Quaerellus. And he would know at last who the true victor was.

EIGHT

Conall arrived home later that week, leading a string of breeding mares behind him. His tour of Valens' estates in Gallia Aquitania had been a complete success. Aside from making Valens a small fortune at the horse auction at Lugdunum, he had found exactly the kind of stock he needed to increase the overall size of the Massalia bloodlines, and these days bigger horses meant bigger prices.

As he accessed the old coast road east of Massalia, his thoughts turned to his son, Cecht. He was a good boy, a strong boy, and like his father, he served their employer well. Valens had already complimented Conall on Cecht's abilities several times, but the biggest compliment had come three weeks ago, when Valens had suggested Cecht could handle Conall's duties while Conall was in Aquitania. He was eager to see his son again and learn how he had handled the responsibility Valens had placed on his young shoulders.

Conall wiped a swatch of sweaty red hair from his brow. It was early evening, and the day had not yet lost much of its heat. Red was Conall's predominant colour: a thin line of red for eyebrows, a bushy red beard with the first patches of grey beginning to appear below his bottom lip, thick red hair on his forearms and chest, and a red glow to his cheeks, especially when it was hot. As he approached the estate he noticed a group of people trudging up the road toward him. They passed him on the left; none of them looked up. He reined in his horse and turned to watch them. Obviously, they were travelling together, but they did not speak or even look at each other. Strange.

He spotted his friend Sukuta at the end of the laneway and raised his hand in greeting. Sukuta was lying in the grass on the side of the road, a stalk of timothy in his mouth and a scroll in his big hands. Sukuta rarely went anywhere without something to read. Conall himself had no desire to learn; he had gotten by for forty-seven years without it, and if the Lord permitted, he would survive another forty-seven years without ever having to darken Valens' library. But when the big Ethiopian slave had offered to teach Cecht the art of letters, he had agreed. It might serve Cecht well when he became Valens' Master of Horses in a few years.

Sukuta rose from the grass as Conall jumped down from the horse, and the two friends embraced. "A fine looking batch of young ladies," Sukuta said, patting the first one, a white mare whose sleek flanks glistened in the late afternoon sun. "You've done well."

Conall laughed. "So have you. Spending your day sitting by the road and reading? How did you manage that?"

"Guard duty." Sukuta pointed at the group Conall had passed, now mere specks on the dusty road. "Christians seeking an audience with the confessors."

Conall nodded. He had come to the *Christos* six months ago, he and Cecht, after attending several meetings at the nearby Manlius estate. He had worried about what Valens might say when he discovered his Master of Horses now adhered to a forbidden sect, but much to his surprise—to everyone's surprise—when Valens returned a few months ago with his beautiful young wife, he was a Christian. Conall had heard bits and pieces about the *lapsi* but had not paid much attention; he had not been a Christian during the persecution, so the controversy did not concern him, especially since many of the tales came out of the cities in the south: Rome, Carthage, and distant Alexandria in Egypt, too far away for a practical man like Conall to worry about. In his absence, however, the controversy had landed on his own front door, and that *did* concern him. "I'm guessing from the looks of their faces that they did not get what they wanted."

Sukuta put his arm around Conall's shoulders. "Come," he said, "I'll accompany you up to the villa and give you the details."

TACITUS WATCHED THE BIG BLACK MAN and his companion walk up the laneway toward the villa from the cover of a stand of old oaks across the road. He and his aides had arrived in the pre-morning darkness. By the time the Ethiopian appeared at the gate, just after dawn, they had hidden the horses and taken up positions around the estate, Tacitus here, where he could watch the legitimate comings and goings of the Valens household, with Martial and Plautus on either side, covering the sides and back between them. Amongst the three of them, they would spot anybody approaching the estate.

They had arrived the previous evening in Massalia. While Plautus and Martial filled their bellies, Tacitus had put his time to good use. Crossing a few palms with the emperor's silver was all he needed to do to get directions to the estate of Julius Valens and a description of its main inhabitants. Aside from Valens and Damarra—he already knew what they looked like; he had been present at the banquet at which the Divine Valerianus had attempted to crucify the man—he learned several other names. The big Ethiopian was Sukuta, the foreman of Valens' local estates. The man who had just arrived with the horses was Conall, the Master of Horses. His informant had tossed a few other names at him, but none of them seemed particularly important to him. Not particularly troublesome, that was. Sukuta and Conall might get in the way; he would have to deal carefully with them.

He dug an apple out of the leather bag that hung from his belt and bit into it. Good. Valens' slaves grew them juicy. He had filled his bag this morning in the *peristylium* while the household slept around him, oblivious to the man intruding in their lives. Munching apples had helped pass the long hours of surveillance, that and thinking about the best way to deliver the emperor's message. He still wasn't sure how to convey it, but not to worry. Time was on his side.

"BY THE GODS, WHERE COULD HE BE?" Dionysius swore. Twilight was on them again, for the second time since Paulus had escaped them in the forest outside of Veluma. At dawn on that first day, they had found his blood trail and followed it partway through the forest, but it had disappeared again and they had wasted the best part of the day searching for it, only to discover that the forest was barely a mile wide and that Paulus had escaped into a meadow and back to the road many hours before. Then the question became, had he gone back to Veluma to tend his wounds? Or had he continued west? It was obvious now to Dionysius that Paulus was making his way to the estate of his old friend Julius Valens. During the meeting between Tacitus and the emperor, Valerianus had told Tacitus that Valens' home estate was near Massalia, and the *Via Iulia* went to Massalia. Yes, there were plenty of places he could turn off and head north, up into Aquitania or even to the Rhine Frontier and the wilds of Germania beyond, but Dionysius' gut told him Paulus was heading to Valens' estate. Paulus had grown up there, and like any injured animal, he was heading back to his favourite den to lick his wounds.

At last, Ulf galloped into view behind him. He had sent him to check a few of the villages they had passed during the night, just in case, but he could tell from the glare on Ulf's narrow face that he had had no luck. No matter. The time for wandering up and down this highway was over. The best option was to go where Paulus would probably go. "Come," he said to Ulf, and they turned their horses to the west. "We will catch up with Licander ahead, then continue on to the estate of Julius Valens. If I am right, Paulus will be there waiting for me, and we can end this before sunset tomorrow."

THE FIRST THING CONALL SAW when he and Sukuta led the horses into the front courtyard was the German warrior Sukuta had told him about. He was definitely Suevi. He wore his long blond hair tied up in a knot on top of his head, an old Suevi trick designed to give the warrior more height and thus make him seem more menacing. The second thing that Conall saw was that the Suevi somehow *knew* him. The moment their eyes locked, the German rushed over to him and grabbed his shoulders. "You come!" he cried, as if Conall were a member of his family that he had not seen in many years.

Suddenly the whole household was there in the courtyard. Cecht, grinning with joy, slipped an arm around his father's waist, and Senator Valens and his wife, who had been sitting on the porch in the cool of the evening studying a scroll, were hurrying over as fast as Damarra could move. "Beautiful mares," Valens exclaimed, his gaze flitting to each in turn, assessing them with a critical eye. "Well, done, Conall!"

Conall passed the reins of his horse to his son and shook Valens' hand. "They will add strength, size, and stamina to your herds, my lord, or I do not know horses."

"You most certainly do," Damarra said.

Conall bowed his head. "Thank you, my lady."

"I can hardly wait to ride one of these. They are amazing!"

Valens patted her abdomen. "Not today. Please!"

They laughed as Cecht led the horses away to the stables. Conall turned his attention back to the German. "Sukuta tells me his name is Gundabar and that he has come from the Suevi for some reason."

"Yes," Valens said. "His Latin is poor, and none of us speak any of the Germanic dialects. We were hoping that you could help."

Conall scratched his head. "It has been many years since I visited Germania. I was a boy not much older than Cecht the last time my father journeyed east to trade with the tribes. But let me try."

He spoke a few words in one dialect, but Gundabar shook his head. He tried a few more before Gundabar's eyes grew big and bright. "*Yiese* . . . yes!" he cried.

Conall nodded. "Germania is a very . . . fluid place, my lord," he said to Valens. "The tribes are in constant motion; their boundaries never cease to fluctuate. The tribes mix, separate, form new tribes, and so their languages mix, separate, and form new tongues. He speaks a form of Suevi, but it is not much like the Suevi I heard in my youth. Still, I think I might be able to—" He began talking to Gundabar again, and the German responded, long strings of words that sounded guttural to ears more attuned to the flowing nuances of Latin and Greek. At one point Conall lifted his hands and gestured for the German to slow down, and he did, for a few moments, but then the excitement burning in his green eyes burst from his tongue again in a staccato of harsh sounding words. Finally the German stopped and looked at each of them in turn. He held out his arms, spread them wide, as if trying to embrace them all. And then he nodded. He was finished.

The others turned from Gundabar to Conall, staring at him expectantly.

"I understand some of it," Conall began.

"Which is more than we do," Valens said.

"He says God sent him a vision, by which I mean the *Christos*. He is a Christian."

"I did not know our faith had reached that far to the north," Damarra said.

Conall nodded. "There were a few Christians amongst the Suevi back when I was a boy. Not many. Our faith does not always sit well with the Germans."

"Why is that?" Valens asked.

"They pride themselves on being warriors. A warrior does not give up his life without a fight. According to their beliefs, one does not join Woden in the halls of Valhalla unless one dies in battle. The *Christos* allowed himself to be killed; he did not fight back."

Damarra took her husband's hand. "Valens had a similar difficulty with the crucifixion—that a god would allow himself to die in such a degrading manner seemed to disprove his divinity."

"It is the same for the Germans," Conall agreed.

"So what was this vision?" Valens asked.

Conall continued: "The *Christos* told him to leave the Suevi and journey to Gallia and find *Sankt*," Conall spoke a few words to Gundabar, who pointed at Valens. "That's you, my lord Valens, and to join *Sankt's* household . . . clan I think is the better word. And when that clan is . . . full, he is to lead them to the . . . dark trees? . . . no . . . uhm . . . black woods, yes, that's it. Lead them to the black woods for a *Thing*."

"*A-zem-bly*," Gundabar added, grinning at Valens.

"A *Thing* is a council of warriors," Conall said. "Under a king, the leader of the clans."

Damarra and Valens glanced at each other. "It sounds like he wants us to go to Germania with him," Valens said.

The German spoke to Conall, nodded. "The *Christos* wants your clan to go to Germania, yes."

"My *clan*?"

"Yes."

"And . . . who is in my clan?"

Conall spoke to the German again. Gundabar nodded and pointed at Valens, then, in turn, at Damarra, Sukuta, Conall, and himself.

"Is that it?" Valens asked.

Gundabar shook his head. He looked around the courtyard, spotted Persephone at the loom and pointed at her, then at Prisca, who was hovering behind her mistress. He looked around again, shrugged, and pointed to the stable and lifted his hand halfway up Conall's chest.

"And Cecht," Conall added.

"And is that all?" Valens asked.

Again Gundabar shook his head. He spoke to Conall, but Conall couldn't quite grasp the meaning of the German's words and asked him to repeat them several times. At last, he shrugged. "It's confusing, my lord. Something about 'another must come' and then 'another must come.'" Conall scratched his head. "As near as I can figure, your clan is not complete. Another must come . . . two others must come, perhaps? Only then, when the number is thirteen, will the clan leave for the black woods."

"And where are the black woods?" Damarra asked.

"That could be anywhere in the wilds of Germania, my lady. Germania is a land of forests."

"Wait a minute," Sukuta said. "That doesn't add up."

They all turned to look at him. He had been standing beside his friend Conall the whole time, listening intently. "What do you mean?" Valens asked.

"The eight of us plus these two 'others' he mentioned. That adds up to ten, not thirteen."

Conall spoke to Gundabar, who shrugged and held up both hands, fingers and thumbs extended, then closed them and added three fingers more: thirteen.

"So let me understand this," Valens said. "The *Christos* came to Gundabar in a vision and told him to come to Gallia to find *Sankt*." He turned to Conall. "What does '*Sankt*' mean?"

Conall grimaced. "Never heard that one before, my lord."

Valens continued: "Once he finds *Sankt*—me—he is to join my clan, and when the eight of us become ten of us become thirteen of us, our clan is to go to the black woods somewhere in Germania for a *Thing*, which is some kind of a council of warriors."

"That is correct, my lord," Conall said with a shrug.

"Well that clears that up then, doesn't it, Master Valens?" Sukuta added with a wink.

FROM HIS HIDING PLACE in the copse of oaks, Tacitus could just make out the sounds of laughter. They had been standing together for the last hour in the courtyard, just inside the open doors, talking, but they were too distant for him to make out any specific words. And now that the last hint of daylight was fading from the western sky, he could barely make them out anymore. There was a sudden flare of light, and Sukuta appeared and lit lamps on either side of the door, both inside and outside.

He was just leaving his cover, planning on sneaking closer to the open doorway so he could hear what they were discussing, when the sound of approaching hoof beats on the road forced him back into the shadows. A lone rider appeared, impossible to tell who in the fading light, but Tacitus saw a glint of metal in the rising light of the moon, and knew the rider was a soldier. He stopped at the gate, seemed almost to waver in the saddle as if he were exhausted, then eased the horse forward, using its broad chest to open the gate. Now perhaps was his chance. He could cross the road under cover of the noise the horse and rider were making. Again, he began to edge from his hiding place, and again he thought he heard something on the road. He froze, turned, gazed into the darkness to his left untouched by the light of the rising moon. Something . . . someone was there. Maybe. Another horse? Someone on foot? Or was it just his nerves playing games with him in the night?

The horseman stopped three-quarters of the way down the laneway and called out Julius Valens' name. A torch appeared in the doorway, and when Tacitus looked back to the road, there was no one there. If there ever *had* been. Silently, he crossed the road, slipped through the gates, and took shelter amongst the olive trees that lined the laneway. Close enough to hear, but out of sight of the group of people who were now pouring out the doorway to answer the horseman's call.

VALENS TOOK THE TORCH FROM SUKUTA and held it up. "Who are you?" he asked. "What do you want?"

The horse trotted closer, stopped again. "Is this the villa of Julius Valens and the lady Damarra?" the horseman asked.

Valens stepped toward him; he glanced back at Damarra. She was shivering, whether from the cool now that the sun had set or from fright, he did not know. "Prisca," he said. "Run to our chamber and fetch Damarra's shawl."

"Yes, my lord," she replied and fled into the courtyard. Persephone, who had left her loom and come to the doorway with the others, took Prisca's place beside Damarra.

Finally the horseman came close enough for them to distinguish his features. He was a soldier, a tribune from his armour, perhaps thirty years of age. His hair and eyes were brown, his nose slightly hooked. He had heard Valens speak Damarra's name, and so he dismounted and pulled a leather pouch from his belt. He stepped toward Damarra, but Valens slipped in front of him. "I am Tribune Marcus Gaius Fortunatus," he said to Damarra, "and I bring you greetings from your brother, the emperor Caesar Publius Licinius Egnatius Gallienus Augustus."

Damarra's sea-blue eyes blinked in the torch light. "My *brother?*" she exclaimed. "The *emperor?*"

Marcus smiled. He was very handsome, the epitome of the gallant soldier. "Yes, my lady. Your brother, the Emperor Gallienus, and his father, Caesar Publius Licinianus Valerianus Augustus, are the new emperors of Rome. Gallienus wishes to assure you—"

But at the name of Valerianus, Damarra had stopped listening.

"No, it cannot be," she breathed, her eyes wide with shock. She touched her stomach and swooned backwards, as if the name itself were a fist that had just struck her to the ground. Sukuta caught her before she could fall.

Gundabar pushed between Conall and Valens and pointed excitedly at the new arrival. "Another," he cried. It was the right Latin word, but pronounced with the German's harsh accent. The others glanced at him, then at Marcus, who was staring down his nose at the German as if he were seeing a ghoul rise from the grave. "Another must come," Gundabar said. "He *another*."

"Are you saying that Tribune Marcus is to join my clan?" Valens asked.

"*Yiese*," Gundabar cried. "Yes! Yes!"

"Excuse me?" Marcus said.

A shrill scream sounded in the darkness behind them. "What *now*?" Valens groaned. He pointed at the tribune. "You, stay here. You," he said to the others, "watch over Damarra." Yanking his dagger from its sheath on his belt, he raced back into courtyard. Ahead, Prisca was fleeing toward him out of the shadows of the porch.

"Master," she cried, when she spied him. "Some—" but he grabbed her arm and shushed her. It might have been nothing more than a bat flitting about the atrium, but whatever it was, he did not want Tribune Marcus to find out; not before he made some sense of what he had just said. He leapt up the porch steps two at a time, grabbing a torch from a sconce beside the door, then headed into the shadowy house.

"Where?" he demanded of Prisca.

"In your chambers," the plump slave whispered. "A man!"

He ran through the atrium, down into the inner courtyard, to their quarters at the far end of the villa. The large oak door at the end of the hallway that led to their bedroom was ajar. Shoulder to the wood, he shoved it open all the way and hurled himself into the room with his dagger ready and torch held high.

His friend Paulus Antoninus Quaerellus stood just inside the room, his back leaning against the wall by the entrance to the terrace. His white tunic was stained with blood. "Valens," he whispered, and began to slide down the wall to the floor.

Valens dropped his knife into its sheath and grabbed Paulus before he could fall. He handed the torch to Prisca. "Say nothing about this!" he ordered.

"Yes, my lord," she squeaked. Her entire body was trembling.

"Valens," he whispered. "We must talk."

He dragged his friend over to the bed. "You must rest; Prisca will tend to your wounds."

Suddenly there was another scream, this one at the door of his bedroom. Valens' hand dropped to the hilt of his knife again as he turned. Persephone stood in the doorway, her delicate hands clenched in fists over her mouth. He shushed her as he poured Paulus into bed. This time he was too weak to protest. "My lord," Persephone said. Her voice was trembling. "Lady Damarra . . . the baby. She has gone into labour. It is time."

Valens groaned again. This could not be happening!

"Persephone, come here."

The slave hurried to the bedside.

"This man is my friend. Make him comfortable. Stop the bleeding. Say nothing of this to the others."

With a nod, she set to work.

"Come, Prisca, the lady Damarra needs us."

They hurried back through the dark house by torchlight, out into the courtyard where Valens could hear Damarra's muffled cries. The others stood around her, trying to comfort her. Even Tribune Marcus was lending a hand. Valens thrust his way into the middle of the group. "Damarra," he cried.

She looked at him, her eyes like shining blue pools of sea water. "It is time, Valens. Your son is coming."

He handed the torch to Prisca again and picked up his wife. With Prisca leading the way he hurried as fast as possible, trying not to jar her and cause her more pain. "The rest of you stay in the courtyard," he called over his shoulder. "Including you, Tribune Marcus. I will return as soon as possible.

He carried her into the atrium, then turned left, toward the slave's quarters. "Where are you taking me?" Damarra asked. Her hand clutched her abdomen, and she bit her lip to stifle a groan of pain. "I want to go to my own bedroom."

"No," he said. "You will be better off in Persephone's room.

Won't she, Prisca?"

"Yes, my lord," the slave agreed. "It is a much better birthing room. You will see. Trust Prisca now."

"All right," Damarra agreed.

NINE

Tacitus crept closer to the entrance to the walled outer courtyard. He halted his advance just beyond the glow of light of the lamps, still invisible but now able to hear the discussion taking place a few yards away. Everyone was focused on the villa; he probably could have marched right into the courtyard unnoticed. He listened for ten minutes, then slipped away, back to his hiding spot amongst the oaks. Nothing to learn right now. Their conversation centred on the woman, Damarra, and the baby she was about to deliver. But what he *had* heard gave him plenty to think about.

Tribune Marcus Gaius Fortunatus. He knew the man, knew *of* the man, more accurately. Tribune Marcus was one of Emperor Gallienus' officers and his friend. The two of them had met in Numidia. The Fortunatus estate was a mile from the estate of Festus Macrinus, the man Emperor Valerianus had chosen to see to his son's education. The two youths had forged a bond of friendship that had carried on into their careers, Gallienus as general and Marcus as his most trusted lieutenant. Marcus had taken a six month furlough to journey to Numidia and set the family estates in order a few years before, after his father's death, but aside from that he and Gallienus had rarely been apart.

Tacitus permitted himself a thin smile. A very interesting situation, this was. Emperor Valerianus had made no mention of

Tribune Marcus delivering a message to Valens and Damarra—that task had been delegated to him—and even if the Divine Valerianus had sent another, it wouldn't have been Marcus, whose loyalty to the Divine Gallienus was unimpeachable. Or so one would think. So Gallienus had *also* sent a messenger and a message. Two emperors, two messages, and neither emperor knew what the other had done. Already a gap of information existed between the two emperors, and it was in such gaps that the collection of intelligence was most essential. And most *lucrative*.

His thoughts were interrupted by the less than stealthy arrival of Plautus. The big man stepped on a dead branch that produced a snap loud enough for Zeus atop Mount Olympus to hear. The people gathered in the courtyard were too intent on the noises coming from inside the house to notice, but just for a moment Tacitus fantasized about slicing open Plautus thick neck and leaving him here for the vultures. "Someone has come, my lord," Plautus whispered.

Tacitus rolled his eyes. "Yes, I see that Plautus. Did you blunder all the way over here to tell me that?"

Plautus glanced at the courtyard. "No, my lord. Someone entered the house from the side."

Now Tacitus was interested. "Did you see who it was?"

"It was too dark. It was a man, I think, and he seemed unsteady on his feet."

"Unsteady?"

"Yes. He fell once, got up, leaned against a tree to catch his breath, then lurched toward the terrace and disappeared inside. I think he was drunk."

"Or perhaps injured?"

Plautus shrugged. "Perhaps."

Excitement trilled in Tacitus' chest. A solitary man entering the villa, not by the front because he did not want to be seen. It could be nothing of course—a drunk slave slinking home to avoid punishment, or a lover come for a midnight tryst. Or somebody much more important. "Show me," he ordered.

Plautus led him out and around the east side of the villa, past the inner garden courtyard to the living quarters at the back of the complex. A terrace jutted out from the large bedchamber that they had already identified as belonging to the lord and lady. When they were twenty yards from the terrace, Tacitus motioned Plautus to stay and then crept forward until he was crouching behind the terrace's half wall. Slowly, carefully, he lifted his head and peered over the wall. The bed chamber was lit by a solitary lamp. A beautiful woman with brown hair and olive skin was leaning over the bed. She was tall and willowy and in the full sheen of her youth; Tacitus was immediately attracted to her. The figure on the bed was obscured by the chamber walls. "Drink more, my lord," the woman said. Her voice was sweet and full of compassion.

The man on the bed moaned. "Must talk to Valens." He was having difficulty speaking; even from this distance Tacitus could hear the pain in his voice, his labouring breath. Wounded, not drunk.

"The lady Damarra is in labour, my lord. He will not leave her now."

"A baby?" The man's chuckle descended into a coughing fit.

"Hush, my lord, rest."

Through the open doorway he saw a hand grab the woman's arm. It was stained with blood; on the third finger was a signet ring. He pulled her down on the bed beside him. "Must give him a message." He paused, breathing hard, then he laughed. "Valerianus' soldiers . . . waiting . . . outside Veluma." His speech had begun to slur.

"Here, drink more," she said.

He drank, sputtered, then spoke again. His voice grew softer with each word. "Someone will come . . . another . . . help." He lapsed into silence, and when Tacitus thought he was indeed finished, he spoke one more time, words so soft and slurred he could barely make them out: "Between . . . rivers."

The woman stood up, bent over the man on the bed, then turned and hurried out of the room.

Tacitus rose from his hiding spot and crossed the terrace. He did not need to look at the man—he had already guessed who it was—but he was paid to be thorough. Quick, quiet steps brought him into the bed chamber, where the woman had left the lamp burning. On the bed lay Paulus Antoninus Quaerellus. The woman had bound his left arm and side in strips of white linen.

He laughed at that. The strips of linen were either bandages or the first tentative loops of a burial shroud—all in the eyes of the beholder. On a small table beside the bed was an empty wooden bowl. He picked it up, sniffed: a light medicinal smell, some kind of concoction of herbs. Paulus' chest rose and fell in slow measures; the former commander of the Praetorian Guard was asleep. With a grin of satisfaction, Tacitus stole from the villa and returned to Plautus.

MARCUS REMOVED HIS HELMET and ruffled his short hair. He set the helmet on a stone bench that sat against the courtyard wall. A loud cry of pain echoed from the villa. The confessor was in the throes of childbirth. Marcus closed his eyes and sent up a silent prayer to the *Christos* for her safety. She must survive. Not only was she the half-sister of the Emperor Gallienus, she was *Amicula Christi*, Friend of the Christ—surely no other person in the empire had the ear of both the emperor of Rome and the Emperor of Heaven as she did. Despite Gallienus' assurances that his father had no intention of persecuting the Christians, he did not believe it. Not at this time, Gallienus had said. But a year from now? Two? Surely that would change. Valerianus' hatred of the Christians was as sure as the rising sun and the ocean tides. For now the sun had set, the tide was out, and there was darkness and quiet and peace, and under those conditions the Christians thrived; but inevitably the sun of Valerianus' hatred would rise again, and in the fiery heat of that day, when the screams of the persecuted once more rolled across the empire like the pounding surf, the lady Damarra might be the sole barrier between that hatred and the extermination of every Christian in the civilized world.

Marcus opened his eyes and glanced at the others. They were milling about, talking together and ignoring him. All except the German: he was gazing at Marcus as if the two of them were old friends reuniting after a long absence, as if he somehow *knew* him. But Marcus had never met the man before; he was *sure* of that. It occurred to him that they might have met on the battlefield, and his hand fell to the hilt of his sword. He had spent the last two years on the Rhine Frontier patrolling the provinces of Germania

Superior and Germania Inferior, with nothing but the thin blue line of the Rhine separating the beleaguered Roman outposts from the seething tribes of the German homeland. In that time he had faced countless raiding parties from across the river; but try as he might, he could not remember ever looking down the blade of his sword at that face. Besides, the German—they called him Gundabar—did not *feel* like an enemy; he felt like a friend. In fact, he felt like more than that.

Marcus drew a fish in a patch of dry dirt with the toe of his sandal. Gundabar's smile brightened even more. He scratched a cross beside the fish with his leather boot. Marcus erased both signs and at last smiled back. The German was a Christian! Of course, there must be a few in Germania. He had heard that the faith had reached beyond the frontiers, to Sarmatia, into sub-Roman Africa, even into the Persian Empire. In fact, it was said that Christians were *welcome* in Shapur's realm. The best that the Christians could hope for in the Roman Empire was to be ignored. In some of the larger cities Christian *ecclesia* were more visible, had actually gone public, a phenomenon that had commenced during the long period of peace the Church had experienced before Decius came to the throne and brought the wrath of his gods down upon their heads. In his travels, Marcus had seen a number of such Christian houses of worship. *Ecclesia* was coming to mean an actual building, rather than the body of worshippers itself, who shifted their worship from apartment to villa to cemetery as necessitated. Most of those permanent *ecclesiae* had been abandoned during the reign of Decius, but now, with the persecution over, the Christians were returning to them again. But even before Decius had shattered their peace, Marcus had seen these new church buildings as a mistake. It was one thing to worship in the shadows; it was another thing to stand in the bright light of day and cry out, *Christianus Sum*. Because unlike Shapur, the emperor was not welcoming the Christians; he was ignoring them—and the more visible the *ecclesiae* became, the harder it became to turn a blind eye.

Suddenly the German was beside him, slapping him on the back. "You another," he said in his thick accent. "You join clan."

Sukuta grinned over at Marcus. "You've made a friend, my

lord."

"He is Christian."

Sukuta's grin evaporated; his expression became wary. "Is he, my lord?"

"Relax, Sukuta. I too am a Christian. And you?"

The big black man shook his head. "Not me, my lord."

"And you, Conall?"

Sukuta stepped in front of his friend. "Forgive me, Tribune Marcus, but perhaps these are matters best discussed when Lord Valens is present."

"Don't worry, Sukuta," Conall said. "He is part of this; Gundabar identified him."

"Yes, and that's another thing. We have no idea what this whole clan marching through the black woods to a *Thing*—"

"*A-zem-bly*," Gundabar interjected, smiling.

Sukuta continued: "Yes, *a-zem-bly*. We have no idea what any of this means."

"It is a message from the *Christos*," Conall said, as if that were explanation enough.

"So you are in fact a Christian," Marcus observed.

Sukuta threw up his hands.

"Yes, my lord. I serve the *Christos*."

"Very well, I promise to refrain from identifying any more Christians in the household, if you will explain to me why Gundabar seems so intent on having me join his clan."

Sukuta glanced at Conall, who shrugged. "It is a long story, my lord," Sukuta said.

Another cry of pain issued from the house. Marcus sat down on the bench beside his helmet. "I think we may have the time," he said.

PERSEPHONE FOLLOWED DAMARRA'S CRIES to her own room in the slave quarters of the house. Damarra sat on her bed under a sheet. Prisca held one hand, Valens the other, while the two of them supported her back. She had just finished a contraction. Her face was red from exertion and specked with perspiration, but she was smiling. "Look, Persephone. See how easy this is!" Damarra rolled her eyes as they helped her lay back down.

Persephone laughed. Her mistress always seemed to see the light rather than the shadows. "I will keep that in mind when my turn comes, my lady."

"Oh no, don't wait; you may take my place now if you wish."

Even Valens laughed at that. He kissed his wife's forehead. "I am stepping outside to talk to Persephone for moment. Just out the door. I will be right back."

Prisca dabbed Damarra's forehead with a cool cloth. "Prisca, tell my husband he does not need to be here. Everything is fine."

Prisca looked up at Valens. "She speaks the truth, my lord. The baby is just where it should be. My lady is healthy and strong; there is nothing to fear."

Valens nodded at the slave then hurried Persephone out of the room, out of earshot of Damarra. "How is he?" he asked.

"I bound his wounds, my lord. He said that Valerianus' soldiers caught him near Veluma. He is weak from loss of blood, but I think with rest he will recover. He is very strong. I gave him a sleeping draught. He should sleep until morning. Sleep and rest are the best remedies for him now."

"Did he say anything else?"

"Yes, my lord, but I did not understand it."

"Tell me."

"He kept saying he had to talk to you. And then he said something about someone coming to help."

Valens' eyes pierced hers. "Someone coming to help?"

"Yes, my lord."

"Someone," he muttered to himself.

"Does that mean something, my lord?"

"What were his exact words, Persephone? Try to remember."

She paused for a moment, closed her eyes, then repeated the memory back to him. "He said, someone will come . . . another . . . help. Yes, that was it, 'someone will come . . . another . . . help.'"

"Another," Valens repeated. "There is that word again."

"My lord?"

He shook his head. "I will tell you later, Persephone, as it involves you."

"Me, my lord?"

"Yes, so Gundabar says." Suddenly there was a cry from the room; Damarra was having another contraction. "Find food and lodging for Tribune Marcus, but keep him away from our bed chamber. When you finish, return here. You may be needed to help Damarra."

"Yes, my lord. Oh, and he said something else, my lord. I almost forgot."

"What did he say?"

"He said, 'Between rivers.'"

Valens blinked at her. "What does that mean?"

"I had hoped you would know, my lord."

With a shrug, he hurried back to his wife.

TACITUS MET PLAUTUS WHERE HE had left him and together they headed back to the irrigation ditch where Plautus had secreted himself for the day. "Who is it?" Plautus asked when they were sitting on the grassy bank.

"Paulus Antoninus Quaerellus."

Plautus' beefy face dropped in surprise. "Commander Paulus? Here?"

"Ex-commander Paulus, you mean, and yes, he is here. Looks to me as if our friend Commander Dionysius got a piece of him. Not a big enough piece, though; he will recover."

"Where is Commander Dionysius?" he asked.

"Somewhere between here and Veluma, by the sounds of it. I wouldn't be surprised if the good commander put in an appearance as well." Tacitus chuckled. "The lord and lady have never had so much or such distinguished company as they have had tonight, I'll warrant."

"What should we do, my lord?" Plautus asked.

"I still must deliver the Divine Valerianus' message." He took a flat leather pouch from his belt and hefted it in his hand. "And I think I know the best way to deliver it now. Find Martial and prepare the horses. I shall meet you there in an hour or less."

Tacitus waited until Plautus had moved off, then he stood up and returned to the bed chamber. Paulus was still asleep. He crept around to the other side of the bed so he could immobilize Paulus' good arm first. Wounded or not, drugged or not, the man was a competent soldier and that made him dangerous. Best not to take unnecessary risks.

Carefully, he placed his knee on the man's right arm, then swung his other leg over top to pin his wounded arm. Paulus did not stir; whatever draught the beautiful slave had given him was very strong. Tacitus tightened his knees, purposefully jabbing his weight into Paulus' wounded side. The wounded man let out a whimper; his brow furrowed, then slowly smoothed again. He slapped Paulus across the face. "Wake up, Commander," he barked.

Paulus groaned.

He slapped him again, harder this time, then backhanded his other cheek. Paulus' eyes fluttered open, began to drift shut again, and Tacitus reached back and dug his fingers into the wound on his side. Now his eyes flew open and stayed open. Tacitus clamped his hand over Paulus' mouth. "If you cry out, I will kill you. Do you understand?"

Paulus nodded.

"Good." Tacitus sat up, released his mouth. He dug his finger into the wound on Paulus' side again, and Paulus bit his lip to stifle a scream. Tacitus smiled down at his ashen face. "Hurts, doesn't it?"

Paulus stared at him, but even now the powerful drug the woman had given him was doing its work, and his eyes began to drift shut. "Not yet," Tacitus said, slapping Paulus' face.

The eyes popped open again. He managed a slurred, "What do you want?"

Tacitus lifted the leather pouch, opened it, and pulled out the document it contained. He held it up for Paulus to see; recognition sparked in his eyes when he saw the red seal. "Yes, that's right, a message from Emperor Valerianus for your friend Valens and the lady Damarra. You are going to deliver it for me." He slapped Paulus face again. "And then you can sleep all you want, drift off to Elysium for a good, long rest, yes?"

As if in answer, Paulus' eyelids drooped shut. This time he didn't bother to wake him. He had had a bit of fun with the once mighty Paulus Antoninus Quaerellus, but now the time for games was at an end. All that remained was to leave Valerianus' message and be on his way.

He placed the letter on Paulus' chest, got up, and leaned over the sleeping man one last time. "Good night and farewell, Commander Paulus," he whispered.

THEY HAD BEEN TALKING FOR ALMOST an hour when the pretty, dark-haired slave reappeared, carrying a tray of food and a jug of wine. Marcus smiled at her as she poured the wine; the young woman blushed in response. She was more than pretty; she was beautiful. And apparently Gundabar thought so, too. He watched her every move until she turned to offer him some wine, and then his handsome face split into a big grin, and from the smile she offered in response, he thought perhaps the attraction was mutual. He sipped at his wine, then set the goblet down on the bench beside him. "So you are destined for Germania," he said to Conall.

"Aye," Conall replied.

"I have visited Germania," Marcus said. "I was stationed in the empire's German provinces across the Rhine from Germania, and we often made forays over the river, usually chasing after some band of adventurers who had ducked into the empire for a quick pillage, then scooted home again."

"Perhaps that's why you are meant to come—your knowledge of Germania?"

Marcus shook his head. "I imagine Gundabar here knows it far better than I do. I have never been further than ten miles east of the Rhine. We usually turn around and head home before that; wouldn't pay to have some war band cut off our retreat. The Lord must want me along for some other reason." He stood up and stretched. "I am just grateful that the Lord has honoured me in this way."

"So you believe Gundabar?"

He handed his empty plate to Persephone and thanked her. "Yes, I do," he replied.

"You must be a Christian, then."

"Why do you say that?"

Sukuta laughed. "You Christians are always, 'The Lord said

this,' or 'The Lord said that.' I hear nothing but the breeze in the trees and the sound of the surf below."

"That's because you don't listen," Conall said to his friend. They both laughed.

"Then let us speak as the Romans do," Marcus countered, "and say that destiny brought us together, or the goddess Fortuna, or would you prefer to read it in the stars like the eastern astrologers: 'The stars say this,' or 'The stars say that?' Is that not how it goes?"

"At least I can see the stars," Sukuta replied. His big chest expanded in a sigh. "Forgive my scepticism, Tribune Marcus. In truth, I must admit that I too believe Gundabar. It is as if something . . . bigger is bringing us together. Maybe the *Christos*, maybe the stars, I don't know. But I know one thing: there is still this 'other' who must come."

The slave girl opened her mouth to speak, then closed it.

"And even Tribune Marcus and this 'other' does not make thirteen," Conall reminded them.

Persephone cleared her throat. "If I may, my lord?" she said.

Marcus nodded.

"Forgive me for interrupting, my lord, but the master wishes me to take you to your room, then return to help with the lady Damarra."

"Of course," Marcus said. He patted his armoured belly. "I am full and content and ready for sleep. My message from the emperor can wait until Damarra is ready to receive it. Lead on, fair Persephone."

With another blush, the slave turned and led Marcus into the house. The room she led him to was small but functional: a simple bed pushed up against one wall, a wash basin, an urn for night toiletries. Persephone lit the small lamp, bid him goodnight, then closed the door behind her. Marcus removed his armour and set it on the floor at the foot of the bed. Next came the sword and sheath, which he stood against the wall beside the head of the bed, in easy reach. Caution was always the best policy, especially in a new environment. The holy confessors might be close, but that did not mean there was no danger. Finally he removed his belt and took out the flat leather pouch secreted in the lining. There were two documents inside. The first was a letter of transit from Emperor Gallienus, giving the bearer permission to commandeer anything he might need for the journey—horses, food, men, all at imperial expense. The second was a letter he had received in Carthage, where he had disembarked to make the overland journey to the family estate near Cirta in Numidia two years before. Smiling, he opened it and read the words written there; then he refolded it, kissed it, and tucked it under the pillow. It was part of his nightly ritual. No matter where he was, he always read it before going to sleep.

He placed his dagger on the little table beside the bed—also in easy reach—then dropped to his knees, and spent a few minutes worshipping the *Christos*. The others could not know how much it meant to him that the Lord had chosen him for Gundabar's quest. For so very long now he had felt a vast silence pressing down on him when he sought out the *Christos*. But now he knew the *Christos* was still thinking of him, that he was somehow part of the Lord's plan. How, did not matter. Just knowing the *Christos* cared was enough.

TEN

As the first broad stroke of red brushed the eastern horizon, Damarra's eyes opened. As she had done so often on waking in the last nine months, her hand reached down to caress her abdomen and say good morning to the life growing inside her. But today she touched nothing, and suddenly the memory of what had happened a few hours before blossomed again in her consciousness, and she smiled and stretched languidly, then turned her head. Beside the bed, her baby slept in its cradle.

Her *baby*.

Damarra tossed back the sheet and sat up. Never had she seen anything so beautiful as the life she and Valens had created together, the little girl that God had blessed them with. She closed her eyes and lifted her hands in prayer. When she opened them again, she glanced around the room. The lamp had burned low, but a flame still flickered on the wick, casting shadows in the gathering light of day. Prisca was sleeping in a chair beside the bed, one hand on the cradle as if protecting her new ward even in her sleep. Valens sat in a chair on the other side of the bed, and she felt a moment of relief seeing him there asleep. His baby had lived; his wife had lived. The fear that had terrorized his heart since the day he had found out Damarra was pregnant had proved unfounded. He had never expressed the fear in words, but it had burned in his eyes every time he looked at her.

She looked at her baby again. So beautiful. She had a full head of hair as white as Damarra's. Her eyes opened and she cooed, and Damarra's breasts filled with milk in response. Gently she picked up the swaddled babe. Holding her close to her heart, she kissed the tiny nose. "Come, little one," she whispered. "Let me show you the garden."

Damarra stood up and slipped out of the room. She felt good and strong; there was no pain. Even the memory of her birthing pains was beginning to fade. By the time she found her favourite bench nestled among the apple trees in the peristylium, she had decided she wanted to have another child as soon as possible. As the baby suckled, Damarra told her about the fun she would have here in the beautiful Gallic sunshine, about riding horses and searching for shells down on the beach, about running through the fields when the hay was high and the golden wheat rippled like yellow waves in the salted breeze that flitted up from the sea.

"You make me want to grow up here again," Valens said.

She looked up at him and smiled. "Did I wake you?"

He stretched, touched her head. "No. I woke up and you were gone. I knew you'd come here."

"I was telling our daughter about our life here."

Valens knelt down and kissed the baby's head. "She is beautiful. You are beautiful."

"Would you like to hold your daughter?" she asked.

He nodded and she passed the baby to him. In his arms she seemed even smaller. He held her up to his shoulder and began to pat the baby's back. Once again her eyes were drawn to the marks on his wrists, and suddenly it all flooded back to her, the tribune who had arrived last evening, the message from her brother.

And Valerianus.

Her hands flew to her mouth and she choked back a sob.

Valens saw the change, and his happy expression faded. "What's wrong, Damarra?"

Her blue eyes shone with tears as she looked at her husband. "Valerianus." She whispered that single word as if it were a black spell that would conjure his actual presence.

Fear leapt into Valens' eyes as well. In their joy they had forgotten what Tribune Marcus had told them, but now the memory resuscitated and the horror metastised through her like a cancer. "*Emperor* Valerianus. Oh, Valens, what will we do?"

He shook his head, and that frightened her even more. Because Valens always knew what to do, always had a plan. "We must talk to this Tribune Marcus," he said at last.

Persephone entered the peristylium from the front of the villa, carrying a tray. "Is that for me?" Damarra asked.

Persephone glanced at Damarra, then at Valens. Valens answered for her. "You may go, Persephone. I'll explain everything to Lady Damarra."

With a bow of her head, Persephone continued on to the back of the garden. Damarra watched her until she disappeared into their living quarters, then asked, "What is going on?"

"Damarra, my love," Valens began.

A scream echoed through the villa.

"Persephone!" Damarra exclaimed.

Valens handed the baby to Damarra and ran toward the rear of the garden. There was a second scream, and then Persephone appeared on the colonnade that surrounded the peristylium. Valens caught her on the steps. "My lord Paulus!" she cried.

Prisca hurried up behind Damarra, wiping the sleep from her eyes. From another room on the same side came Tribune Marcus, wearing only a tunic. In his hand was a dagger.

Paulus?

Damarra handed the baby to Prisca and hurried over to her husband. "Did she say Paulus?" she asked.

Valens rushed into their quarters without answering. She and Marcus and Persephone, now sobbing into her hands, followed. The first thing Damarra saw when they burst into her bed chamber was Valens on his knees beside the bed, his fists raised to the heavens, and a look of anguish on his face that she had not seen since that day, two years before, when Valerianus had murdered Baradoc, Valens' dearest friend, before his very eyes.

The second thing she saw was a man lying on their bed with a knife protruding from his chest.

Paulus Antoninus Quaerellus. The man who had saved their lives.

Dead.

PAULUS IS DEAD.

Valens' mind whispered the words, but they could not pierce the whirlwind of memories that swirled through him: boyhood games fighting the Germanic hordes that never troubled their sleepy, seaside home . . . army life in Britannia and on the Rhine Frontier . . . nights of gambling and drinking . . . covering each other's backs . . .

. . . *saving each other's lives* . . .

Paulus had saved his life two years ago. Valerianus had tried to crucify him, and Paulus had been there to cover his back, just like old times.

But he had failed to cover Paulus' back and now Paulus was dead.

Paulus is dead.

From somewhere far away he heard a keening wail, the sound of grief so stark and potent that it wrenched his heart, until he realized that *he* was making that horrible sound, and the grasping fingers of anger slipped around his anguish and began to throttle it. He stood up, wiping the tears from his eyes with the back of his hand, and bent over his friend, and it was then that he noticed that something was attached to the knife.

A piece of parchment with a red seal.

He grasped the knife and pulled it out of Paulus' chest. It made a sucking sound as it came loose. Pulling off the parchment, he tossed the knife aside.

"What is it?" Damarra whispered.

Lost in his own grief, Valens didn't hear her. The back of the parchment was slick with blood. He withdrew his dagger, slit the seal, and opened the document. A single sentence was printed there in ink as black as the abyss into which Valens' heart now glared:

Be sure that we will meet again
when I have set my house in order.
V.

The letter slipped from Valens' hand.

"What did it say?" Damarra asked.

Valens turned to look at his wife, but his eyes found Marcus instead. Tribune Marcus. The man who had come with a message from the emperor.

"*You*," Valens hissed. His fist tightened over the hilt of his dagger.

Marcus looked into his eyes. "Excuse me?"

"You *killed* him!"

Marcus touched his chest. "*I* killed him? No, I—"

Valens vaulted over the body of his dead friend and caught Marcus in the stomach with his shoulder, slamming him into the wall. Somewhere far beyond the rage that had sprung to voracious life in his soul, Damarra was begging him to stop, but the words had no meaning. Marcus shoved back, got his knife up, but Valens lunged with his own and caught Marcus' side. Blood oozed from the wound, staining the torn tunic red. Valens let loose the ululating battle cry that he had learned from his friend Baradoc, and then he and Marcus were locked together, their arms clasped around each other's necks, tumbling out of the room with Persephone and Damarra following behind. They rolled down the corridor, neither man able to get the best of the other. Marcus lost his knife, managed to break free, and tried to scoop it up again, but Valens got him first. His arm encircled the tribune's neck, tightening, the rage giving him strength beyond any he had ever had, and Marcus began to gag and lost his grip on Valens' wrist. His hand free now, Valens flipped the knife so that he could plunge it into Marcus' chest, into his black heart, just as Marcus had done to his friend, Paulus.

Before he could drive the dagger home, someone grabbed his wrist; not Marcus, whose hands were clawing at Valens' arm as Valens choked the life from him, but someone from beyond the reality of his mindless rage. The knife was wrenched from his hand and tossed aside. The world swam back into focus and he saw the face of Gundabar. "No," he commanded in his guttural tongue. "This man another. No kill another."

Valens twisted in Gundabar's grip and slammed into him with his shoulder, knocking the German aside. Gundabar tumbled down the steps into the peristylium. The distraction was only momentary, but it was long enough for Marcus to twist in his arms and head butt him. Lights exploded in Valens' head and he staggered backwards. Marcus leapt at him, struck him in the midsection, and together they flew through the air, landing mere inches away from Gundabar, who was already back on his feet. Suddenly Conall and Sukuta were there, dragging Marcus away, and Gundabar had his arms wrapped around Valens in a massive bear hug that squeezed the air out of his lungs. At last the men released their holds and both Marcus and Valens dropped to the ground, panting with exertion. Gundabar and Conall stepped between them. "No," Gundabar ordered again.

Valens got up on his hands and knees, glanced over at Marcus, who was shaking the fog from his head. "He killed Paulus," he snarled and staggered to his feet again.

"I did no such thing," Marcus replied, pushing himself up.

Conall braced his hand on Marcus' chest; Gundabar gathered Valens' tunic in his fist. "*Enough!*" yelled Conall.

Valens heard the sound of his daughter crying and the fight went out of him. He glared at Marcus, then nodded.

"What has happened?" Conall asked.

"My friend, Paulus, is dead."

Conall's face paled. "Commander Paulus? Dead?"

"Yes, he arrived last night, just after Tribune Marcus. He was wounded. Persephone bandaged his wounds and gave him a sleeping draught. This morning she found him dead."

"He died in his sleep?"

"Yes," Valens' eyes flashed at Marcus, "with a knife sticking out of his chest."

"Where?" Sukuta asked.

"In our bed."

With a nod, Sukuta hurried off to their bed chamber.

Now that the fighting had stopped, Prisca brought the baby to Damarra. She took the squalling infant into her arms and the baby settled. Tears swam in Damarra's blue eyes. "How do you know Marcus killed Paulus?" she asked.

He sent Persephone back to the room for the letter. When she returned with it, he opened it and showed Damarra the message written there. Her face became as white as her hair. "Valerianus," she breathed.

Valens read the letter to the others. When he finished, he pointed at Marcus. "He said he came with a message from the emperor." He shook the letter at the tribune. "This is the message. He stuck it on his dagger and plunged it into a sleeping man's chest. The *coward*."

"I swear by all that is holy that I did not kill your friend," Marcus vowed.

"You show up and that same night my friend is murdered, and you expect me to believe it is just a coincidence?"

"Yes."

Damarra turned to study Marcus; his eyes dropped under the confessor's gaze. At last she turned back to her husband. "He speaks the truth," she said. Her voice trembled.

"You believe him?" Valens asked.

"Yes, I do." She turned back to Marcus. "Who is this Gallienus of whom you speak?"

Marcus looked surprised. "He is Valerianus' son. You did not know he had a son?"

"No."

"And yet you grew up on Valerianus' estate."

"His African estates, yes."

"You never went to the family estate in Italy?"

"The one near Ostia?"

"No, in Etruria, in central Italy."

Damarra shook her head. "Never."

"Still, one would think," Marcus muttered to himself. For a moment he was lost in thought, then: "In all that time you never heard anything about Valerianus' family?"

"Whispers. That he had had a wife, that she had died long ago. No one mentioned her name. Or a son."

"Two sons, in fact. Gallienus and Gaius."

"And what is the message you bring from Gallienus?" Valens asked. Anger still ripened his words.

"The Emperor Gallienus sends greetings to his sister, the lady Damarra. He wishes to assure her that she is ever in his thoughts, and that she need not fear any violence while he sits upon the throne. He wishes me to say as well that he and Empress Nina will visit the lady Damarra in Gaul when the duties of the imperial office permit such pleasantries."

Damarra and Valens glanced at each other, then at Marcus. "Two emperors," Damarra stated.

"Indeed. Gallienus is emperor of the West; Valerianus is emperor of the East. Even now, Valerianus is planning a campaign to recover territories annexed by Shapur of Persia. He will leave as soon as preparations permit." Marcus grinned at Damarra. "Gallienus is your emperor, not Valerianus. You are quite safe."

"And yet my friend Paulus lies dead in our bed," Valens reminded him.

Marcus looked troubled. "Who was this Paulus?"

"Paulus Antoninus Quaerellus."

Understanding dawned on Marcus' face. "*That* Paulus—the Commander of the Praetorian Guard."

"Yes."

"Then forgive me for being blunt, but it is not unusual for a new emperor to execute certain high-ranking officials, especially—" Marcus hesitated.

"Especially?" Valens prompted.

With a sigh, Marcus continued: "Especially an official who has openly declared himself an enemy of that new emperor."

"By saving our lives."

Marcus nodded.

"And you still think we are safe from this madman?"

Marcus shrugged. "Yes, I do."

Sukuta returned. "My lord," he said. "There were two sets of footprints outside your terrace. One came from the northeast. Someone wounded; there was blood. I followed the back trail to a horse tied to a tree just inside the eaves of the forest to the north."

"And the other footprints?"

"Led back to the eastern irrigation ditch, and from there two sets of footprints led out to the stand of oaks across the road. I found several apple cores nearby, and the underbrush was trampled flat, as if someone had stood or sat there for a long time."

"Watching the villa," Conall added.

"My thoughts exactly," agreed Sukuta.

Valens glanced at Sukuta. "Could it have been more of the *lapsi* seeking an audience with the lady Damarra?"

"Perhaps," Sukuta said, but from the tone of his voice he did not believe it.

Valens was silent, pensive. He stared at the bench where he and Damarra had spent so many mornings in prayer. At last he looked at Damarra. "Do you think you can ride?"

"My lord," Prisca exclaimed. "My lady has just had a baby. She must rest for several days."

"Yes," Damarra replied.

"My lady, no," Prisca insisted.

Damarra shushed her and said to her husband, "I think I can ride. Why?"

Valens clapped his hand on Conall's shoulder. "Ready horses for all of us. The Lord sent Gundabar to lead us to Germania, so we will go to Germania. This very day."

COMMANDER DIONYSIUS SAW A PARTY of three riders access the *Via Iulia* ahead and ordered a halt. They were a few miles outside of Massalia, no more than ten miles from the Valens estate. Behind them, the sun sat on the eastern horizon like a large yellow ball, blinding the horseman galloping toward them. They were still a hundred yards away when Dionysius realized who it was.

Tacitus and his men.

Dionysius waited until Tacitus was almost on top of them, then shouted the smaller man's name. Immediately Tacitus reined in his horse, turned it; his men followed suit. Their horses danced up beside them, then the two parties dismounted for a quick conference.

"Have you concluded your business?" Dionysius asked.

"Oh, yes," Tacitus replied. "And while I was there, I met a stunning young woman named Persephone. Delightful, interested in medicinal herbs. Absolutely gorgeous."

Dionysius laughed. "You sound smitten, Tacitus."

"Quite. The gods sent her to me, I'm sure of it. I intend to marry her."

"That's fast work!" Dionysius laughed again. "I hope you invite me to the wedding."

"We haven't set a date yet, but I'll remember you when we

do."

Funny. Tacitus almost seemed . . . *serious*, but he *must* be joking. Dionysius shrugged and changed the subject. "So you delivered your message?"

"Yes."

"Emperor Valerianus will be pleased."

"Very. And so will you."

"Me? Why me?"

Tacitus answered Dionysius' question with a question of his own: "Have you dispatched Commander Paulus yet?"

"No, but it is just a matter of time. I know where he is."

Tacitus flipped open his saddlebag and took out two apples. He handed one to Dionysius and bit into the second. "And where is that?" he asked.

"Where you just came from—Valens' estate." Dionysius bit into his apple. It was delicious.

Tacitus took three quick bites, then tossed the rest of the apple into the ditch. "You are right, Commander. He is there."

"You saw him?"

"Yes."

Dionysius ordered his men to mount up.

"Where are you off to?" Tacitus asked.

Dionysius saw Plautus and Martial, Tacitus' aides, grinning at each other and scowled. "To deal with Paulus, of course." Dionysius' eyes narrowed. "What's going on here?"

For a moment Tacitus stared up into Dionysius' blue eyes, then he began to laugh. "My apologies, Commander—just having a bit of fun. You might as well turn around and head back to Rome with us. Paulus is dead."

"Dead? How?"

Tacitus explained the events of the previous night. Dionysius had already decided that he liked the commander of the *Agentes in Rebus*—he was soft-spoken, polite, and efficient, the kind of man who did whatever task needed doing without complaint. But after hearing how Tacitus had dispatched Paulus, his respect for the man increased. By the end of the story, Dionysius was laughing. "Brilliant," he said. "Just brilliant."

Tacitus bowed. "Thank you, Commander." He pointed east,

into the rising sun. "Shall we?"

Dionysius stroked his square chin. "You are sure he is dead?"

"Quite."

"Valerianus will demand proof."

Tacitus opened his saddlebag again and removed another apple and a bundle wrapped in black cloth and tied with string. He bit into the apple as he handed the bundle to Dionysius. "Will this suffice?" he asked.

Dionysius looked at the bundle in his hand. It was small, perhaps three inches in length. The bottom was wet and sticky. He untied the string and rolled the cloth open to reveal the contents: a severed finger. Just below the knuckle was a signet ring that bore three letters: PAQ.

Paulus Antoninus Quaerellus.

Tacitus mounted his horse and turned to the east. "I understand there is an establishment in Forum Julii that specializes in quail. If we hurry, we can be there in under an hour."

Dionysius wrapped up the severed finger again and tucked the bundle into his belt. "My treat," he replied.

"NO!" GUNDABAR EXCLAIMED. "No go black woods!"

Valens turned to the German warrior. "We must leave, and we must leave now. Paulus is dead. We are next."

"You are safe," Marcus said again. "Emperor Gallienus has pledged your safety."

"That means nothing, not when Paulus lies dead in my bed chamber."

"It means everything!" Marcus exclaimed. Anger rose in his voice. "Emperor Gallienus is an honourable man. If he pledges your safety, then you are safe."

Valens waved the remark aside. "We go to Germania."

Gundabar spoke excitedly to Conall, who nodded. "Gundabar says it is not time."

"Not time?"

Conall nodded. "Another must come, my lord. Remember?"

"Besides," Marcus said. "I cannot go to Germania now. I am a Roman soldier and a friend to the Emperor Gallienus. I am bound by duty."

"There, Tribune Marcus refuses to come," Valens said to Gundabar.

Gundabar laid his hand on Marcus' shoulder. "*Yeise*. He come."

Marcus cleared his throat. "I did not say I would not come; I said I cannot come at this time."

Valens turned to him. "You mean, you *will* come?"

"Yes."

"Why? Why would you leave your career and your homeland to traipse through the forests of Germania with us?"

"Because the *Christos* wishes it."

Valens started. "You are . . . a Christian?"

"Yes, my lord Valens. I serve the *Christos*."

"And you are Emperor Gallienus' friend?"

Marcus bowed. "That is true."

"And does the emperor know you are a Christian?"

"Yes."

Damarra and Valens looked at each other. Knowing Marcus was a Christian and that the emperor knew it as well defused the sense of imminent danger that had gripped Valens since he had found Paulus dead. "When will this 'other' come?" Valens asked Gundabar.

Conall translated Valens' question, then translated Gundabar's answer. "He says 'at a different time.' I think he means later, not now."

Valens considered his options. His gut told him to flee before a unit of soldiers showed up at his front door with orders to arrest them. Or worse. For years he had followed his gut, and it had rarely let him down. His heart, on the other hand, was telling him something very different. His heart was saying stay. More, his heart told them that if he fled to the wilds of Germania now—if he followed his gut and not his heart in other words—that the results would be catastrophic. Before he had made the decision to serve the *Christos*, Damarra had told him that God's timing was perfect. He had not understood that statement at the time, but later, when he had begun to grasp how the *Christos* had been working in their lives all along, that statement had become a truth by which he had pledged to live his life. God had sent Gundabar to lead them to Germania for a *Thing*, and one day he would do just that.

But not today.

"All right," Valens said. "We stay."

The entire group released a collective sigh, as if in each of their hearts they had come to the same conclusion Valens had.

Not yet. The time was not right.

"And what do we do in the meantime?" Damarra asked. She kissed her sleeping baby's forehead and cuddled it close.

Conall spoke to Gundabar. The German's ubiquitous smile returned as he replied to Conall's question with a single word.

Conall turned to the others and shrugged. "Wait," he said.

AND SO THEY WAITED.

Marcus went back to Rome, pledging to return "when the time was right." Valens ordered Conall to keep their horses saddled and ready, so that they could flee at a moment's notice. He posted guards around the estate, at the gate, and up and down the road in both directions; he even set two slaves to watch at the port down in Massalia, in case their executioners disembarked there.

And life went on.

Insulated from the great sweep of events on their rural estate, they nevertheless heard the rumours. Barbarians swarmed over the frontiers. Plague and famine were rife. Harvests failed. The world around them was crumbling, burning, devoured in a great conflagration that threatened the lives of every citizen in the empire. The days turned into weeks and the weeks turned into months, and Valerianus did not strike; and so they settled into an apprehensive existence, a life of waiting for the thunder of hoof beats in the laneway, for the sudden hammering on the door in the middle of the night.

And while they waited, that great ravenous beast—Chaos—opened its vast jaws and consumed the world.

PART II
IN A MANGER LAID

"Great good and great evil begin in the same place: the cradle."
ANONYMOUS

"Who is the liar? It is the man who denies that Jesus is the Christ.
1 JOHN 2:22

"Sin, when it is full-grown, gives birth to death."
JAMES 1:15

ELEVEN

THE DANUBE FRONTIER, UPPER PANNONIA
JUNE A.D. 255

What proof do you have?" Marcus asked.

Emperor Gallienus gestured for Marcus to calm down. "Let us hear Commander Festus out," he said.

Marcus glared at the commander of the praetorian guard, whose lip curled in a smirk. "What do you care either way, General Marcus? Unless," Festus gave a mock gasp, "unless *you* are perhaps affiliated with these atheists?"

Marcus sat down, glowering at the table about which Gallienus' officers sat. The emperor's tent was the largest in the encampment, larger even than his father's tent, which had been pitched beside it. Ten officers sat around the table, their gaze flitting from Festus to Marcus and back again. This was not the first time that Gallienus' two main councillors had disagreed on policy—they always seemed to be at loggerheads—but never before had the animosity between the two men seemed so tangible. "I do not wish to see anyone condemned without evidence," Marcus said.

Festus ran a hand through his silver hair. "Ah, yes, the infamous Marcan integrity. How admirable! And yet, I note that you have avoided answering my question."

"Enough!" commanded Gallienus.

Festus bowed; Marcus nodded.

Gallienus turned to Festus. "And what *is* your proof of this accusation?"

Festus held up a scroll. "This was found in Hunderic's possession." He opened the scroll. "Should I read it out loud, Your Excellency?"

Gallienus gestured for him to proceed.

Festus cleared his throat:

> *To Hunderic the Great, King of the Buri:*
> *Valerianus withdrew the Pannonian legions into*
> *Italy to support Emperor Gallus against Aemilianus.*
> *Pannonia is defenceless. Our prophetess predicts vic-*
> *tory if you strike now.*
>
> *IXΘYE*

Festus handed the scroll to Gallienus, who gave it a cursory glance, then passed it to a slave, who took it to the covey of scribes sitting at their writing desks in the corner, recording the proceeds of the meeting. "And how can you be sure that this is the work of Christians?" Gallienus asked.

"Perhaps General Marcus will answer that question, Your Excellency."

"I bow to your superior knowledge, Commander Festus."

"As you wish." Festus addressed the emperor: "The document is signed *IXΘYE*, a Greek word which means 'fish.' It is an old Christian trick, an acrostic. Each letter is the first letter of a Greek word, which, when put together, produces the Greek phrase, '*Iesous Christos Theou Huios Soter.*'"

Gallienus chuckled. "'Jesus the Christ, God's Son, Saviour.' Very clever."

"Well, I'm convinced," Marcus said. His voice was rife with sarcasm. "Bring the great Hunderic to us, so that we might question him about his alliance with the Christians."

"Alas, Hunderic was killed in the battle," said Festus.

Marcus smirked. "How unfortunate. Now all we have is your word that the Christians are to blame."

Festus' hand fell to the hilt of his sword. "Are you impugning my honesty, General Marcus?"

"Do you have any honesty to impugn?" Marcus countered.

"Why, you young whelp!" Festus snarled and drew his sword. "I will teach you the last lesson you will ever learn."

Marcus jumped up, his own sword out and pointing at Festus' chest, and then all the officers were up and shouting at each other. Gallienus glanced at his father, who was sitting beside him, grinning at the mayhem. No help there. "Enough," Gallienus bellowed.

Instantly, there was silence.

"Sit down. All of you."

The officers resumed their seats at the table. Festus slipped his sword back into its sheath and stood in front of the emperor, legs slightly apart, hands clasped behind his back. "Who is the new chief of the Buri?" Gallienus asked.

"Hunderic's son, Gaeseric," replied Festus.

"Bring him."

Festus nodded at one of the guards standing just inside the tent's flaps. With a salute he marched out and returned a few moments later with a tall, thin warrior. His long brown hair was tied back with a leather thong. He wore a leather shirt and breeches. Patches of beard dotted his long cheeks and chin. The warrior stopped beside Festus and gave a sharp bow. "Hail, Augustus Gallienus," he said.

Gallienus rose, went to Gaeseric and embraced him as a brother. "Greetings, Gaeseric, King of the Buri."

The officers glanced at one another.

Gallienus ordered a slave to fetch food and wine for Gaeseric. His officers began to murmur amongst themselves, but a sharp, backward glance from Gallienus silenced them. "Shall we talk while we wait for your refreshments?" Gallienus asked.

"Yes."

"Good. Let me begin with a question, then: why did you invade Upper Pannonia?"

"We learned that the legions had been withdrawn to Italy." The German spoke with an accent, but his Latin was excellent.

Festus smirked at Marcus.

"Who told you this?"

"My father, King Hunderic."

"And who told him?"

King Gaeseric shrugged. "He did not say and I did not ask. We are warriors," he proclaimed proudly. "We would have come even if a hundred legions awaited us."

Gallienus smiled at the barbarian's bravado. "You came to pillage," he said.

"Yes."

"And you leave with nothing."

This time Gaeseric was not so quick to answer. Nor so haughty. "Yes," he said through clenched teeth.

"You will return to Germania, defeated. You have lost face; the Buri have lost face. You will become the laughing stock of the Goths, the Franks, the Alamanni—all Germania will mock you."

Gaeseric thumped his chest. "We are Buri. No one will dare mock us—we will destroy them."

Gallienus patted the king's shoulder, like a father comforting a wayward child. "Of course. The Buri are brave. The Buri are the greatest warriors in Germania."

Nodding, Gaeseric relaxed.

"Which is why we wish you to remain in Pannonia."

Gaeseric's brown eyebrows furrowed. "Remain here?"

"Yes."

"As slaves," Gaeseric said. Anger had returned to his voice.

"No, as *foederati*."

Amazement lit Gaeseric's face. "*Foederati*? The Buri and the Romans . . . allies?"

"And why not? The other tribes are slowly throttling the life out of the Buri. What other choice do you have?"

Gallienus silenced Gaeseric's cry of outrage with an upraised hand. "We are not totally in the dark about political trends in Germania, King Gaeseric. Each year your neighbours grow richer and larger at Buri expense. You are beset by enemies, who are devouring your homeland one piece at a time. Soon the Buri will be no more."

Gaeseric glared at Gallienus.

"Your father knew this to be true. Why else would he have risked everything on an invasion of Pannonia? He was not interested in booty. He wanted a new homeland for the Buri, a place for his people to live and thrive without fear, where the honour and dignity of your people could be restored. Is that not what you want for your people?"

Gaeseric hesitated, then his eyes flicked to Gallienus. "Yes," he whispered.

"Good," Gallienus said. "For that is what I am offering you. There is a desolate stretch of northern Pannonia not far from here. No frontier forts protect it; no Roman soldiers patrol the area. Nothing stands between it and the tribes of Germania except the Danube."

Gaeseric grinned with understanding. "And now, the Buri."

"Precisely. We will assist you in settling the area, provide tools, seed, all your needs until you are established. And in return—"

"We keep *our* enemies on their own side of the Danube."

Gallienus grinned back. "Allies?" he said and held out his hand.

Gaeseric grabbed him by the forearm and slapped the emperor's shoulder. "Allies!" he agreed.

"One more detail," Gallienus said. He turned to his officers and summoned one. A tall, middle-aged man got up and joined them. He was bald and sported a closely trimmed beard. "King Gaeseric, this is your new neighbour, Commander Ingenuus."

Gaeseric and Ingenuus shook hands.

"Commander Ingenuus is one of our finest officers." He laughed. "A senator who actually deserves his position. Imagine that!"

Gallienus' joke met with polite laughter from his officers, several of whom were senators as well.

"Commander Ingenuus will be in charge of Lower Pannonia, to your east. He will also be responsible for the education and training of our eldest son, Caesar Cornelius Licinius Valerianus. Our young Valerianus will be the imperial representative for the Pannonias and the Danube frontier."

Gaeseric's brows furrowed and Gallienus laughed. "A figurehead, King Gaeseric. The legions that occupy the Danube frontier are more . . . *cooperative* with an emperor present. They feel . . . ne-

glected when we spend so much time on the Rhine frontier. Our young son's presence will placate them."

Gaeseric's food arrived, and while he ate and drank the emperor's health, they discussed their new alliance, then Gaeseric left, a much happier man than he had been when he entered. As soon as the Buri warrior was out of earshot, Gallienus' officers began to voice their objections. Gallienus demanded silence, then approached the table. He gazed at each man in turn, then finally at his father, Emperor Valerianus, who had been uncharacteristically silent throughout the proceedings. When at last Gallienus began to speak, his voice was full and strong, which lent an authority to his words that demanded the respect and compliance of each of his officers. "The world has changed," he began. "For fifty years, imperial policy regarding barbarian incursions has remained the same: defeat them and send them home, back to Germania. Nor is the policy wrong—for the health of the empire, for the purity of the empire, they must be kept out." He paused, looked again at each of his officers, then continued. "But the time has come to modify that policy, adapt it to present circumstances. In fact, the entire defensive policy of the empire must adapt to present circumstances. We must adapt or fall—those are our only choices. Which do you prefer?"

Although the question was rhetorical, his officers answered in one voice: "Adapt!"

"Some of the tribes we must continue to defeat and send back, for to allow them to remain in the empire would be dangerous. But other tribes, tribes like the Buri, can be of use to us. The Buri have traded with the Romans for many years. They have acquired a taste for Roman luxuries. They envy the Roman way of life. And so we will give it to them," Gallienus grinned, "and in the giving make them more Roman than Buri. So that when one of the other tribes comes knocking at their door, they will bar the way to protect what they have. Protect what *we* have."

The officers began to murmur again, but now it was with understanding and agreement.

Gallienus held up his hand for silence. "Other changes are necessary and will be made when the time is right. For now, prepare to break camp; we leave at first light."

As his officers filed out, Gallienus returned to the chair beside Valerianus. "Commander Festus and General Marcus, stay," he ordered.

When they stood in front of the two emperors, hands clasped behind their backs, Gallienus asked Festus to apprise him of the current situation in Rome. Festus reported on the activities of the fire brigade, policing actions, work crews involved in temple restorations and upkeep of government buildings, distribution of bread and wine to the unemployed masses, the whole gamut of urban administration involved in the operation of a city the size and stature of Rome. Gallienus listened attentively, until Festus finished. "And what about the plague? Are the numbers still high?" he asked.

"Approaching three thousand per day, Your Excellency," Festus replied.

Gallienus shook his head. "It is getting worse, then."

"Yes, Your Excellency."

"What measures are you and the city praefect taking?"

"We have increased the number of clean-up crews to fifty. Each crew is responsible for one section of the city. They pick up whatever bodies are found in the streets and take them to the garbage pits outside the city, where the bodies are cremated. The fires burn night and day, and still the crews cannot keep up."

"Increase the number of crews then."

"Yes, Your Excellency."

Gallienus heard something in Festus' tone. "What is it, Commander?"

"It is difficult to find men to man the crews."

"Why is that?"

Festus looked almost embarrassed with his answer: "Because crew members keep dying of the plague, Your Excellency."

Gallienus nodded. He tried whenever possible to hire jobs out to Roman citizens; but no citizen, no matter how poor, no matter how high the pay, wanted to work at a job that would kill him. "We will use slaves then." He turned to Marcus. "How many captives do we have?"

"Four thousand, but half of those are Buri," Marcus replied.

"Release the Buri captives and turn over the others to Commander Festus." He turned to Festus. "Take the captives back to Rome and put them to work on the clean-up crews. When those are gone, we will send others." He gave a heavy sigh. "We fear there will soon be many more to send your way."

"You are not planning to return to Rome with me, Your Excellency?" Festus asked.

"No. We have decided to tour Germania Superior and Germania Inferior. We have received news from the frontier that the tribes are massing on the east bank of the Rhine. Another invasion is imminent."

Festus bowed. "Yes, Your Excellency."

"You are dismissed, Commander."

Festus bowed again and went to the exit, then he turned and held up the scroll. "And what about this, Your Excellency?" he asked.

"We will consider the matter."

Festus nodded his head gravely, then: "May I speak, Your Excellency?"

Gallienus gestured for him to continue.

"The Christians are a problem that will not go away." He touched the scroll. "This proves it, and it is but one, small example of their treachery. They will not go away; we must *make* them go away."

"We will consider the matter *closely*," Gallienus assured him.

Festus tucked the scroll into his belt, saluted, and left the tent.

Valerianus rose from his seat. "Emperor Gallienus, we wish to talk to Commander Festus before he leaves for Rome, so we too will bid you farewell."

"You are leaving in the morning?" Gallienus asked.

"Yes. The time has come to deal with Shapur. He has taken Armenia, raided Roman Mesopotamia repeatedly, and now word has reached us that he has captured Antioch, the capital of Syria. If we do not meet him soon, all the East will be lost." Valerianus smirked. "And then we will have nothing to rule, and you will have to share the West with us."

"Let us pray to the gods that day never comes," Gallienus replied.

They both laughed.

Gallienus snapped his fingers and a slave standing beside the scribes, who were still scribbling madly on their parchments, hurried to his side. He carried a silver platter, upon which sat a leather bag, tied at the top with a piece of gold string. Gallienus picked it up and flipped his hand at the slave, dismissing him. "A present for you, Emperor Valerianus," he said. He handed the bag to Valerianus. "A going away gift. A little something to remind you of our time together in the last year and a half."

Valerianus looked pleased. "What is it?" he asked and made to untie the string.

Gallienus grabbed his hand, stopped him. "For another day, when we are apart," he said.

With a shrug, Valerianus tucked the bag into his belt. "How very mysterious, Emperor Gallienus. Will you at least give us a hint?"

Gallienus' smile was strained. "If I must. It is a bag of coins, minted by us to . . . celebrate our family name, you might say. You will understand when you see them, and you will know where our loyalties lie."

Valerianus gave a regal bow. "A fine gift, my son. A small fortune, no doubt."

"Not much of a fortune," Gallienus laughed. "They are silver *antoniniani*, but the silver content is very low. Really they are bronze coins covered with a silver wash." He laughed again. "Enough to trick the merchants, we hope. Still, we have discovered that the imperial coffers are more often empty than full."

"Decreasing the amount of silver and gold in your coinage is one way to save money; but there are better ways to generate income."

"Yes," Gallienus nodded. "I heard you had levied a new tax on wine revenues in the East. I plan to follow your example here."

"A wise move, Emperor Gallienus." He gazed into his son's eyes, then asked: "May we offer you a piece of advice, father to son?"

Gallienus gestured for him to proceed.

"We have served in the upper echelons of imperial administration for more than ten years, and we have discovered ways to squeeze money out of the empire that would have surprised most of our predecessors. So when we advise you to follow our lead in financial matters, we do not advise idly. The choice is yours, Emperor Gallienus, but if you are truly wise, you will watch us and learn. Empty coffers will not keep the barbarians in Germania nor buy the loyalty of your legions, but they *will* shorten your reign. Remember that, and do not be too quick to reject an opportunity to augment your finances just because it seems ignoble. Better a live emperor than a noble corpse."

"I will remember," Gallienus promised.

Valerianus left and Gallienus tuned to Marcus. "Must you argue with our Praetorian Praefect at every opportunity?" he asked.

"He argues with me," Marcus said.

"Wonderful. You sound like a little child: *He started it first.*"

Marcus chuckled.

"I thought you Christians loved peace?"

"I am trying to preserve the peace. Festus seems determined to blame the Christians for everything. I overheard him say that the Christians were responsible for the plague, that they had prayed it down on Rome's head as punishment for the persecution Decius waged against us."

Gallienus nodded gravely. "We have heard those whispers, too."

Marcus' eyes narrowed. "You almost sound like you . . . agree."

Gallienus didn't answer.

"Surely you don't believe them?" Marcus cried incredulously.

Gallienus' eyes flashed. "We do not know what we believe yet," he snapped.

"My apologies, Your Excellency," Marcus said. His voice was stiff. "I can assure you that I, as a Christian, have never prayed vengeance down upon Rome's head."

Gallienus gave a weary sigh. "No, Marcus, we apologize. In the last two months we have repelled three invasions, and we suspect that we will have to deal with many more before winter sets in again. We are too busy fighting the enemy crashing through our door to worry about the enemy already inside."

"We are *not* your enemy, Your Excellency."

"The document Festus showed us suggests otherwise."

"A forgery."

"You are so sure. How do you know?"

"I just . . . know."

"And what would Festus gain by convincing me that the Christians must be dealt with?"

Marcus shook his head. "I don't know. Except, perhaps, that he wants you to eliminate the Christians?"

"We do not believe that," Gallienus said. "We spent many years with the man. He was our teacher, and more, he was like a father to us. And yes, like many Romans he disliked the Christians. He also disliked Mithraists and Epicureans. But we never in all those years heard him talk of eliminating any sect, even those he disliked. Never did we detect in him the virulence and hatred that motivated our real father."

"And which now seems to be mysteriously absent."

Gallienus looked troubled. "Yes. Absent. Since our initial meeting almost two years ago he has made no mention of the Christians. None at all."

They were both silent for a moment, thinking, then Marcus asked, "So what will you do? About the Christians?"

"We have not decided yet." He smiled at his friend. "But as we told you before, whatever becomes of the Christians, you have nothing to worry about."

"Nothing to worry about," Marcus echoed in a whisper.

Gallienus did not like the look on his friend's face. He slapped his shoulder. "We know what will make you smile again: a visit to one of your holy confessors."

Marcus glanced up and did, in fact, grin. "You mean the lady Damarra?"

"Yes. Send word to Empress Nina to meet us in Massalia in the new year. We will tour our northern defences, and then, when the barbarians take their winter rest, we will proceed to the Valens estate. The time has come for us to meet our little sister."

THE LARGE FRONT ROOM of Valerianus' tent had been converted into a sumptuous dining chamber. Golden goblets glimmered like diamonds in the torchlight. The earthen floor was covered with furs, the dining couches draped with silks, and rich tapestries had transformed the ordinary canvas walls into a gallery of delightful scenes from Roman mythology. Valerianus and his friend Festus Macrinus lay upon two dining couches, sampling the dainties that the emperor's dining staff had created for their pleasure: stuffed peacock, quail eggs, and fresh trout served with garum, the sauce made from fermented fish innards that was Rome's favourite staple. They complemented the feast with a vintage Falernian, and then Valerianus dismissed the slaves and staff so that they might enjoy their final meal in peace.

Afterwards, when both men were stuffed fuller than the peacock had been, Festus raised his goblet and toasted Valerianus. "May you rain down the very thunderbolts of Jupiter on Shapur's head, old friend."

Valerianus raised his own goblet. "The Persian will rue the day he set foot on Roman soil."

The two men drank, and then toasted each other's health and drank again.

"I wish I were going with you," Festus said as he set his goblet down. "Like the old days, eh? You and me, knocking Persian heads together. Remember that village near Ctesiphon, where we met those two beauties?"

"Could I ever forget that night?" Valerianus said and laughed. "Or that time in Alexandria? Remember?"

"The priestesses?"

"Yes."

Festus howled laughter and slapped his knee. "You told them we were gods come to earth to find new consorts."

"And they believed us!"

"You always had a way with the women," Festus said.

Valerianus stared into his goblet, suddenly silent, and Festus knew that whatever memories had bolstered his mood had been shut away again. Valerianus had always been that way: up one moment, quiet and brooding the next. More of the latter than the former as he grew older.

"You will serve the empire better by remaining in Rome," Valerianus explained.

"Of course, Your Excellency." He sighed. "I am just reminded of the . . . pleasures of our youth. An old man's predisposition, I fear—I find myself looking backward more than forward these days. Forgive me."

Valerianus waved the confession away. "Shapur will not return the territories he stole without a fight, so we may be in the East for some time. Years perhaps. While we are away, you will be our representative in Rome."

"Yes, Your Excellency."

"Our son may need your perspective to guide him."

"I am one of his most trusted advisors, Your Excellency. Sometimes he accepts my advice; sometimes he rejects it. He has a mind of his own—the product of his excellent education, no doubt."

Valerianus smiled at Festus' little joke. "You are as crafty as you are humorous, old friend. We trust in your ability to . . . mould Gallienus' thoughts and policies in our absence."

"With the assistance of the *Agentes in Rebus*, and Tacitus in particular, that should not be a problem."

"The *Agentes* are at your disposal, Commander Festus. But we have need of Commander Tacitus ourselves; do not include him in your calculations."

Need of Tacitus? Before his old friend had assumed the imperial purple, Festus had never even *heard* of Tacitus. He was familiar with the *Agentes in Rebus*, of course. Who in the empire had not heard about the *Agentes*, who functioned as imperial "watchdogs" at every level of society and in every province of the empire. But the man in charge of the *Agentes* had been an unknown, just another bureaucrat in a bureaucracy top-heavy with them—until the attention of Emperor Valerianus brought him into the light of day. Tacitus still remained an enigma to Festus, who was one of the few people who even knew he existed. In fact, Festus only knew two things for certain about Tacitus: one, he had the uncanny ability to ferret out information where others failed; and two, Emperor Valerianus had sent Tacitus on several undisclosed "assignments," all of which he had completed successfully. "I understand, Your Excellency," he said.

"Good."

"With your permission, Your Excellency, I will retire now. It is a long journey back to Rome. I should leave at dawn."

Valerianus rose with Festus and the two old friends embraced. "My advice? Send Shapur to Hades!"

"Excellent advice, as always," Valerianus said with a laugh. Then he pursed his lips and furrowed his black brows. "Gallienus will spend more time on the frontiers than in Rome, but even at a distance he will continue to seek your advice. He respects you. You were more than his teacher; you were like a father to him. So when he asks your advice, give it to him. Do not hold back. The good of the empire comes first."

"I would not steer him wrong, Your Excellency."

"No, Festus, you would not." He grasped Festus' shoulders. "We are counting on that."

WHEN FESTUS HAD DEPARTED, Valerianus returned to his dining couch and reclined again. He sipped at the wine in his goblet. Excellent. Perhaps the best Falernian he had ever had. To think that his steward could find a wine so fine out here in the wilds of Pannonia. What an amazing accomplishment. He put the goblet down and licked his thin lips. "Join us," he commanded.

The curtains which separated the tent's main room from the second room, where he slept, swirled open. Tacitus and Dionysius, the commander of his personal bodyguard, entered. "You heard?" Valerianus asked them.

Both men nodded.

"Commander Dionysius, we have a special assignment for you. Is there another man you would trust to command our bodyguard?"

Dionysius thought for a moment, then: "Linus. He is a decorated veteran with many years of experience. The men respect him and will follow his orders without question. More importantly, he is loyal to you, Your Excellency. Were you to command him to die for you, he would do so gladly."

"Very good. Inform Linus that he will command our bodyguard in your absence. We leave for the East in the morning. You will remain in the West. Select several of your most trustworthy men to assist you." He took a leather pouch from the folds of his purple toga and handed it to Dionysius. "This contains two imperial letters of transit, one for you and one for Tacitus. You may commandeer whatever you need to complete your mission." Dionysius took the pouch and Valerianus turned to Tacitus. "Has the Divine Gallienus made use of your services, Commander Tacitus?" he asked.

"He has consulted our reports and used them in determining provincial policy, Divine One," Tacitus replied.

"But you personally?"

"No. As you know, he has spent very little time in Rome. The frontiers have demanded all his attention."

"Excellent. Then you will be assisting Commander Dionysius."

Dionysius and Tacitus exchanged nods. "And what is our mission, Your Excellency?" Dionysius asked.

"You are to keep Julius Valens and Damarra Valensia under surveillance. We want to know everything they do and their exact location at any given moment. When the time comes, we do not want to have to hunt them down. Do you understand?"

Dionysius saluted. "Yes, Your Excellency."

"And you, Tacitus. I want you to get one of your men inside the estate."

"A spy, Your Excellency?" Tacitus observed.

"Yes. A permanent one. Or at least until the time comes for our little family reunion."

"As always, Divine One, I am at your service," Tacitus said.

TWELVE

MASSALIA, GALLIA NARBONENSIS
JANUARY A.D. 256

Valens was on his way home from Massalia when they spotted the dead man lying in the ditch.

It was early morning and cold. Frost was a rarity in this part of Southern Gaul, but when *Aquilo*, the North Wind, blew down from the far north in January, it often brought near freezing temperatures with it. Yesterday afternoon, when they had received the message from the emperor and hurried into town to purchase the extra supplies they would need, the day had been warm and, aside from a few *lapsi* at the gate, which Valens had quickly rousted, the road—and the ditch—had been empty. Sometime in the night, the dead man had been attacked. The ground around him was white with frost, and there were patches of frost on his torn cloak.

Valens halted. His horse, the black stallion that had once belonged to his friend Paulus, danced on the gravel, its nostrils flaring at the scent of blood. "Easy, Asclepus," he murmured. He pointed at the body in the ditch. "Have a look," he ordered.

Conall set the wagon's brake, and he and Sukuta got down. Two slaves sitting in the back of the wagon jumped out and grabbed staves. Valens had purchased them last night at the slave market in Massalia. Didymus, the old trader from whom Valens regularly purchased slaves, had assured him that both men had military training. Valens watched them as they scanned their surroundings, the field across the road that rolled down to the Mediterranean, the horse pasture on the north side, before focussing their attention on the forest that stretched east and west fifty yards north of the road. Yes, if trouble came it would come from that direction. Didymus had never steered him wrong before, and it looked like his reputation was still pristine—both men knew what they were doing. They would make excellent guards.

Sukuta stretched his large frame, then peered over the edge of the ditch. "Looks badly beat up, my lord. Probably the bandits," he said.

Valens grunted in agreement. A troop of bandits had begun to ply their trade on this section of the Old Massalia Road back in November. Since then a unit of soldiers out of Massalia had been assigned to patrol the road twice daily, and some of the local landowners, including Valens, had organized their own patrols. So far the bandits had eluded capture.

"I'll make sure he's dead," Sukuta said and scrambled down into the ditch.

Valens almost told him not to bother. Then he remembered the *Scriptura* he and Damarra had studied yesterday—the parable of the Good Samaritan. And wouldn't he feel like a Pharisee if he went on his way and the man in the ditch turned out to be alive?

The two slaves with the staves watched the tree line carefully. Local rumour placed the bandit camp in that forest, but so far all their search parties had turned up nothing but dirt and old leaves. What rankled Valens the most was that the bandits had forced him to change his habits. No longer could he jump on a horse and ride into town whenever he wanted. It had become too dangerous to travel the road alone. Now when he went, he had to take several armed slaves with him. Just in case.

Sukuta dropped down on one knee and took the man's hand. "Warm," he muttered. He pulled back the man's eyelids, first the left, then the right. "He still lives, my lord."

Valens jumped down from Asclepus and hurried into the ditch. The man's tunic and cloak were in tatters. His hair and beard were matted with blood, and his face was cut and bruised, but he did appear to be breathing. "Let's get him up to the wagon," Valens said.

Sukuta and Valens carried the man out of the ditch and set him gently at the very back of the wagon, where the new slaves had been sitting. He told them to follow behind—it was less than a mile to the estate—and mounted Asclepus. In ten minutes, they were turning into the villa's laneway. The estate was a hive of activity. In their absence, some of the emperor's staff had arrived and raised a cooking tent in the long pasture across the road, which Valens had decided was the best place for the emperor to set up camp. At the entrance to the courtyard, slaves engulfed the wagon like a swarm of locusts and carried off the foodstuffs. Local senators and landowners were huddled together in clutches along the laneway, waiting for the emperor's arrival. Excitement shone on every face—an official visit from the emperor was a rare event and would provide sufficient material to keep the gossips chattering for the next decade.

Valens ordered Sukuta to equip the new guards with swords and javelins, then summoned two slaves to carry the unconscious man into the villa. "Where's Persephone?" he asked Cecht, who was unhitching the horses from the wagon. Thanks to her knowledge of herbs and medicine, Persephone was the estate's recognized expert in medical matters. She was competent at everything from lancing boils to setting broken bones, and Valens and Damarra thanked the *Christos* daily for her gifts.

"In the vineyard with Gundabar, my lord," the boy replied.

He found the two of them sharing a picnic lunch under a Bay Laurel tree at the far end of the vineyard and told her about the wounded man. She excused herself and hurried off to see what she could do, and Valens and Gundabar returned to the courtyard. Sukuta had just given the new slaves weapons and was instructing them on their duties. "I would like a word with them," Valens said.

Sukuta bowed. "Of course, my lord."

The two slaves snapped to attention.

"Your names?" he asked.

"I am Regulus, my lord," replied the bigger of the two. He was tall and stocky with huge arms that bore the scars of many fights. His head was bald, but he had a bushy black beard. He told his story quickly and without embellishment: he had been a gladiator on the provincial circuit for several years. In his last bout, a sword wound in the calf had left him with a permanent limp. "They couldn't use me in the ring no more, so they sold me off and shipped me to Gaul." He drew himself up straight; there was pride in his posture. "But I'm plenty fast and strong for your needs, my lord. I will serve you well."

"I have no doubt, Regulus," Valens said. He turned to the second slave. He was tall, but shorter than Regulus and thinner. His brown hair was straight and short, his eyes hazel, his face pleasant, less severe than his companion's. He looked to be in his mid-thirties. "And your name?" Valens asked.

The slave gave a very stiff bow that made Valens smile. "My name is Alexander, my lord. I was a soldier."

"A legionary?"

"Yes, my lord."

"Where did you serve?"

"Germania Inferior, my lord—Thirtieth Ulpian Legion."

Thirtieth Ulpian. A well-respected legion. They had supported Septimius Severus' rise to the imperial throne some sixty years before, and had seen action in the East during Emperor Alexander Severus' campaign against the Sassanids in Persia. "And how did you end up here?" Valens asked.

"As a slave, you mean?" Alexander shrugged. "A simple roll of the dice, my lord. The gods favoured my opponent."

"A simple roll of the dice, was it?" Valens said. He could not help but chuckle. Twice his life had been permanently altered by a "simple roll of the dice." The first time he had won Baradoc, the man who had become his business manager and best friend and whom Valerianus had murdered before his very eyes. And the second time, Damarra, won from Valerianus himself, but in reality a gift from the *Christos* Himself, the woman who had taught him how to live again. How to love again.

"Well, Fortuna has smiled on you this time, Alexander," Valens said. "I served with the Sixth Legion at Eboracum in Britannia, and I can promise you as one soldier to another that if you serve me well, you will be rewarded."

Alexander raised his fist in a salute. "I will serve you well," he vowed.

THE LANDING IN SYRIA went uncontested, just as the gods had told Valerianus it would. The beachhead was empty, the surrounding villages deserted, and the advance scouts had found no sign of a Sassanid presence between the Mediterranean and Antioch. In short order Valerianus' army began to disembark. Horses were quartered in a large pasture not far from the sea and guards were set to watch them. Calvary was important, but not essential to Valerianus' strategy. The cavalry was not an independent unit, as were the Sassanid Cataphracts, the heavily armoured war horses that drove the Persian army into battle. Roman cavalry was a support unit, meant to provide cover for the Roman infantry, which had always been the backbone of the Roman army and, as far as Valerianus was concerned, always *would* be.

From the comfort of his throne, which slaves had set up under the shade of a canopy, Valerianus watched the disembarkation of his army with a sense of pride. Here was Rome's best, standing once again on the shores of Syria, despite Shapur's rantings about Sassanid superiority, and his prediction that he would grind the Roman army into the very dirt they were trying to reclaim. Braggadocio. Nothing more. Shapur was a blowhard, a fact that Valerianus counted on. Actually, his entire strategy pivoted on that fact—that was the beauty of it. Shapur thought that the mere presence of his troops in the city of Antioch meant that he had won all of Syria; he thought that he owned Armenia because his troops had overrun it. But that was only property. The real Antioch, the true Armenia, lay in the hearts of the people that lived there, and those hearts were Roman through and through. Shapur had marched a thousand Romans into one of Antioch's biggest theatres, up onto the stage where once the comedies of Aristophanes and Menander had entertained their audiences, and butchered them one by one. A tragedy, a true tragedy. And yes, Shapur's barbarism had cowed many Roman hearts—but he had not *won* them. Those hearts still belonged to Valerianus and the distant city that had birthed the Empire, and so Antioch remained a Roman city, even though Shapur's soldiers controlled it; and so Armenia remained a Roman ally, despite the elephant corps and Cataphracts and light infantry Shapur had stationed there.

Half of Valerianus' army of seventy thousand men was here, not twenty miles from the Syrian capital of Antioch where Persian soldiers now strutted through the streets, drunk with power. The other half Valerianus had sent up through the Bosphorus, into the Black Sea. Soon they would be landing on the shores of Pontus, then a quick march to Armenia, and Shapur would find himself caught in a Roman vice, and like the barbarian whelp he was, he would run back to Ctesiphon with his tail between his legs. But this time he would not be allowed to brood in the shadows and grow strong again. This time Valerianus would finish Shapur off once and for all. And then what? The whole Persian empire. Or even the greatest prize of all: India?

Valerianus sipped wine from a gold cup, grinning. Alexander had once forged an empire out of the East that reached into India, and for his troubles history had dubbed him Alexander the Great. One day that appellation would belong to him as well: Valerianus the Great. He liked the sound of that. *Loved* it.

All the soldiers had disembarked now, and the real work had begun. Even though there were no Persians in the immediate vicinity, work crews would set up the standard army camp, complete with moat and palisade. It always paid to be careful. Losing an army of thirty-five thousand men for the sake of a few hours of hard labour was unacceptable. The army engineering corps was busy unloading and assembling the prefabricated siege weapons—high, armour-plated siege towers, onagers and ballistae for hurling stones and other projectiles, and of course the huge battering rams that could burst open even the strongest city gates. By the time the army reached the walls of Antioch early next week, everything would be ready.

It was at that moment, when Valerianus was contemplating the triumphs soon to come, that he remembered the leather pouch of coins his son had presented to him when they had parted the previous June. He had placed the bag in his trunk that night, and in the ensuing excitement had forgotten all about it. Summoning a slave, he had the bag brought to him. It was heavy, and when he hefted it, he could feel the coins moving inside. He had had commemorative coins minted as well: Valerianus and Gallienus standing back to back on the obverse, with the two-faced god Janus on the reverse. The coins, a series of *denarii* which symbolized the unity and divinity of father and son, were already in general circulation in the East, although very few of them would have made it into Gallienus' dominions yet. He ordered one of the slaves waiting nearby to send a bag of his new coins to Rome on the next transport. Not that Gallienus would get them there—reports placed him along the Rhine Frontier the entire campaigning season—but Festus would redirect the coins to Gallienus, along with all the official correspondence his scribes were preparing.

Valerianus nodded his head with satisfaction. So far more than two years had passed, and their joint reign had met with unparalleled success. Plague was still a problem; it was spreading out of Italy and had made an appearance in Asia Minor (it had actually arrived in Syria before he did). But so far Gallienus was keeping the Germans at bay, and Shapur would soon suffer the consequences of his arrogance. Which left the enemy within, the enemy that bred in the shadows cast by Valerianus' magnificent empire, and fed on its host's body like a parasite.

The Christians.

When Aemilianus had arrested him after the death of Decius at the Battle of Abrittus, Valerianus had thought their plan to eliminate the Christians had failed. But that failure had actually been a near triumph. Decius' persecution had left the Church in ruins. The unity of the Christians had proved as fragile as glass—it had shattered beneath the hammer of imperial interdiction. Most of the Christians had *raced* to the altars of sacrifice, as if they believed that being the first to deny the *Christos* would win them a prize. There were even instances where one of the Christian *episcopi* would bring his entire congregation to sacrifice *with* him. And there was the perfect strategy for dealing with any enemy: target the leaders first. That was why he was sitting here on the shores of the Mediterranean watching his army prepare for war, after all. If he destroyed Shapur, the Sassanid war machine would grind to a halt.

Destroy the head, destroy the body—the incontrovertible

medical dictum that formed the backdrop for all Roman politics, international and domestic.

And her religious policy.

Laughing, Valerianus opened the leather bag his son had given him, reached inside, and took out a single coin.

At first he was struck by the quality of the piece. It was an *antoninianus*, sometimes called a double denarius, because it was larger than the denarius and was supposed to be worth twice as much. The coin shone a brilliant silver in the hot Syrian sun—obviously it had been handled very little. Its edges had been clipped and sanded down to make the coin almost perfectly round and smooth to the touch. Then he noticed the image on the front of the coin and his heart climbed up into his throat. For a moment he could not breath, could not speak, as if a monster had just leapt out at him from its hiding place and frightened him almost to death.

And in a way that analogy was true . . .

Somehow he found his feet and ordered slaves and scribes and the bodyguards that always stood nearby to leave. He stumbled into the privacy of his tent, collapsing onto one of the dining couches, and dropped the coin on the table, threw it down as if it were poison, and then closed his eyes and willed his breathing to return to normal.

When he opened his eyes again they darted to the coin, which glimmered in the torchlight. The image had not changed. It was Mariniana. Gallienus' mother and Valerianus' wife.

His dead wife.

Even without the inscription that circled the edge of the coin, Valerianus would have recognized that face. It was a hauntingly accurate depiction of Mariniana, right down to the rows of curls that she had always worn along the sides of her head, just above the ears. The artist had caught her profile perfectly, her simple beauty, the sweet smile that had so often brightened her face, and for just a moment Valerianus' heart ached with longing, a response that surprised, then angered him. Mariniana had left them when Gallienus was eight years old, and yet his young mind had preserved her image in startling detail. How could he have remembered her face so well after all these years?

Valerianus read the inscription that encircled his wife's image: "*Divae Marinianae*." He flipped the coin over. On the reverse was a picture of his wife mounted on a flying peacock. One hand was raised as if in greeting, and the other held a sceptre. The inscription read: "*Consecratio*."

Valerianus emptied the entire bag of coins onto the table. There were over a hundred of them, and they were all the same. He gazed at the one in his hand again and whispered the entire inscription front and back: "The Consecration of the Divine Mariniana."

His wife was a goddess.

Gallienus had had his mother deified . . .

Valerianus hurled the coin into the dirt. "You insolent *fool*," he bellowed. Immediately two guards burst into the tent, their swords drawn and ready. Valerianus jumped to his feet. "Get *out*!" he screamed. "Get out! Get OUT!"

The guards left without a word, but he could see the consternation in their eyes. And he did not care. How *dare* Gallienus? How *dare* he? He had given his son everything—a good name, a good home, a good education, a good career—and now, he had taken him to the heights of the empire and given him the imperial throne. And how did he repay his father's love and trust? By taking that . . . trollop out of the grave and thrusting her into the heavens, and making a laughing stock of his father and his family name in the process. Mariniana had betrayed him, betrayed her family, betrayed them all, and for what? For *what*?

Valerianus hurled the table aside; the coins showered the earth in a silver rain.

As was his right as a husband, he had passed the *damnatio memoriae* on her: no one in their household, no one connected to the Valerianus name, no matter how remotely, was permitted to mention her again. Even Gallienus had been forbidden to speak her name.

So what was the point of this . . . this *outrage*? What was Gallienus trying to prove? What would he say when the questions started? When people began to ask him, what happened to the *divine* Mariniana?

She is dead.

Oh, how sad . . .
It happened a long time ago.
Oh, how very sad . . .
Twenty-seven years ago.
Sad, sad, sad . . .
When I was eight.
Oh, you poor boy . . .
She went away.
Sad little boy . . .
She went away and she died.
How did she die . . .
You will have to ask the Divine Valerianus the answer to that question.

Trembling, Valerianus sank down into the soft embrace of the dining couch. Questions whirled through his mind. Why now? Two and a half years ago, when they had decided the future of the empire in a tent outside the city of Narnia, he had said nothing about Mariniana. But suddenly, *this*? When things were going so well? When it actually seemed that the two of them might be able to set the troubled empire on its feet once again? Now, he decided to manufacture more trouble, to chisel a wedge out of memories that was powerful enough to drive them further apart, instead of uniting them and the empire. It made no sense. It was as if Gallienus had intentionally set out to make his father his enemy.

"Trust me, my son," Valerianus whispered. "You do not want me for an enemy."

DAMARRA WAS IN THE GARDEN playing with Ruth when they carried the wounded man inside. The little toddler saw the man and began to cry. "What is it, Ruth?" Damarra asked. She was such a good child, hardly every cried, so when she did one knew there was something truly wrong.

Sniffling, Ruth held up her chubby arms, "Mom-mee-ee," she sobbed.

Damarra's heart expanded in her chest. All children were a miracle from God, but Ruth was *their* miracle, hers and Valens', and gazing into her teary blue eyes made her insides ache with love. How was it possible to love someone as much as she loved her little girl? "Come on, my dove," she cooed and plucked the child up. Ruth nestled into her neck and the crying dwindled to tiny, erratic sobs.

Persephone entered the garden from the front of the villa. She saw Damarra and hurried over. "What has happened?" Damarra asked. "Who was that wounded man?

"Lord Valens found him in the ditch up the road, the victim of bandits."

"But who is he?"

Persephone shook her head. "No one knows. You can barely see his face with all the blood. The master has ordered me to tend to him."

Damarra called Prisca, who had been sitting quietly on a bench enjoying the winter sunshine. Ruth had fallen asleep in her mother's arms. Damarra handed the little girl to Prisca and sent her to put the child down for a nap. "I'll help you," she said to Persephone.

The two young women hurried into the slave quarters, where the slaves had taken the wounded man. They found them in one of the spare bedrooms, gently placing him on the bed. The man was still unconscious.

Persephone asked the slaves to bring warm water, and in short order they had removed his torn garments, washed him, and made him as comfortable as possible. The man groaned once, but did not regain consciousness. His wounds were less severe than they had at first believed. Most of the blood was from cuts on his forehead and cheeks. Whoever had beaten him was probably wearing a ring. His left eye was blackened and there were bruises on his cheeks and his shoulder. Clean, his hair was thick, straight, and shaggy, not overlong, about mid-neck length, and brown. His shaggy beard was brown. "Perhaps he is a bandit," Persephone suggested. "Maybe his gang beat him up and left him to die for some offense."

Damarra's eyes darted to the empty doorway. "Or perhaps one of the pilgrims on his way to see us?" She still could not bring herself to use the term *"lapsi,"* with its derogatory connotations.

"If that is true, the master will turn him out."

Sorrow welled in Damarra's chest. At first Valens' attitude towards the *lapsi* had simply shocked her, like touching a dead ember and finding it still hot. But now that ember had become a flame burning between them: she could not understand the hardness in his heart; he could not understand the forgiveness in hers. She had explained it to him until the words were an acid in her throat, but he would not listen, and so she had stopped trying to make him understand. The argument was a high wall in their lives that neither could scale or break down. Instead, they lived around it. With Persephone's help, Damarra had taken to meeting secretly with the *lapsi*—when such meetings could be arranged without Valens' knowledge—and Valens, for his part, continued to turn the *lapsi* away when he or his guards got to them first. And Persephone was right. If this man turned was one of the *lapsi*, Valens would cast him out, injured or not.

"Unless he is a true pilgrim," Persephone added.

That was another possibility. Some of the Christians who came to see them were not *lapsi*. Some just came to pay their respects to the confessors, especially to Valens, who bore the marks of the *Christos*. Valens did not enjoy the attention, but at least he was willing to talk to the true pilgrims. And show them the marks that they so earnestly wanted to see. And touch. And kiss.

The wounded man groaned and opened his eyes. They were hazel, more brown than green. His eyes flitted about the room, then came to rest on Persephone's face. "Are you an angel?" he asked. His voice was hoarse.

Persephone laughed. "No, my name is Persephone, and this is the lady Damarra," Persephone told him.

"And you are quite safe," Damarra added. "What is your name?"

The man smiled. It looked like it hurt. "Paulus," he replied.

Damarra's mind flashed to the other Paulus, their friend and the former commander of the Praetorian Guard who had died here over two years ago on the night little Ruth had been born. Sadness crept through her again. It was always the same when she thought of Paulus. He had saved their lives, and they had loved him as a brother. She still mourned for him and knew she always would, just as Valens always would, not because he had died so horribly, so . . . *pointlessly*, but because he had died without coming to know the *Christos*. He had died the Wayward Seed, and they would never see him again—his soul was forever lost.

"What happened to you?" Persephone asked.

Paulus scratched his head, winced. "I was walking along the road when someone struck me from behind. I don't remember much after that. Did they . . . take my purse?"

"You had no purse when my husband found you," Damarra said.

"My money! All gone!"

Damarra patted his hand. "Not to worry, you are among friends here. We will look after you."

That seemed to calm him. "Where am I?" he asked.

"The estate of Julius Valens," Damarra replied.

Paulus' eyes widened. "Then you are *that* Damarra. The confessor!"

Damarra and Persephone exchanged troubled glances. "You are . . . a Christian?" Damarra asked.

"Yes."

"You seek . . . a Certificate of Peace?"

He laughed and winced. "No, I am not one of the *lapsi*." Gingerly he prodded his side until he found the culprit—a bruised rib—then winced again. "I am a retired soldier. I had a homestead on the Rhine Frontier, but I grew tired of defending it against the Germans, so I sold it off."

"Then what are you doing here?" Damarra asked.

"I heard stories about you and Lord Valens, and since I was in Massalia on business, I decided to come and see you for myself. It is an honour to meet you, my lady."

"How did you fare in the persecution, Paulus?" Persephone asked.

Damarra shook her head sadly. There was a time when two Christians meeting for the first time would exchange the peace and express joy at finding another believer. Since the persecution, however, such meetings had become restrained, because they now necessitated the same awkward question: "How did you survive the persecution?"

"I was a centurion with the First Minervia in Germania Inferior during the reign of Decius. We were much too busy repelling barbarians to worry about a few Christians in our ranks." He laughed. "I already know what happened to you, Lady Damarra," he turned his hazel eyes on Persephone, "but you, Persephone? What happened to you."

"We were blessed here. One of the men on our commission—I will not name names—was the husband of a Christian; he simply convinced the other members that the decree was foolishness, and the commission spent its days playing dice and drinking wine and left us alone."

Paulus laughed. "You were blessed indeed!"

Suddenly Gundabar appeared in the doorway. His blue eyes narrowed at the man on the bed, then they found Persephone and he smiled. "Gundabar, this is Paulus," Persephone said.

Damarra had a sudden thought. "Is he the other we've been waiting for, Gundabar?" she asked.

Gundabar stepped into the room and went to the side of the bed, opposite Persephone. His chainmail rattled as he bent over Paulus. He studied him a moment before shaking his head. "No, not other."

Damarra sighed. For over two years now they had been waiting for this "other" that Gundabar had assured them would come. They had raised their little girl, attended the duties of the seasons, read the *Scripturae*, loved each other, tried to get on with their lives. Tried. But no matter what they did, the future hung over them like a curse. Someday this "other" would come, and they would have to give it all up and flee to the wilds of Germania. In the meantime, the days and weeks were passing and the Clan was waiting. Life had become waiting.

"Emperor come," Gundabar said.

"He is here?" Damarra asked and her heart fluttered in her chest.

"Yes, you come, Lady Damarra."

Damarra and Persephone squeezed each other's hands. This was the first bit of real excitement they had had in months. "How do I look?" Damarra asked.

Persephone looked her up and down. Damarra wore an elegant blue *stola*, the long gown that was the traditional garment of the Roman matron. A gold belt set with semi-precious jewels was tied about her narrow waist. Her long white hair was piled up on top of her head and held in place by a thin band of gold. Ringlets hung down on either side of her head, framing her delicate features. An armlet of beaten gold encircled her left bicep, and on her right wrist were three golden bracelets, gifts from Valens for their first anniversary. "You look . . . nervous, my lady," Persephone teased.

Damarra slapped her hand playfully.

"My lady, you look wonderful, as beautiful as Helen of Troy," Persephone said.

"I was aiming for somewhere between nervous and Helen," Damarra admitted.

Persephone hugged her. "Then you have succeeded, my lady. I do not think the emperor will care either way. I imagine he will be pleased just to meet his little sister."

"I hope so."

They said their farewells to Paulus, then followed Gundabar into the outer courtyard and out into the front laneway. Across the road, several tents had already been erected. Many of the local landowners had come to meet the emperor, and already a large crowd was milling about, mixing with members of the emperor's entourage. Slaves were moving through the crowd carrying trays of wine and food. Entertaining an emperor was considered a great honour, but it also incurred great expense. Not a few Roman noblemen had found themselves honoured out of their family fortunes by an imperial visit. Fortunately, Julius Valens was one of the richest men in the empire and could entertain a hundred emperors without feeling the loss.

Damarra recognized Tribune Marcus, now General Marcus from the cut of his dress uniform, and waved at him. He hurried over and greeted her with a regal bow. "Blessed Confessor, it is an honour to see you again."

Damarra laughed. "And you, Lord Marcus."

Marcus grinned at Persephone. "And the beautiful Persephone, as radiant as ever."

Persephone blushed and curtsied.

"Where is he?" Damarra asked.

Marcus glanced around the crowd until he spotted Gallienus. "There," he said, "over by the great oak. Come, Holy Confessor, I will take you to him."

Marcus led her through the crowd to the oak which stood by itself, just outside the doors to the courtyard. The oak was massive, perhaps ten feet across at its base. By itself it produced more acorns than the entire household used, and most of the surplus went to feed the pigs. Slaves had spent the morning raking away old acorn shells, twigs and dead leaves, making the space as tidy and smooth as possible so that thrones might be set up in the oak's shade. A canopy had also been erected to protect the royal heads from any errant acorns that might pick that moment to fall.

The emperor and the empress were standing in front of their thrones under the canopy, talking with Valens. They were dressed in regal splendour for the occasion. The Empress Nina was in purple and blue silks and decked with gold and precious jewels. Upon her head sat a coronet of gold with silver rays, as if she were the sun goddess, shedding her glorious light for the benefit of her subjects. She was a beautiful woman, olive skinned, with soft brown eyes and a magnificent mane of auburn hair. Her features were sharp, and could have lent her an air of cruelty were they not softened by her smile. Her husband, who was laughing at some joke he had shared with Valens, wore a circlet of gold with silver rays as well, although his crown was thicker and larger. He wore a purple tunic and cloak, golden greaves and sandals, and at his side was a sword with a jewelled hilt. The breastplate of his armour was breathtaking, gleaming gold into which a master craftsman had etched a scene out of Roman mythology: Romulus and Remus, the twin founders of the city of Rome, being suckled by a she-wolf. The wolf's eyes were glittering green emeralds. He was slighter of build than his father, shorter but more muscular, and his hair was the same shade of brown Valerianus' had been before age had salted it with grey. She thought he looked like a younger version of his father, but his features were softer, without the angles and gauntness that characterized his father's face.

When he saw Damarra approaching, he grinned and turned to his wife. "Nina," he said, "is that Helen of Troy?"

The empress glanced at Damarra and her face broke into a

stunning smile. "Aphrodite, I think, my lord emperor."

Damarra's heart beat like a blacksmith's hammer as she curtsied. "We are honoured by your presence, your excellencies," she said. She heard her voice tremble and prayed that they had not.

Gallienus laughed. Growing up in the Valerianus household, she had learned quickly that the master's laughter was a lie, a presage of wrath and punishment. Gallienus' laughter was true, the sound of real joy, and despite her nervousness, she began to laugh herself. "Little sister," he said and opened his arms. "I have waited many years to meet you, and my time here is short. So let us not stand on formality."

Damarra stepped into Gallienus' embrace, amazed at how willing this man was to accept her. Not only had she been born a slave, but she was a known Christian, and despite the fact that the persecution was over, being a Christian was still a crime punishable by death. Most Roman aristocrats would have been embarrassed by her at the very least, a skeleton to be buried in the furthest recesses of the family closet and avoided at all costs, and yet here was Gallienus, one of the most powerful men in the world, openly and *publicly* accepting her as a member of the imperial family. Her life was living proof of the existence of a God of miracles.

"You are as beautiful as the rumours claim," he whispered in her ear. He released her and kissed her cheeks. "And I am proud to call you my sister."

THIRTEEN

The emperor's visit to Massalia lasted one week. Much of that time was spent on matters of state. Gallienus cut the ribbon on new baths located in the north quadrant of the city and officiated over the opening ceremonies of the restored Temple of Aphrodite. The centrepiece of the temple was the new twenty-foot statue of the goddess that graced the altar room, where sacrifices were offered daily on behalf of those seeking the goddess' intervention in matters of the heart. During the ceremony Gallienus commented to the empress that the statue bore an uncanny resemblance to his sister, and after appraising the statue herself, Nina agreed. Later, when they returned to the Valens estate and mentioned the similarity to Damarra, she blushed and changed the subject.

On the last evening of their visit, Gallienus requested to review Valens' horses. General Marcus had praised their quality and size—he had had the opportunity to assess them on his first visit—and Gallienus wanted to see for himself. So Gallienus and Valens, along with Empress Nina, Damarra, and Marcus (and the ubiquitous guards who accompanied the emperor wherever he went), rode out to a large corral in the middle of a fine pasture where Valens' prime breeding stock was spending the winter with his largest stallion. Conall was there, making sure the horses had plenty of hay and water. Since it was Conall who had designed and implemented Valens' breeding program, Valens introduced him to the emperor. Gallienus' eye roamed over the spirited mares in the corral. "These are some of the finest horses we have ever seen, Conall," he admitted. The ladies wandered over to the split rail fence to pet a black mare, which was tied to the fence's top rail by a rope bridle.

Conall bowed. "Thank you, Your Excellency."

"How many do you have of this size?" Gallienus asked.

"This size? Perhaps fifteen hundred all told, here and on several other estates in the area. We will have double that by next year."

"We will take them all," Gallienus said.

Valens and Conall gasped in surprise. Even Marcus gave a start. "All, Your Excellency?" Valens asked.

"Yes, these fifteen hundred, the fifteen hundred that will be ready next year, and any others of the same size and breeding you might be able to acquire for us."

"Forgive me, Your Excellency," Valens said, "but most of these horses are spoken for. In these troubled times, many landowners are creating cavalry units for self-protection."

Gallienus waved away his objection. "Precisely why we need them. As your emperor, we claim the right of pre-emption."

Valens bowed, "Of course, Your Excellency—the horses are yours."

Gallienus grinned. "Do not worry, Julius Valens. You will be paid handsomely for these fine beasts. If you were not already a wealthy man, you would be so when our business is concluded."

"I know of breeders up in Gallia Aquitainia who can provide stock of the same quality, Your Excellency," Conall said.

"How many?"

"Two thousand head, perhaps more."

"You will act as our agent in this matter. A commission on each head purchased."

Conall glanced at Valens, who nodded his permission. "Yes, Your Excellency," Conall said.

"If I may be so bold, Your Excellency, what need do you have for so many horses?" asked Valens.

"A good question," Marcus agreed. "I, too, would like to learn the reason for your sudden interest in horses."

Gallienus studied the horses in the corral for so long that the others thought he had decided not to answer the question. At last he sighed and turned to Valens. "Last spring, while we were near Bona in Germania Inferior, we received news of a raiding party that was pillaging the countryside around Castra Vetera, a frontier town and fort no more than thirty miles north of Bona. We left immediately and by forced marches were able to make Castra Vetera in two days.

"The town itself was fine; the raiding party—Franks apparently—was small, too small to penetrate Castra Vetera's walls. Instead, the raiders had attacked and pillaged several of the small villages in the nearby countryside. We entered one village, Bona Fortuna, it was called," the emperor's laugh was bitter, "the village of Good Fortune, a misnomer as it turned out. The six or seven huts that comprised the centre of the village were smoking ruins. Bodies were strewn everywhere, old women, children, a few old men, several infants. The raiders had butchered the young and the old and taken the rest as slaves. Not a single inhabitant of Bona Fortuna survived the raid. There was nothing left. No food, no metal implements, no animals—nothing.

"This was hardly the first time we had come across such devastation. It is a common sight on the frontiers. For every raiding party we intercept and destroy, three more pillage and escape before we arrive. Something had to be done to change those odds, but we did not know what until that day.

"We were surveying the carnage when we saw an old centurion digging through the rubble of one of the huts, looking for survivors. His name was Attalus, a thirty-year veteran. We asked him if there was a way to stop this devastation." The emperor paused and stared again at the horses, shaking his head. "Why we asked him, we do not know. Perhaps exasperation prompted us. Or perhaps we believed that after thirty years the veteran may have garnered some insights into this endless game of cat and mouse we were playing with the barbarians. Attalus thought for a moment, and then he replied, 'We must get to the enemy faster, Your Excellency.'

"I grinned at that. The enemy appears, they rape, they pillage, then they vanish before we can march to meet them. That is the endless cycle that we face, and to tell us we needed to reach the enemy faster was like telling a drowning man he needs to breathe—no great insight. But then the veteran glanced down at his sandaled feet, gave a grim chuckle, and said, 'These old feet are too tired and too slow; if only they had Mercury's wings!'"

Gallienus laughed. "And that is when it came to us. 'Not Mercury's wings,' we replied. 'But the wings of Neptune Equester.'"

Valens, Marcus, and Conall stared at the emperor, uncomprehending. "The god of horses?" Valens said.

Gallienus laughed again. "Attalus looked at us exactly the same way. What we are proposing is a new military unit: a stand-alone cavalry. We will continue to use cavalry to support the infantry, especially mounted archers, after the Palmyrene model. But we shall introduce a variant of heavy cavalry, like the Persian Cataphracts, but with one main difference—our cavalry will be more lightly armoured."

At last Valens nodded with understanding. "To make it more mobile," he said.

"Yes. An armoured cavalry with its own weaponry—bow, javelin, and sword—that can cover the same distance as the infantry in a fifth of the time."

"Thus the need for larger, stronger horses," Valens added.

"Precisely. They must be able to carry armoured riders great distances without tiring. Our new cavalry will operate out of Mediolanum in Northern Italy for now, ready and able to race to any point on the Rhine-Danube frontier as soon as they receive news of a raid. No infantry to slow them down."

"A brilliant strategy, Your Excellency," Valens said.

"Indeed," Marcus agreed.

They worked out some of the details of the transaction, then returned to the villa for their final meal together. The cooks had prepared a sumptuous banquet for the imperial family and their guests. They met in a canopied dining room, set up in the open air with a view of the Mediterranean to the south, and Valens' vineyards to the north. As the sun set, they reclined on dining couches and the feast began. It was a joyous occasion. Massalia and Arelatum, further to the west, the two most important cities in the province of Gallia Narbonensis, had both pledged their support to the new dynasty by building temples in honour of Gallienus and his divine consort, Nina. Gallienus had made connections with many of the province's most important senatorial and equestrian families, and he had acquired the horses he needed for his new cavalry in a single transaction. The emperor's visit had been both successful and profitable, and the emperor was in the mood to celebrate. The guests were few: Valens, Damarra, and Marcus. A slave dressed in a green silk tunic attended the emperor and empress and Marcus, while Persephone attended Valens and Damarra. A bodyguard consisting of four soldiers stood nearby, guarding the royal family; Gundabar and the new slaves, Regulus and Alexander, provided protection for Valens and Damarra. The fourth member of their guard was Paulus, the man they had found in the ditch the week before. Although his face still bore the bruises of his beating, he was back on his feet again, and Valens, upon learning of his military background, had hired him on permanently as a guard.

The celebration was well underway in the long Gallic twilight when four people trudged out of the dusk and stopped at the villa gate. Valens ordered Gundabar to find out what the new arrivals wanted, although from the scowl on his face, Gallienus deduced that his sister's husband already knew. Gundabar hurried to the gate and spoke to them in his halting Latin. After a few moments he drew his sword, and the group turned around and headed back in the direction they had come.

"Let me speak to them, Valens," Damarra whispered. He could hear the pleading quality of her words.

He shook his head, "Not now."

Damarra lowered her eyes and nodded sadly.

Gundabar returned and whispered a word that his friend, General Marcus, had mentioned on several occasions. "*Lapsi*," the emperor repeated.

Marcus looked up from the plate of roast boar he was eating and glanced at the four people Gundabar had turned away, who were just disappearing into the darkness.

"Forgive the interruption, Your Excellency," Valens said.

"Not at all." He set his empty cup down on the table. The

slave in the green tunic filled it again. "What are these *lapsi* I keep hearing about?"

"They were once Christians—"

"They are still Christians," Damarra corrected.

Valens rolled his eyes. "They are fallen Christians, Your Excellency. Nothing to worry about."

"Ah, yes, Christians. We had forgotten that you and our sister are Christians. You seem so . . . " he paused, looking for the word.

"Normal," Nina offered.

They all laughed.

"Yes," Gallienus continued. "Normal. But who are these *lapsi*?"

Valens said nothing, so Damarra explained the term and how it had come about.

When she had finished, Gallienus picked up his cup and drank deeply. "Fine wine," he said to Valens.

"Our own stock," Valens replied. "When you leave I shall send ten amphorae with you. A gift."

"Our thanks," Gallienus said. He thought for a moment, then: "Emperor Valerianus told us that the Christians were divided, fighting amongst themselves. Now we understand why."

"And what do you intend to do about the Christians?" Damarra blurted out.

Gallienus had been expecting that question all week. As they were leaving the next morning, he had begun to hope that the subject would not come up, but now it could not be avoided. "Our policy remains the same as our predecessors," he replied.

"And what does that mean?" Valens pressed.

"As the great Trajan stipulated, the Christians are not to be sought out. If they come to the attention of a magistrate, they are to be given the chance to recant; if they refuse to recant, they are to be executed."

"And what of us?" Valens asked.

Gallienus laughed. "I have no plans to execute either of you or Marcus at present."

There was laughter, but on Damarra and Valens' side it was strained.

"So the Christians are to remain in the shadows," Valens said.

"The government pretends we do not exist unless we make ourselves too obvious to ignore."

"For the present, yes. But I want to assure you that no matter what changes the future may bring, you and my sister will be safe. I will allow no harm to befall you."

Valens' eyes narrowed. "Excuse me, Your Excellency, but that sounds like there is a possibility that you will return to the more aggressive policy followed by Decius."

Gallienus hesitated, then: "It may come to that."

"But why?" Damarra cried.

"There are certain elements in your sect that have become more . . . radical. Dangerous, even."

"Christians?" Damarra said, flabbergasted. "No, it cannot be."

"We have proof. For example, Christians instigated the Buri invasion of Pannonia last year."

"Forgive me, Your Excellency," Marcus interrupted, "but that source was never satisfactorily verified."

Gallienus held up his hand. "Christians have also been implicated in recent food riots in Alexandria and Carthage, but more damaging, there is evidence to suggest that Christians have been stirring up the tribes in Germania."

"What evidence?" Valens asked.

"Franks, Marcomanni, Alamanni, Juthungi, Sueves," Gallienus counted them off on his fingers. "In the last ten years, Christians have infiltrated each one of these tribes—and many others—an incontrovertible fact."

"Missionaries," Valens objected. "Travellers in the Way, who dedicate their lives to taking the love of the *Christos* to the peoples who do not know Him."

Gallienus shook his head. "No! They have stirred up the tribes! Is it just a coincidence that each tribe that has received one of these so-called 'missionaries' has subsequently raided the empire? Pillaged our towns and cities? Butchered our citizens? We think not!"

Damarra touched her husband's arm, and when he looked at her, she shook her head. Valens sighed. "Your Excellency, I can only say that your interpretation of what Christians are doing in Germania is misguided, and I hope that you will not permit these 'facts,' as you call them, to form the basis of any new imperial policy regarding the Christians."

Gallienus raised his cup to Valens. "We thank you for your honesty, and as we said before, no matter what happens, you will be safe."

"Perhaps this will change your mind," Valens said. He removed a piece of folded parchment from his belt and handed it to Gallienus. "What is it?" Gallienus asked. The back of the parchment was stained red. He unfolded it and read the words written there out loud:

> *Be sure that we will meet again*
> *when I have set my house in order.*
> *V.*

"What is the meaning of this?" Gallienus asked.

"Do you recognize the seal?" Valens replied.

Gallienus turned the paper over and studied what remained of the red wax. "Difficult to tell. The stain has obscured it."

"It is your father's seal," Valens said.

"It might be."

"And the message?"

Gallienus read it over again and shrugged. "Somewhat obscure. It could mean anything?"

"And the signature?"

"'V' could be my father . . . or many other people." He laughed. "It could even be *you*, Valens."

"The letter was found attached to a knife that had been plunged into the chest of my friend Paulus Antoninus Quaerellus as he lay wounded in my bed."

"Ah! That *does* sound like my father's handiwork," Gallienus admitted. "But you must understand, Valens: Commander Paulus was an enemy of the state. Once Valerianus assumed the purple, Paulus' death was only a matter of time."

"I do understand, Emperor Gallienus. Just as I understand that your father used the assassination of his political enemy to deliver a message to my wife—your sister—and me."

Gallienus looked at the parchment again, then set it on the table. He glanced over at his friend Marcus. They had been together since he turned thirteen, and until this moment he had planned to keep Marcus by his side until the end, but knowing what his father had in store for Valens and Damarra had changed things. He trusted Marcus more than any of his officers, more than any other human being, with the exception of Nina, so he was the best person to whom he could entrust the safety of his sister. He would not allow Valerianus to destroy her too. "General Marcus, we have new orders for you."

Marcus rose from his dining couch and saluted. "Yes, Your Excellency."

"You will stay here and protect our sister."

"Yes, Your Excellency."

"No," Valens cried. He pointed at Gundabar and his three subordinates. "We have everything well in hand. Forgive me, General Marcus, when I say that we have no need of you." He saw Marcus' worried face and added, "Not at present, anyway."

Gallienus glanced from Marcus to Valens. Something had passed between the two men, an unspoken agreement, as if they were sharing some secret that neither could speak of in present company. He turned to his sister. She too was looking at Marcus and Valens, only there was doubt in her eyes. Finally she smiled at Gallienus and said, "For now, Your Excellency, we are fine. By all accounts our . . . father has yet to set his house in order."

"True. Dealing with Shapur will take some time." Gallienus sighed. "Very well, we will keep General Marcus with us for now. But should the need arise, you must send for him. And if at any time we feel our sister is in immediate danger, we will send him to you without waiting for your permission."

"He will be most welcome then," Valens said.

Gallienus took Damarra's hand and squeezed it. "We will not permit Valerianus to harm you. You have our word."

"Thank you, Your Excellency."

NIGHT HAD FALLEN, and in the villa and the emperor's camp, sleep was once again victorious. There were a few, however, who still resisted its charms. Damarra lay in the darkness, listening to the sound of Valens' breathing, her mind a whirl that would not let her rest. At last she rose from their bed, took the lamp from her desk, and slipped out into the garden. A single torch still burned at the far end, where the pillared portico that surrounded the garden met the entrance into the front of the villa. On those rare occasions that sleep eluded her, she often came out here to the garden to pray or read. Tonight, she felt compelled to go elsewhere, why she could not say. Using the torch to light her small lamp, she made her way through the long hallway and out into the front courtyard. In the shadows, at the opposite end of the courtyard, she spotted a figure on his knees. Although she could not tell from this distance, she thought it was Marcus. Maybe the Christos was prodding her to speak to him for some reason. Maybe that was why her usual bench in the garden had felt wrong tonight.

"A beautiful night, my lady," whispered a voice behind her.

Her heart lurched with surprise as she spun around. She hadn't passed anyone in the hallway, yet she *must* have. A man stepped into the light. It was one of the new slaves Valens had purchased the previous week. He bowed. "Forgive me, my lady; I did not mean to frighten you. Alexander and I drew second watch tonight."

She placed a hand on her chest. "No, that's fine, Regulus. I just didn't see you there."

He jerked his head toward the praying figure at the other end of the courtyard. "General Marcus," he said, keeping his voice low. "I did not realize he was also a Christian."

"Yes, he is."

"Does the emperor know that his best general is a Christian?" Regulus asked.

Damarra nodded.

Regulus grinned. "That bodes well for the Christians then, doesn't it?"

"I hope so, Regulus."

"Well, good night, my lady."

"Good night, Regulus."

The guard headed back into the villa. Damarra walked down the steps into the front courtyard. Marcus heard her coming and glanced back over his shoulder. When he saw it was her, he stood up and bowed. "Greetings, Confessor," he said.

She smiled up at him. "You couldn't sleep either?"

He looked up at the bowl of stars glittering overhead. "No. So I came out here to pray to the God who made those," he said, pointing up.

"You are troubled, Marcus." It was a statement, not a question.

His eyes narrowed. "How did you know?"

"I was restless, unable to sleep. When I finally gave in and got up, I felt compelled to come out here, as if the Holy Spirit wanted me here. When I saw you praying, I knew I must talk to you." She placed her hand on his arm. "What is it, Marcus? What troubles you?"

He glanced up at the stars again. In the light of her lamp, she could see his eyes glistening. It took him a long time to finally say the words: "I . . . am afraid."

She could not imagine General Marcus being afraid of anything. Even here in the Gallic countryside, they had heard tales of his exploits on the battlefield. He was handsome, gallant, and brave, a combination that loosened the tongues of many young ladies in the empire. "Afraid of what?" she prompted.

He looked at her again, and yes, those were tears in his eyes. "I am afraid . . . that Valens will not . . . want me to accompany the Clan to Germania when the time comes," he blurted out.

"But Marcus, it is not a question of if he wants you to come. The *Christos* has chosen you—you are one of the Clan," she laughed humourlessly, "whatever that may mean. You *must* come. Valens cannot turn you away. And why would Valens do such a thing? I know the two of you started poorly, but that was a misunderstanding."

Marcus sighed. "I think it best that I show you," he said and, taking a piece of folded parchment from his belt, he handed it to her. "Read this," he said.

She handed him the lamp and unfolded the document, then read aloud the words written there:

> *Know that we have granted peace to Marcus Gaius For-*
> *tunatus, whose behaviour since the commission of his*

*crime is satisfactory; and we desire to make this known
to other episcopi also. We wish you to maintain peace
with the holy martyrs.*
   Lucian the Confessor Wrote This

Damarra looked up into Marcus' eyes and saw his pain and
his turmoil, saw the sleepless nights he had spent in prayer and
self-condemnation, the agony of his doubts and the joy and
blessed relief he had felt when this Lucian had lifted all that from
his shoulders with the stroke of a pen. "Oh, Marcus," Damarra
whispered, and then Marcus Gaius Fortunatus—lifelong friend of
the emperor Gallienus, veteran of too many campaigns against the
Germans to count, a general respected by his colleagues and
feared by his enemies—began to weep.

"Oh, Marcus," Damarra whispered again, and pulled the crying man into her arms. He was taller than she by more than a foot,
but he crumpled in her embrace like a hurt child. His head found
her shoulder, and great sobs wracked his chest.

"I'm so sorry," he groaned through his tears.

"It's alright; you're forgiven."

"I . . . I didn't want to deny him."

She stroked his hair. "I know, Marcus."

Damarra held him until his sobs died, then she took his hand
and led him to the bench by the door. For a long while they sat
together in silence, Damarra holding his large hand, Marcus with
his eyes closed and head bowed, either praying or embarrassed by
his outburst. Damarra guessed it was embarrassment. At last she
said to him, "Tell me how it happened."

He opened his eyes, nodded. "We were in Hispania, in the little village of Fortuna Marcus near the city of Toletum. Have you
heard of it?"

Damarra shook her head.

"Not surprising. Not much to see, really—a blacksmith, a
butcher, a few small shops, and an inn. The inn was what interested us. We were on leave, the five us, Gallienus and myself, and
three other officers." He laughed. "I can't even remember their
names now.

"They were all making fun of me, because my name was similar to the name of the village. Good natured ribbing, you know. 'Hey, did they name Fortuna Marcus after you, Marcus? What kind of fortune do they mean, good fortune or bad fortune? Good luck or bad luck, Marcus, which is it?'

"We'd seen the commission in the village square on our way into the inn. Some local baker had just refused to sacrifice, and they were dragging him off to see if a good beating would change his mind. One of the company suggested we let the commission decide if my luck was good or bad. Gallienus thought it was great idea, and before I knew what was happening I was standing in front of the commission being asked to sacrifice to gods."

"Didn't Gallienus know you were a Christian?"

"No, not then. None of them knew."

"What did you do?"

An expression of pain crossed Marcus' face. "I did what any coward would do: I pretended to be drunk, leaned over, and threw up. My friends thought it was hilarious. They picked me up and carried me off to the inn and threw me in a bed to sleep it off. A few hours later, Gallienus came back. He apologized to me, said if he'd known he never would have gone along with the others. 'I don't know what you're talking about,' I said. But he'd figured it out; I couldn't fool him anymore. He handed me a piece of parchment. 'I pulled some strings,' he said. 'All you have to do is sign it,' and then he left the room.

"It was a *libellus*, a Certificate of Sacrifice, with my name on it, and already signed by all the judges. I figure he threw his father's name at the commissioners and scared them into signing, but he never told me how he got it, and I never asked." He paused, took a deep breath that seemed to catch in his throat. "All night I held the certificate in my hand, read it over and over again, prayed about it, begged God to tell me what I should do. A part of me wanted to run back to the town square and tell the commissioners I refused to sacrifice, but in the end I gave in to the fear and signed my name. I knew it was wrong, I knew I was denying the *Christos* just as much as if I had sacrificed to the gods, but I convinced myself it wasn't *quite* as bad as sacrificing and I signed . . . signed my soul away. Before the ink even had time to dry, I regretted my choice. I tried everything I could think of to make it up to *Chris-*

tos—I even took a vow of chastity. Yet still I lived with that regret hanging over me until I met Lucian in Carthage on my last trip to North Africa. Lucian gave me a Certificate of Peace and it was like . . . God's light pouring into my soul again. It felt so good to be free of the guilt. But sometimes . . . sometimes the guilt comes back. Sometimes I wonder if this little piece of parchment signed by a very brave man in Carthage really means *anything*."

"God has chosen you to be a member of Valens' Clan, Marcus," Damarra reminded him. "He still loves you. He still has work for you."

Marcus' smile was bright. "Knowing that has eased my guilt more even than Lucian's Certificate of Peace." His smile faded. "But Lord Valens is a Novatianist, my lady. If he finds out I was one of the *lapsi*, he will cast me out."

Damarra reached up and patted Marcus' cheek. "Then we must take care that he never finds out, mustn't we?"

Marcus' smile returned. "Thank you, Holy Confessor."

"Have you asked the *Christos* to forgive you, Marcus?"

"Yes . . . many times."

"Then believe you are forgiven and work for him all the harder."

"Yes, my lady."

"Good." She took his hand again and squeezed it. "The only other advice I can give is to get some sleep. I believe you have a long journey ahead of you in the morning."

MARCUS PICKED UP THE CLOAK upon which he had been kneeling and accompanied Damarra back into the villa. In the garden they said their goodnights, then returned to their bedrooms. In a few moments the villa was still again, silent, save for the distant howl of a wolf and the nervous response of a horse in the stable. In the outer courtyard, Alexander emerged from the porch, where he had been standing in the shadows, listening to Marcus and Damarra talk. "*Lapsi*," he said, savouring the word like a fine wine.

It just went to prove that looks could be ever so deceiving. When he had first seen Marcus riding down the laneway on his horse, he had pegged him as a product of senatorial patronage—just another officer whose career depended on *who* he knew, not *what* he knew. A mistake. The man had the respect of his colleagues and the love of his men. Then he had turned out to be a Christian. What a surprise *that* was—a Christian general!

And now a *lapsi*. Which meant a coward, according to Julius Valens . . .

Marcus Gaius Fortunatus was full of surprises.

Gundabar emerged from the villa behind him. Even though he wore a mail shirt and a sword, the German had moved so silently through the darkness that Alexander had not even heard him. Gundabar yawned and slapped Alexander's shoulder. "My watch," he said.

"Yes, Commander."

Here was another surprise: a Suevi warrior in charge of security at the estate of a Roman senator. And there was something going on with that, too. He hadn't worked out all the details yet, but it sounded like they were planning some kind of trip. They were just waiting for someone else to come before they left, and apparently that "someone else" wasn't him.

He grinned. Of course, it wouldn't be him, would it!

"Nothing to report, Commander. Quiet as the grave."

"Good," Gundabar said. "You sleep now."

"Yes, Commander."

Gundabar grabbed the torch out of the sconce on the wall and walked off toward the large, heavy doors that led to the laneway outside. Alexander watched him go, cursing under his breath. How could a goddess like Persephone be interested in a Suevi warrior who stank of bear grease and peat moss? It made no sense! But then nothing else on the Valens estate made sense, either!

"Strange goings on here, and that's for sure," he muttered, shaking his head.

"What's so strange?" asked a voice behind him.

Alexander jumped, spun around. "By the gods, Regulus!" he exclaimed.

Regulus laughed.

"I hate it when you do that!"

"That's how I survived all those years in the arena: my opponents never heard me coming."

"You'll have to teach me that trick," Alexander said. His pulse returned to normal. Actually he was glad to see Regulus. They had met on the docks in Massalia. Didymus had been looking for men with a military background for a customer who wanted to purchase guards for his estate. Regulus and Alexander had the right qualifications. A little dickering, a bit a silver, and they were on their way to their new home. By the time they reached the estate of Julius Valens, they had struck up a friendship. "Are you done your watch?" Alexander asked.

Regulus nodded. "Paulus relieved me a few minutes ago."

"What do you say to a cup or two of wine before bed?"

"Only if you'll tell me about these 'strange goings on.'"

Alexander slapped the bigger man's back. "It's a deal," he agreed.

FOURTEEN

Valens was gone when Damarra woke at dawn. The emperor had ordered the horses to be sent to Mediolanum in Northern Italy, where he had already made arrangements to establish a "cavalry school" to train his new cavalry, so Valens and General Marcus had left before dawn to ride into Massalia and hire men to drive the herd to their new home. Damarra got out of bed, washed and dressed, then went to check on Ruth. Prisca, who served as Ruth's nursemaid now, was sleeping in a rocking chair outside Ruth's room. Damarra tiptoed by the sleeping slave and peeked in on Ruth. She was sound asleep, her thumb in her mouth and her other hand twined around her long blond hair. Damarra smiled, then headed back out to the garden to the little bench amongst the apple trees, to pray.

She had been there about ten minutes when a voice interrupted the quiet: "Should I come back another time?" it said.

She opened her eyes and found her brother smiling down at her. She quickly rose and curtsied, "Your Excellency, good morning."

He waved a hand at her, a gesture of dismissal. "I think when we are alone that a simple Gallienus will suffice." He grinned at her. "Or brother, if you prefer."

"Please, join me," she said, pointing at the bench.

Gallienus wore a purple tunic and sandals. A thin gold crown graced his brown hair. "I realized this morning that although I have been here a week, you and I have not had the chance to speak alone."

"Nor will we now," Damarra said. She pointed at the guards who had accompanied him into the garden. They were keeping their distance, but they were still visible.

"Pretend they are not there," he advised her.

Damarra laughed. "I shall consider them gone," she said. For a moment she looked at her brother—still amazed that she had a brother and even more amazed that he was the emperor—then she asked, "May I ask you a question, Gallienus?"

"Of course."

"I do not understand how it is that I never met you, that I never even knew you existed. How can that be?"

He laughed, but there was no humour in it. "Valerianus never mentioned me?"

"Valerianus said very little to me . . . until the last year of our acquaintance. Before that, I saw him two or three times at most, usually when he was dispensing punishment."

"Of course. I forget sometimes that you were but a slave on one of my father's many estates, an estate he rarely visited before becoming Governor of North Africa. I'm sure even Valens has slaves he has never met, nor ever will meet."

"True, but my mother travelled with Valerianus for many years, and yet she never once mentioned a son to me either. Nor did anyone else on the estate ever mention a son."

"Ah yes, your mother. I understand she and her new husband died last year. My condolences."

"Thank you," Damarra said. She had received a letter from her mother last June, a typically chatty account of their daily lives, despite Drusus' obvious editorial work. She had seemed so happy. She had accepted the *Christos* as her saviour, thanks in the end to Drusus' ultimatum: "You must be a Christian or we cannot wed." So, she had became a Christian and the two of them had married the next day. They had honeymooned in Naples and were planning to visit Massalia in September for the grape harvest. Everything was wonderful. *More* than wonderful. Her mother was happier than she had ever been in her life . . . and she could hardly wait to see her little dove again.

Three days after she sent the letter by imperial post, both she and Drusus were dead. Two more victims of the plague. "It was quick for both of them, which is a mercy. And my mother knew the *Christos*, so she is in Heaven now. As is Drusus."

Gallienus stared at her one eyebrow arched high, then: "That is a consolation to you, I suppose." He cleared his throat. "So you never heard of me or my brother?"

"No."

"Or my mother, Mariniana?

"I heard it whispered that the master . . . that Valerianus had once had a wife, and that she was long dead. No one ever mentioned her name. It was Mariniana?"

"Yes."

"A beautiful name."

Gallienus took a coin from his belt. "I carry this with me wherever I go," he said and handed it to her. "That is my mother: Mariniana."

Damarra looked at the coin, at the woman's face. Young, beautiful, graceful, elegant—she wondered how much of the image was real and how much of it had been manufactured by his memories. "She was very beautiful," she said and handed the coin back. "When did she die?"

He tucked the coin away again. "When I was eight—twenty-seven years ago."

She touched his arm gently. "I'm so sorry."

"She was a wonderful woman." He smiled. "Like you. I think she would have liked you, Damarra."

"You honour me. How did she die?"

Gallienus stood up, turned away. When he finally spoke, his voice was hoarse. "You could say she was sick, I suppose. My *father* sent her away." He spat the word 'father' venomously.

"Why?"

He shook his head. "I'm not sure."

"Not sure?"

"Valerianus claimed that she betrayed him. Roman law states that a wife who betrays her husband may be put away, and that is what he did. He sent her into exile. I don't know where."

"Then how did she die?"

"I do not know the answer to that question either, only that she grew sick and died within a year." He looked at Damarra; his face was flushed with anger. "That was the official version Valerianus told me. But I have my own theory about what her sickness was."

"What do you think it was?"

"The man she loved sent her away. Never again would she see her home or her husband. Or her children. She could not stand the pain of separation, and so she grew sick and finally died. My mother died of a broken heart." He paused, looked away again, then said, "That was her sickness—a broken heart. But my father gave her the sickness, Damarra. He killed her; that is what it amounts to."

"I am so sorry, Gallienus."

"Thank you, Damarra." He smiled at her. She thought it was the saddest smile she had ever seen. "And that is why I want to assure you that you are safe. Valerianus took my mother away from me; I will not permit him to take my sister, as well."

Damarra kissed his cheek. His words sounded wonderful, and she could tell that he actually believed them. But they also sounded naive. When it came to Valerianus, she suspected she knew more about the evil he was capable of than Gallienus did. "Just be careful, Brother. Valerianus plays to win, and when he does not win, his wrath is epic. I should know."

"Yes," he said, "I suppose you do."

MASSALIA WAS A TRULY COSMOPOLITAN CITY. Once a Greek colony, even after it became subject to the Romans in 49 B.C., it never lost its taste for Greek culture. Schools of philosophy, from old school Stoics to cutting edge Neo-Platonists, argued and debated in the forum. Greek tragedies and comedies performed by some of the finest thespians in the empire were available for the theatre buff, and there were fine dining establishments for the gourmand.

The inn in which Commander Dionysius sat, nursing a cup of *mulsum*, wine sweetened with honey, was not one of those establishments. The stench of rotten eggs and fish that was several days past fresh wafted from the kitchen and connected to the common room by an arched entrance that was black with the soot from the kitchen fires. Dionysius had already decided he would not risk eating here. He had found a little place down by the harbour, Ursula's the locals called it, where the food was good and the women were better, but this was where he had told Ulf to meet him, because it was outside this inn that they had parted three days before. Had he known what the place was like inside, he'd have chosen Ursula's instead. Next time, they'd meet there.

Two men had started a fight over one of the barmaids. The inn's bouncer, a burly Briton with blond hair and blue eyes who went by the name of Lugh, picked both men up by the scruff of their tunics and tossed them into the street. Without asking, one of the barmaids brought Dionysius another *mulsum*. He passed her his empty cup and waved her away. He wore a simple tunic and sandals; there was no sign of his military profession, except per- haps for the severe cut of his black hair. During his stay in Mas- salia, he was Dionysius the Greek merchant from Athens. Nobody in the city knew his real occupation or his connection with the emperor; that was a card he would only play if it were absolutely necessary.

Ulf entered the inn, spotted him at the corner table, and trudged over. Like Dionysius, he wore the disguise of a merchant, or, in his case, the disguise of a merchant's freedman. Ulf dropped into the table's other seat and ordered a cup of wine. When the barmaid dropped it off, he sipped at it, grimaced, then set the cup on the table. "Been here long?" he asked.

Dionysius shook his head. "Let's hear your report."

For the next twenty minutes Ulf told Dionysius about recent events at the Valens estate. Getting into the estate had been sim- ple. He had disguised himself as a slave—Valens' slave when the emperor's guards inquired, the emperor's slave when Valens' guards enquired. The organized chaos involved in an imperial visit had made the gathering of intelligence very easy. When the emperor's party left the estate this morning, he had accompanied it as far as the *Via Iulia*, then had slipped away and hurried back into Massalia.

"And this journey they are planning, there was no indication as to where?" Dionysius asked after Ulf had given his report.

Ulf shook his head. "Not yet, but I will find out."

Finally Dionysius slapped Ulf's back. "You've done well, Ulf," he said.

"It pays to have a man inside, doesn't it, Commander?" Ulf said with grin.

"As his excellency predicted," Dionysius said with a laugh. "And I suspect that when Emperor Valerianus receives my report, it will pay very, *very* well."

FAR TO THE NORTH AND THE EAST, in the ill-defined frontier between Germania and Sarmatia that roughly corresponded to Europe and Asia, Kniva King of the Goths opened his eyes in the darkness. Surprise had stopped his breath in his throat, and it was a full minute before he realized what had happened and ordered his lungs to breathe again. White wisps of cold air exploded from his mouth and nose and he inhaled hungrily. The whirl of questions in his mind narrowed down to one: why had The-God-With-The-Blood-In-His-Fists returned now, after all this time?

He threw the skins back and sat up on his sleeping platform. His hut was large and usually warmed by a central fire, but the fire had gone out in the night and the February wind that blew down from their ancient homeland in the north carried a bitter cold with it. He groped on the floor until he found his leather shirt and tugged it on over his head, but he couldn't find his boots. "Guards," he called and instantly two Goth warriors entered the hut each with a torch and drawn sword. "You," he said to the man on the left, a young warrior whose brown beard was still patchy on his cheeks. "Fetch my counsellors."

The guard saluted and darted out. He had the second guard light his torch, then sent him out to wait for the others. He found his thick leather boots, pulled them on, and tied them in place. Next came his chainmail and the golden belt from which his sword hung. The belt was part of the vast treasure he had taken from the empire the first time The God-With-The-Blood-In-His-Fists had spoken to him in a dream. It had once encircled the waist of an emperor. Kniva had won it at the Battle of Abrittus, stripped it from the fallen body of Decius himself before he cut off his head as a gift to Decius' successor and a warning to the empire: fear the Goths; fear their great leader, King Kniva.

He quickly combed out his long blond hair and pinned it back on each side of his head with elaborate combs, made of gold and silver by Goth smiths. A warrior's hair must not obscure his vision, and The-God-With-The Blood-In-His-Fists had called his people to be warriors again. For the last three years they had lived on the shores of the great inland sea that the Greeks had called Pontus Axeinos—the Inhospitable Sea—but was now generally referred to as the Black Sea, biding their time, growing strong again. Last year a Roman had come across the sea in a ship—he called himself "Servant of the *Christos*"—and told them that this *Christos* and The-God-With-The-Blood-In-His-Fists were one. They had sent the Roman away instead of killing him—if the *Christos* and The-God-With-the-Blood-In-His-Fists were the same, then they could not risk his wrath. Kniva did not care who the god was; all that mattered was that this god was a god of power, and that he was summoning them as he had before. "Before" had made them the richest tribe in Germania; now they would be richer still.

Kniva rose and checked his appearance in the polished bronze shield that served as a mirror. Although he was fifty-three, he retained the vigour of his youth. His blond hair and beard were untouched by grey. His features were like smooth stone, unlined except for the scar on his left check and another that ran down the middle of his face, from the top of his forehead to the tip of his nose. The middle scar looked like a seam dividing his face into two halves. His people saw the scar, which a Carpi chieftain had given him in his youth, as a sign of power, proof that he had the favour of the gods. His dreams were also proof of his power, especially the ones that brought guidance from The-God-With-the-Blood-In-His-Fists.

He heard a commotion outside and stepped out of his hut. A slave hurried in behind him to build up the fire again. The moon shone bright and full above, the stars crisp and sparkling in the frosty air. His counsellors had come from their huts, wrapped in furs against the cold, looking half asleep but anxious. When Kniva called in the middle of the night, it usually boded well for the tribe. Marrak, Clovis, and Kuror stood before him, silent. Expectant.

"The-God-With-the-Blood-In-His-Fists has spoken," Kniva announced.

Counsellors and guards began to murmur excitedly. Kuror reached a hand out from the warmth of his furs to slap Clovis on the back. Marrak stood apart from the others, staring at Kniva with his deep, black eyes.

Kniva silenced them. "When the moon again rises full, we will strike."

"Where?" Kuror asked.

Kniva glanced at Marrak, who had still not responded. "Speak, Marrak. What troubles you?"

"Are you sure, my King, that it was the God who spoke?"

Kniva frowned. Three years ago the Goths had invaded the Moesias, on the grounds that the Emperor Gallus had not paid the tribute he had promised after the Battle of Abrittus. That time, The-God-With-the-Blood-In-His-Fists had *not* been with them, and they had suffered a major defeat at the hands of Aemilianus. Since then they had brooded in their huts on the northern shores of the Black Sea, too weak to trouble the Romans. But no longer. This time, The-God-With-the-Blood-In-His-Fists was calling them, and they would have victory. "Yes, Marrak, it was The-God-With-the-Blood-In-His-Fists—we fight for Him again."

Assured, Marrak grinned. "Victory," he yelled, and the guards and the officers took up the cry. "Victory! Victory! Victory!"

"GREAT SHAHANSHAH, the Romans are leaving the field."

Shapur shaded his eyes from the scorching Syrian sun and gazed across the battlefield. The enemy was indeed retreating back to their encampment, not victorious and yet not beaten. But beaten he would be. Shapur had already beaten two Roman Emperors. He had defeated the Emperor Gordianus more than ten years ago at Misiche on the Euphrates, a defeat which had cost Gordianus his life at the hands of his own soldiers. Then he had forced Gordianus' successor Philip to ransom safe passage for his paltry army, five hundred thousand *denarii* so that he might withdraw with his life and claim, when he was beyond Shapur's long and mighty arm, that *he*, Philip, was the true victor, that *he* had defeated Shapur and not the other way around. And now this old man, Valerianus, had come in his folly to test his strength against Shapur.

"What do you command, mighty Shahanshah?" his general asked. The title "Shahanshah" was a Sassanid creation meant to convey the multicultural makeup of the Sassanid Empire and the majesty of its bearer. He was Shahanshah—King of kings—the greatest power on earth; the King before whom all the petty monarchs in the empire bowed; the King who established law, who *was* law in his domain. Like Ahura Mazda, the god of the universe, god above all other gods, Shapur was King above all other Kings, even those kings who were not yet under his sway. Such as the Roman king. Valerianus did not understand that. But he would.

"What news from Antioch, General Aheer?" Shapur asked. Shapur wore full battle armour, banded metal plates to protect his torso and legs. The golden belt about his waist had sheaths for his sword and war daggers. As with the Cataphract cavalry which was the backbone of the Persian military, a lance sheath dangled from his horse's saddle, although Shapur's horse was only armoured with metal plates at the neck and chest, thus giving the Shahanshah greater speed and mobility. His black hair and beard were rolled into long curls that stood out from his head and chin like the rays of the sun. Beneath his armour he wore a silk tunic of royal blue and red, silk trousers.

"The walls and gate still hold, O Great One, but for how much longer, none can say. News has come from your son, Hormozd, as well. The Romans have repelled his raiders from Cappadocia but he still holds Armenia. The Romans have now entered Syria in the north and are marching south to join up with Valerianus again."

Shapur quickly calculated his options, then nodded at General Aheer. "We shall withdraw from Syria, Aheer."

The look on the general's face expressed disapproval, but Aheer would not dare voice his opinion.

Shapur grinned. "A slow withdrawal, Aheer, fighting as we march. Everything is to be destroyed in our wake. I want nothing left for Valerianus to use—not so much as a grain of wheat."

The general understood and nodded. "A wise decision, O Great One."

"We will draw the Romans to some suitable spot in Mesopotamia, the banks of the Euphrates will work. A year from now Valerianus' supply lines will be stretched tight and the emperor's army will be starving, and if history is any indication, some general will rise up and cut Valerianus down and save us the trouble."

"And pay us handsomely to allow them to run away," Aheer sneered.

"Exactly."

"Shall we destroy Antioch as well, O Great One?"

Shapur pondered the question, then shook his head. "Hold it as long as possible, then plunder it and withdraw—but leave the buildings intact. Once the Romans have run for home, we will retake Syria and use it as the capital from which we will administer our new territories."

"As you wish, O Great One."

FIFTEEN

S pring came early that year, and with it came the Germans. The Franks were the first to risk the cold waters of the Danube, this time invading Germania Superior, and made it deep into Roman territory before Gallienus' fledgling cavalry, under its commander, Aureolus, fell upon them out of nowhere and sent them scurrying for home. A Juthungi raiding party tried its luck further north, in Germania Inferior, but Gallienus' legions cut them to pieces. It was a good start to the campaigning season, but Gallienus already knew the year would be propitious. The priests had performed their auguries on a herd of sheep, and according to almost three Roman miles of intestines, his success was assured. Only one troubling incident occurred. Amongst the Juthungi dead, they had found a corpse that was decidedly Un-Juthungi—a man with short hair and a bag of Roman coins, a man with a letter of introduction to the Juthungi chief written by a Christian *episcopus* in Gallia. "More proof of Christian complicity in these barbarian raids," Festus Macrinus said when he joined Gallienus at Augustabona at the beginning of April.

"So it would seem," Gallienus agreed. He ordered a slave to bring more wine, then picked at the delicacies that Cook had prepared for the imperial palate. The tent flaps were thrown back to allow the bright spring sunshine inside. "You seem to have developed a deep dislike of the Christians in recent years, Festus. Do we detect the influence of our father?"

"Bah!" Festus exclaimed. "I do not need your father to detest the Christians. They are a thorn in the empire's side. They stand in contempt of our gods, and they will not participate in the imperial cult—they say you and your father are men, not gods."

"We *are* men, Festus."

"Did I not teach you better than that, Your Excellency? Once a man assumes the imperial purple he is above other men, greater than them, holier, more divine. He becomes a god, he *is* a god. So say our forefathers, and so say I. If they will not worship you or our gods, they should be exterminated."

"And what of the Jews? They will not worship our gods, nor will they worship their emperors as gods. Remember Caligula? When he tried to place his image in their temple, they rebelled."

"The Jews are different. The antiquity of their religion protects them. Their belief in Yahweh predates the empire, and Yahweh's proscriptions against worshipping any other god are clear and ancient. The Jews entered the empire as devout followers of Yahweh, and so we permit them their odd beliefs, even where they disagree with our own. But this Christianity is a novelty, barely two hundred years old. Christians choose to turn away from our beliefs, to follow after some criminal who claims he is the son of god. They are not just rebelling against our gods, they are rebelling against our way of life, the Roman way, and for that alone they must be punished." Festus popped an egg into his mouth, a signal that his diatribe was over.

Gallienus thought over Festus' argument. It made sense . . . and yet the malodorous influence of Valerianus burned in his nostrils. Their joint reign was almost three years old and *still* Valerianus had not brought up the "Christian Problem." At first his father's silence had puzzled him, but now he thought his silence was damning. He suspected Valerianus was using others—like Festus—to goad him into persecuting the Christians. But there was no proof. And at this stage it really did not matter—a large-scale persecution was financially impossible. "Perhaps you are right, Festus, but the fact is we cannot afford to launch a persecution right now."

"You cannot afford it?" Festus struck his knee with his fist.

"You cannot afford not to!"

"Hear us out, Festus. The cost of empire is astronomical. We have spent millions of *denarii* on our new cavalry alone, and on top of that we must sedate the Roman mob with bread, wine, and circus, pay our legions and bureaucrats, maintain aqueducts, public buildings, and temples, the costs go on and on. Even in good times, taxes barely cover imperial outlay. But in these evil days? No, we are in debt to the moneylenders, and each day that passes sinks us deeper. To persecute the Christians just compounds that debt."

Festus began to laugh, hardly the response Gallienus had expected. "Why are you laughing?" Gallienus asked with a scowl.

"Forgive me, Your Excellency, but you are looking at this all wrong."

"And how is that?"

"I can think of few better ways to fill the imperial coffers than persecution."

"Fill our coffers!" Gallienus exclaimed with a laugh. The commissions Decius had set up to expose the Christians had cost the empire millions in the final accounting. To claim the opposite was ludicrous. "How do you accomplish that by persecuting Christians?"

Festus had brought with him from Rome a dispatch bag full of reports, intelligence, and other documents demanding the emperor's attention. He opened the bag and took out a single piece of parchment, which he handed to the emperor. Gallienus scanned it quickly. The document was a list of estates and buildings and their owners. On the far right was a number, which, according to the heading at the top of the page, represented an approximation of the value of each of the items. At the bottom was a figure that made Gallienus' eyebrows rise in appreciation: two billion *denarii*. "Impressive," he said and set the document down on the couch beside him. "But what does it mean?"

"Do you know what all those names have in common, Your Excellency?"

Gallienus picked the document up and ran his index finger down the list of names. Some he recognized, wealthy senators and equestrian businessmen, a large number of wealthy widows, but many of the names on the document were unknown to him. "No," he said, "what do they have in common?"

"According to the most current information available, every man and woman on the list is a Christian."

Again Gallienus' eyebrows rose, this time in surprise. He had had no idea there were that many wealthy Christians in the empire.

"And that list accounts for known Christians in Italy *only*, Your Excellency. There are many more in the Gauls, Hispania, Britannia, Greece, North Africa, and the other western provinces. Many *many* more."

Gallienus' eyebrows rose a third time, now in understanding. And with that understanding came his father's voice, whispering once again the advice he had given him before he marched east: *Do not be too quick to reject an opportunity to augment your finances just because it seems ignoble: better a live emperor than a noble corpse.* "I see," he whispered.

"Billions of *denarii* waiting for you to appropriate."

"Yes . . . billions."

"If you feel their crime is not worthy of death, simply exile them and confiscate their holdings. Alive or dead, it makes no difference. All that money will be yours." Festus laughed. "Why, the Christians would be helping to *save* the empire for a change!"

Gallienus pictured all those Christians in chains trudging off to the salt mines, imagined his treasury filled to overflowing, a golden rain that could save the empire from destruction, and he grinned. But on the tail of that fantasy came another voice, a dearer voice, the advice his mother had given him on the day his father had sent her away: *Genuine thoughtfulness lies in putting the needs of others ahead of your own. That is true nobility, my son, and that is the Roman way. Never forget it.*

Two opposing suggestions, two opposing life philosophies, both weighed against the cold, hard, and very heavy fact that the Western Empire was facing financial ruin if he did not find some way to get the money flowing again. What to do? "We will consider it," he said at last.

Festus' mouth dropped open. "*Consider* it? What's to consider, Your Excellency? Do it! Do not wait for things to get worse."

"We said we will consider it, Commander Festus," Gallienus snapped.

Festus immediately retreated into a respectful posture. He bowed his silver head. "Forgive me, Your Excellency, I spoke out of turn."

Gallienus scowled at him for a moment longer, then his anger dissipated. It was impossible to stay angry at Festus Macrinus. The old man had raised him; he was certainly more of a father than his own father had *ever* been. "No, forgive us, Festus," he sighed. "We find ourselves . . . wary of any plan proposed by our august fellow emperor."

"Well then, rest assured, the idea is mine, not Valerianus'."

"Yours?"

"Yes, Your Excellency."

Interesting. This little plot had all the earmarks of a Valerian conspiracy, and yet perhaps he was wrong? After all, news from the East suggested that Valerianus was not yet in a position to start dealing with the Christians. The siege of Antioch was taking much longer that Valerianus had anticipated, as was the recovery of Syria. They had fought many indecisive battles and skirmishes, with both sides taking turns advancing and retreating through the Syrian countryside. The latest report claimed that Shapur was at last retreating, and that Antioch would fall to the Romans in a matter of days. Now that the two prongs of Valerianus' army had come together again, his strategy was to drive Shapur back beyond the Euphrates before the end of the year, and then on to Ctesiphon on the Tigris in the spring, if not sooner. In his last imperial message to the West, Valerianus had vowed to hang Shapur from the highest battlements in Ctesiphon, plunder the Sassanid capital's vast wealth, then march its inhabitants home for the empire's slave markets. He could see Valerianus turning on the Christians when he was sure of victory, but not before that. So maybe this idea was Festus'; and maybe he should not dismiss it so readily. Not when there was so much at stake.

Maybe.

"Send details of this plan of yours to our august colleague. Let us see what his feelings are on the matter."

"Very wise, Your Excellency," Festus said. "I am sure your father is a better advisor in these matters than I am."

"Meaning?"

"Meaning nothing, Your Excellency."

Anger heated the back of Gallienus' neck. "Are you trying to insinuate that we require Valerianus' advice in matters of state? Do you think such a childish ploy will work on us?"

"Certainly not, Your Excellency. I would not presume to insinuate anything of the kind."

"Good. Then as we commanded, inform Emperor Valerianus of your plan and we will await his thoughts on the matter before we make a decision. " He gestured for Festus to go. "Now leave us and let us enjoy our dinner in peace.

THE *CLASSIS MOESICA*, the largest fleet on the Danube river, was located at Noviodunum in Moesia Inferior, where the Danube flowed out into the Black Sea. It served two functions: one, to patrol the east end of the Danube and the Danube delta; and two, to ensure safe shipping at the northwest end of the Black Sea. The fleet consisted of *triremes* and *liburnae* for the most part, with one or two larger *quinqueremes* to assist in troop transport, all ships capable of traversing the deeper waters of the Black Sea, as opposed to the smaller ships stationed further west on the Danube, which were used mainly for patrolling the shallower and narrower river channels. The Procurator in charge of the *Classis Moesica* was named Antius Lupus and was of equestrian rank, one of the up and coming middle class Romans who owed their advancement to the emperor and not to senatorial patronage. Most of the equestrians chosen for such positions were intelligent and capable—and entirely loyal to the emperor rather than the senate. But the wealthy Antius Lupus was, in the estimation of his colleagues and the soldiers under his command, a cretin and a fool, whose incompetence was only exceeded by his stupidity. It was rumoured that Antius had purchased the position with a massive donation to the emperor Decius' war chest, which had blinded Decius to his almost total lack of experience (said experience consisting of several hours rowing around a pond in a small rowboat when he was ten), and that Decius' successors had simply neglected to replace him in their scramble to deal effectively with more immediate problems.

It was an oversight that was to have far-reaching consequences.

Antius reclined in his office overlooking the docks where his fleet was anchored. His slave and chief cook had created an amazing feast for him tonight, a veritable festival for his palate, goose done just the way he liked it, with a side of those salty sturgeon eggs which were a delicacy in this region of the Danube. Life was good for Antius. He had the prestige of his position, while his officers did all the work. Like tonight. He could lie here in comfort, enjoying the full moon shining on the rippling Danube, while his officers were off chasing down some rumour about a party of Germans that had been sighted a few miles to the north. Tribune Licinius had wanted to leave half the men in Noviodunum, but he had insisted that they all go. They'd had it easy all winter, hanging around camp and getting into trouble in town. A midnight march would do them good, toughen them up. Besides, he had posted guards on each of the ships, and that was security enough: if the rumour was true and there were Germans about, then they were north of here, not in the dockyard.

His slave entered the room with more sturgeon eggs. He loved the taste of them; couldn't get enough. Snatching the bowl from the slave, he used the last bits of bread to sop the salty eggs up. He had finished the dish before he realized that the slave had not moved. "Why are you still standing there, Cyrus?" he snapped.

"My Lord Procurator," the slave said. Something in his voice made Antius look up. Cyrus was trembling; his face was white.

Antius gave an exasperated sigh. "I'm not going to beat you, Cyrus. Just bring me the next course."

Still the slave did not move, and Antius decided that perhaps a beating was required after all. He could not stomach insubordination. He was about to inform Cyrus of this when he noticed a figure standing in the doorway. "Who is that, Cyrus?" he asked. "Who's there?"

The figure entered the room. He was tall and muscular and dressed in leathers and chainmail. His long hair was held back from his face by a comb on either side of his head. The man had a peculiar scar, a very . . . disconcerting scar, that ran down the centre of his face from his hairline to the tip of his nose.

He also had a sword.

Antius scrambled up off the dining couch. "Who are you and what do you want?" he cried. For the first time in his life, he knew fear.

The man stared at him with icy blue eyes. "I am Kniva," he said; his voice was deep, his accent guttural.

Antius' bladder let go. Urine dribbled down his leg and pooled on the floor. He had heard of Kniva; *everyone* had heard of Kniva.

Kniva glanced at the puddle, his mouth pulled up in a sneer. "We have business, yes?" Suddenly two more Goth warriors entered the room. They held daggers in their hands. "You have something I want. I have something you need."

"What . . . what do you have that I . . . need?" Antius asked.

Kniva grinned as the tip of his sword found the tender meat under Antius' chin: "Mercy," he replied.

ANOTHER DISPATCH FROM VALERIANUS was waiting for Festus Macrinus when he returned to Rome. He sat in the office that had once belonged to Paulus Antoninus Quaerellus and read Valerianus' message for the fourth time, his face scrunched up in an expression that could only be described as glee. Except for the Persian garrison at Antioch, which still held on, his friend had at last evicted Shapur from Syria and was steadily pushing him across Mesopotamia, the area the ancients called the Land Between Two Rivers, back to his hiding hole at Ctesiphon on the banks of the Tigris. He set the dispatch down on his desk and laced his hands together over his slim belly. How he wished he were there with Valerianus teaching Shapur a lesson, the same lesson they had taught Shapur's father in their youth.

A mellow smile lit Festus' face. Those had been good days, the best days of his life. Two men in the vigour of youth, strong and healthy and passionate. Oh, the *passion*! Passionate about battle, about drinking, about simply being *Roman*, and sharing the privilege of fighting for the greatest empire the world had ever known, ever *would* know. Ah, and those dark and sultry eastern women! The glory of battle was an aphrodisiac. Combine that with the confidence that comes from knowing you're invincible, and few women could resist their charms. And those that did resist, well . . . a good friend was always willing to lend a hand. Festus felt a twinge in his lower back and shifted in the chair. Maybe not so invincible anymore, eh?

True friendship. That was the greatest passion of all. Few people ever experienced it, because two people had to face death together to form a bond that intense and lasting. He and Valerianus had faced death—and conquered it—many times. He remembered one night in particular. The emperor had sent them out on reconnaissance, and they had come upon a party of five Persian warriors sitting around a campfire, out on reconnaissance themselves. The ensuing skirmish had been short and bloody: four Persians dead, the fifth mortally wounded; Valerianus and himself with a few scratches. A rabbit was cooking on the fire. They dragged the bodies aside and helped themselves to the Persians' dinner and wine. "No dessert," Festus bemoaned after they finished. He belched and tossed the bones from his dinner into the fire.

Although Valerianus had been boisterous until that moment, he was suddenly unresponsive.

Festus glanced up at him. Valerianus was staring into the fire as if he were searching its flickering flames for some message, for some . . . sign. A shiver crawled up Festus' spine. There was an intensity in Valerianus' gaze that Festus had never seen before. "What is it?" he asked.

At last Valerianus looked up. Flames danced in his brown eyes. Festus felt himself shrivelling under his friend's scrutiny. It took all his will to hold his hard gaze, and even that finally failed him, and he knew he had to look away or the fire reflected in his eyes would consume his soul. His eyes dropped to the cup in Valerianus' hand. Then Valerianus asked him a question, the last question he had ever expected his friend to ask: "Do you love me, Festus?"

He tried to laugh off the question. "You've had too much to

drink," he replied.

Valerianus drew his dagger and got up. "Do you love me, Festus?" he asked again.

The intensity of his words could not be ignored. He stood up. "What is it?" he asked and managed to look into his eyes again. "What's wrong?"

"Do you love me?" he asked a third time. "It is a simple question, Festus. Either you do or you do not."

In an instant, their long friendship flashed before his eyes, the battles they had fought, the women they had won, nights of drinking and feasting and laughter, and most of all, the times Valerianus had saved him from that final ride across the River Styx. Without this man he would be dead, and that fact alone prompted the simple answer, the only answer, to his "simple question." He grabbed his friend's arms: "Yes, I love you. You know I love you. I would die for you, my friend." It was a proclamation and a vow, not a statement.

Valerianus grinned and the intensity burning in his eyes now set fire to his words: "We are brothers, bound by love, bound by friendship. We are one—only our blood is different."

Valerianus' passion had infected him now. In that moment he would have done anything Valerianus asked of him.

Valerianus tossed the contents of his cup into the fire. "Bring a torch and your cup," he commanded. Festus plucked a brand out of the fire and followed Valerianus into the shadows. The bodies of the Persians lay where they had heaped them, except for one. He had managed to crawl a few feet further from the campfire, but he had spent himself and now lay in the dirt gasping for breath. "Roll him over," Valerianus ordered.

Festus shoved the dying Persian with the heel of his sandal and he rolled onto his back. His dark eyes were glazed by the approach of death. He grunted something in his language, then summoned up enough saliva to spit on Valerianus' foot. Valerianus ignored the insult. He knelt down and placed his dagger on the Persian's throat, "For the glory of Rome and Valerianus," he whispered. Then he sliced.

Blood spurted from the wound. Valerianus reached up without shifting his gaze from the Persian's neck. "Your cup," he said.

Festus gave him the cup. Valerianus filled it, then his own, then stood up and handed Festus his cup back. In the light of the torch the contents gleamed a deep crimson. He raised his cup. "Pledge eternal loyalty to me, friend Festus," he whispered.

Festus raised his cup. "Eternal loyalty," he vowed. Then he put the cup to his lips and drank. The blood was hot and tasted like copper in his mouth. When he finished, he tossed the cup into the darkness.

With a smile Valerianus raised his cup. "Eternal loyalty," he vowed. And then he drank.

Sitting at his desk, lost in the memories of the past, Festus chuckled. He would die for Valerianus; Valerianus would die for him. It was that simple. From that day onwards their friendship had transcended all other bonds in their lives. It had become divine, a god that they worshipped. Together they had planned their subsequent careers. Together, with a few well chosen allies, they had conspired to set the Roman world to rights, to rid it of its enemies, both foreign and domestic. The conspirators had chosen Decius to lead them, although Festus had cast his ballot for Valerianus. Decius had won the imperial throne and attempted to rid the state of its enemies.

And Decius had failed.

Now the lot had fallen to Valerianus. And where Decius had failed, Valerianus would not.

Festus picked up the letter again. The most informative part was at the end: Valerianus felt the time had come to address the Christian Problem. Phase one would begin in the spring; he felt confident that by then he would have Shapur sufficiently contained. Only one obstacle remained.

Gallienus.

Valerianus wanted to know if Gallienus would be ready to begin in the spring. Of course, what he actually meant was had Festus persuaded Gallienus to participate in an empire-wide persecution of the Christians?

Almost, Festus thought. The cup of wine he had poured for himself sat untouched on the desk. He picked it up and drained the contents, then poured himself another. Gallienus was not an idiot. Festus himself had made sure of that by ensuring that the boy had the best education possible. So Festus had tread carefully, a suggestion here, a question there, and thus by manipulation and subterfuge he had coaxed and cajoled Gallienus to the very edge of compliance. The chasm of persecution was before him—all he needed was one more push to send him over the edge.

And in his letter Valerianus had suggested the perfect stratagem to induce Gallienus into taking that final step.

Festus shook his head. He was in awe of Valerianus. The man was a master of manipulation who could hold the strings of a thousand plots in his hand and work them all at one time or separately as needed. Festus' own relationship with Gallienus was the perfect example. When Valerianus had sent Gallienus to him for his training, Valerianus had told him *never* to reveal to Gallienus his true feelings for the Christians. At the time, he had not understood why, but he had complied, as he had always complied with Valerianus' requests. So, on those rare occasions that the conversation turned to the Christians, Festus had made sure the boy heard him simply dismiss the sect as silly. Never any vituperation, never any acrimony, never any sign that he believed as Valerianus did: the only solution to the Christian problem was the final one.

Genocide.

Now he understood why Valerianus had instructed him as he did. Somehow Valerianus had known even then that Gallienus would be inclined to rebel against his father's wishes; somehow he had known even then that Gallienus would be inclined to listen to his mentor, Festus.

There was a knock at the door.

Festus set the letter down on the desk. "Enter," he ordered.

The door opened and two praetorians marched into the room. Each of them held one arm of a tall, slim man in his early forties. His tunic was filthy and torn and he smelled as if someone had emptied their night waste out of the window he had been sleeping under. A jagged scar ran down his right arm beside a tattoo that read *Legio IX*.

The shorter of the two praetorians saluted. "The man you asked us to bring, Commander," he said.

Festus waved them away. "Leave us. Strato and I are old friends. Isn't that right, Strato?"

The man answered with a quick smile.

After the guards left, Festus pointed at a chair in front of his desk. "Sit, Strato," he ordered.

Strato complied. He looked calm, but Festus knew the man's heart was beating like a charging rhinoceros.

"In trouble again, Strato," Festus said.

Finally he spoke. "Still, you mean."

They both laughed at his little joke, although Strato's laughter was insincere. "I understand you're in debt."

He nodded.

"And that your debtors are planning to sell your wife and your children into slavery to pay it."

His calm expression became pained. "I don't know how to save them," he said, his words anguished.

Festus leaned over the desk. "What if I told you that I could save your wife and children?"

"How?" Strato spit out the question like a drowning man grabbing a lifeline.

"I need your skills, Strato. You were the best at one time. Are you still the best?"

"If it means saving my family, then, yes, I am."

"You would do anything to save them?"

"Anything."

There was a scroll on the desk. Festus turned it lengthwise and rolled it to Strato. Strato caught it before it fell off the desk. He opened it and his eyes bulged. He looked from the scroll to Festus and back again. "Is this what I think it is?" he asked.

Festus nodded. "Yes, a receipt. Your debt has been paid in full."

Relief shone on his dirty face. "Thank you, Commander!"

"I saved your family."

"Yes!"

"And in return—"

"Yes, yes, whatever you want."

Festus grinned. "You're going to help me save the empire."

SIXTEEN

At the end of summer, Gallienus received astonishing news in a dispatch from Rome. In a brazen manoeuvre that would have shaken the entire Roman world had the authorities not had the foresight to keep it a secret, Kniva, the king of the Goths (whom many Romans now referred to as "Decius' Bane"), had marched into the dockyards at Noviodunum while its legion was off chasing shadows and stolen an entire Roman fleet right out from under its commander's snivelling nose. By order of Valerianus the commander had been executed, and ships had been sent out to search for the missing fleet. But as Decius had discovered when he came up against the same foe five years before, Kniva had a knack for vanishing. They spent the summer and much of the fall scouring the Black Sea for signs of Kniva's new navy with no success.

Also amongst the papers in the dispatch was an invitation from the senate asking Gallienus to return to Rome and attend a series of games in honour of the third anniversary of his reign. He had not intended to return to Rome this year—activity on the frontiers had doubled in the last few months and he felt his place was there, with his men—but in the end he decided it would be politically expedient to attend. Gallienus' relations with the senate was anything but cordial. He had generally ignored them in their capacity as counsellors (he saw them as simpering sycophants whose advice was worthless because of it), and had made little use of them in his bureaucracy. In fact, at the provincial level he had begun to remove senators from government positions and replace them with the equestrian businessmen who were the real backbone of the empire. He suspected the senate had deduced his ultimate goal: to reduce the senate to what it actually was—a group of doddering old fools who did not deserve the power they believed was their birthright. So they had decided to flatter him with games in his honour. And he had decided to permit their flattery—the best way to placate the senate and blind them to the changes he was making was to allow them to think their flattery was working.

The end of September was glorious in Rome. The sun beat down on the city with the same virility as at mid-summer. Days were hot; nights were cool. An atmosphere of guarded optimism buoyed everyone's spirits, from the richest senator to the poorest pauper. Despite the slow progress of his colleague in the East, Gallienus seemed to be on top of the challenges the West faced. Although the death toll from the plague continued to rise, there was little sign of it in the city proper, thanks to the crews which worked through the night to remove corpses while Rome slept. There was plenty of food in the imperial granary, plenty of wine in Rome's many inns, and of course there were games. Lots and lots of games. Every day of the year there were things to do and see and cheer, and that made it easier to forget Germanic raiders in the north. Besides, it had been centuries since an enemy had infiltrated that far into Italy—Hannibal and his elephants were the last. And these days? The Persians might have elephants, but the Germans didn't, and even if they *had* elephants, there was no way Rome would *ever* see an army of long-haired Germans howling at her gates. Inconceivable.

Festus Macrinus met Gallienus and his entourage a few miles north of the city the night before his official arrival to finalize details for his grand entrance into Rome. The next morning a massive crowd formed along the *Via Aurelia* and inside the Aurelian Gate. Children riding their fathers' shoulders waved as the emperor rode by in all his majesty, his golden *lorica* gleaming, his crown dazzling with its stylized rays decked with jewels, the sun god himself bringing his bright splendour to Rome. A few women fainted from the heat; others swooned as their handsome ruler rode past and sometimes even *looked* their way. The flowers cast on the pavement by the adoring crowds were crushed by dancing hooves and the hob-nailed sandals of the unit of praetorians who marched in full dress uniform behind Gallienus and Commander Festus. Men cheered, women screamed, a cacophony of joy so loud, so focused on the emperor, that nobody noticed the archer standing on top of the Aurelian Gate until it was too late.

The arrow hit Gallienus' back, high up on the right side. Had his armour been true armour it might have turned the arrow, but it was dress armour, a stunning amalgam of gold and silver and precious gems that was beautiful to behold but afforded no real protection. At that close range the arrow pierced the armour and the emperor, spinning him around and knocking him from his horse. The sudden silence was as sharp as the arrow, as if all of Rome had inhaled at the same moment and was holding its breath. Gallienus could see the gaping horror on their faces as he fell, and as his turn reached 180 degrees, he saw his assassin on the gate, his face a blank of concentration, one hand reaching into the quiver on his back for another arrow, and then the assassin was gone, lost from view as the momentum of the arrow continued to twirl him—240 degrees, 300 degrees—until at last he completed a full turn. A moment later his shoulder hit the ground, the shoulder in which the arrow was embedded, and the force of that blow shoved the arrowhead the rest of the way through his shoulder and out the front of his armour.

Suddenly the crowd's throat opened in a scream.

The praetorians surrounded their fallen emperor. The assassin had time to loose a second arrow that bounced harmlessly off the cobblestones. As he reached into his quiver again an arrow pierced his chest. His bow flew from his hand and he dropped from the top of the gate and hit the pavement with a heavy *thud*. Dead.

Gallienus glanced up at the man who had killed the assassin and saved his life. Festus Macrinus, his mentor, stood over him, the bow still in his hand. "Thank you," Gallienus whispered, and then darkness took him down into its black embrace.

WHEN HE WOKE HE WAS LYING on an altar, like some animal about to be offered up to the gods. Physicians were huddled over him. They had removed his lorica and the arrow. His fall had made it an easy procedure. With the arrow all the way through, they had simply broken the tail feathers off, then pulled the rest of the shaft out through the wound. They had bandaged the wound front and back and applied one of the foul-smelling poultices for which they were famed.

And hated.

Gallienus shooed them away and sat up on the altar. He looked around for Marcus, then remembered he had left his friend in the north, to guard the frontier in his absence. Festus Macrinus was there, and he was surrounded by praetorians who had been watching the physicians closely to make sure they did no more damage to their emperor. One of the praetorians held the arm of a gnarled old man in a ragged and dirty tunic. On the floor at Gallienus feet lay the body of his assassin. The arrow still protruded from his chest. The entire front of the man's tunic was red with blood. On his right arm was an old scar and a tattoo: *Legio IX*. A soldier. Why would a soldier try to assassinate him? For a moment paranoia snapped its teeth at him hungrily. Had the legions turned on him? Or his father? Or the senate?

"You look much better, my boy," Festus said.

"Where are we?" Gallienus asked.

Festus stepped closer. "A temple near the Aurelian gate. We carried you hear after this animal attempted to take your life."

Gallienus stared at the corpse. "Who is he? Why did he want to kill me?"

Festus shook his head. "Who he is, we do not know. But why he wanted to kill you, that I believe I *do* know." Festus shoved the body of the assassin with his foot, and it flopped over like a sack of grain. Gallienus saw the tattoo on the man's other arm: the word "fish" in Greek letters across the biceps—*IXΘYE*.

"Do you see now?" Festus said and his voice was trembling with anger. "Do you finally understand the danger?"

Gallienus stared at the tattoo in disbelief. *IXΘYE*. An old trick, an acrostic. Each Greek letter was the first letter in a word:

Iesous Christos Theou Huios Soter.

Jesus the Christ, the Son of God, Saviour.

Gallienus' assassin was a Christian.

"No," Gallienus whispered. "It cannot be."

Festus signalled the praetorian to bring the old man over. Festus looked down at him from beneath silver brows and asked, "Where were you when this filth tried to kill the emperor?"

The man looked frightened to death, but he answered: "I was on the top of the gate, cheering."

"Did you see this man?"

"Yes, Your Excellency . . . but I didn't know he was planning to kill the emperor, Your Excellency. I swear it!"

"Of course not. Did you hear him say anything?" Festus asked.

The old man nodded enthusiastically.

"What did you hear him say?"

"As he let go the arrow, Your Excellency, he cried out."

"Yes," Festus prompted.

"He cried out, 'For the *Christos*,' Your Excellency."

Festus waved him away and the praetorian escorted the old man out of the temple.

"For the *Christos*," Gallienus murmured. And suddenly it all made sense. The Christians *had been* stirring up the Germans. The Christians *were* the enemy that Festus had warned him they were.

Gallienus jumped down off the altar. His face was pale and sweaty, but he wore a determined scowl. For the last three years he had focussed on the enemy hammering on the empire's gates, but there was already an enemy inside and the time had come to deal with them too. "The Christians," he hissed through clenched teeth.

His father had been right all along.

THE GRAPE HARVEST HAD COME again to Gaul and the Valens estate was a hive of activity, as it was every September. This year the work had doubled because another consignment of horses had to be delivered to Emperor Gallienus. Conall had been especially busy, dividing his time between caring for Valens' burgeoning herds and business trips to Aquitainia to purchase more horses for the emperor. He had even visited the cavalry school in Mediolanum, now in full operation, to give the Master of Horses there the benefit of his experience. True to his word, the emperor had paid handsomely for the horses, and Valens had added another fortune to his already immense holdings, although the emperor was slower to pay his bills than other buyers. But that was part of dealing with the imperial household.

Life had gone on as usual at the Valens estate. Little Ruth was approaching her third birthday and had become a miniature version of her mother, with the same bright blue eyes and snowy blond hair, and, like her mother, she had won Valens' heart from the moment he first laid eyes on her. Every time he returned home and saw his little girl come running toward him crying "Daddeeeee" at the top of her lungs, his heart swelled a size larger. He wondered if the human heart could burst from too much love, while at the same time knowing that he didn't care; if he had to die, as he would someday, there could be no better way to enter eternity than to be able to proclaim, "I was loved to death!"

They had fallen into a routine. Valens, always accompanied by at least two guards—the bandits that plagued the Old Massalia Road had not yet been apprehended—rode into Massalia once a week for news. Several days each week, Sukuta visited Valens' other estates in the area, and Valens often accompanied him. On occasion, Damarra and Ruth joined Valens on these inspection tours, but normally she preferred to stay home. When Valens was away, Damarra and Persephone spent a good deal of time together, Damarra running the household with Persephone's assistance. When Valens was home, their little family was inseparable. Early mornings found them in the garden reading *Scripturae* and praying. Late in the morning they often went to the beach down at the end of the front meadow, where they collected seashells with Ruth or played in the surf. In the afternoons while Ruth napped they retired to the library. Damarra still enjoyed weaving—she found the back and forth movement of the shuttle relaxing—so they moved one of her looms into the library so that she could weave cloth while Valens read to her from one of his books or poured over his extensive collection of maps. In the evenings they gathered together with the Christians in the household to worship the *Christos*, or went to the nearby Manlius estate to meet with the other Christians in the area.

It was a wonderful life. Valens was happier than he had been since his first wife Julia's death, and sometimes (although he worried that it might be unfair to Julia's memory) he believed he had never been this happy or content. The single point of contention between them were the *lapsi*. Most of the visitors who came now were pilgrims, come to pay homage to the confessors who had once stood before Valerianus himself and proclaimed *Christianus Sum*. But even five years after the persecution ended, there were still *lapsi* who sought them out and begged them for a Certificate of Peace. The very sight of them turned Valens' stomach. He suspected Damarra met with them when he was away. He could have verified that suspicion. All he had to do was ask Gundabar or one of the other slaves or even Damarra herself. Any one of them would have told him the truth, but he knew the truth would lead to another argument and drive the wedge of conflict deeper, separate them further, and so he pretended not to know, as Damarra pretended not to disobey.

The question of Gundabar's prophecy still hung over their heads unresolved. Being the man he was, Valens had called together the "Clan" on a number of occasions to discuss the matter, hoping to squeeze out any new morsel of information that might help him make sense of it all. He knew he had to wait on God, even suspected that it was taking so long because God was teaching him *how* to wait, but that could not stop him from wondering, planning, sometimes cajoling God with his prayers. Once he had taken Gundabar into his library to show him one of his maps. Most of his maps depicted the Roman Empire in varying degrees of accuracy, but this one was a map of the "known world" (as it was known eighty years before when its creator had drawn it), and included Persia, India, distant China, a portion of sub-Roman Africa, and Germania and Sarmatia. Assembled as the map was from the tales of sailors and travellers with a penchant for embellishment, the map's accuracy lessened as it moved further away from the empire, but the wilds of Germania were closer to home and better documented. With Conall's help—even daily exposure to Latin had not improved Gundabar's Latin markedly—he had directed Gundabar to Germania and asked him the question that they all wanted to know. Where? Where in Germania did the *Christos* want them to go? Where was the *Thing* to be? But Gundabar had just smiled his pleasant—and to Valens, increasingly irritating—little smile and shrugged. And what about this "other"? When would he arrive? Another shrug; another irritating little smile. He was waiting on God just as the rest of them were.

One morning towards the end of September, Valens was in the front courtyard with Conall when Paulus entered from the laneway to inform Valens that another group of pilgrims had arrived at the front gate. Paulus had proven himself an efficient guard, and was now Gundabar's second in command. He had even begun to look like Gundabar—since joining the household he had let his brown hair and dark beard grow long, and on occasion tied his hair up in a Suevi knot on the top of his head, much to Gundabar's delight. Valens caught Gundabar's eye—he was over at Persephone's loom talking to the slave girl as she worked—and summoned him with a wave of his hand.

"Pilgrims," he told the German.

Gundabar nodded. He had heard that word enough times to learn its meaning. "We go," he said.

Along with Paulus, who was still on gate duty, they headed out of the courtyard and down the laneway. The sun was bright and large in the eastern sky, the day already warm. Slaves and the local freedmen that Valens' hired for the harvest and winemaking were busy amongst the vines. Sukuta was keeping track of this year's yields on a wax tablet. He waved as Valens passed.

A group of men and women were huddled together on the road. As soon as he walked through the gate they began to murmur together. He held up his hands for quiet, but the nail prints on his wrist produced the opposite effect.

"*Holy Confessor!*"

"*Marks of the Christos!*"

"*Bless me, Holy One!*"

Valens glanced at Gundabar, who was carefully studying each face. At last he looked at Valens and shook his head. The other was not among them. Gundabar strode up in front of Valens, put both index fingers in his mouth, and let out a piercing whistle.

Immediately the pilgrims silenced. All eyes turned to stare at the German. Gundabar nodded at Valens and moved aside.

Valens smiled at the crowd. "How many of you are here for a Certificate of Peace?" he asked.

Two of the seven held up their hands—a man and a woman, both dressed in sackcloth.

"I am sorry, I cannot help you," he said. "You must take up the matter of forgiveness with God, not me."

Their faces fell. The woman turned away, but the man stepped forward. "Please," he begged, "may we speak with Confessor Damarra?"

Obviously they had heard his wife was more amenable. "Please leave," he asked, keeping his voice as free of emotion as possible. After many months of dealing with the *lapsi* he had learned to control his anger and disgust. But just barely.

"If we could but—"

"Leave now," he commanded, accentuating each word.

With a nod, he turned and took the woman's hand. Together they trudged back down the road.

Valens spent the next hour with the pilgrims, answering their questions, praying with them, allowing them to touch the scars on his wrists. The attention still felt awkward, but he had come to accept it and even understand it. Romans loved their heroes. Gladiators and charioteers were idolized by the masses. Fans accosted them constantly, threw gifts and money at them, even offered *themselves*, their bodies, their hearts, their very souls. And the Christians? They too wanted heroes, men and women to look up to and emulate, and as long as it went no further than that, Valens was happy to play that role. His fear was that they would start to *worship* him. Long ago the Children of Israel had faced a similar choice. God had appointed Judges to rule over them in His name, but they had decided they wanted to have a king like all the other nations. God had warned them of the consequences of rejecting Him in favour of a king, but they had not listened, and so he had given them their kings, and eventually those kings had led them to division and ruin. Now the Christians wanted heroes, just like all the other nations, even though they already had the one hero above all heroes—the *Christos*. And Valens, for one, did not want to be the one who led the children of the *Christos* to division and ruin.

Division and ruin . . .

The words echoed in his head. For just an instant his mind churned up an image—the *lapsi* trudging back down the Old Massalia Road after he had rejected them—but righteous indignation chased the scene away.

Division and ruin . . .

One by one the pilgrims bid him farewell and left, some returning to their homes, some with plans to visit other confessors in Gaul. He prayed for their safety as he watched them go. At one time the Old Massalia Road had been the epitome of safe, but with the bandits still living in the forest and preying on travellers, that was no longer true. For so long, he had thought of this estate as a refuge against the storm that was tearing their world apart, but *that* was no longer true, either. The bandits were proof of that. In the last few months several hundred people in Massalia had died of the plague. And despite the success of Gallienus' new cavalry, the Germans were attacking the empire all along the frontier, and each time they came they were a little better prepared, a little better armed, a little bigger in numbers, and they managed to infiltrate a little deeper, push the defenders back a little further. Evil was pressing in on all fronts, and he could not escape the feeling that eventually it would crush them.

Just a matter of time.

Please, Lord, he prayed, *spare my child. Spare my wife.*

He heaved a heavy sigh as the last of the pilgrims disappeared from sight. Suddenly Gundabar grabbed his arm. "There," he said, pointing at the copse of oaks across the road. "Something move."

Valens drew his dagger.

Paulus stepped in front of them and peered into the trees. "No, my lord. Nothing there. A bird, perhaps."

Gundabar shook his head. "No. Man."

Paulus took a few steps, then stopped and studied the trees again. After a few moments he shook his head. "Nothing there now. Maybe a deer? Or a dog?"

"I look," Gundabar said, drawing his sword.

Paulus grabbed his arm. "Forgive me, Commander, but I

should be the one who looks." He grinned. "That's my job."

Gundabar grunted agreement.

Paulus slipped across the road, then made his way stealthily through the long grass. As he approached the trees he drew his sword. He leaned around the trunk of the outside tree like a child playing hide and seek. Suddenly he leapt in front of the trees, disappearing from view, but they heard him cry out: "You there! Don't move!"

Gundabar and Valens hurried over to join Paulus. He was standing over a man who was sitting with his back against one of the oaks, a half-eaten apple in one hand and the other raised in surrender. Despite the tip of the sword lifting his chin, the man wore a gentle smile, as if he were enjoying the sunshine and not in imminent danger of death. His skin was dark, not black like Sukuta or olive-skinned like Persephone, but a rich brown that reminded Valens of the soil in his vineyard. Long, straight black hair framed an oval face that was pocked across the cheeks, the scars of some childhood malady, yet was handsome nonetheless. His beard and his eyes were black, too. He wore a long brown tunic that fell to his knees over a pair of breeches that were pleated in ballooning, horizontal segments all the way down to his brown boots. The combination of skin, hair, and dark clothes made Valens think of a long twilight just dwindling into the black of true night.

"Are you a bandit?" Paulus asked.

The man laughed. "I have been called many things in my life, my hairy friend, but bandit is not one of them." His voice was a low tenor, but with an accent Valens had never heard before. His Latin was impeccable. He seemed anything but dangerous.

"Put away your swords, Paulus, Gundabar," Valens said and dropped his dagger into its sheath. "What is your name?" Valens asked the man.

"I am Xerxes," he replied. He gestured for permission to stand and Valens nodded. When he was on his feet, he swiped down the back of his clothes, then held his hand out to Valens. "And you are the confessor Julius Valens, are you not?"

Valens' eyes narrowed. "Are you *lapsi*, here for a certificate?"

Xerxes laughed. "No. Where I come from, we do not have

lapsi. There is no need for them."

Valens took his hand and shook it. "You are a pilgrim, then?" Valens asked.

Again Xerxes laughed. "I suppose I am." He took another bite of his apple, then wrapped it in a piece of cloth he took from his belt and dropped it into a large leather satchel at his side. "And I am also a messenger."

"From whom?"

He bowed. "I was sent by the great Shahanshah, the King of kings, Shapur, Lord and Master of the Sassanid Empire. I bring greetings from Shahanshah Shapur to the confessors Julius Valens and Damarra Valensia, and I bring an invitation. Shahanshah Shapur invites you to come to the Persian realm and meet with him and know safety and joy in his presence."

Valens was so flabbergasted that he could not speak. An invitation from Shapur? How could that be? How could Shapur have heard of them . . . and why would he want them to come?

Fortunately, Gundabar was still able to talk. He suddenly barged in front of Valens, almost knocking him over in his rush, and grabbed the Persian in his arms and hugged him fiercely. Paulus, like Valens, looked on in total amazement. Gundabar drew away and began to speak to Xerxes in rapid-fire Suevi. Xerxes nodded and smiled at the German. It was obvious he could not understand him, but he was responding to his affectionate display. At last Gundabar looked over his shoulder and grinned at Valens. Tears were flowing down both cheeks into his beard. "Another!" he cried. "Another has come!" Then he turned around and shook Xerxes by the shoulders as if he were trying to make the Persian understand. "You another! You come!"

Again Valens was too flabbergasted to speak. His gaze fell on Xerxes, who was laughing at Gundabar's excitement. Xerxes was the man they had been waiting for all this time.

The other had finally come.

THEY LED XERXES BACK TO THE VILLA, and when they appeared in the courtyard there was a flurry of activity as the members of the Clan Gundabar had already identified appeared one by one, as if the Persian were an irresistible magnetic force. Marcus alone, still in the north guarding the frontier, resisted the pull. Gundabar flitted to each of them in turn, crying "another" over and over again, his face beaming with such excitement that soon they were all laughing, even Xerxes, who had no idea what was going on. Paulus asked Gundabar for permission to leave, but Valens asked him to stay. Then came the explanation. Many of them jumped in with details as Valens relayed the story of Gundabar's arrival and the subsequent revelation about the Clan and the impending journey to Germania for the *Thing*. When Valens finally finished, they all turned to look at Xerxes. In the silence, he gazed around the circle. His dark face was composed, even serene, as if the strange story they had just shared with him were as commonplace as a shopping list or a favourite recipe. "The *Christos* has his hand upon you," he said at last.

"You . . . are a Christian?" Damarra asked. Little Ruth squirmed in her arms and held out her hands to her daddy. Valens took the child from his wife.

"Shahanshah Shapur thought it best to send a Christian ambassador to reassure you." He lifted his hands. "And here I am."

"But *why* did he send you?" Valens asked.

"About a year and a half ago a man arrived in Ctesiphon and requested an audience with Shapur. The man turned out to be a Roman soldier. He carried with him a communication from the commander of your praetorian guard, a man named Paulus Antoninus Quaerellus."

A murmur rippled through the Clan. Damarra gasped.

Valens snapped his fingers. "That's it! Between rivers! Do you remember what Commander Paulus told you, Persephone?"

The maid thought for a moment: "He said that someone would come to help and 'between rivers.'"

"Mesopotamia!" Valens exclaimed. "It's the region between the Tigris and the Euphrates rivers, the ancient Persian homeland and now an area of dispute between the Persians and the Romans. The word Mesopotamia literally means 'the land between two rivers.' Paulus was trying to tell us that someone would come from Persia to help us!"

"Ah, and that someone is me," Xerxes said, and then he continued. "Commander Paulus narrated the events which led up to Valerianus' attempt to crucify you." He bowed reverently to Valens. "The commander noted Valerianus' obsession with you and the confessor Damarra and that your lives would be in danger now that Valerianus was emperor. The Shahanshah dispatched me, although he feared that I would find you already dead when I arrived. I must say I feared the same. I am most glad you are still alive."

"As are we," Valens said. The others chuckled. Ruth laid her head on Valens' shoulder and closed her eyes.

"Paulus requested the Shahanshah's aid on your behalf. I memorized what he wrote." Xerxes cleared his throat, then quoted Paulus: "There is nowhere for Valens and Damarra to hide, no place in the empire beyond Valerianus' wrath. But in your realm, mighty Shahanshah, they may reap the benefits of your benevolence and at last know safety." He grinned. "Your friend was most eloquent on your behalf, yes? The Shahanshah could hardly refuse such a polite request."

"And so you are here to escort us to Persia," Valens concluded.

"Precisely."

"But we cannot go to Persia."

"Obviously. The *Christos* is directing us elsewhere."

"And . . . that's fine with you?"

"Of course."

"Will the Shahanshah be angry if you come with us instead?"

Xerxes laughed. "I am not here to steal you away. The Shahanshah offers sanctuary; it is your choice whether or not to accept that offer. As far as I am concerned, the orders of the *Christos* supersede the orders of any earthly ruler. And besides, all we know is that we must attend this *Thing* somewhere in Germania; who knows where the *Christos* will send us after that? If He does direct us to Persia, the Shahanshah will be waiting to greet you with open arms, as will the Christians who openly worship the *Christos* under his enlightened rule."

Conall cleared his throat. "Begging your pardon, Lord Valens, but may I ask a question?"

"Of course, Conall."

"Forgive me, Lord Valens, but you are one man and one woman far, far away from Persia—why would the emperor of Persia care about any of this?"

Xerxes laughed. "Ah, my friend, Conall, you see, Shapur is very wise. He knows that if his enemy Valerianus desires something, *he* should desire it, too. He wishes to protect Lord Valens and Lady Damarra because Valerianus wants them dead, you see? Having you under his wing will anger his enemy, and an angry enemy is more likely to make mistakes."

Conall shrugged. "I suppose that makes sense if you're a ruler of men. I'm just a horseman, and it all seems foolish to me." He sighed. "But it is good to know that at last we can begin this . . . *quest* that the *Christos* has set before us."

Paulus, who had stood by listening for the last hour, spoke up, "Lord Valens, may I ask why you wanted me here?"

Valens nodded. "Yes." He turned to Conall. "Ask Gundabar if the guards may accompany us on our journey."

Conall asked Gundabar, and, after a moment's hesitation, Gundabar launched into a long explanation. Finally Conall nodded his head. "Yes, Lord Valens. The guards may accompany the Clan, but they are not *part* of the Clan. Gundabar wanted me to stress that."

"Fair enough." Valens turned to Paulus. "You understand the plan?"

Paulus scratched his beard. "Yes, Lord Valens, and quite frankly I'm relieved. I admit I've heard bits and pieces in the last few months, just enough to confuse me. But now it all makes sense."

Valens nodded. "Good. Gundabar informs me that you are an excellent guard, and I want you to come with us. We may have need of your skills in the wilds of Germania. Alexander and Regulus are coming as well. But you, Paulus, are a freedman and must decide for yourself if you will accompany us or not."

Paulus did not even hesitate. "I will come, my lord."

"Excellent," Valens' gaze travelled around the group. "We leave tomorrow morning."

Suddenly Gundabar stepped into the centre of the circle and raised his hands. "No! No leave tomorrow!"

Sukuta rolled his eyes at Conall. Everyone else groaned. "Why not?" Persephone asked?

"Clan not full."

Sukuta slapped his forehead. "That's right. Remember, my lord? The riddle? When the eight of us become ten of us become thirteen of us! With the addition of Xerxes we are now ten, not thirteen."

It was Prisca who piped up next, which surprised them, as the midwife rarely spoke unless spoken too. "Actually, we are eleven now, my lord, if you count our dear Ruth. And it occurs to me, my lord, that that is what the riddle means." She paused, looking around the circle, her cheeks red. Valens urged her to continue. "Two more children, my lord. It won't be time to go until you have two more children. Then the eight will become ten will become thirteen. You see?"

Valens glanced at her, amazed. The timid little midwife had figured it out. They had all overlooked the obvious.

Except for Prisca.

"I think you're right, Prisca," Valens admitted. "Well done!"

Prisca glowed with her master's praise.

"Then what do we do now?" Persephone asked.

All eyes turned to Damarra. "What?" she asked.

Suddenly everyone looked away, as if embarrassed.

Damarra laughed. "I'm not pregnant, if that's what you're all wondering. You're just going to have to wait."

"That could mean years still," Conall observed.

Valens grinned and threw his arm around his wife. "We'll try our best to speed things up," he offered.

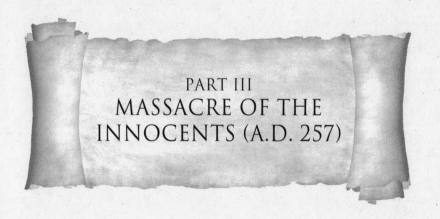

PART III
MASSACRE OF THE INNOCENTS (A.D. 257)

"A voice is heard in Ramah, mourning and great weeping,
Rachel weeping for her children and refusing to be comforted,
because her children are no more."

JEREMIAH 31:15

SEVENTEEN

SYRIA
DECEMBER A.D. 256

Before the mild Syrian winter set in, the Roman siege towers at last breached the thick walls of Antioch, and the remaining Persian defenders were slaughtered by the victorious Roman legions. Two days after the actual capture of the city, Valerianus entered in triumph. Riding in the back of a golden chariot and arrayed as the sun god in shining gold and silver, he allowed the ecstatic screams of his subjects to wash over him, cleansing him of the anger that had been building within him since the landing in Syria. Everything was proceeding as planned, behind schedule perhaps, but that insignificant Persian runt, Shapur, was on the run now, and Valerianus planned to chase him all the way to Ctesiphon. Antioch was his, Syria was his, and the Persian empire lay before him, a rich prize that the gods had assured him would one day belong to him. And on that day, when the subjects of both Rome and Persia bowed down to worship and adore him, his rise to deity would be complete. He had no delusions that his deification by the senate had somehow transformed him into a true god — their decree was nothing but empty words, despite how seriously some of his subjects took the imperial cult. But the gods could and did elevate mere mortals to divinity, and he knew that was his destiny. One day the gods would admit him to their company, and he *would* be a god: the god Valerianus.

But first . . .

A dispatch from the West reached him on the day he left Antioch to rejoin the rest of his army in Mesopotamia. That night when they made camp, he dismissed his slaves and his officers and retired early, so he could study the contents of the dispatch in private. The news from Festus was excellent. The "attempted assassination" of Gallienus had produced the predicted results: Gallienus had finally conceded that the Christians were a threat to the security of the empire. The dispatch also contained a communiqué from Gallienus himself in which he related the details of the "attempted assassination," assuring his father that he was recovering from his wounds, and informing Valerianus that he was prepared to "open a dialogue about the Christian Problem."

Valerianus put down his son's letter and grinned. It had taken more than three years to turn Gallienus and make him see things as he should. Thank the gods for Festus. His old friend was a master manipulator, dropping hints here, planting evidence there, leading Gallienus ever on through the muddle of facts and fantasy until, like Theseus in the Labyrinth, he arrived at the monster at the centre of it all—the Christians. They were the Minotaur that haunted the maze called the Roman Empire, and Gallienus had finally seen them for what they were: repulsive, evil atheists who must be destroyed if the empire was to be saved. The Christians themselves had helped Valerianus' cause. They had infiltrated Germania to spread their noisome creed, a fact that Festus had easily reinterpreted as proof that the Christians were plotting with the Germans against the empire. And who knows, perhaps they *were* assisting the Germans? What did it matter in the end? Roman law proclaimed that the name of Christian was punishable by death. All Valerianus wanted to do was to appease the gods by upholding the law. What could be more pious and just than that?

Valerianus finished reading his son's letter, then put it back in the dispatch pouch and sat pondering his next move. How was he to interpret Gallienus' decision to "open a dialogue about the Christian Problem?" A phrase like that was pure bureaucratese; it said much without saying anything. How far was his imperial colleague willing to go? Certainly he wasn't suggesting a set policy— he could be considering anything from a slap on the wrist to complete extermination. No way to tell. He only knew that if he pressed Gallienus too far too fast that his son would balk, and the persecution would have to be postponed even longer.

In the end, Valerianus decided a gently escalating approach to the "Christian Problem" would work best. He settled on the two phase attack that he and Festus had developed after Decius' failure. Phase one involved enlarging the rifts created by Decius' persecution. They would attack the leaders of the sect, the *episcopi* and the elders that assisted them. Turn them, turn their followers. If they could not be turned, they would be exiled—at this stage he wanted converts, not martyrs. Break down their organization, isolate them, forbid them to congregate—no more meetings in their cemeteries or these *ecclesiae* that had begun to spring up across the empire. Even meetings in private homes would be forbidden.

Once Christian unity had been shattered, the persecution would enter its second phase. All Christians, but especially those Christians of senatorial and equestrian rank, would be required to sacrifice. If they refused, their lands, goods, and monies would be confiscated. If they continued to refuse, they would pay with their lives. Festus had wanted the confiscation of property to begin immediately, in phase one, but Valerianus had vetoed the idea. Although he desperately needed the funds, starting with confiscation would look like a land grab instead of a religious revival. The emperors must first appear to be benevolent fathers, trying to correct their wayward children.

Then let the blood and money flow.

Valerianus called for parchment, pen, and ink, then wrote a letter to his son, outlining the two phase plan and suggesting they begin phase one in the spring. On a second piece of parchment, he drafted an edict of persecution in both their names and signed it at the bottom. He would have his most trusted scribe make a copy before he sent the letter and edict by imperial post to Germania Inferior. All Gallienus would have to do is pick a date and sign it to make it official.

The third document in the dispatch pouch was a report from his surveillance team in Massalia. On the first read through he could make no sense of it—the details were simply too bizarre to comprehend. He had to read it again and a third time before he was able to bypass his incredulity and piece together the revelations the document contained. Apparently his daughter and her husband believed their God wanted them to go to Germania. Worse than that, Shapur had sent an ambassador to take them to safety in Persia, if they so wished. And to top it all off, General Marcus, Gallienus' right hand man, was a Christian, just as Festus had suspected!

Valerianus stared at the document, his mind a whirl of dark thoughts. Why would Shapur offer sanctuary to Damarra and Valens? His heart suddenly spasmed, as if the cursed Persian had reached into his chest and clutched it with his bare hand. If Damarra and Valens ran to Persia they would be beyond his reach! He could not let that happen!

He jumped up and began to pace back and forth in front of his desk, his hands clenched behind his back. Slowly calm returned, and his mind began to impose order on the chaos. Shapur's defeat was predetermined. Valerianus would stand in glory in Shapur's throne room in Ctesiphon—the gods had foretold it. So even if Damarra and Valens did escape to Persia, they would not escape *him*. One day he would *be* Persia, as he was now Rome. It was his destiny.

Valerianus sat down again, comforted as he always was by the prophecies the Oracle at Delphi had given him so many years before. It was tempting to order Dionysius to execute Damarra and Valens and be done with it. But why should he deprive himself of the pleasure of seeing them die? Everything was going according to plan. *Better* than planned. Besides, executing them would alienate Gallienus. According to one of Dionysius' earlier reports, Gallienus had visited his "sister" and pledged to protect her, so as long as she stayed put on their Massalia estate, Valerianus could not touch them without arousing Gallienus' suspicions. Better to wait them out. Valerianus smiled deviously. Maybe he could turn Gallienus against Damarra and Valens somehow. Yes, he'd write Festus and get that scheming brain of his working on that.

On the other hand, if they decided on the alternate course and disappeared into the wilds of Germania, what then? They would be much more difficult to find there, and it would be years before he was ready to launch a full scale invasion of Germania and pacify the tribes once and for all. He drummed his fingers on the table. What to do? What to do?

In the end he decided to maintain the status quo. He would order Dionysius to continue surveillance. If Damarra and Valens made a move, follow them; otherwise, watch and wait for further orders.

WHEN GALLIENUS LEFT ROME at the beginning of January, the weather was cool but comfortable. There was no respite from the plague, as often happened in northern cities during the winter. For some reason that not even the physicians understood, cold seemed to slow the plague down, but it was never cold enough in Rome for that. He and the Empress Nina and their three children—along with their guard, the officers who had accompanied him to Rome for his anniversary celebration, and a long train of slaves, cooks, priests, and hangers-on—proceeded to the family estate in Etruria. After a week's stay, Gallienus left his family and continued north. The weather in northern Italy was still mild, although they met snow and cold in the Alpine passes, and southern Gaul was even warmer. He and his entourage made good time, and by mid-February they were back in Germania Inferior, where the snows were deep and the cold harsh. Because of his wounds he decided to winter in Augusta Trevia, in a large villa donated by one of the town's leading citizens, where he could stay warm and continue strengthening his shoulder with daily exercise.

His wound had healed over. All that remained were puckered scars front and back. At times it still pained him, especially when the cold was deep and biting. Theophilus, one of the physicians that had tended him in Rome, and the only physician he had ever met that he actually respected, had given up a thriving practice to join his entourage as the official imperial physician. When the pain was bad, Theophilus mixed a tea from the bark of the Aspen tree that helped to dull the pain without dulling the senses, unlike the opiates they had given him in those first few weeks after Strato had tried to kill him. The opiates had caused hallucinations and left him feeling out of touch with his own body. He preferred the pain to that ugly sensation.

Gallienus sat before a fireplace with his legs stretched out. A fire crackled before him, sending strong waves of heat up through his legs and into his torso. It felt good, relaxing, and the pain was in the background, easy to ignore. A dispatch pouch was waiting for him when he arrived in Augusta Trevia, and he was taking a few quiet hours alone to deal with his correspondence. Festus' final report on his assassin, Strato, was vague on details, mainly a repetition of what he had already uncovered. Strato was a retired cavalry officer, an archer who supported the infantry when they were advancing into battle. He was "gifted" with the bow, a true marksman: his former commander claimed he could pierce the eye of a fleeing rabbit at seventy-five yards. Gallienus rubbed his wounded shoulder—he could certainly attest to Strato's gift. Since leaving the cavalry he had drifted to Rome, taking odd jobs, living off the dole. No family, no ties, no connections . . . except to the *Christos*.

A slave had set up a small, portable desk beside his chair. Gallienus reached for the cup of wine the slave had left there and took a drink. He still had a hard time believing that Strato had tried to kill him "for the *Christos*." It didn't make sense. Everything he knew about the Christians, which, he had to admit, was very little, suggested that they would not condone assassination. And yet the evidence was irrefutable.

He read the report again, then shook his head. Something wasn't right. A fact, a detail, something missing, or something that *he* was missing, something in the report that did not add up. It was there on the tip of his consciousness, but no matter how many times he read the report, he could not grasp the . . . error? Inaccuracy?

Deception?

He had had doubts about the official story from the beginning. Before leaving Rome he had launched his own investigation of this Strato character. It was not that he did not trust Festus or his sources; it was simply that the attempted assassination had shaken him to the core of his being, and he wanted as much information on the man and his motivations as possible. So he had sent for the commander of the *Agentes in Rebus*. Thus far in his reign he had made little use of the *Agentes*, although he had requested detailed reports on the activities of certain prominent senators at Rome during his long absences from the city. Tacitus was a handsome man with a tiny, black moustache and an air of efficiency about him. Gallienus had directed him to dig up more information on Strato. Quietly and discreetly. Tacitus was to answer to Gallienus and no one else.

Gallienus searched through the dispatch bag for a communication from Tacitus, not expecting to find one. He was not disappointed. It would take some time to root out more details about Strato.

Assuming there was anything more to find.

The other document of interest was from his father. After Gallienus had given his father the bag of coins that celebrated the divinization of his mother, Mariniana, Valerianus' communications had been abrupt, barely cordial. His father had made his outrage plain by what he had *not* said, and Gallienus had been delighted by that little victory. Valerianus had forbidden the world to remember Mariniana, so Gallienus had not only honoured her memory, but *worshipped* it, by making her a god. No one could forget her now, not even Valerianus. It was childish perhaps, but he believed he owed that to his mother. More, he believed Valerianus owed it to her.

This letter was different. It was chatty, full of details about his campaigns and the administrative woes he was encountering in the East. He expressed his shock at the attempt on his son's life . . . and his even greater shock that the Christian sect was responsible. He sounded sincere. Even his plan for dealing with the Christians seemed moderate. Gallienus had expected vituperation, a call to liquefy the entire cult. Instead, Valerianus offered him a reasonable approach. Deal with the leaders first, try and get them to deny their atheism and return to the gods of their forefathers. Only later, when resistance became stubborn and refused to yield any further, would they turn to more severe measures. It seemed impossible, but perhaps the mantle of the imperial office had cooled his father's passions. Matured him.

Gallienus thought of his friend Marcus, to whom he would have to break the news. Marcus was not going to like it, but there was no other choice. The Christians had definitely been in Germania stirring up the tribes. The Christians would not worship the gods, nor participate in the imperial cult, which brought unity to the empire. And now the Christians had made an attempt on the life of the emperor himself. Marcus would deny it, but until there was evidence to the contrary, it was his duty as emperor to act. The *Agentes* had already prepared lists of known Christian leaders, and his father had drafted an edict. All he had to do was choose a date and sign the edict to make it official. He thought for a moment, then settled on the third day before the kalends of June, the anniversary of the day he and Nina had wed. An auspicious day to begin. He picked up a stylus, dipped it in ink, and wrote the date on the document. Then, without any hesitation, he signed his name on the bottom, next to his father's.

Done. Finished. Official.

Gallienus remembered a lesson Festus had taught him many years ago: all great leaders have one thing in common—once they identify a problem, they solve it. The Christians were the problem and he had solved it. He had done his part. Now it was up to history to decide if his solution was right.

EIGHTEEN

GALLIA NARBONENSIS, SEVENTH DAY BEFORE
THE KALENDS OF JUNE (MAY 26 A.D. 257)

A noise woke Valens from a nightmare.

The dream had been vivid and horrifying. He and Damarra had been summoned to an imperial audience at Rome. They entered a vast hall hand in hand. The roof stood on the shoulders of high, marble columns that marched up both sides of the hall from the entrance doors to the foot of a dais. Statues occupied the spaces between the columns. To the right, the greatest emperors of Rome: Augustus, Tiberius, and Vespasian, then Nerva, Trajan, Hadrian, Antoninus Pius, and Marcus Aurelius, known as the five good emperors, and Septimius Severus, who had died some forty years before and was the last emperor to receive such an honour. To the right, the spaces were occupied by imposing statues of the gods, from mighty Jupiter the Thunderer with his bronze thunderbolt lifted high, ready to strike down anyone who dared to disobey an imperial command, to the crippled Vulcan with his leg brace and hammer and anvil.

They stopped at the foot of a dais that seemed a thousand feet high, and yet they could see the thrones and the men . . .

. . . *gods* . . .

. . . who occupied them as if they were a few feet away.

Valerianus and . . .

At first Gallienus sat on the second throne. But then he

changed, aged, thinned, became a gaunt, snarling reflection of Valerianus, *another* Valerianus. The two Valeriani were laughing, hurling insults down at them from the heavens; and then the insults became real, physical, hideous forms with mass and weight, each heavier than the last, until they gave birth to an insult so monstrous and heavy that the weight of it would crush them. Screaming laughter, the Valeriani hurled it, and as it descended it blocked out the universe, and the crash of its impact shattered his eardrums.

And woke him up.

He held his breath and listened, positive that the noise was real, that it had reached into his nightmare and pulled him out. Damarra breathed softly beside him. Drapes fluttered in the breeze. Normal night sounds. Nothing at all to worry about.

His fingers touched the hilt of his knife on the bedside table and he gripped it in a tight fist. "Is someone there?" he whispered.

"*Yeise*," came the whispered reply. A familiar voice.

"Gundabar?"

"*Yeise* . . . yes. You come."

Valens flicked back the blanket and rose from the bed. He slipped his tunic on over his head, found his belt, then followed Gundabar from the room.

A torch burned in a sconce outside their bed chamber. Gundabar must have put it there before sneaking into the room to wake him. When Gundabar turned, Valens saw his face in the torchlight. He was pale; sweat stood out on his forehead, although the night was cool. "What is it, Gundabar?" Valens asked, but even as the question left his mouth, he knew.

He *knew*.

Gundabar placed a trembling hand on Valens' shoulder. "*Christos* say time to go," he replied.

Valens closed his eyes. He allowed himself a moment of self-pity, a moment to think, *I'm happy here. I don't want to go. Please, Lord, can't we stay?* Then he opened his eyes and did what his military training had taught him to do: he took command. "Wake the Clan and the guards and get everyone to the library immediately. I'll go wake Damarra."

DAMARRA AND VALENS WERE THE FIRST to arrive in the library. Valens had explained as much as he knew while Damarra dressed in a *stola* and shawl, then they had hurried to the meeting place and busied themselves lighting lamps while they waited for the others. They did not have to wait long. Before a quarter of an hour had passed, they were all present, standing around Valens' map table upon which he had unrolled a map. The last to arrive was Prisca; she had a sleeping Ruth in her arms. "I wasn't sure if I should bring her or not," the plump slave told the room.

"That's fine, Prisca," Damarra said. She looked about, then pointed at a long couch with scrolled arms that sat near the fireplace, where Alexander was now starting a fire to take the edge off the cool night. "Put her there."

Prisca put Ruth down on the couch. The little girl curled up into a ball and stuck her thumb in her mouth. Damarra removed her shawl and draped it over her, then leaned over and kissed her small cheek.

Alexander finished with the fire and joined the others at the table. "Regulus, Alexander, do you know why you're here?"

Regulus nodded. "Yes, my lord." He glanced at Paulus. "Paulus told us after Xerxes arrived."

"Did you?" Valens asked Paulus.

"Yes, my lord. I . . . didn't think it was a secret. You said they'd be coming."

"Well, it's probably for the best, anyway." Valens paused and looked at the others. "Apparently, the time has come."

A murmur ran around the table.

Valens gestured to Gundabar. "Gundabar, if you please."

All eyes turned to the young Suevi warrior. With Conall's help, he explained what had happened. The *Christos* had appeared to him in a dream and instructed him to tell *Sankt* it was time to lead the Clan to Germania. They were to leave tomorrow, no sooner, no later.

Regulus raised his hand and Valens nodded at him. "Begging your pardon, my lord, but who or what is *Sankt*?"

Valens pointed at himself. "That's me. We don't know what it means."

Regulus raised his hand again and again Valens nodded.

"Begging your pardon once more, my lord, but are you really planning on going to Germania because Gundabar had a dream? No offense to Gundabar intended, my lord." Regulus cocked his bald head to the side, then added, "No offense intended to you either, my lord."

"Yes we are, Regulus."

"Oh."

Which Valens interpreted as meaning, "You're all insane." And certainly to someone who did not know the *Christos*, the whole affair would seem *insane*. Ludicrous, in fact. And yet most of the people in this room believed in what they were about to do. Even the non-Christians like Sukuta and Prisca had accepted Gundabar's dreams as mandates for action.

"What about the riddle, my lord?" Conall asked. Before any could answer, he turned to Gundabar and repeated the question in Suevi. Gundabar grinned from ear to ear, then hurried over to Damarra and pointed at her belly.

Damarra inhaled a sharp breath, then a look of wonder brightened her face. She touched her abdomen, which was as flat and taut as it had been before her first pregnancy and showed no sign of another. Her eyes met Valens' and gleamed with excitement. "I don't feel pregnant at all. There's been no signs."

Gundabar nodded. "Yeise! Baby!"

"Babies," corrected Prisca. Valens and Damarra both stared at her and her cheeks turned red. "It must be twins, my lady. The eight shall become ten shall become thirteen. If Ruth is eleven and your god says we don't go until we're thirteen, then it *must* be twins."

"Twins!" Damarra exclaimed and threw her arms around her husband. "Isn't that wonderful, Valens?"

"Yes, wonderful," he agreed. But the image in his head of a very pregnant Damarra trudging through the endless tracks of Germania was not wonderful at all. It frightened him to death. How could he take his pregnant wife on this long, long journey?"

Trust in the Christos, his mind whispered.

Yes. He *must* do that. There was no other choice. Something told him that to tarry here any longer would be more deadly than all the terrors that Germania had to offer. He kissed his wife's temple, held her tight for a moment, then directed everyone's attention to the map he had unfurled on the table. "Over the last several months Xerxes, Gundabar, and I have put our heads together to create this map. We started with a map of the empire, then added Gundabar's knowledge of Germania and Xerxes' knowledge of Persia and the entrances to that realm. We know we are going to Germania first, but after the *Thing*, our destination is unclear. It may be that we will continue on to Persia," he gestured to Xerxes, "to take Shapur up on his generous offer of asylum. Or the *Christos* might direct us elsewhere. All we know for certain is that we must leave tomorrow. Most of you prepared for this day many months ago—bring only what you need. Remember that winters in the north are brutal."

"How long will the journey take?" Alexander asked.

"We don't know. We're not even sure where or when the *Thing* will take place, only that it is in Germania." It occurred to Valens just how little they *did* know about this journey, and again his mind whispered the same consolation: *Trust in the Christos.*

"We will travel by day, to begin with. There is no need for secrecy, at least not yet, but do *not* tell anyone our destination. We are simply a band of travellers heading north."

Valens paused. His eyes drifted over the map, then: "According to the most current information available, Gallienus is here," he jabbed his finger at the map, "in Germania Inferior, near the German Ocean that runs between the mainland and Britannia. My plan is to head north to Germania Superior, at which time we will send Conall on ahead while we follow. Conall will find the emperor and inform General Marcus that the time has come to leave. Marcus will make some suitable excuse and join us here," he jabbed the map again, "at Castra Vetera on the Rhine frontier. That's when we will meet our first real challenge—entering Germania unseen. We will cross the Rhine near Castra Vetera, perhaps disguised as a caravan of merchants."

Gundabar struck the map with his fist. "No!" he exclaimed.

Everyone turned to look at him. Gundabar rarely raised his voice in anything other than excitement. For the first time he seemed stressed, even angry. "What's wrong, Gundabar?" Conall asked.

Gundabar jabbed the map just as Valens had done, but much further south. "Here," he told them. "We go here!"

Valens and Conall leaned over the map to see where Gundabar had pointed. When they stood back again, each man wore the same worried expressions.

"What's wrong?" Damarra asked.

It was Sukuta who answered. "We can't enter there, Lady Damarra," he replied. "It's impossible."

Damarra studied the map, and it was plain from the confusion on her face that she had no idea what the problem was. It all looked like the same frontier to her.

"That is the *Agri Decumates*, Damarra," Valens explained. "We can't enter Germania there."

"But why not?"

"Our northern frontier is protected by two rivers—"

"The Rhine and Danube," Damarra said.

"Yes. But that protection is incomplete. The Rhine begins in Germania Superior and flows north to the German Ocean; the Danube begins in the province of Rhaetia and flows east to the Black Sea. In between the headwaters of the Rhine and the Danube there is no river boundary. That area is called the *Agri Decumates*, and it is one of the most heavily fortified regions on the frontier. There are frontier forts and watchtowers all through the area. There is *no* way we can enter Germania through the *Agri Decumates* unobserved." He looked at Gundabar and shook his head. "It's *impossible*."

Gundabar stuck his finger on the map in the same place; this time he kept it there. One by one he looked at each member of the Clan and the guards. "Here," he said, his voice firm. "*Christos* say here."

"*Christos* say?" Valens asked.

"*Yiese!*"

And that was that.

ULF YAWNED WITH WEARINESS and rubbed his bleary eyes. It was at times like this that he regretted giving up his position in the Praetorian Guard. Sure, he liked the status that came with being a member of the emperor's personal bodyguard, and the money was excellent. But if he were in Rome right now he'd be lying in a cot sleeping the night away, instead of standing here in the cold darkness waiting for something to happen. Nothing had changed in the months since they had begun surveillance of the Valens estate. His day—well, his night, actually—was always the same. At sunset he met Licander at the ramshackle old shed that stood in an otherwise empty field a few hundred yards south of the Old Massalia Road. After Licander updated him on the day's events— usually nothing—Licander would head back into Massalia. Ulf would wait until full darkness, then sneak over to the copse of oaks directly in front of the estate. From there he had clear line of sight of the entrance to the front courtyard. Not much to see at night, except the guards making their hourly rounds. Most nights passed without anything happening. But some nights the signal would come: one wave of the torch meant information; two waves of the torch meant important information.

Tonight there had been two waves.

When he had received the signal he had hurried back to the old shed to wait for the informant to come. His orders were simple: listen, then report to Dionysius. And he had thought military service would be exciting! Was *that* ever a mistake.

"Are you there?" a voice whispered in the darkness. At last.

"Right here," Ulf said.

Ulf smiled to himself as he listened to the informant. They always met like this, under cover of darkness. If he turned now, he could probably catch a glimpse of the spy, but that was against orders. Why Tacitus wanted it played this way, he had no idea, but he had ordered the informant's identity kept a secret—even Dionysius did not know who it was, although the big man had some suspicions. No matter. Ulf loved life too much to disobey Tacitus. He had seen what the commander of the *Agentes-in-Rebus* was capable of, and he wanted nowhere near the man's bad side.

At last the informant finished his report and vanished back into the night without even a farewell. Typical. But at least this was news worthy of reporting. The Clan, as they called themselves, was leaving for Germania sometime tomorrow. And they were planning to go by way of the *Agri Decumates*! He laughed at their audacity. Trying to sneak through the *Agri Decumates* without being noticed was like trying to sneak out of Ursula's without paying your tab! With all those forts and soldiers waiting for them? Not a chance. Still, if they were leaving, it meant his stint on the night shift was finally over.

He left the cover of the shed and made his way to another shed half a mile further down the road, where they kept their horses when they were on duty. There was no point in waiting out the night. Commander Dionysius would want this information as soon as possible. And then a little wine, a little food, and a nice warm bed. Life didn't get much better than that.

A MESSENGER ARRIVED SHORTLY after dawn with a letter. Valens was already up, directing preparations for the long journey that would begin the next day. There was much to do. Conall and Gundabar were readying the horses, while Valens and Sukuta worked on the inventory of weapons and provisions they would need. Valens had an estate in Germania Superior just south of the *Agri Decumates*, so they would head there first. Moving from one estate to another was customary for a wealthy senator like Valens and would not arouse suspicion. Once the inventory was complete they would load everything into two wagons. They planned to plod along, taking their time, until they reached the estate in Germania Superior. After that they'd have to carry whatever they couldn't pack on the horses—there were few roads in Germania, so the wagons would have to stay behind.

The messenger was a soldier from the garrison at Massalia, one he knew by name. Valens opened the letter absently, without looking at the seal. His business interests were vast, so it was a rare day when a message did *not* arrive. Usually it was the same old thing, a request from one of his other estates, an accounting of wine sales or horse sales or grain sales. But this letter was from Emperor Gallienus. He was sending General Marcus to them; he'd arrive before the kalends of June. The emperor wanted to assure them that they had nothing to fear. At this time only the leaders of their sect, the *episcopi*, presbyters, and elders would be targeted. Regular Christians were safe . . . unless they continued to meet with their fellow Christians. Meetings were forbidden—nothing new there. Meetings had *always* been forbidden by law . . . and now that law would be strictly enforced. No more congregating in cemeteries or ecclesiae or houses or barns or catacombs or any of the other secret and unwholesome places that Christians liked to meet. Henceforth, if two or more gathered in the name of the *Christos*, they would suffer the consequences of imperial wrath.

But not you, of course! You and my sister, the lady Damarra, are safe.

Valens looked up, just as Damarra and Ruth entered the courtyard from the villa. His heart wrenched with anguish as Damarra smiled at him and little Ruth toddled toward him with her arms wide open. Gallienus had wanted to reassure them, but Valens' mind burrowed between the lines and read the death sentence hiding there.

At this time . . . forbidden . . . cemeteries . . . catacombs . . . wrath.
Persecution.

His wrists ached with the memory of the nails.

The smile fled Damarra's face when she gazed into his eyes. He swept Ruth up and crushed her to his chest. "Love you, Daddy," the little girl cried. Tears traced lines down his cheeks.

"Love you too, Ruth," he whispered.

Damarra touched his shoulder. "What is it, Valens?"

He handed her the letter, watched her read it, watched her face turn the colour of sun-bleached marble and her hand creep up to cover her mouth and lock the horror inside. When she finished reading, her eyes found Valens'—they were wide and wet and fearful.

The shock kept him glued in place for a few more moments, then the administrator in him took control and urged him to action. He called the others over, explained what was coming, then began to issue orders. "Conall, ride into Massalia and warn *Episcopus* Pius. He needs to gather the elders and vanish, into the catacombs, into the countryside, somewhere where they won't find him. Sukuta, you ride to Arelatum and tell the *episcopus* there the same thing. You won't make it back before we leave in the morning, so find us on the road. And have Massalia and Arelatum send out riders to as many *episcopi* as possible—maybe we can get most of the Christian leaders in Gallia to safety before the persecution starts."

"Are we not going to wait for General Marcus?" Sukuta asked.

Both Valens and Gundabar replied, "No." Valens continued on his own. "The *Christos* commands us to leave tomorrow, so we leave tomorrow. It is imperative that we follow His direction at all times, but *especially* now. God will lead General Marcus to us. Have no fear."

CENTRAL GALLIA, THE FIFTH DAY
BEFORE THE KALENDS OF JUNE (MAY 28)

MARCUS REIGNED IN HIS HORSE and left the road a few miles south of Alesia. Night had fallen hours ago, but he had ridden on, relying on his horse to keep to the road while he dozed in the saddle. He had almost fallen twice now, and he knew the next time he would for sure. A few hours sleep and he would be on his way. He hated to lose the time, but he'd be no good to the Clan if exhaustion killed him.

About ten yards in, he came to a stone fence that ran parallel to the road. He followed it until it turned to the right and headed off into darkness. Ahead was a pasture, nothing but a few skinny cows and a hovel that obviously served as a barn. Dismounting, he led the horse in behind the hovel, tied the reigns to a tree, then dropped to the ground. He was too tired to bother with his bedroll. Turning over on his side and slipping his hands under his cheek, he fell into a deep sleep.

How long he slept, he did not know. When his eyes opened again it was still dark, with no sign of light on the eastern horizon. He sat up, looked about. His horse was munching contentedly on grass. The night was quiet, no crickets, no night birds, not even a breeze stirred the grass. And yet he knew he was not alone. "Who's there?" he asked.

A voice replied. Not out of the darkness, or from the hovel, or from some late-night traveller passing by on the road, but from inside of him, and he jumped to his feet in surprise. The voice was not a sound in his head or in his heart; it was a light, bright and hot, that flooded him with its brilliance, and in that light was a message, not spoken but understood. The message was simple; the power behind it was infinite.

East

"Yes, Lord," Marcus whispered.

He untied the reigns and led his horse back to the highway and continued south. At the first crossroads, he set his face to the rising sun and rode on into the dawn, bound for Germania Superior and the *Agri Decumates* beyond.

NINETEEN

THE THIRD DAY BEFORE THE
KALENDS OF JUNE (MAY 30 A.D. 257)

Valerianus and Gallienus did not repeat Decius' mistakes. Provincial governors, procurators, and local magistrates were told well in advance on which day to begin the persecution. Lists of known Christian leaders were issued to simplify matters even further, and in those cases where the lists were incomplete, local knowledge helped fill in the missing names. Each unit of soldiers was assigned a specific target. By dawn on the third day before the kalends of June, everything was ready to proceed.

The initial sweep for Christian leaders caught almost everyone by surprise. No sooner had the edict of persecution been posted in forums from one side of the empire to other than the first arrests were made. Soldiers descended on known Christian meeting places before the sun cleared the eastern horizon. *Episcopi*, presbyters, and elders were taken into custody and brought before judges; many were tried, found guilty, and sent into exile before noon. Of course, not all the meeting places were in use at the time, and so some Christian leaders were able to slip away before they could be apprehended. And there were a few places, such as Rome and southern Gallia, where news of the persecution had leaked out ahead of time, and the leaders went into hiding before the persecution started.

Some of the arrests were particularly high profile. Cyprianus of Carthage, who had gone into hiding during Decius' persecution and had been criticized because of it, redeemed himself admirably during his trial. When Proconsul Paternus ordered him to return to the religion of his forefathers, Cyprianus declared, *"Christianus Sum,"* then refused to reveal the names of any of his presbyters on the grounds that being an informant was prohibited by Roman law. "After all these years I finally found a use for my law degree," he told a presbyter later with a wink. Exasperated by Cyprianus' inflexibility, Paternus exiled him to Curubis, a little backwater town some forty miles from Carthage. Novatianus of Rome went into exile, but his rival at Rome, Sixtus, evaded the initial dragnet. Dionysius of Alexandria, another *episcopus* that had the respect of Christians everywhere, was arrested with several of his presbyters and tried before the deputy-praefect, who exiled them to Cephro, a small village in the middle of nowhere.

All in all, both emperors were pleased with the initial results, which demonstrated a degree of organization and planning that the persecution of Decius had lacked. There was one result, however, that they had not foreseen. Up until the new persecution began, Christian leadership had been divided over the question of the *lapsi*. Some, like Novatianus of Rome, clung to doctrine "once lapsed, forever damned," although less hardline Novatianists were willing to allow that the decision was ultimately God's. Others, like many of the confessors who had become the heroes of the faith, felt that a note from them would be enough to convince God to grant forgiveness. In the middle were men like Cyprianus of Carthage and the new *episcopus* of Rome, Sixtus, who believed that the lapsed could be forgiven only after a long period of penance.

The imperial position on the debate was that Christians were Christians were Christians, and so they arrested and exiled *all* Christian leaders, no matter what their stance on the *lapsi* happened to be. Thus the emperors, who were trying to increase the divisiveness of the Christian sect, actually achieved the opposite: Novatianists and Confessors and the leaders in the middle all found themselves under arrest and discovered that they were not that different after all.

DURA-EUROPOS, EASTERN FRONTIER, SECOND
DAY BEFORE THE KALENTS OF JUNE (MAY 31)

VICTORY IS A POWERFUL APHRODISIAC, Valerianus told himself as he stood on the city walls looking down at the Euphrates River some seventy feet below. A chill ran up his spine and out his arms, as if this sensation of power were trying to burst from his fingertips. Never had he felt so alive, so *sure* of his own omnipotence. His friend Festus Macrinus talked endlessly about the adventures they had shared in their youth, and those memories still thrilled him. But this moment, *this* time in his life, was more, greater. His star was ascendant. Destiny within his grasp. He reached his hand out toward the horizon, where the rising sun was a bright, red blade slicing its way out of the earth. If his arm were a little longer, he could pluck the sun from the sky and swallow it. Never had his divinity seemed more real than it did at this moment.

He turned from his dreams and visions and descended the wall. Dura-Europos sat on a sheer cliff that plunged to the Euphrates. No enemy would attack it from that side, but the other walls needed reinforcements, especially the western wall by the Palmyrene Gate. Accompanied by his bodyguard and officers, he began marching through the town toward the western wall. The town was laid out in standard block formation, with straight streets that ran north to south and east to west. Many of the townsfolk had turned out to cheer their emperor's entrance via the Palmyrene Gate, and as he walked along, crowds began to form again along his route, as if somehow advance notice had been given of his destination. He smiled. Perhaps they did know; perhaps they had seen this coming.

They had arrived yesterday, the first day of the persecution of the Christians, after a long, quick march through Mesopotamia, snapping at Shapur's heels all the way. Shapur's strategy had become plain months ago. The retreating Persians had destroyed everything in their path, towns and villages flattened, crops burned, the livestock killed and left to bloat in the hot Mesopotamian sun. Only Death thrived in their wake. Valerianus admired his foe's resolve, but he cursed him for the difficulties it caused him. Troops had to be left behind at strategic points to defend the ever-lengthening supply lines. Sometimes supplies failed to arrive on schedule, and his soldiers started grumbling about half-rations and the lack of wine. Fortunately, his enemy had bypassed Dura-Europos and there was plenty of food for everyone.

Valerianus arrived at the final crossroad before the Palmyrene Gate. Like most Roman cities, many of the streets in Dura-Europos were named by occupation—Fuller's Street, Baker's Road, Wine-seller's Way. This street also had a suggestive name: Street of the Gods. From one end to the other, the buildings were dedicated to the many sects that made up the religious mosaic of the Roman Empire. A crowd had formed near Tower 17 on the wall. Obviously, they had divined his intentions. Something about that irritated him. Gallienus had failed to see where Valerianus had pushed him, yet here, they knew. Was he that easy to read?

He sloughed off the troubling thought as he came to a halt in front of a large building that backed onto the western wall. A unit of soldiers stood by the door guarding three men. The man in the middle was taller than the other two and overweight. He wore a tunic with a green belt and sandals. His double chin was beardless, his grey hair had receded on the sides to form a widow's peak in the middle of his forehead. Both his eyes were bruised. Two guards held him by the arms. "You are the *episcopus*?" Valerianus asked.

The man bowed. "*Episcopus* Pertinax, my lord emperor."

"This is your temple?"

"Our *ecclesia*. Yes, Your Excellency."

Valerianus pointed at the open doorway. "Show us," he said and gestured for the guard to release him.

Pertinax and his two associates led Valerianus and two members of his bodyguard inside. "This is the original house, Your Excellency," Pertinax explained. "Years ago, we held our meetings here, but when our numbers grew too large we purchased the building next door and knocked out the wall here." He gestured to an arch on the right and raised his eyebrows over his swollen eyes, as if to say, *Would you like to see more?*

Valerianus nodded and followed the portly *episcopus* into the second room. It was much larger, more of a hall than a simple room. At the west end of the room, where the ecclesia butted up against the city walls, was a stone altar. Metal candelabras on either side of the altar and at regular intervals along the walls provided light. The walls were covered with frescoes. "What do these signify?" Valerianus asked, pointing at the artwork on the walls.

"Ah," Pertinax sighed. Despite the circumstance, he grinned with real pleasure. "These frescoes tell the stories of our faith. Over here, Adam and Eve, the first man and woman created by God and the founders of the human race."

"This one here with the giant?" Valerianus asked.

"Another story from the *Scripturae*: David and Goliath. When David was but a youth he killed the mighty giant Goliath with his sling."

Valerianus laughed. "We do not believe that. We believe the giant would have crushed him. We believe the giant always wins, *episcopus*."

Pertinax glanced nervously at Goliath, then continued his description of the frescoes. "Over here are scenes from the life of the *Christos*: the healing of the paralytic, the *Christos* and Peter walking on water, and this one," he traced his finger lovingly over the wall, which showed three women walking towards an open tomb, "depicts the Resurrection."

"And what of those?" Valerianus asked, pointing at an open cabinet made of wood. Many scrolls rested on its shelves.

"Those are the *Scripturae* and books by other Christian authors."

"*Scripturae*?"

"Yes, Your Excellency. Holy books that tell the story of the Christos and some of his followers."

Valerianus gazed one last time around the hall, then turned his eyes on Pertinax. "You were arrested yesterday, you and your ..." He pointed at the two men with him.

"My presbyters. Yes, Your Excellency."

"You know why you were arrested?"

"Yes, Your Excellency."

Valerianus stood in front of the *episcopus*, his hands on his hips. "Explain the reason," he ordered.

"You ordered all Christian leaders to be arrested and sent into exile, Your Excellency."

"Why?"

Pertinax hesitated, then, "Because Christianity is illegal, Your Excellency."

Valerianus put out his hand to the tall guard who stood behind him, glaring at the prisoners. The guard pulled a long, double-edged knife from the sheath on his belt and handed it to the emperor by the hilt. The emperor stepped to the left. "Are you a Christian?" he asked the first presbyter.

"*Christianus sum*," he replied.

"Then I exile you to Hell," he decreed, and slit the presbyter's throat.

The presbyter dropped to his knees, his hands clutching at his throat. Blood pumped out between his fingers and splattered Valerianus' toga. As the man fell forward onto the floor, Valerians moved to the other presbyter. "Are you a Christian?" he asked the second presbyter.

The man's eyes darted to his companion, who lay dead on the floor, then jumped back to Valerianus. "*Christianus sum*," he said with a shaky voice.

"I exile you to the same place," the emperor decreed, and slit the second presbyter's throat. The man fell backward with his neck gaping open and was dead before he hit the floor.

Valerianus stepped in front of Pertinax. He plucked up the hem of Pertinax's tunic and cleaned the blood off the knife. "And you, Pertinax, tell me: are you an *episcopus*?"

Pertinax squared his shoulders and stared resolutely at the fresco of David and Goliath on the wall. "I am," he replied.

"You *were*," Valerianus corrected, and drove the knife into Pertinax's chest and through his heart.

As Pertinax crumpled to the floor, Valerianus handed the guard back his knife. "Have the bodies and those scrolls taken to the garbage dump outside the gate," he ordered."

The guard saluted.

Valerianus left the *ecclesia*. The crowd outside had multiplied. General Eutropus, his second-in-command, had arrived while he was touring the Christian temple. He was an efficient administrator and a brilliant strategist, whose ties to Syria and Mesopotamia made him indispensable. "Your Excellency, we must speak," he said.

Valerianus pointed to the ecclesia. "Christians," he spat, making the word sound like an obscenity. "Confiscate this *ecclesia* and all the other temples that back onto the western wall, and then have them filled with rubble. Shapur likes to undermine walls during a siege—so let's make it harder for him. If the Christians own any other properties in the city confiscate them, and appropriate any monies they have on deposit with the bankers. Use the proceeds to pay off the temple priests, that way the gods will not be angered."

"Yes, Your Excellency," General Eutropus said. He issued the orders to his tribune, then said to Valerianus, "News from the provinces, Your Excellency."

Valerianus' saw alarm creasing his general's brow and his heart dropped, but he allowed no sign to show on his face. "What news?" he asked.

"King Kniva, Your Excellency. The Goth fleet appeared off the shores of Galatia a few weeks ago. The Goths are roaming through Cappadocia, Galatia, and Bithynia unchecked, plundering one city after another."

Valerianus cursed.

Suddenly another of his generals elbowed his way through the crowd. The alarm on his face mirrored Eutropus'. "Shapur has returned!" he exclaimed. "The Persians are crossing the river. And they have siege towers this time."

Again Valerianus cursed. This morning as he stood on the wall gazing east he had seen the dawn glinting blood red on the towers of Ctesiphon, Shapur's capital. It had been a fantasy, a vision of victory to come, victory he had thought was almost in his grasp. Now he was at war on two fronts—Shapur ahead, Kniva behind.

Victory postponed.

Valerianus issued orders to General Memnon, who had brought him news of Shapur's attack. "Prepare for a siege."

Memnon yelled orders to his tribunes and hurried away.

Valerianus turned to General Eutropus. "We will leave Dura-Europos before Shapur encircles the city. Decius misjudged Kniva and lost his head; now I will have Kniva's head as trophy. Ready the legions, General: we march west to destroy the Goths once and for all."

GERMANIA INFERIOR
KALENDS OF JUNE (JUNE 1)

GALLIENUS' HORSE LUNGED OUT of the trees onto the grassy slope and broke into a gallop. The grass, already as high as his horse's knees, whispered as he passed, but the sound was lost beneath the crash of swords. The slope ended abruptly and he jerked in the reins. Three officers and a unit of bodyguards halted behind him. He urged the horse forward onto a flat, granite shelf that looked down on a narrow valley some thirty feet below, the perfect vantage point from which to witness the battle.

Two of his officers appeared on either side of him. There was no room on the outcropping for the third. The officer on his left, Tribune Cecropius, was young, late twenties, minimal experience. This was his first taste of real battle, and from the look on his face, he was wishing he had stayed on the family estate in Sicily. Gallienus disliked him. He was nothing but a senatorial brat whose father had used his influence and his money to assure his son's ascent up the ranks. After the campaigning season, he would transfer him, possibly to Africa, where he could do minimal damage. In fact, he was considering banning senators from *all* military command. How many times in the history of the empire had a senator abused his command to usurp the imperial throne? Even in the last fifty years it had happened too many times to count. Put a senator in charge of a few legions, and he started to wonder what he would look like draped in purple.

He grunted a laugh. His own family was an excellent example. Valerianus was the patriarch of a respected and wealthy senatorial family, and true to those roots, he had lusted after the imperial throne all his life. Fortunately, Valerianus was an able administrator and an adequate general, an exception to the rule which stated that senators rose to positions of power by patronage (and bribery) rather than ability. Gallienus wanted to replace aristocracy with meritocracy—merit rather than birthright—and thus had shown a distinct preference for equestrian commanders. The senate had already sent him several "official" and numerous individual complaints. It had not taken an augury for that august body to divine its future if Gallienus continued on his present course.

The man to his right was a different matter. General Aureolus was his Master of Horses, the man who commanded his new cavalry. Aureolus was a frontier man from Dacia who had started as a groom in the imperial stables, but had shown himself such a brilliant horseman that he had quickly moved up the ranks. He had been Gallienus' first, best choice for Master of Horses for his cavalry and had proved himself a capable commander. As a strategist he was unorthodox, but as long as Aureolus continued to win battles, Gallienus did not care.

Gallienus cursed under his breath. Why had he not told Aureolus to bring the cavalry when he had ordered the man north for a meeting of his generals? He stared at the carnage below. A line of Frankish warriors ran forward and hurled their throwing axes at the advancing Roman phalanx. The heavy iron axes shattered shields and sliced through limbs, leaving the Roman line open and vulnerable. With a war cry that echoed off the sheer valley walls, the Franks swooped in with their swords, hacked what remained of the Roman line to pieces, then pulled back to allow the axemen to open up the next line for them. And so the battle went, with the Franks rolling forward, and the Romans stumbling back.

"I estimate twenty-five thousand, Your Excellency," Aureolus said.

Gallienus gave a grim nod of agreement. "Where did they come from?" It was a rhetorical question that Aureolus attempted to answer.

"Back in Dacia when I was a boy, I heard stories about a great chief who formed a war band out of many different tribes and called it the *Franci*, which means 'fierce ones.'" He shrugged. "I don't know if it's true or not."

Gallienus winced as another volley of throwing axes shattered Roman shields. Men screamed in agony. "We have had small raiding parties of Franks before, but this . . ." He swept his hand across the battle field below them, letting the gesture finish the sentence for him.

"There," Aureolus said, pointing to the other side of the valley. Three Franks on horseback were darting in on the flanks of the Roman lines, swinging their axes then retreating before the Roman infantry could reply. "The large one in front is Merovech, the Frankish chief."

Gallienus studied his opponent. He was young, no more than twenty-five. Combs on either side of his head kept his long blond hair out of his face. The warriors beside him wore mail and iron helms, but Merovech was dressed only in leather breeches and a leather shirt. As if he thought he were invincible.

Merovech wheeled his horse around and galloped back to the mass of warriors and began yelling orders. In response, the Frankish vanguard formed a wedge, with the main host pushing in behind, as if the entire army were an axe aimed at the centre of the Roman lines. They charged forward and the front line buckled, hammered again and the line collapsed, and twenty-five thousand screaming Franks broke through the opening and swept all Roman resistance aside.

"Sound the retreat," Gallienus ordered.

It was an hour before the last of the Frankish warriors scrambled out the far end of the valley. Gallienus' officers were riding through the ranks, restoring order, numbering the wounded. He had already sent for reinforcements; they would set up camp here and await their arrival.

Gallienus rode across the battlefield with his bodyguard and General Aureolus, assessing the damage and planning his next move. Since assuming the imperial purple, he had spent most of his time repelling barbarian invaders. This was different. The Franks were organized, strong, united under a single, capable leader, and they had the numbers and desire to do irreparable damage. His initial strategy had been simple: bottle the Franks up in this narrow valley and destroy them. But they had broken through, and now all of Gallia lay before them, ripe for the plundering. Gallienus had no choice but to pursue them once reinforcements arrived. And he had already received news from his son—the Pannonian legions had taken to calling him Valerianus the Younger—and Commander Ingenuus informing him of an imminent invasion of Pannonia by the Marcomanni and the need for reinforcements there. So he must meet that challenge as well. Obviously, he had to send Commander Aureolus to Pannonia. But if he sent Aureolus east to Pannonia while he chased Franks into the west, it would leave the centre undefended. His advisors had assured him that all was quiet on the central frontier, but since those same advisors had assured him the Franks were not a threat, their advice did not inspire him with great confidence.

He halted and shifted in the saddle so he could see his Master of Horses. "Our meeting is cancelled for obvious reasons. Return to Mediolanum, then ride on to Pannonia. We have received word that the tribes will attack there soon."

"Yes, Your Excellency."

"Leave half the cavalry at Mediolanum."

"Yes, Your Excellency." Aureolus saluted, then wheeled about and galloped off.

Tribune Cecropius trotted over to inform him that his tent was ready. Gallienus grunted at him, then nudged his horse forward. He was exhausted and his shoulder ached. He'd have Theophilus, his physician, make him some of his special tea to ease the pain. His shoulder reminded him of the Christians, and he wondered absently how the persecution was proceeding. Very little news yet, but it had only started a few days ago. The chief magistrates at Castra Vetera and Augustabona had submitted reports that were almost identical. In both towns, the *episcopus* and his presbyters had been arrested, tried, and exiled.

At last Gallienus arrived at his tent. He dismounted and a groom led his horse away to be fed and watered. Inside, he ordered a slave to find Theophilus, then collapsed onto his dining couch and closed his eyes. His father had talked about converting the Christians back to the traditional Roman rites, but for the first time Gallienus wondered if that was likely under the present conditions. The threat of exile had not caused the *episcopi* of Castra Vetera and Augustabona to scramble to the altar and sacrifice to the gods. Sterner measures were necessary. Perhaps they should move the second phase of the persecution forward. Start it sooner.

He pushed himself up off the dining couch, went to his desk,

and rifled through the papers until he found the one he was looking for, the list that Festus Macrinus had prepared for him. Two
billion *denarii*, the estimated value of Christian holdings in Italy.
He thought of the Franks raping Gaul at this very moment, and
the men and weapons and horses that two billion *denarii* could
buy. He set the document back on the desk, then returned to the
couch.

Again he closed his eyes, and this time his mother's voice rang
in his ears:

Put the needs of others ahead of your own. That is true nobility. But
whose needs mattered most in this case? The needs of the Christians? Or the needs of the men and women and children that the
Frankish host would butcher if he could not raise an army large
enough to destroy them? Two irreconcilable choices.

Gallienus laughed at himself. That was a lie. He was trying to
use the Frankish invasion to justify the confiscation of Christian
property earlier than planned. But Valerianus was right—the persecution must not look like an attempt to fill the imperial coffers.
The *ideals* of the persecution came first: identify the lost, give them
the opportunity to return to the fold, and then punish them if they
resisted, but gently, like a father disciplining a child. Only when
every attempt to save them had failed would they lose their property, their wealth, and, ultimately, their lives. He would not permit greed to sully those ideals.

That was true nobility.

TWENTY

The Clan arrived at the Neckar River in Germania Superior just after dark. Here the Neckar, which flowed into the Rhine further north, was not too wide or too deep. They could ford it, but they had come to this spot to use the bridge, the *only* bridge that crossed the Neckar. From previous experience Valens knew that the Neckar bridge was the easiest way to cross the river. Certainly the *driest* way. On his last visit, the bridge had not been guarded. But things had changed since then. Now there was a unit of soldiers on the far bank. Obviously they were there to protect the bridge in the event that raiders made it through the maze of defences along the frontier. They would not stop the Clan crossing the bridge; it was not illegal to enter the *Agri Decumates*. The problem was that the soldiers would *see* the Clan crossing the bridge, which contradicted their goal of entering unseen. And if by some miracle they did cross without being seen, they still had to get by the *Limes Germanicus*, a defensive line that ran for several hundred miles and included sixty forts and over nine hundred watchtowers.

Valens glanced at Gundabar, who lay beside him in the darkness. The German shook his head. They crawled back from the slope which led down to the bridge, then, when they were sure they couldn't be seen, they got up and went back to the others.

"Well?" Damarra asked.

"The bridge is lit up with torches and guarded by soldiers," Valens replied.

"So we cannot make the crossing here."

"No."

"What do we do?"

Valens shrugged. "Pray for a miracle."

"I've been praying for that all along," she told him and kissed his cheek.

Valens turned to the others. "Rest while you can."

Gundabar and his guards dropped their heavy packs, then slipped into the darkness to keep watch. They had stopped at a small clearing in the trees covered by a soft, orange carpet of pine needles. Damarra, Persephone, and Prisca sat down and stretched out. Ruth was asleep in Damarra's arms, and in a few moments Damarra was asleep, too. Cecht, Conall's son, slipped his pack off and sat down with his back against a slim willow tree, and soon he was asleep as well.

Conall, Sukuta, and Valens crouched down to discuss their options. They had arrived at the estate in Germania Superior three days ago. The trip north from Massalia had been uneventful. Once a unit of soldiers had hurried past on their way south, but otherwise the road had belonged to them and a few farmers and merchants. The first day of the persecution was something of an anticlimax: there was no indication on the road that the persecution had even started. Their first evidence that imperial policy had changed occurred near the city of Noviomagus. Two soldiers were guarding the entrance to a small building beside the road. A third soldier was clapping chains on the wrists of an elderly man dressed in a roughspun brown tunic. The placard hanging from the man's neck read, *Christianus Sum*. The sight of that sign stirred old memories for Valens. Damarra too, from the look of fear that had marred her beautiful face.

They had spent a day resting at his estate, then redistributed the provisions they had brought in the wagons, which they were leaving behind. This morning, before dawn, they had begun the last stage of their journey. Now they were here at the Neckar River on the doorstep of the *Agri Decumates*. And he had no idea what to do next.

Please, Lord Christos, he prayed. *Show us the way.*

A branch snapped behind him and he glanced over his shoulder. His hand fell to the hilt of his sword. Gundabar emerged from the trees and they stood up. "What is it?" Valens asked.

"A rider," Gundabar whispered.

Quickly they woke the women and Cecht and everyone moved into the trees and crouched in the shadows. A minute passed and then they heard it: the dull clop of iron-shod hooves on the soft earth. A horse and rider came into view, framed in the light of the rising moon. Halfway across the small clearing he reigned in his horse. His head turned right, then left. "I think I smell my Clan," he chuckled.

Damarra jumped up. "Marcus," she exclaimed. Then they were all up and surrounding him. He jumped from the horse, and they spent the next few moments hugging and shaking hands, and talking excitedly—but quietly—with the new arrival. "How did you find us?" Sukuta asked.

Marcus smiled. "That God of mine you don't believe in told me where to look."

Sukuta shook his head. "Luck," he grunted.

Marcus explained what had happened, how Gallienus had sent him to Gallia to look after Damarra and Valens, and how the *Christos* had come to him and told him not to continue south to Massalia, but to turn east and ride to the *Agri Decumates*. "I knew as soon as He told me that that the Clan had finally set out for Germania." He glanced around. "Which means the 'other' finally arrived. So where is he? Or her?"

Valens sent Gundabar to fetch Xerxes. When Valens had discovered that Xerxes was a cavalry officer with the Persian Cataphracts, he had put Xerxes to work as a guard, too. Gundabar and Valens had organized a training regimen for all the guards that combined the best techniques of Germanic and Roman warfare, and since Xerxes' arrival the guards had trained daily in preparation for this journey. Valens wanted them thinking and acting like a team.

Valens had left Gundabar in charge of security—they were about to enter his homeland where his knowledge would be one of their primary assets. He had contemplated leaving Paulus as second-in-command, but after prayerful consideration had settled on General Marcus instead. Paulus was an excellent guard, but he was not a member of the Clan—the *Christos* had not chosen him—and Valens knew in his heart somehow that key positions must be held by Clan members. How he knew, he could not say, but he did know it and would abide by that . . . instinct? Divine revelation, perhaps?

Now that General Marcus was here, he would serve as Gundabar's second. Valens and Marcus had gotten off to a rocky start, and Valens still had some reservations about the general, but Marcus was an experienced soldier and strategist, and that made him an asset to the Clan.

Gundabar returned with Xerxes and Valens introduced him to Marcus. It was the first time all the Clan had come together, and a part of Valens expected something extraordinary to happen, but the darkness around them stayed dark and the crickets continued their night song. Marcus asked to see the bridge and the soldiers guarding it, so he, Valens, and Xerxes crept up to the top of the slope and lay there on their bellies and studied the scene below. "How deep is the water here?" Marcus asked.

"Deep enough," Valens replied. "We could cross on the horses, let them do the work, but it would mean building a raft to keep the provisions and our gear dry. We'd need to go upstream or downstream to do that, out of earshot of those soldiers."

"A distraction," Xerxes suggested. "I jump up, show myself, then while the soldiers are chasing me, the rest of the Clan crosses the bridge. I then lose the soldiers, double back, and meet you on the other side."

Valens shook his head. "It would take more than one man to lead all those soldiers away."

"A good point," Marcus said. "Not all of them would chase you. They would leave some behind to guard the bridge."

Xerxes smiled. "What if I told them the Shahanshah Shapur had sent me?"

Valens and Marcus laughed. Xerxes had a delightful sense of humour, something the Clan had learned quickly after the Persian arrived.

Suddenly there was a commotion below. They heard shouts and saw lights bobbing through the trees on the far side of the bridge. A soldier appeared, carrying a torch, and began talking excitedly to the guards. From their vantage point they could not make out any words, but the results were obvious: suddenly the entire unit drew their swords and ran off into the woods in the direction from which the soldier with the torch had come. The *entire* unit.

The bridge was now unguarded.

Marcus and Xerxes glanced at each other and grinned. "The *Christos*," Xerxes whispered, and Marcus nodded his agreement.

They scurried back to the others and told them what had happened.

"Why did they go?" Paulus asked.

Valens shook his head. "We don't know why, but we need to cross now, while there's no one to see us. Let's go."

They grabbed their packs and their horses and hurried up the hill, then down the far slope to the bridge. Torches flickered on both sides. The fire reflected off the sluggish waters of the Neckar. The world was suddenly quiet. The crickets had ceased chirping, and even the water flowed by without a sound. They crossed the bridge in single file; the echo of their horses' hooves off the stone seemed unnaturally loud in the silence. On the other side of the bridge was a small stone hut. Valens looked inside as they filed past. A table, a wineskin, a few javelins standing in the corner—a guard hut. But no guards.

Valens grinned as he lead the Clan back into the woods. He had prayed for a miracle and the *Christos* had delivered one: they had entered the *Agri Decumates* unseen. His mind whispered doubts at him, *Only sixty forts and nine hundred watchtowers to go,* as if the need for an even greater miracle somehow negated the miracle they had just witnessed. But he shut out the despair before it could take hold. He was "*Sankt*," the Clan Chief, and leadership could be a lonely, thankless task; but he was also a servant of the *Christos*, the Chief of chiefs, and if the *Christos* wanted them to go to Germania—and He did—then they would go to Germania. And not even Valerianus and all his legions could stop them.

THE FOREST REMINDED ULF of his home in the north, a land of pines and brambles and cold winters. He slowed to duck under a low branch, then picked up the pace again. As a child, he had loved running through the trees in the moonlight like his namesake, the wolf, with the quiet of the night whispering in his ears. Sometimes he regretted leaving his homeland, but what else could he have done? He was the fifth son of a poor Saxon farmer who had sold three of his own children to Roman traders, just to try and keep the other six alive. Ulf had no desire to spend his life scratching a living out of the tough northern soil like his father had, and even *less* desire to end up a slave. So, at the age of fourteen, he had crossed the Rhine and joined up. He had not been back to Germania since, but he was going back now and he was thrilled about it. He would never tell Dionysius or Licander that, but it was true.

He leapt over a rotting log into the clearing where the others were waiting. Dionysius saw his jump and stood up. Like the rest of them he wore civilian clothes—tunic, sandals, and a short cape. It was not wise to enter Germania in uniform, unless you had an army with you. "What took you so long?" he snapped.

Ulf kept the grin from his face. There were seven of them all together—Ulf, Licander, Dionysius, and the three soldiers they had requisitioned from the barracks in Massalia. Tacitus had insisted that one of the *Agentes* accompany them, so he had sent a big man in his thirties named Siricius. Dionysius was the only one who seemed angry to be here. For a year and a half now, they had been keeping Valens and his beautiful wife under surveillance. Most of that time Dionysius had spent at Ursula's, drinking wine and playing house with the owner. Now he had to leave all that wine and the bed he shared with Ursula for a hike through Germania with six men. Was it any wonder he was annoyed? "I had to wait until they made a move, Commander."

Dionysius grunted.

"They crossed the Neckar by the bridge."

"I thought they didn't want to be seen?"

"That's the strange part—the guards at the bridge ran off somewhere, left it unguarded. The Clan just walked across the bridge like they owned it.'

Dionysius picked up his pack. "Then I guess we should do the same."

ON THE RIGHT BANK OF THE NECKAR, a trail led off to the northeast. The Clan led the horses into the woods and picked a path parallel to the trail, but far enough away from it that they would not be seen. Soon the trees, mostly pine and spruce with a smattering of large beech, began to thin out and they made better time. They had travelled about a mile when they heard shouting off to their right and stopped to listen. The language was Latin, but they could not make out what was being said, so they edged forward until they were close enough to hear a few words. From the tone, the speaker was issuing orders. They heard "man" and "coming" and then silence again. The Clan withdrew and continued northeast.

They saw their first watchtower ten minutes later. It was rectangular and about twenty feet high. Beneath its peak roof, a gallery circled the tower; torches were lit at each corner. Three soldiers stood on the gallery gazing north, an arrow nocked in their bows. They were so still they looked like statues.

Damarra's hand slipped into Valens' and he turned to look at her. Her face was just visible in the moonlight. "What's going on?" she whispered.

He shrugged and squeezed her hand.

A man stepped out of the trees just north of their position. He must have been there all along, but they had not seen him. Nor had the soldiers in the tower. His tall body moved cat-like through the shadows until he reached the door at the tower's base. A knife appeared in his hand; he held it up, let the moon glint off its blade, then froze like the soldiers on the gallery.

"Alamanni," Gundabar whispered.

A flaming arrow sailed out of the darkness and struck the tower just below the gallery. Instantly the dry wood burst into flames. The soldiers on the tower returned a volley of arrows. A second fiery arrow arced back in response, piercing a soldier's leg and igniting his tunic. Screaming in pain, he dropped and rolled, but instead of extinguishing the flames, the fire spread to the gallery. A third arrow set the tower roof ablaze, and the two remaining soldiers dropped their bows and raced into the tower and down the stairs. A few seconds later they scrambled out of the burning tower, only to have their throats cut by the warrior waiting outside.

"Alamanni raiding party," Marcus said.

Suddenly the northern horizon was ablaze with light in a line that stretched out to the east and west as far as the eye could see. A battle cry erupted from the Alamanni host, a sound so loud that it shook the earth beneath the Clan's feet. Valens glanced at Marcus who was gaping at the advancing Alamanni line, then at Damarra who was clutching his hand so hard that it hurt. "By the gods," Sukuta swore behind him. Persephone began to pray out loud, but her voice was drowned out by the rumble of Alamanni feet racing toward them. Gundabar drew his sword and took Persephone into his arms.

"What do we do?" Paulus cried at the top of his voice.

"Pray," Valens yelled back.

"Pray?" Paulus screamed, and even through the crescendo of the Alamanni advance, Valens could hear his incredulity.

Valens closed his eyes, pulled Damarra and Ruth into his arms, and began to pray. There was nothing else they could do now. It was too late to run, too late even to mount their horses and ride in the opposite direction. This was not just some raiding party out for a quick pillage: this was an invasion. The entire Alamanni nation was sweeping into the *Agri Decumates* like a tidal wave, and when it crashed down on them they would be swept away.

DIONYSIUS AND HIS PARTY had just crossed the Neckar when they heard feet running down the trail toward the bridge. Three soldiers raced out of the darkness. Dionysius readied his patented explanation as he dismounted: *We are merchants going to Germania to establish trading ties with the Alamanni.* If that didn't work, he'd pull out the emperor's letter. But that was a last resort.

The soldiers didn't slow down, didn't even look at Dionysius and his men. In less than a minute they crossed the bridge and were racing up the bank on the far side. "What was that all about?" Licander asked.

More soldiers emerged from the darkness. Some were running down the trail; others stumbled out of the woods. Most were making for the bridge, but a few crashed down the bank and jumped into the Neckar without stopping to remove their armour. Soon there were fleeing soldiers everywhere. Dionysius spotted one wearing nothing but his tunic. He had obviously tossed away his armour and weapons so he could run faster. Dionysius grabbed the front of his tunic in his big fist and lifted the struggling man up to his face. "What's happened?" he asked.

"The Alamanni are attacking!" he exclaimed.

"How many?" Dionysius asked.

"All of them!"

Dionysius set the man down. "All of them? Are you sure?"

The man nodded. "And the Juthungi, too. They're destroying everything in their path. The watchtowers and forts are burning. The whole line is gone. If you're smart you'll get out of here now." And with that he fled over the bridge.

Ulf looked nervously at Dionysius. "Are we smart, Commander?" he asked.

With a grunt of disgust, Dionysius led his men back over the bridge.

JUST BEFORE THE ALAMANNI host reached them, Valens drew his sword. He was one man against ten thousand, probably twice that, but he would take down as many warriors as he could before they killed him. He had vowed to give his life for Damarra and his child, the way the *Christos* had given His life for His children. Now the time had come to keep that vow. He opened his eyes. One of the Alamanni warriors was almost on top of him. He could see the man's deep blue eyes, the scars on his cheeks, the wild designs tattooed on his forehead.

And then the man was gone.

Valens jerked his head around. There was the warrior, behind them, as if . . . as if he had run right *through* them! Valens turned back and saw more warriors screaming towards him, hundreds of them, *thousands* . . . and yet he and his family, the horses, the entire

Clan, remained untouched. The warriors were flowing around them, over them, through them, as if they were nothing but dreams without form or mass. Wave after wave of Alamanni crashed down upon them and then were gone without drawing a single drop of Clan blood. Finally the last few stragglers of the host raced by them, yelling curses at the Roman dogs, threatening the wrath of Odin upon their cowardly heads. The watchtower collapsed; fire flared and sparks shot up into the darkness. The night quieted again, crickets began their love song, and one by one the members of Valens' Clan began to stir.

"What just happened?" Sukuta asked. Valens had never heard such wonder in the slave's voice.

"They went right by us, right *through* us," Conall said.

"Impossible," said Paulus.

Valens dropped to his knees and began to pray out loud, praising God and thanking him for the miracle they had just witnessed. Damarra and Ruth dropped down beside him, then Persephone, Gundabar, Conall, Marcus, Cecht, Xerxes, and, finally, Paulus. The others stood by quietly, respectfully—they were not believers, but they could not deny that something miraculous had just happened. They should all be dead, but instead they were all alive.

For some reason the Alamanni had not been able to see them.

After their prayers of thanksgiving, the Christians rose and embraced one another, and then they moved on. They no longer worried about attracting attention. There was no one here to see them now. Except for the Clan, the *Agri Decumates* was devoid of human life. A few hours later they came upon another line of watchtowers, or what was left of them. All of them had been torched by the advancing Alamanni host. Here and there they passed the bodies of soldiers, even a few Alamanni warriors. But most of the legions stationed in the *Agri Decumates* had fled before the unexpected Alamanni attack.

At dawn they came to a stone protruding from the ground like a single tooth in an old woman's gums. The stone was three feet high and painted white; a single word was carved into the stone's face. Valens dismounted, traced his finger over the word, then whispered it aloud:

GERMANIA

A simple white stone. Such an insignificant thing. And yet the division it represented had plunged the Roman world into a crisis that might lead to the destruction of the empire. He turned to the Clan. "Do we spend one more day in the empire?" he asked, then stepped to the other side of the stone. "Or our first day in Germania?"

"Or half and half," Xerxes said. "We can camp right on the line."

The Clan laughed.

Damarra picked up Ruth and went to her husband. She touched his cheek, and he bent over and kissed her. "Rome or Germania," she said. "It doesn't matter as long as we're together."

"What do you think, Ruth?" Valens asked. "Rome or Germania?"

The little blond girl looked around and asked, "Where are we, Daddy?"

"Germania," he said.

"Stay here," Ruth said. "I too tired to go to Rome."

Valens and Damarra laughed at Ruth, who gave them a bright smile, then laid her head on Damarra's shoulder. "I too tired, too," Valens said. He stroked his daughter's snowy blond hair. "So let's spend the night in Germania."

TWENTY-ONE

Like *locusts,* Dionysius thought as he watched the mass of Alamanni and Juthungi warriors swarm past their hiding place. He had spent several years in sub-Roman Africa in his youth, as a one-fifth partner in a slaving venture, and he had once seen locusts swarming. The swarm had been so vast that it blackened the sky when it was on the move, and wherever it touched down it consumed everything—not a blade of grass was left in its wake.

Out on the plain, a Roman general rallied his troops and made a stand, but nothing seemed to hinder the barbarian's forward momentum. The Alamanni trampled the Romans beneath their stampeding feet and carried on to the rich pillaging fields of Germania Superior and Rhaetia. By sunset all that remained of the Alamanni was the memory of their passing, written in crushed grass and the bodies of fallen Roman legionaries.

They emerged from their hiding place in the trees and set up camp. There was no point in continuing in the dark—there might be no point in continuing at all. Valens and his Clan could not have survived the Alamanni onslaught. The Alamanni had taken no prisoners. They had either trampled the Clan to death or butchered it. But Dionysius had to be sure. His career and his life depended on it.

Early the next morning they broke camp and rode back to the

Neckar River. The surface of the bridge was scuffed white by the passing of so many feet. Dead saplings littered the woods; the undergrowth was crushed. The trail leading up out of the Neckar River valley had been grass covered; now the grass was gone and the black dirt showed the prints of thousands of warriors.

They spread out into the trees, looking for some sign of the Clan. The first watchtower was a smoking ruin. Ulf found three sets of footprints by the base of the tower, but two of them bore hobnail imprints—Roman soldiers—and the third had been wearing leather boots—an Alamanni warrior. He deduced that the charred remains near the prints belonged to the two soldiers.

No sign that the Clan had been here.

Dionysius and his men pushed on, studying the prints on the ground as they went. The Alamanni had come without their females, so any smaller prints they found had to belong to one of the women—Damarra, Persephone, or Prisca—or the child, Ruth. Spotting their small prints beneath those left by the Alamanni host was impossible, but they tried anyway.

At midday Dionysius ordered the men to take a break, and he threw himself down on the loamy earth and closed his eyes. He was at an impasse. Logic told him that the Clan was gone. Dead. Nothing standing in the path of the Alamanni host had survived, and they had found no evidence that the Clan had gotten out of the way, no evidence of the Clan at all. He could hear the men grumbling; they thought he was asleep. He heard Licander whisper, "This is pointless," and he felt the same way.

And yet . . .

His instincts were nagging him, screaming at him, and his instincts had never steered him wrong. Somehow the Clan *had* survived. He had no proof, but he knew it was true.

He sat up. Instantly his men quieted and turned to look at him, waiting for orders. He read their discouragement in the stoop of their shoulders, but none of them complained out loud. They wouldn't dare. Tacitus' man, Siricius, was big—6'2" and two hundred fifty pounds, but he was tiny compared to Dionysius. Yet it wasn't his size that made his men obey. They respected him, even liked him. He knew how to have a good time when he was off duty, but on-duty he was a different man, serious, conscientious, a professional who was proud of his ability to transform any ragtag group of men into a unit of soldiers that knew how to follow orders and get the job done. "Let's go," Dionysius ordered, and pushed himself up.

They found their first sign that the Clan had survived the Alamanni onslaught an hour later. Dionysius had sent Ulf, who was the best tracker of the unit, on ahead to forage for clues. He returned with a piece of torn, white cloth and a grin on his narrow face. Dionysius took the cloth and examined it, but it was what it looked like: a piece of cloth. "I found it tied to a branch," Ulf said.

"Tied?"

Ulf nodded.

Dionysius grinned back at the Saxon. 'Tied' meant 'on purpose.' Someone was marking the path, showing them the way. So their informant had survived and some of the Clan, too.

At dusk they found a campsite, just past the boundary stone that marked the frontier between the empire and Germania. A thin wisp of smoke curled up from the embers. There were prints everywhere—the Alamanni host had obviously entered the empire here—but right next to the fire Ulf found two small footprints the size of his palm.

Ruth.

The Clan had camped here.

"Make camp for the night," Dionysius ordered. The men dismounted and sloughed off their packs. Siricius and Matthias, one of the soldiers from Massalia, went off to find firewood while the others began setting up the tents. Dionysius turned east and studied the route they would take in the morning. Low mountains studded with trees rolled out before him. They had dried rations, enough to last for weeks if need be, and after that there was plenty of game. They would not starve. With Ulf's tracking skills, following their quarry would be easy. Valerianus' most recent orders were very explicit: if the opportunity arose, he wanted Valens and Damarra brought to him. Alive. And *only* if it could be done without arousing Gallienus' suspicions.

A tall order. Impossible, he had thought. But not anymore. Now that the Clan was in Germania, they were beyond Gallienus' protection. Dionysius could arrest them at any time without Gallienus ever knowing, but he had no intention of doing that. Right now his plan was to keep out of their way, let them attend this gathering they were going to, a *Thing*, the German had called it. Every mile they travelled east was another mile closer to Valerianus. So they were saving him the trouble of transporting prisoners!

THE CLAN STOPPED EARLY THAT EVENING, a full hour before sunset. By Valens' calculations they had travelled fifteen miles since dawn. Since Gundabar had supplied no set destination, Valens had no idea whether to push the Clan or just plod along. He liked the idea of plodding, taking their time. Thanks to the Alamanni invasion they had entered Germania unseen. No one knew where they were, and only the *Christos* knew their destination. Might as well enjoy the journey.

Gundabar organized the men into three teams for guard duty and hunting: Gundabar and Alexander, Marcus and Regulus, and Xerxes and Paulus. Valens complained that he should take a turn as well, so Gundabar created a fourth team: Valens and Sukuta. The first three teams he sent out to hunt; Valens and Sukuta remained with the women. All three teams were successful—five rabbits between them—and so that night they feasted on rabbit and saved their dried rations for another day.

Afterwards, as the sun slowly sank into the west, they sat around the campfire talking and laughing. Everyone's spirits were high. Xerxes entertained them with some humorous anecdotes about his homeland, and Gundabar sang a song in his native tongue. Gundabar had a beautiful tenor voice that enthralled them all from the very first note, even though they couldn't understand the words. As near as Conall could make out, the song was about a young Suevi warrior searching for his lost love, who had been snatched away by a band of raiders. After he finished, Ruth climbed up in his lap and gave him a hug, then fell asleep in his arms. "You will make a fine father one day," Persephone told him and kissed his cheek.

Gundabar blushed.

Marcus got up. "In all the excitement, I forgot that I have a message for you, Lord Valens," he said.

"The imperial post is so efficient it can find me in Germania!" Valens joked.

Marcus laughed as he went to his horse. He returned with a dispatch pouch and handed it to Valens. Valens opened it, then took out the contents. On top was a letter asking Valens and Damarra to join the emperor in northern Gaul "for their own safety." Beneath that was a letter of transit, which they could use to pay for the journey, if they decided to take Gallienus up on his offer. *A lot of good that'll do us out here*, Valens thought as he shuffled the first two letters to the bottom of the pile.

The third document was a letter of imperial protection. He read it twice. Basically it forbid anyone to harm the bearer of the letter on pain of death. Of course, like the letter of transit, the letter of imperial protection was useless out here. They could hardly stop a charging warrior and hand him the letter and expect him to obey. Valens shuffled that document to the bottom as well.

He glanced at the next document and sucked in breath. "What is this?" he asked Marcus.

Marcus looked across the fire at him and shrugged. "I'm just the bearer; I didn't read it."

Valens held up a piece of parchment. "This is a Certificate of Sacrifice. With *my* name on it."

Marcus furrowed his eyebrows. "Let me see."

Valens handed the document to Damarra on his left and it went around to Marcus. He studied it, then looked up at Valens. "You're right. It is." He handed it back around the circle.

Valens fanned out the rest of the papers. They were all certificates of sacrifice. One for Damarra, one for Ruth, one for Marcus, the rest unnamed but signed by the emperor himself. Fifteen of them altogether. Valens felt a surge of rage that he just barely contained. "Why would he send these?" Valens asked.

Marcus shook his head. "I'm . . . not sure. He told me they were only targeting Christian leaders." He hesitated, then, "These certificates suggest he's planning to target *everyone*—just like Decius."

Valens read the one with his name on it again. "How *dare* he put my name on one of these filthy documents."

"Think of it as a gift," Marcus suggested. "Gallienus was just trying to help."

"I do *not* need that kind of help," Valens scoffed.

Marcus gave an exasperated sigh. "All I am saying is that you should thank him for caring instead of—"

"*Thank* him?" Valens cried. He crumpled the certificate in his fist and threw it in the flames. "I will not deny the *Christos*," he said through clenched teeth. "I will not sacrifice, and I will not *pretend* to have sacrificed." He held up the second certificate and turned to his wife. "Damarra?"

She shook her head. Her eyes pleaded with him to control his anger, but he was already past that point. He tore her certificate and Ruth's to shreds, then threw the pieces into the fire. Then he gave a certificate to each of the non-Christians—Sukuta, Regulus, Prisca, and Alexander.

Sukuta shrugged. "Don't really need one out here anyway," he said, and tossed his in the fire. The others followed suit.

Finally, he addressed the other Christians. "Gundabar?" he asked.

The German laughed, and his certificate went into the fire.

"Persephone?"

Into the fire.

"Xerxes?"

Into the fire.

"Conall? Cecht?"

Into the fire.

"Paulus?"

Into the fire.

Finally, he turned to Marcus. "And you, General? Will you take this *gift*, or resign it to the flames where it belongs?"

"Do I have a choice?" Marcus asked.

"Do you need one?" Valens replied.

The voices grew hotter and louder with each word. Ruth woke with a start and began to cry; Gundabar cuddled her closer.

"*Enough*," Damarra snapped. She snatched the remaining certificates from her husband, handed one to Marcus, then tossed the rest in the fire. Marcus threw his in as well. "There is no point in getting everyone worked up about this," she said.

Valens grunted an apology, then stood up and strode off into the trees. Marcus got up and went the opposite direction. Damarra rolled her eyes at Persephone. "And *that* is what happens when you marry a stubborn man," she warned.

AFTER BREAKING CAMP THE NEXT MORNING, Valens consulted Gundabar on where they should go next. Valens was Clan leader, but by unspoken consent Gundabar was the navigator—it was he the *Christos* had contacted in the first place, and until the *Christos* declared otherwise, they would follow Gundabar's directions. And so for the next several weeks they continued due east. The landscape remained hilly and thickly forested. Pine and beech predominated, but on occasion they would pass through a stand of ancient oaks with a canopy so dense that it blocked out the sunshine. Streams were so abundant that they were tempted not to fill their leather water bags, but Gundabar insisted. Sometimes when the trees thinned out they were able to ride and cover a greater distance, but normally they walked and led the horses. None of them felt the need to hurry.

Valens tried to coax Damarra into riding even when the horses had to be led. She still did not look pregnant, although one night she had confided excitedly to her husband that she had missed her monthly flow, but he wanted to make sure that Damarra and their baby—*babies*—remained healthy. Ruth preferred to ride on Sukuta's shoulders when they had to walk—he was the tallest and she could see the most from that perch. As far as Ruth was concerned, Sukuta was the most interesting person in the universe. He knew the names of all the flowers and the trees, and he kept her enthralled for hours on end with his stories and poems. Gundabar usually led Persephone's horse or walked with her in the cool of the morning, often holding her hand as if they were two young lovers out for a stroll in the forest. It was obvious to everyone that Gundabar and Persephone had feelings for each other, and that those feelings were growing stronger day by day. Valens had also noted some of the other men looking at Persephone—she was beautiful and unmarried, after all. Twice he had caught Paulus staring sidelong at her, and he had overheard Sukuta tell Conall that when he read the Iliad, he always pictured Helen of Troy with Persephone's face. Alexander seemed especially smitten with her. Whenever Gundabar rode off to scout ahead, Alexander took his place at Persephone's side. Even Conall's son Cecht was not immune to her charms—he had taken to leaving flowers by her bedroll each morning.

The biggest surprise was Xerxes and Prisca. In Gallia they had never so much as looked at each other. But from the moment the Clan entered Germania, they had been inseparable. They usually rode together, or she would ride and Xerxes would lead her horse as well as his own. He shared his adventures in the Persian cavalry, and she regaled him with stories of all the babies she had delivered (which he openly admitted was far more frightening than anything he had encountered on the battlefield). At times he talked to her about the *Christos*. His family had been Christian for four generations. In fact, he was proud to say that his ancestor was the very first Persian Christian, converted by Thomas himself as the apostle travelled through Persia on his way to India. Prisca had never thought much about Christianity, even though her owners were Christian. But having thousands of Alamanni warriors run past her as if she were invisible had piqued her interest in the sect, that and the warmth in Xerxes' rich, black eyes when he talked about his God.

One day about mid-afternoon Valens found himself walking beside Marcus. They had had little contact since their argument that first evening, but now they were together and chatting as if nothing had happened. Valens had forgotten about it, but then a memory of Marcus stalking away from the fire flashed before his mind's eye. "I want to apologize to you, Marcus," Valens said.

Marcus veered to the left, to avoid a fallen tree. "For what?" he asked.

Evidently, he had forgotten the incident, too. "The certificates of sacrifice? I should not have gotten angry with you; it was not your fault. And you're right—Gallienus was just trying to help."

"All is forgiven," Marcus said.

"May I ask you a question?" Valens asked.

"As long as I may refuse to answer."

Valens laughed, as did Damarra, who was resting on horseback while Valens led. "Good for you, Marcus," she said.

"Isn't the good wife in Proverbs supposed to be silent while her husband is talking?" Valens teased.

"Isn't it true that the Devil can quote scripture?" Damarra countered.

Valens winced. "You win, my love." He winked at Marcus. "You may refuse to answer if you wish."

"Then, please, ask your question." They came to a spring bubbling up out of the ground and Marcus stopped to drink. "You should try it," he said. "It's sweet."

Valens tasted it and agreed. They emptied their water bags and filled them from the spring. When they were on their way again, Valens asked his question: "What made Gallienus start another persecution?"

"An attempt was made on his life."

"And what bearing does that have?"

"The assassin was a Christian."

"A Christian assassin? How can that be?"

"I asked myself the very same question."

"How did they know the man was a Christian?"

"He had a Christian symbol tattooed here." Marcus touched his biceps.

Valens thought about it, then shrugged. "I suppose if I were Gallienus, that would have convinced me."

Marcus nodded. "And there were other factors."

"Gallienus mentioned Christians stirring up the tribes."

"And he was right—the Christians *were* stirring up the tribes. But not in the way he thought they were. They were missionaries, trying to stir up the German heart for the *Christos*, not the German hatred of Rome. But I could not make Gallienus understand the difference. To him Christianity is illegal, so any contact Christians have with Rome's enemies is just further proof of their treason."

They heard twigs snapping in the trees to their right. "A deer," Marcus whispered and grabbed his bow.

Instead of a deer, Paulus suddenly dashed out from behind a thicket of wild raspberries. Sweat dotted his bearded face. His long hair, which he normally kept tied back with a strip of leather, was loose. He was winded. "What is it?" Valens asked.

He bent over, hands on his knees, sucking in air to catch his breath. "Someone . . . is . . . following us . . . Lord Valens," he gasped.

TWENTY-TWO

SOUTHERN GALLIA
MID-JULY A.D. 257

The Franks were done marauding in Gallia.

For the last month and a half they had run rampant across the southwestern reaches of the province. They had sacked cities and towns and looted their wealth. They had burned fields of summer wheat and destroyed vineyards that had provided the empire with some of its finest wine. They had slaughtered cattle for their feasts, kidnapped and raped maidens and called it love, and now Gallia was groaning under the weight of the butchers who were cutting her up and consuming the pieces. Gallienus had chased them from one nest to the next. He had accosted their rear endlessly. He had met them in battle on four separate occasions, but each time Merovech had slipped through his grasp. And when they counted the dead at the end of the day, the tally always favoured the Franks.

Gallienus stood at the edge of southwestern Gaul, staring up at the Pyrenees, the mountain range that separated Gallia from the rich province of Hispania. The earth here was stripped raw, chafed by the feet of its tormenters as they marched up into the mountain fastnesses. The emperor's heart urged him to press on, pursue the Franks, run them to ground, exterminate them.

But the Franks were done marauding in Gallia.

Behind him the Alamanni and Juthungi were laying waste to

Germania Superior and Rhaetia. The Rhaetian legions had taken a chunk out of them, slowed them down, but they had not stopped them, and south of Rhaetia lay a province Gallienus could not permit the enemy to pillage, a province that no barbarian army had entered in hundreds of years.

The province of Italy.

Rome itself.

If the Alamanni did to Italy what the Franks had done to southern Gallia, then Gallienus was finished. The Roman psyche would never recover from such a blow to its ego. He could hear those old fools in the senate now:

Barbarians on Italian soil?

Barbarians at the gates of Rome?

That would not happen if I were emperor . . .

Gallienus shivered with rage. If he could not protect Italy, a usurper would rise to take his place. And he would come from the senate; they always came from the senate.

Gallienus heard a rumble, as if some giant buried at the root of the mountains had stirred. Rocks bounced down the slope, starting an avalanche of scree. He jumped aside to avoid the rockslide.

The gods warning him not to pursue the Franks any further.

"Tribune," Gallienus said.

Tribune Cecropius snapped to attention.

"Inform my generals—we make for Rhaetia."

Tribune Cecropius saluted, then jumped into the saddle and raced back to camp. Gallienus' mouth twisted in a sneer. Cecropius. Another senatorial darling. He was too young now, too inexperienced, but some day Cecropius would succumb to the delusions of grandeur that motivated all senators and make a bid for the throne. But Gallienus was bored by that cycle and intended to put a stop to it once and for all. He mounted his horse and returned to camp.

His legions were already breaking camp, but Gallienus' tent had not yet been taken down. He summoned his scribe, then went to his desk and dictated a letter to Festus Macrinus at Rome, warning him of the potential Alamanni invasion. Part of the Praetorian Guard had accompanied Valerianus east to supplement his bodyguard and his elite infantry. The rest had remained at Rome and in the barracks south of the city. Gallienus ordered Festus to call up the guard and prepare to defend the city against the Alamanni. The size of the guard was insufficient to stop the Alamanni host, but that did not matter. Even if the Alamanni did invade Italy, the chances of them reaching Rome were few. The cities of northern Italy were rich prizes that would occupy Alamanni greed long enough for Gallienus to get his legions to Italy and sweep down on them from behind. But the senate must see that their emperor had not left Rome totally undefended. They must see the praetorians standing between them and the barbarians. They must not set aside their dedication to the pursuit of pleasure and consider more serious subjects, such as defence or attack.

Or rebellion.

DURA-EUROPOS
MESOPOTAMIA

Spies from the city had given Shapur the news early that morning: Valerianus had slipped away just before the siege of Dura started; he had returned to Asia Minor. The fool had chosen to deal with the Goth King instead of the King of kings himself.

Shapur had learned of the Goth invasion of the provinces of Asia Minor long before Valerianus. Several years ago, Shapur had sent ambassadors to Kniva. Kniva sat on the shores of the Black Sea and could harass Persia's northern frontier, if he so chose. Shapur saw him more as an irritant than a potential threat, and so he had sent the balm of gifts to soothe that irritation before it became inflamed. Silks, gold and silver jewellery, all the little treasures that the barbarians lusted after. His ambassadors had watched the king, studied him, and they had returned with assurances that Kniva had no designs on Persia: his eye was on Rome and would not stray further east. Shapur believed his ambassadors and had crafted his own strategy on their revelations. If they were wrong, they would pay with their lives.

Up on top of Dura's western wall, a row of archers waited for any Persian foolish enough to stray into range. Now that the spies had confirmed that Valerianus was gone, some of his generals wanted to abandon the siege of Dura and pursue the emperor. Their new strategy was simple: Persians attack the rear, Goths attack the front. Between the two of them they would crush Valerianus' army. Finish him off.

Shapur had vetoed the plan. Unlike his generals, Shapur had studied the Goths and their leader, as he studied all potential opponents, and he knew that Kniva was playing a different game than they were. Kniva's attacks usually followed a pattern:

1. Appear out of nowhere.
2. Plunder city.
3. Destroy aqueducts.
4. Raze temples.
5. Burn crops.
6. Generally terrorize citizens.
7. Vanish when the emperor arrives to mete out punishment.

From which Shapur had deduced that Kniva's goal was to aggravate the emperor. Shapur was happy to permit Kniva his fun, especially since it inadvertently helped Shapur to obtain his own goal—the conquest of Roman territories in the East—but he would not base his strategies on Goth assistance, since they were unreliable. Thus, before he moved west in pursuit of Valerianus, he would destroy Dura-Europos as a potential threat to his rear, and as a staging ground for a Roman campaign aimed at his capital, Ctesiphon.

Shapur's horse danced nervously and he had to tighten the reins to calm her down. Strange. His horse was battle trained; neither the clash of weapons nor the smell of blood bothered it. For just a moment his mount seemed to shift, as someone had pushed it, and then shouts were raised in the city. Some of the archers on the wall withdrew; those that remained spread out to fill their places. Shapur spurred his horse and rode north until he was directly opposite Tower 19. And then he waited.

Dust billowed out from the base of the wall just to the left of the tower and Shapur cursed. "Light cavalry, forward," he ordered, and the unit of mounted archers that had been awaiting his

signal darted forward and loosed their arrows at their counter-
parts up on the wall, then zipped back out of range before the enemy could sight them. Persians emerged from the base of the wall,
engineers and soldiers and workers scrambling up and out of the
tunnel that had just collapsed. Men were running toward the Persian position, zigzagging to make themselves more difficult tar-
gets. The last two were carrying a man on a stretcher made of
shields and javelins. The man at the back took an arrow in the
shoulder, staggered, then caught himself and kept running. Finally they were all out of range, and Shapur's mounted archers
withdrew. Fifty men had been sent in to work on the tunnel; ten
men had escaped.

Shapur stopped the soldiers carrying the makeshift stretcher.
The man in the rear was replaced by another soldier. The man lying on the stretcher was Shabdiz, Shapur's chief engineer and his
friend. Shapur dismounted and bowed his head to Shabdiz. "You
have survived. I shall erect a fire altar to Ahura Mazda to com-
memorate this auspicious moment."

Shabdiz coughed. He was covered in white dust; all of the
men who had escaped the tunnel were covered in dust. "We had
accessed the Roman tunnel system just inside the city walls, O
Great One," Shabdiz said. "But then the earth moved and our
tunnel collapsed and they saw us and fought us back. They have
buttressed the tower and blocked off the entrances—undermining
Tower 19 is no longer an option."

Shapur grinned at the older man. "There are many towers on
the western wall. We shall try another."

"Yes, O Great One." Shabdiz struggled to get up, but Shapur
pushed him back down.

"Others will begin while you rest." Shapur was about to dismiss Shabdiz, but instead he reached down and touched the man's
shoulder. "You are sure this will work, old friend?" he asked.
Forty men had died under Tower 19 so that Shabdiz might try the
new weapon he had developed. Shapur did not want to risk more
lives on foolishness.

"Yes, O Mighty One."

"Every one of them must die. You understand that?"

"I understand, Your Excellency. If even one soul escapes, he will raise the alarm. But have no fear, Your Excellency: every digger, every soldier, even their water bearers will die—no one in their tunnels will survive. Those up above in the city will not know the tunnels are ours until it is too late."

"And my soldiers will not have to lift a finger?"

"They will need no weapons until they are in the city."

Shapur shook his head. When Shabdiz first explained his idea, Shapur had laughed. A weapon that needed no soldier to wield it? A weapon that could not be seen? Shapur was Shahanshah, King of kings, a man of might and power; he did not believe in ghosts or fairy tales. But Shabdiz swore by Ahura Mazda himself that his new weapon would clear the tunnels and permit his soldiers to enter the city, and Shabdiz was neither a liar nor a braggart. "Where do you suggest we try next?" he asked.

Shabdiz thought for a moment, then said, "Tower 14, the last tower on the western wall. There is a ravine below it. The men can start the tunnel there and work unseen and unprotected. Trust me, mighty Shahanshah, if you follow my directions, Dura-Europos will be yours by the end of the month."

RUMOUR OF KNIVA MET VALERIANUS wherever he went. Cities the Goth spared offered sacrifices to the gods in thanksgiving; those he attacked considered themselves lucky he had stolen their wealth and not their lives. The cities on the coast of Asia Minor that bordered the Black Sea lived in constant fear. Like a storm that suddenly bursts from a pale, blue sky, Kniva's navy descended on a target without warning, only when he crashed into a harbour town he left more destruction in his wake than wind and water damage. Naughty Roman boys and girls were told that Kniva would come in the night and steal them away if they did not behave. Had Kniva known that he had become the boogeyman for an entire generation of Roman children, he would have been proud, but no Roman captive ever had the courage to tell him.

Valerianus marched from Dura-Europos to the city of Sinope in Galatia on the coast of the Black Sea. When he had first landed in Syria, he had ordered his fleet up into the Black Sea with the other half of his army. Ever since then, the fleet had been waiting at Sinope for new orders. Now he was glad he had left it there. The only way to stop Kniva's fleet from ravaging the coast of Asia Minor was to chase it down with another fleet. If for some reason he could not find Kniva—he was a slippery opponent, as Decius had discovered—he could at least order the fleet at Sinope to actively seek out Kniva's fleet and attempt to locate his base of operations, which they knew was somewhere on the northern shore of the Black Sea. End of problem.

On his way to Sinope, he made imperial visits to a number of inland cities in the provinces of Cilicia, Galatia, and Cappadocia. The imperial cult was popular in the provinces of Asia Minor— historically those provinces had strong connections to the East, where the deification of rulers was customary, and the fine line separating man from god was much more blurred than in the West. Temples to the god-emperor Valerianus had sprung up in most of the cities, and he was greeted by crowds of worshippers at every stop he made along the route. In Asia Minor he experienced the true adoration of his subjects. He felt loved as he had never felt loved before, except perhaps in the early years of his marriage to Mariniana, before everything went tragically wrong. Some nights as he lay in his tent waiting for sleep to claim him, he took out one of the coins Gallienus had sent him and stared at her image. He remembered the nights they had shared, talking together, laughing, making love under the stars. He remembered the sound of her voice, its sweet cadence, her professions of eternal love. She pinched her cheeks to make them redder; she sang lullabies to Gallienus . . . and sometimes to him when he couldn't sleep; she loved to ride horses; she preferred apricots to peaches; she thought he looked handsome in green, boyish in red, and purple was just not his colour.

And she had betrayed him.

Valerianus let her memories go, but not the anger they invoked; that, he used to prepare himself and his troops for Kniva and his Goths. He gave a stirring speech to his legions about Kniva's less than regal heritage, noted how much a Goth army resembled a swarm of little girls out for a hike, and generally denounced the enemy as idiotic and cowardly. His troops roared their approval and marched on with new determination, singing songs of blood and retribution, songs of battles won and barbarians who ran before the glory of Rome's legions. And when the first signs appeared that their quarry was near—the garbage the Goths cast aside as they marched and the bruises their booted feet left on Roman soil—Valerianus' men readied their weapons and prayed to the gods that before that day ended, they would sheath their swords in Goth blood.

They caught the Goths late that afternoon. Scouts returned with the news that the Goths were making camp at the mouth of a long wadi, less than a mile from the Roman position. Valerianus sent the scouts back; he wanted to know the length of the wadi, the size, how many openings there were. When the scouts returned again, the news was excellent. The wadi was actually a canyon with deep sides that ended in a high wall half a mile from its mouth. A box canyon. Thanks be to the gods! A sudden attack from the front would drive the Goths into the canyon. Once inside there was no other way out. He would block their exit, then send archers up to the top of the canyon walls and let them pick off the enemy one at a time. That would end the Goth threat for at least a generation. If not forever.

Valerianus vowed to raise an altar to Mars after the Goths were destroyed. He sent the cavalry first, with orders to ride out and around, to position themselves so they could block the right flank in case it tried to flee. He split his infantry in two. General Eutropus took half out to cover the left flank. Valerianus himself took the centre. He wanted to see the shock on Kniva's face when the Goth king realized he was trapped. When all was ready, Valerianus advanced.

They were in sight of the Goths before the enemy realized what was happening. The Goths had pillaged the provinces of Asia Minor without meeting any effective resistance for so long that they had gotten careless. There were no Goth scouts, no advance guards, no protective measures around their camp at all. As far as Valerianus knew, it was the only mistake Kniva had made in his entire military career. But one mistake was all it took.

The Roman line was close enough now to see shock on some of the enemy's faces. The Goths were scrambling for armour and weapons. Warriors were screaming at each other and pointing at the mass of Roman soldiers marching down on them, as if trying to cast blame. One contingent of warriors had already solidified into a line at the mouth of the canyon, and they were backing into it as the Romans advanced. Just what Valerianus had planned. The Goths were finished.

Suddenly, there was a loud rumble and everything stopped. Roman, Goth, Emperor, King, everyone froze in place. Heads swivelled back and forth as men tried to locate the source of the rumble. The sudden quiet was unnatural—thousands of men stood side by side and face to face, and yet there was no rattle of weapons or creak of metal, no whispering, not even the sound of breathing broke the silence. A flock of birds burst out of the canyon and flew overhead; the sound of their flapping wings was somehow more frightening than the silence had been. A solitary deer appeared, stood for a moment between the two armies, looking first at the Romans, then the Goths, and then darted away.

"By the gods—" Valerianus whispered.

The earth beneath his feet shifted. He looked down. A cloud of dust billowed up into his face.

Suddenly, there was a load *snap*, as if some monstrously huge god had reached down and slapped the ground with the palm of his hand. A roar began deep in the bowels of the earth, then crescendoed until it was deafening. A shaking began, gentle at first, and then increasingly violent. Valerianus toppled over—his entire *army* toppled over, and try as they might, they could not get their feet under them again. A jagged crack in the earth ran up between the two armies, then heaved and widened, a few inches, a foot, a yard, before the walls slammed back together again. No sooner had the crack closed then it widened a second time, faster and further than the first time, and the Romans began to crawl away, fearing that the earth would swallow them whole.

And the Goths? They were still on their feet, as if on their side of the crack the earth had not rebelled against them. Valerianus saw Kniva mount his horse and signal the retreat. The earth erupted beneath Valerianus' feet and a shower of rocks and stones sprayed out of the crack. He saw Kniva grin, raise his hand in farewell, and then a rock struck the back of Valerianus' head and he saw no more.

THE DAY HAD STARTED like every other in Rome. Patrons met with their clients, then sprinted off to the law courts and the senate house in the forum. Matrons went about the business of organizing their homes with the help of their slaves. The poor congregated in the streets to talk about yesterday's games or tomorrow's chariot races. As usual, the workshops of the fullers stank, the bakeries made mouths water, and the taverns opened their doors at first light and let the wine flow. Plague deaths were more noticeable—the work crews were falling behind. The sick lined up to see physicians, or lined up at the temples for a blessing. Some people sacrificed to the gods in hopes of a cure, or purchased an amulet of protection from the temple priests. Some people went away relieved, some people dropped dead while waiting their turn, and other people caught the illness they were trying to avoid from the person standing next to them.

Just before dark, Rome began to shake.

Earthquakes were not uncommon in Italy. The Apennine mountain range, which ran down the centre of the Italian boot like a backbone, was a conduit for geological stresses in the Alpine range in the north and in the Mediterranean basin to the south, and had helped produce some significant geological events—the periodic eruptions of Mount Etna in Sicily and the infamous eruption of Mount Vesuvius which had buried Pompeii and Herculaneum two hundred years before. Compared to those catastrophes, the earthquake that struck central and northern Italy that day was relatively mild. The damage was more severe in Rome because it was more densely populated. Tenements in one section of the city were flattened, which began a rumour that the gods were angry at the poor. News soon filtered out of some of Rome's better neighbourhoods that villas had been toppled and their rich owners buried beneath the rubble, and that brought a sigh of relief; obviously the gods were angry at *everyone*, which was the normal state of affairs these days.

Just after dark, Senator Sextus called an emergency meeting of the senate in the Curia Julia—untouched by the quake. Present at the meeting was the praetorian praefect, Festus Macrinus, who placed the Praetorian Guard at the senate's disposal for the duration of the crisis. Together with the praefect of the city, they organized relief efforts. Fires were burning in every district, so many that the fire brigade was unable to keep up, so the senate increased their numbers. Crews were designated to dig through the rubble in search of survivors, while other crews were organized to begin the long process of removing the rubble permanently. Inspectors were sent to check for damage to the bins where the dole was stored—everything was fine. Before dawn the day after the quake, Rome was well on its way to full recovery, thanks to the cooperation of Rome's ruling elite.

Which for several of the participants turned out to be an even bigger catastrophe than the earthquake.

TWENTY-THREE

Valens called a halt and they gathered around Paulus to hear his story, all except Alexander and Regulus, whom he had sent ahead to scout out a suitable site to set up camp for the night. "What did you see, Paulus?" Valens asked.

"I was at my usual place in the rear, my lord." He laughed. "I was thinking how strange it was that we have not encountered any Germans yet, when I saw something flit through the trees."

"A deer?" Sukuta suggested.

"That's what I thought, especially as the colouring was the same. But then a thought nagged at me: 'Maybe the colour's the same because Germans wear buckskin.' So I strolled along pretending I hadn't seen anything, and then a little ways later I zip behind a big tree to watch. Ten minutes pass, and I'm about to give up, when I see this head peeking out from behind a bush not ten feet away. Dark tangled hair, blue eyes—it's a boy, not more than ten. He steps out, slinks toward me, and when he's close enough I grab at him! But I missed. He runs off cursing me in some language I never heard before, but he dropped this." Paulus withdrew a knife from his belt and passed it to Valens by the hilt.

Gundabar took the knife from Valens and examined it. The hilt was of braided metal, long enough to be held in a fist. The blade was one-sided and very sharp. Snakes were engraved in the metal. "Franks," Gundabar said.

"We're too far east for the Franks," Conall noted.

"Trade," Gundabar added.

"If it was a child, there must be a village nearby," Damarra said.

"Then let's see if we can return this knife," said Valens.

They moved on, picking the path of least resistance through the trees and searching for signs of human habitation. Five minutes later they came to a stream, a few yards wide but shallow. Fording the steam, they climbed up the far bank and discovered a rutted path. The path followed the stream, and the Clan followed the path until it came to a bridge, which led back across the stream, which was much deeper and wider now. They crossed, then continued on. Soon the trees began to thin out on either side of the path, until at last they came to a large clearing in the middle of a stand of ancient pines. In the clearing was a village.

The path was the village's solitary "street." There were clusters of huts on either side. The huts were constructed of wattle and chinked with mud and moss, making them look like round humps growing out of the earth. Each hut had a chimney opening at the top to allow smoke to escape. A few of the huts had racks erected beside them for drying fish. Most of the huts had stables at the rear. A large oak tree grew in the middle of the village to the right of the path. It was laden with acorns. A pig trotted out of the woods, grunted at them as it crossed the path, then trotted off again.

"Where are the people?" Persephone asked.

They were about to call out when a young boy stepped out of the closest hut on the left. He went to the middle of the path and stood there with his hands on his hips. His hair was dark and matted with leaves and pine needles, as if he'd been lying in the forest. "That's the boy I saw," Paulus said.

Gundabar held up the knife that Paulus had found. The boy's face showed surprise, then distrust. Gundabar walked forward; the boy backed up. Gundabar set the knife down in the middle of the path, then returned to the Clan. The boy looked at the knife, then the Clan, then grinned. He retrieved the knife, then began to chatter. Gundabar interrupted him, asked several questions, then spoke to Conall.

"The boy's name is Irmun; they are Hermunduri. Gundabar says they are related to the Suevi, but distantly, and he does not understand all the boy says."

"Ask him where everybody is," Valens said.

Gundabar asked the boy. Valens heard the word 'Alamanni' in the boy's reply.

"The men went with the Alamanni and the Juthungi," Conall explained. "They have not yet returned. He says they must be doing well since they are still away. He says the Romans are weak." Conall paused to listen to the rest of Gundabar's translation. A shadow darkened his face. "Irmun is the chief while the men are away. The women and children and old ones are here, in the huts. They have the sickness."

"The plague?" Valens asked.

Behind him he heard Alexander mumble to Regulus, "We don't want nothing to do with the plague."

"I will check, my lord," Persephone offered.

Persephone and Prisca were the Clan's "physicians." Both were knowledgeable in herb lore. Valens nodded.

Persephone got a leather pouch from her horse in which she kept a supply of dried herbs. "Come," Gundabar said, "I take you."

Persephone smiled at him and nodded. Gundabar spoke to the boy, whose face brightened. He gestured for them to follow him, and led them to the hut he had emerged from. They ducked to go in through the low entrance. A little while later Persephone came out again. "Not plague, my lord," she said.

There were several sighs of relief.

"Irmun's mother and grandmother are both ill. They have a high fever and a rash around the neck and chest and on the tongue; the rash is spreading to the rest of their body. I have seen this fever before, my lord. With proper care they will live."

"And without it they will die," Damarra concluded.

"Yes," Persephone said. "And Irmun says there are sick people in all the huts."

Valens put his pack down and turned to the others. "The Lord has brought us to these people because they need our help. So we will help them. Persephone and Prisca are in charge. Do as they say."

ULF RETURNED FROM HIS SCOUTING with news of the Clan. Generally they had followed them from campsite to campsite, staying about one day behind them. But one evening there had been no campsite and the trail had just vanished. Thinking perhaps the Clan had decided to push on through the night for some reason, they searched well beyond the twenty miles per day the Clan averaged and again found nothing. By then Dionysius had been sure they had missed something and had sent Ulf back to look, and sure enough the German had sniffed them out. They were at a Hermunduri village not too far north of the Danube. Ulf took Dionysius to the edge of the village and showed him. A few huts, some animals, nothing too exciting. He saw the beautiful slave girl with the olive skin emerge from one hut, then enter the next, followed by the lady Damarra. The men were chopping wood, skinning game, drying fish. Conall's boy was playing with a barbarian child about the same age. "Looks like they plan to be here awhile," Ulf whispered.

Dionysius grinned at him and slapped his shoulder. "Ever been to Quintiana?"

Ulf shook his head.

"There's an inn there called the Sword and Shield, prettiest barmaids in the empire."

"I like it," Ulf said. "Where is it?"

Dionysius pointed south. "Three miles that way."

Ulf's eyes widened. "Don't jest with a man who's been wandering through the wilderness for a month and a half."

Dionysius laughed. "May the gods strike me dead if I'm lying."

"Let's go!" Ulf tried to get up, but Dionysius pulled him back down. "Commander! Please! Who knows when we'll get this close to a real Roman inn again. And barmaids!"

"Go get Siricius and Matthias," Dionysius ordered. "They can keep watch while we drink."

DURA-EUROPOS, THE EASTERN FRONTIER
EARLY AUGUST A.D. 257

AT LAST THE TIME HAD COME. The engineers had dug under Tower 14 and accessed the Roman tunnel system that ran the length of the wall. Shabdiz had promised he would deliver the city to Shapur before August began, but the delay was not his fault. A series of earthquakes further west had caused intensive damage through Asia Minor, and although the shocks they had felt here at Dura were minor in comparison, they had still disrupted the digging and caused a number of collapses that required precious time to repair. But at last the trap was ready to be sprung. Shapur and two members of his elite bodyguard entered the tunnel that led under Tower 14. Normally he would not enter the tunnels. As Shahanshah, his place was on horseback riding through the city gates. But this amazing new weapon Shabdiz had created! He must see it up close. Shabdiz had assured him that neither he nor his men would be in danger. "The Roman tunnels will draw like a chimney, O Great One," Shabdiz had explained.

Whatever that meant.

Shapur wore the High Crown of the Shahanshah on his head and had to duck beneath a support beam as he and his escort worked their way down the tunnel. He would soon enter Dura as conqueror and he was dressed the part, High Crown, shimmering silks of royal blue and fire red, leather boots embedded with gems. As he walked he could feel the draft whistling past his cheek. All the air was indeed being drawn into the Roman tunnel works.

At last he arrived at the end of the tunnel. A unit of Dailamites stood to one side, waiting for the order to attack. The Dailamites were Shapur's elite infantry—the best of the best. Each man had a shield, sword, and javelin, and had sworn by Ahura Mazda that he would die for the Shahanshah. Shabdiz was also there, holding a metal tray with a lid shaped like a funnel and like a funnel open at both ends, with one end wider than the other. The end of the tunnel looked like a solid wall of dirt and rock, but in fact it was only a few inches thick and could be broken down with a few kicks. At face height was a single hole, about the size of a man's fist. The hole opened into the Roman tunnel system inside the city.

"Thank you for coming, mighty Shahanshah," Shabdiz said with a bow.

"All is ready?" Shapur asked.

In response Shabdiz lifted the lid off the metal tray. Inside were crystals of various hues; they looked like children's playthings. "That is it?" Shapur said incredulously. For a moment he could not believe he had risked everything on a tray of crystals.

Then Shabdiz grinned, and Shapur knew he had made the right choice. He put the lid back on the tray, then lifted it, so the lid's funnel opening covered the hole in the wall. A young boy, Shabdiz's grandson, handed him a small torch. "Now watch, O Mighty One," Shabdiz said.

GENERAL MEMNON STOOD ATOP Dura's wall studying the Persian army that had assembled just beyond the range of the Roman archers. In the centre, a unit of Cataphracts waited like metal statues. They were the elite heavy cavalry, the main weapon in the Persian arsenal. The rider was encased in metal plates from head to toe, and the horse wore a blanket of metal plates that protected everything but the hooves. Only the strongest men were chosen for the Cataphracts because only the strongest of men could bear the weight of the armour and still wield sword or javelin. Beside the Cataphracts were armed archers and a token war elephant. Most of the troops were infantry, which was unusual. Shapur would not place that many infantry at the front . . . unless . . .

Memnon jumped down from the wall and hurried over to the tunnel entrance by Tower 14. He got down on his knees. "What's going on down there?" he shouted.

"Nothing, as usual," a voice replied. A man appeared at the bottom of the opening, looked up, and recognized General Memnon. He saluted. "Nothing, General."

"Run down to the end and check," he ordered.

With another salute, the soldier raced off. A few seconds later Memnon heard a sound, a grunt, as if someone had fallen over and winded themselves. "Soldier," he called out.

No answer.

"Soldier," he yelled louder.

Still no answer.

A tribune stood nearby, watching him. Memnon waved him over. "In the hole, Tribune," he ordered. "See what's happening down there."

The Tribune jumped down, walked two paces, and then fell over backwards.

Dead.

"What the—" was all Memnon managed.

SHABDIZ PRESSED A LEVER on the top of the metal container and two plates slid down, blocking off the holes in the funnel. "It is done, O Mighty One," he said.

Shapur motioned at the wall. Two diggers with pick-axes knocked the wall down with a few well-placed blows, then they stepped aside and the infantry poured into the Roman tunnels. There were no shouts of surprise, no sounds of battle; the Romans in the city above had no idea that their tunnels had been compromised. Shapur ducked inside the tunnel for a look. All along the base were dead Roman soldiers. One man who had been sitting on a rock having a drink, still held the cup in his hand. Amazing.

"How does it work, Shabdiz?" Shapur asked.

He showed him the metal container. "The crystals are bitumen and sulphur. When burned together they create vapours that cannot be seen, but one breath is enough to kill a man," the old engineer pointed at the Roman tunnels, "or many men."

Shapur laughed. "Poisonous vapours! What a wonderful idea."

Up in the city of Dura-Europos, the Romans began to scream.

SOUTHERN RHAETIA
MID-AUGUST A.D. 257

GALLIENUS HAD REACHED SOUTHERN RHAETIA when he learned that his worst fears had come true: the Alamanni had crossed the Alps into North Italy. When the messenger announced the news, Gallienus did not let the emotions roiling in his chest show on his face. He dismissed the messenger, dismissed his officers, who were with him planning strategy for the recovery of Rhaetia, then went into his tent and threw himself down on his bed. His shoulder ached; his head ached. More than that, his *heart* ached. More than anything he wanted to lay aside the imperial mantle and just go home. Take his precious Nina into their bed chamber and lie in her arms and listen to her sweet voice assuring him that everything would be alright. And yet it was Nina and his children who kept him going. If the Alamanni moved south into central Italy, they might very well march past his family. Worse, they might not march past at all. He could picture them swarming into his estate, killing his children and raping Nina before setting his home on fire. That he could not permit.

As his army marched south toward the Alps, he thought of Rome. Nina called her "the other woman," or even "Mistress Roma," and though Nina meant it as a joke, it was true. Rome was his mistress, and in the last year she had endured horrific abuse. She had been assaulted by plague, shaken to pieces by the earthquake that had rocked Italy and Asia Minor, and now she had been violated by these vile barbarians. And worst of all, she was batting her eyes at a new lover.

Festus Macrinus.

The fool had placed the Praetorian Guard "at the senate's disposal" during the aftermath of the earthquake. Did he not know that granting the senate control over that many soldiers was tantamount to *asking* it to rebel? And who would they put forward to usurp the throne? That idiot Sextus? No, there was only one man in Rome whom the senate would back for emperor: Festus Macrinus. And maybe that's what all this "cooperation" between Commander Festus and the senate was about? Rebellion. Usurpation.

Emperor Festus Macrinus.

A year ago he would not have believed it possible. Festus Macrinus was his father's oldest friend. He was Gallienus' mentor, the man who had educated him, raised him. But power was seductive; *Rome* was seductive. And perhaps their beauty had blinded Festus to his duty to the Valerian dynasty?

He had written Festus a scathing letter of reproof after learning of the cordial relations he now shared with the senate, but he had not sent it. The more he thought about it, the more he realized that he needed to discuss the matter with Festus face to face. He needed to gaze into Festus' eyes and see if deception and rebellion lived there, and he needed to teach the senate once and for all who their master was.

No matter what happened with the Alamanni, the time had come to return to Rome.

SENATOR SEXTUS BURST INTO FESTUS' OFFICE without knocking. He and the senators who accompanied him—fifteen in all—crowded around the front of his desk, all chattering at once like a gaggle of geese. Sextus, the oldest of the group, was red-faced and sweating; his cheeks puffed in and out as he caught his breath. Festus stood up, gestured for quiet, but their volume increased. Exasperated, he slapped his desk with an open palm. All fifteen of them gave a start and fell silent.

Festus pointed at Sextus. "You, Senator Sextus. Explain. What's going on?"

"The Alamanni are marching on Rome."

Festus felt his chest constrict. "Are you sure?" he asked.

"We just received word from Pisae. The Alamanni are marching down the *Via Aurelia*; they will arrive at Rome in three days."

Festus sat back down and pondered his options. Gallienus had not prepared for this, and why would he? The last barbarian to visit Central Italy had been Hannibal, five hundred years ago. It was impossible that any enemy would march on Rome, would *dare* to march on Rome. But in these troubled times the impossible happened over and over again. The world had stopped making sense. "Are the praetorians enough?" Sextus asked.

Festus shook his head. As per Gallienus' order, he had called up the Praetorian Guard and placed it north of the city, between Rome and the Alamanni, in case the Alamanni decided to attack. But it was for show, to instil confidence in Gallienus' regime. "Valerianus took half the praetorians east, leaving twenty-five hundred. The Alamanni have five times that number."

"Then we must supplement the guard," Sextus said.

"Supplement it?" Festus laughed. "From what? Shall we sow dragon's teeth like Jason and harvest the crop of soldiers that grow from the ground? No, my friend, there is no way to supplement our forces. The closest legion is the Third Augusta in Africa Proconsularis—it would take weeks to ship them to Italy, and we have less than three days.

"Then we supplement them from the city."

Festus raised an eyebrow. "From the city?"

"Yes, we call up the senators—"

"Most of you are older than sixty!"

"I did not say the 'senate.' I said 'senators.' There are many young senators in Rome; some of them have military experience. For that matter, there are young equestrians and young plebeians—the city is full of young people. We choose the biggest and the strongest, give them weapons, and when the Alamanni arrive, we fight!"

Festus liked the idea. It had merit. Under the circumstances, it was probably the only option. If they did not find warm human bodies to stand between the Alamanni and Rome, the city would be sacked, and that was a catastrophe from which the empire would never recover.

Festus smiled to himself. He was commander of the Praetorian Guard, but what did that mean with Valerianus and his son sharing the throne? A pretty uniform. The respect of a few senators. Cutting ribbons, attending banquets. Bah! Action. That is what he *really* wanted. One more chance to relive his glory days and feel the heat of battle burning in his blood. No more ceremony and mindless obligations.

He stood up and strapped on his belt and sword. For the first time in years he noticed the weight of the weapon hanging from his side, its *presence*, and its true purpose. "Battle calls, Senator Sextus," Festus said, and slapped the old man's shoulder.

Sextus winced, then smiled. "To the glory of Rome!" he cried, and his colleagues took up the cheer.

"To *my* glory," Festus muttered as he pushed through the senators and marched out the door.

GENERAL MARCUS STOOD ON THE BRIDGE outside the Hermunduri village watching the water slip downstream. He saw a fish just below him, its tail undulating slowly back and forth as it fought to stay in place. A trout. A good sized one, too. But they had more than enough trout dried and salted and stored away in a nearby cave. The Hermunduri used it to keep their food cool. There was even a deep hole in the cave where water froze, even in the heat of August.

Marcus loved it here. It was quiet and peaceful, so unlike the bustling metropolises of the empire. Or even life in an army camp. Out here, you could hear God speaking in the babbling brook, in the leaves that rattled in the breeze. He heard footsteps on the trail and turned to see Persephone walking towards him. She smiled and waved. What a beautiful young girl she was! Not that he was interested in her *that* way—he took his vow of chastity very seriously. But Gundabar, now he *was* interested in Persephone. You could see it in his eyes every time he looked at her. Even the lady Damarra had commented on the young German's infatuation. And from the way her eyes sparkled whenever Gundabar was around, it seemed pretty obvious that Persephone felt the same way about him.

"Good afternoon, General," she said. She rested her back against the railing and crossed her arms.

"And a good afternoon to you, Physician," he teased. "How are the patients?"

"Most have recovered. A few are still ill, but the rashes are beginning to peel, so it should not be much longer."

"Good! We've been here many weeks."

"Do you feel we should be going?"

"Yes and no." He looked around and smiled. "I love it here; I could spend the rest of my life here. But—"

"But you're starting to feel like we should be moving on."

"Exactly. If we don't go soon, we'll have to spend the winter."

"Yes, I believe the Lord wanted us here, but now, I feel a stirring in my heart, telling me to go. I wonder if any of the others feel the same way?"

Marcus considered her comment. It was mid-August. They could safely travel for another two months before winter became a real threat. If they knew what their destination was, aside from a "*Thing*" somewhere in Germania, it would help them gauge better. But that was the point, wasn't it? Not knowing. Having to trust in God, not themselves. He wished he could speak to Gundabar about it, but the language barrier was still impassable. If they had ever needed the gift of tongues, it was now! He patted Persephone's slim shoulder. "I think it's time the Clan had a meeting," he said.

GUNDABAR STOOD IN THE COVER of the trees watching Marcus and Persephone on the bridge.

"You see what I mean?" Alexander whispered in his ear.

Gundabar looked over his shoulder and shrugged, touched his ear.

Alexander grinned. "Oh, you don't need a translator for this. You're not a complete idiot, my little Suevi warrior."

Gundabar touched his ear again.

Fine. Let him play it that way. Alexander was done, anyway. All Gundabar needed was someone to point him in the right direction. Eventually the German would grope to the appropriate conclusion all on his own. The plan was simple: Marcus versus Gundabar for the hand of the fair Persephone. And while they were fighting over the prize, Alexander would slip in and steal her for his own. He licked his lips and wondered again what her lips would taste like. Strawberries, he thought. One way or another he would find out. And soon.

"I just figured you should know, Commander," Alexander said. "Now I'll return to guard duty."

Gundabar waved him away. He was too busy watching Marcus touching Persephone's shoulder to notice Alexander's soft chuckle as he walked off into the trees.

TWENTY-FOUR

ROME
AUGUST A.D. 257

The Alamanni host was huge but unorganized. It was loosely controlled by the Alamanni King, Chrocus, but his hold over the other tribes that had joined in this venture—the Juthungi and the Hermunduri were just two—was minimal and dependent almost solely on victory. While Chrocus won battles, his host stayed together; when he started to lose, it was every tribe for itself. Thus King Chrocus had chosen a target which would win him the most respect among the tribes with the least trouble.

Rome.

He had planned this venture for years, winning the support he needed from various chiefs by promising each of them a share of the spoils. He had constructed a complicated web of alliances based on those promises and solidified by numerous political marriages—he had too many daughters for any man's good, he always told his friends, but they had come in handy in the end. And when everything was finally ready, he waited for a sign from Woden. He did not have to wait long. The moment he heard about the Frankish invasion of Gallia and the merry chase on which Merovech was leading Emperor Gallienus (not to mention his many legions), he knew Woden was telling him it was time to strike. And if it was not Woden, then it was just common sense.

Chrocus was anticipating the vast wealth waiting for him at Rome. The city was undefended. There were some walls, the Servian Wall, for example. It had been erected hundreds of years ago. Since then Rome had expanded so much that the Servian Wall was practically useless—most of the city was outside those walls, not protected by them. Gallienus was probably in Spain by now, chasing Merovech down, so Chrocus expected no trouble from him. There were a few thousand praetorians, but what was that against his host?

Chrocus' first indication of trouble was the appearance of several chiefs whom he had sent on ahead to negotiate Rome's surrender. Only one of them was Alamanni—his son, Altan. The others were Juthungi and Hermunduri, and they looked upset. They rode up, yanked on the reins, and began to shout curses at him. Altan rolled his blue eyes. "There is a problem, King Chrocus."

"Yes?"

"An army."

"*What*?" Chrocus bellowed.

The chiefs with Altan began to curse again. It was times like this he was glad he did not speak their languages. Altan could, but he was not translating. Altan was fifteen, but he was wise for his age.

Chrocus spurred his horse forward and galloped to the front of his army. Which had stopped marching. Ahead was an army twenty thousand strong. Lots of very big, very angry looking Romans. A few of them had come to battle in togas, which normally would have made him howl with laughter, but their scowls and the swords and javelins they carried demonstrated they were taking this very seriously. So were his chiefs. They had ridden up behind him to continue their harangue in front of the whole host. He spun in the saddle and gave them a cutthroat gesture to shut them up, then he spurred his horse forward again into the breach between the two armies. Across the way, a man wearing praetorian armour rode forward. He was silver-haired, like Chrocus himself, and looked very fit. His arms were muscular and his bearing was regal. The man drew his sword as he approached Chrocus. Chrocus drew his in response.

"Are you here to surrender?" Chrocus asked. A little bravado never hurt.

The man laughed. "Are you?"

"I am Chrocus, King of the Alamanni."

"I am Festus Macrinus, Praetorian Praefect, and I will have your head if you do not leave now."

"Bring me the wealth of Rome and I will leave."

"Prepare to die," Festus said, and rode back to his army.

Army! Could it really be called that? Was it any more than rabble plucked from the streets of Rome?

And is your army any more than rabble plucked from the forests of Germania?

Suddenly a trumpet sounded and Chrocus looked up. The Romans were advancing! Unbelievable! Somewhere a drummer began to beat to their marching feet. An old man in the front wearing a blindingly white toga was carrying the Roman standard. Chrocus rolled his eyes. His little jaunt to Rome had gone sour. With a sigh, he turned his horse and raised his sword and cried, "To battle!"

HE WAS STANDING ON A ROCKY SHORE, gazing out across a boiling sea. A fleet of ships was sailing into the horizon. One voice began to chant, one of his generals or a tribune, he wasn't sure where it started, but the voice became two, then a hundred, and then every Roman soldier in every Roman army was joining in. Like the plague that was decimating the empire, it spread—to governors, to city magistrates, to the gladiators fighting for their lives in the arenas, to the charioteers who raced for riches and glory and fame, to every fan who cheered them on, to every temple priest and prostitute, to every child, slave, matron, farmer, merchant, senator, equestrian, and plebeian. One mouth had begun the chant, now every mouth took it up, and for once there was no counterpoint, no dissonance, no variations on a theme, just a perfect unison chanting its horrific message into his ears:

Valerianus' Bane . . . Valerianus' Bane . . . Valerianus' Bane . . .

He opened his eyes, but part of the nightmare was true. Kniva's ships were already specks on the horizon, heading north to his den in Germania or Sarmatia or wherever it was he spent his winters. Surely every soldier was thinking that chant, as every Roman would think it when they heard the news. How much more of this would it take for the nightmare to become prophecy? How much longer before Decius' Bane became Valerianus' Bane?

Valerianus turned his back on the sea and marched back to his tent. He felt the eyes of his officers following him, but looked neither left nor right, afraid he might see reproof in their eyes, afraid of what he might do to his own men if he *did* see reproof. They needed a victory, something to remind them that they were the conquerors, not the conquered. Kniva had never won a battle against them; that was the aggravating part—where he excelled was in the ability to keep one step ahead of his opponent. Because of that, the Goths had done well in Asia Minor, which was rich with plunder. *Was* rich with plunder. How much was left after Kniva's depredations? Enough to lure him back in the spring? Or would he go somewhere else? Further east would be perfect—let Shapur deal with him for awhile.

Back in his tent, Valerianus ordered food and wine and then reclined on his dining couch. He sighed. A month ago, south of Sinope, he had almost had Kniva. If not for that earthquake, Kniva would be dead. Instead he had gone on to pillage one city after another while Valerianus rode his trail like some defective hunting dog, always scenting the Goth's stink but never running him to ground. That opportunity had come and gone the day of the earthquake. Kniva was too wily to let himself be caught again.

Valerianus let the waves of hate and anger roll over him. Those emotions had always given him strength, and he basked in them now, allowed them to lift his spirits and infuse him with their power. Immediately a feeling of peace settled over him. His mind calmed, order returned to his thoughts, and he was able to plan out his next move. He must protect Asia Minor from future raids, that was essential. Despite the gloominess of his prior assessment, Kniva *might* be back in the spring—he had only pillaged a small percentage of the cities here. Valerianus' fleet was still searching for Kniva's home base in the northern Black Sea region. The *Classis Pontica*, the fleet that patrolled the southern Black Sea region—the northern coast of the provinces of Asia Minor—had been placed on high alert and the number of its ships doubled.

Similarly the *Classis Syriaca*, the fleet which patrolled the southern coast of Asia Minor, had also been placed on high alert and augmented. With three Roman fleets actively pursuing Kniva and protecting the provinces of Asia Minor, Valerianus was confident that the Goth's reign of terror in Asia Minor was at an end. It would take a miracle for him to elude all those enemy vessels.

That left Shapur. After destroying Dura-Europos, Shapur had massed his troops on the border of Mesopotamia . . . and then dug in. He was still there now, as if he were waiting for some sign from his god. Or goading Valerianus to come after him. Too bad. Valerianus intended to winter at Antioch and allow his troops to rest. If Shapur wanted him badly enough, he could march his army to Antioch. Otherwise, let him sit there until spring.

MARCUS AND PERSEPHONE FOUND Valens and Damarra by the great oak tree in the centre of the village, pouring over Valens' map with Brunhilde, Irmun's mother and the wife of the village's Headman. She was a large woman in her forties, tall and wide, with long brown hair that she wore in braids. When the Clan first arrived she had been very sick, so sick Persephone had feared she might die. Thanks to Persephone's care, she had made a full recovery. Brunhilde was fluent in Latin—she often accompanied her husband to the Roman settlement of Quintiana on the south bank of the Danube to trade—and so she became Persephone's assistant. She was particularly interested in Persephone's herb lore. Persephone had taken her into the woods to help her learn to identify and harvest any medicinal herbs that could be obtained locally.

Brunhilde grinned down at Persephone and pointed at Marcus. "You must teach me how to harvest that kind of herb before you go."

They laughed at Persephone's blush, then Valens held up the map. "Brunhilde has shown us the best route for our journey." He touched the map. "This is the village of Singone, which lies just beyond the great southward bend of the Danube. If we leave tomorrow we can reach Singone before winter sets in."

Marcus studied the map. "Singone is in Quadi territory. They are not fond of Romans."

Damarra laughed. "You don't look much like a Roman any-more, Marcus," she said. She reached up and ran her fingers through Valens' hair. Like Marcus, Valens' hair had grown longer since they entered Germania, and both men now had bushy beards. "None of the men look Roman anymore."

Valens chuckled. "It doesn't matter, Marcus. Brunhilde is Quadi and she is sending messages with us to give to the chiefs at Singone. We will winter with the Quadi."

"Actually, my lord, we were coming to discuss our depar-ture," Persephone said.

Valens raised his eyebrows. "Really? Damarra and I talked about it this morning. We both woke up with the feeling that it was time to go."

"Perhaps that is the *Christos* talking to you," Brunhilde sug-gested. Aside from herb lore, she had been quizzing Persephone on Christianity.

"You're right," Damarra said. She took Brunhilde's hand and squeezed it. "The *Christos* talks to us in many ways. Sometimes it is a simple urging we feel inside to do a certain thing. Or not to do it." She looked at each of them. "And I think, yes, the *Christos* is urging us to go."

Brunhilde frowned. "We will be sad to see you go."

Damarra hugged her. "We'll miss you, too," she said.

"Tonight, we have a farewell feast to say goodbye to our new friends," Brunhilde pronounced.

It was settled. Brunhilde, Damarra, and Persephone headed off to find Brunhilde's mother-in-law and make preparations for the feast. Valens went to find the others, and Marcus headed back to the hut he had been sharing with Gundabar, Conall, and Cecht. At the entrance, he spotted Gundabar coming out of the woods and waved. The German scowled and marched off in the opposite direction. Marcus shrugged and entered the hut. Gundabar had looked upset, but he obviously did not want to discuss it right now. Maybe he just wasn't feeling well?

Marcus put it out of his mind as he started gathering up his things. He inventoried his pack—everything was there—then took his belt and laid it out on his bedroll. Since arriving at the village, he had stored his belt at the bottom of his pack. Now that they were leaving, he'd start wearing it under his tunic again. He turned the belt over and pulled back the seam, which revealed the hidden pocket where he always kept a few gold coins for emergency, his travel papers, and, most importantly, his Certificate of Peace, signed by the confessor Lucian at Carthage. He opened the pocket to check the contents. Tipping it up, five gold coins fell into his hand. All there. Next he pulled the papers out and checked them. The letter of imperial protection and the letter of transit, both signed by Gallienus, were there.

But where was his Certificate of Peace?

He shuffled the letters, opened them. No certificate, He put his hand into the belt's pocket and traced his fingers up and down the seams. No certificate.

His heart crashed against his ribs. Where was the certificate?

Again he shuffled the papers and felt about the pocket. He checked his bedroll in case it had fallen out, then emptied his pack and searched its contents.

Gone! His Certificate of Peace was gone!

KING CHROCUS CHARGED BACK to the Alamanni host, which had not responded to his command. He galloped across the front line, bellowing at them to follow orders. His son Altan was yelling the same thing, but their words were falling on deaf ears.

Stubborn ears.

He glanced over his shoulder. The Roman army was continuing its advance, slow and steady. He doubted if some of the old men in the front line were capable of moving any faster. Altan rode in behind him. "This is ludicrous," he said.

"My thoughts exactly, boy."

"The chiefs say there is no honour in fighting old men and children."

"Some of those children are carrying large swords."

"We should have left the Hermunduri and Juthungi in Germania."

Chrocus ground his teeth. His son had argued that from the beginning. Since entering Italy it had become his favourite song.

"Then let's send them home," he snapped.

He had meant it sarcastically, but Altan turned and raised his sword. "Juthungi! Hermunduri! Your oaths are filled. You are released."

"What are you doing, boy?" Chrocus cried.

The Juthungi and Hermunduri warriors began to mutter to each other.

"I have had my fill of these quarrelsome fools," Altan said, "and I say we do not need them. We are Alamanni. All that stands between us and glory is an army of old men and children. How many nights have we sat in our halls and dreamed of Rome's destruction? Now it is within our grasp; the wealth of Rome is within our grasp."

"Well, my boy," Chrocus laughed, "when you put it that way." Chrocus raised his sword to the chiefs and cried: "Your oaths are filled; you are released. Begone!"

The Juthungi chief spat in disgust. He whispered to his Hermunduri counterpart, who nodded, then turned to face his men and yelled: "We will return to Northern Italy and sack Verona, as we should have done from the start."

A great shout went up from the Juthungi and Hermunduri, and then a third of the host peeled off and began the long trek north. Chrocus scowled as he watched them go. "When this is done, I will have their heads," he swore.

"But they are your son-in-laws," Altan replied with a laugh. "Would you deprive your own daughters of their husbands?"

Chrocus grunted. He had wasted two daughters on those fools.

Altan slapped his father's shoulder. "Instead, we will sack Rome, and all the tribes will know that the Alamanni are the greatest warriors on earth, and that the Juthungi and Hermunduri are cowards. It is a gift from Woden."

Suddenly, the Roman army cried out in one voice: "*For Rome!*"

"For Chrocus!" Altan wailed in response, and in the crash of swords and clubs and the screams of dying men, battle was met.

CHROCUS' CONFEDERATION HAD succeeded thus far because of sheer volume. The sudden appearance of the Alamanni had surprised the defenders of the *Agri Decumates*, but it was their numbers that had caused those seasoned veterans to turn tail and flee. Their numbers had also cleared a path through Germania Superior and Rhaetia—that and the fact that both Gallienus and Valerianus had fattened their own armies by pilfering soldiers from the legions that defended those provinces. By the time the Alamanni host entered Italy, they had come to think of themselves as invincible. In actuality, they had not yet faced any serious resistance.

Chrocus and Altan were right about one thing: the army thrown together by Festus Macrinus and the senate did have a fair number of "old men and children." What they did not know, however, was that most of the older men had military experience, while many of the teenagers were in training for the military, so they were more than the "old men and children" that the Alamanni saw. In addition to these "old men and children," Festus' army also had soldiers on leave, ex-gladiators, large, angry plebeians whose livelihood (and entertainment) depended on the survival of the state, and the well-trained bodyguards of numerous wealthy citizens (whose livelihood also depended on the survival of the state). Plus twenty-five hundred praetorian guards, each handpicked because of his prowess and bravery, and who together comprised the finest fighting force the empire had ever known.

The battle was short and decisive. In the first clash of weapons, Altan lost his head to an old man who had served under the emperor Septimius Severus in Britannia fifty years before. A child managed to flay the skin and muscle from Chrocus' left forearm, which he later lost to gangrene. Fortunately, the right-handed Chrocus was able to lift his good hand to his mouth to amplify his voice when he ordered the Alamanni host to retreat. It was rumoured that the Alamanni retreated so quickly that they actually beat the Juthungi and Hermunduri to Northern Italy.

The Battle of Rome, as the skirmish was called by the senate, lasted five minutes—anywhere from five hours to five days depending on who told the story—and, according to the senate, effectively ended the threat to the empire posed by the Alamanni (in fact, the end of the Alamanni threat was yet to come). Festus Macrinus was the hero of the day, and at the moment that the Alamanni turned and started running in the opposite direction, someone in the army had the bright idea that the day's hero should be running the empire, and began shouting, "Festus for emperor!" The chant quickly spread to every member of the makeshift army.

The chant washed over Festus like a warm and gentle rain, and for a brief moment his daydreams about past glories flipped into fantasies about glories to come. Emperor Festus Macrinus entering the forum to the cheers of the Roman mob. Young ladies tossing rose petals at his feet as he glided up the steps of the senate house to greet the kneeling and prostrate senators and accept their flattery and gifts. His mind flashed on the brilliant triumphs of his career: the annihilation of the Germans tribes, the construction of a new amphitheatre in Rome capable of seating five hundred thousand spectators, the extermination of the Christian atheists, the subjugation of Persia and India, and the final, most momentous victory of all—his ascension to Mount Olympus, where he would take his rightful place beside Father Jupiter and receive the adoration of the entire world. And then he remembered the blood oath he had made to his friend and brother, and now his emperor, and he raised his hands for silence. "I cannot accept this honour."

His army screamed its incredulity and he silenced them again. "I have sworn a blood oath, eternal loyalty to Emperor Valerianus. I will not break it."

"Gallienus is not Valerianus," a voice shouted. And the army took up that chant.

"Gallienus is like a son to me!" He yelled it to make himself heard over the cacophony of voices. "He is like a son to me!"

The elderly Senator Sextus commanded silence, and Festus' army closed its mouth. "Sometimes," Sextus cried, turning to the four corners of the world to demand their attention. Finally, he stared into Festus' grey eyes. "Sometimes a father must sacrifice his son for the good of his people."

The army focussed on Festus, waiting for his answer.

"Sometimes," Festus agreed. "But I am not that father."

TWENTY-FIVE

MARCOMANNI TERRITORY, GERMANIA
SEPTEMBER A.D. 257

The Clan found it easy to fall back into the rhythm of travelling after their long stay with the Hermunduri. They kept the Danube to their right and followed a course that was generally southeast to avoid the mountain range that marked the southern edge of Marcomanni territory. The mountains were beautiful . . . as long as they didn't have to climb them. At some point they would turn northeast, away from the easy trail of the river in order to skirt the province of Dacia. Until God informed them differently, the plan was to keep moving east and avoid reentering the empire.

They were passing through flatlands that eased down to the Danube River. Trees were plentiful, as they were most everywhere in Germania, but many of these trees were stunted by the cycle of icy winter winds from the mountains and the spring flooding of the river. The underbrush was thick and made walking difficult, even for the horses. After a few days of fighting the vegetation, they moved away from the river into the forest, where the underbrush was less substantial. After that, they made good time.

The mood of the Clan had changed. Before their stay with the Hermunduri, there had been jokes and songs and stories shared as they hiked along. For all the seriousness of their journey, the atmosphere had been festive, more like a group of friends on a holiday outing than refugees in hostile territory. But now a silence settled over them, and with it, a tension. They did not discuss it, but each Clan member felt it and wondered at it in his or her heart. Paulus, Alexander, and Regulus seemed unaffected, as if the feeling of malaise had targeted only Clan members.

Marcus was even more withdrawn than the others. The mystery of his missing Certificate of Peace tormented him most of his waking hours and kept him from sleep at night. Why would anybody take it? What use was it to anyone but him? Probably it had fallen out of his belt, and it was lying in the trees somewhere in Germania. The years would cover it with leaves and dirt and it would eventually dissolve, the words lost forever; but that did not matter, because the words were printed on his heart and soul. If only he knew for certain.

Losing the certificate was not what bothered him anyway. The fear that really haunted him was having the certificate turn up in Valens' hands. He cringed every time he pictured it. What would Valens do if he found out Marcus was *lapsi*? How many times in the last few years had he seen disgust in Valens' eyes when he looked at the *lapsi*, and heard it in his voice when he turned them away?

That evening they made camp in a small clearing in the pines. Gundabar and Alexander took first watch; Marcus and Regulus drew second. They sat around the campfire chatting in low voices. Valens was rubbing Damarra's aching shoulders while Ruth played with the little doll that Gundabar had carved for her out of a piece of wood. They prayed together as they did each evening— Regulus sat quietly and looked up at the stars, but Prisca began to join in the prayers—then they planned out the next day's journey, which took only a few minutes as each day was more or less the same as the one before. Marcus rubbed his head and got up.

"A headache?" Persephone asked.

He nodded. He had had one most of the afternoon. "I thought I would take a nap before Regulus and I relieve Gundabar and Alexander."

She stood up, wiping off the back of her tunic. "I'll make you some tea, Marcus."

He smiled at her. After entering Germania, he had insisted she call him Marcus, rather than "general" or "my lord." She had finally gotten used to the idea. "That would be wonderful, thank you."

He went to his bedroll, stretched out, and instantly fell asleep. Marcus was a consummate napper—his years in the military had trained him to take his sleep whenever the opportunity arose. When he opened his eyes fifteen minutes later, Persephone was standing over him with a cup of her special tea. She said it was a blend of willow and aspen bark. All he knew was that it worked, and as he took the cup he was once again grateful that the *Christos* had wanted Persephone to come along on this quest. He got up on his knees, realized that his sandal had come undone, and set the cup down. As he was tying up the sandal, Gundabar emerged from the forest.

Gundabar yelled something in Suevi, then strode across the clearing to Marcus and Persephone. Conall, who was sitting by the fire listening to Cecht read from one of the scrolls that Sukuta had brought along, heard what Gundabar yelled, jumped up, and tried to intercept Gundabar, but the Suevi warrior reached Marcus first. Marcus stood up and Gundabar began screaming at him. Marcus stepped back, a look of puzzlement on his face, and then Gundabar drew back his fist and punched Marcus in the nose. Marcus fell over backwards, the puzzlement replaced by surprise, then anger. "Are you insane, Gundabar?" he yelled.

Conall turned to Marcus. "Stay down! Don't get up!"

Persephone looked from Gundabar to Marcus, her face white.

Gundabar pushed Conall aside and began yelling at Marcus again. Blood was oozing from Marcus' nose.

Conall tried to talk to Gundabar, but the German shoved him aside and drew his sword.

Persephone backed up. "Gundabar!" she exclaimed. "What are you doing?"

Conall threw himself between Gundabar and Marcus. Sukuta joined him, then Valens. None of them had ever seen Gundabar worked up like this.

Marcus got up. "Conall," he said. "Why is Gundabar angry at me?"

Conall had his hands lodged against Gundabar's chest. Sukuta had grabbed the German's sword arm and was holding onto it. Conall cranked his head around. "He says you dishonoured Persephone and now you must die."

Marcus' mouth fell open. "I *what*?

"He saw you dressing on your bedroll in front of Persephone."

Marcus groaned. "Tell him nothing happened."

"Don't you think I did that?" Suddenly, Gundabar shoved Conall aside and lunged at Marcus. Sukuta's grip on his arm tightened, and Valens grabbed his other arm.

Gundabar began a rapid-fire scolding of his captors, which they did not understand and Conall wisely left untranslated.

"Can I fix it somehow?" Marcus asked.

Conall shrugged. "German law changes from tribe to tribe. Some tribes place a *weregild* on a woman's virtue. A set fine based on the woman's place in the tribe. Persephone is a slave so her *weregild* will be less than Damarra's. The *weregilds* are meant to replace blood vengeance—money instead of murder." Conall sighed. "But from the look in Gundabar's eyes, I doubt all the gold in the empire would suffice." Conall turned to Gundabar and spoke a few words in Suevi. Gundabar glared at him for a moment, then spat back, "Yes."

"I asked him what the *Christos* would do," Conall explained. "I asked him if the *Christos* would forgive Marcus."

"But I didn't do anything," Marcus exclaimed.

Conall shook his head. "That doesn't matter right now. All that matters is calming him down, so he can see reason." He smiled at Gundabar. "We see Gundabar as a Christian and a Clan member; we forget sometimes that he is a Suevi warrior, with a warrior's passions. Right now the warrior is in charge. He has vowed to protect Persephone's virtue, and for some reason he believes you are trying to . . . deflower her."

"Tell him I have taken a vow of chastity."

They all looked at him. "A vow of chastity?" Sukuta said.

"Yes."

Conall and Sukuta glanced at each other, then at Marcus. "I did not know that," Conall said.

"Nor did I," said Valens and Sukuta together.

Before the rest of them could comment, Marcus said. "It is my gift to the *Christos*, not information I share with others . . . except under these circumstances. The point being that it is impossible for me to . . . treat Persephone in the manner Gundabar thinks I did—my vow prevents it."

Conall cleared his throat and translated Marcus' revelation to Gundabar as best he could. Gundabar's glare dimmed. "I think he understands," Conall said with a shrug.

"Good." Marcus picked up his tea. It was cool now. He drank it down in one gulp and handed the wooden cup to Persephone. "I'm on guard duty now with Regulus, so if you'll excuse me." He turned to leave, but Gundabar yelled at him to stop. Marcus turned back. "Now what?" he asked.

Gundabar was still frowning, although it was obvious Marcus' revelation had deflated his anger. He spoke quickly to Conall, then his eyes locked on Marcus.

"He says you must apologize to Persephone."

Marcus blinked at Conall. "Apologize? For what?"

"You placed Persephone in a situation which brought her virtue into question."

"*I* placed!"

Conall shrugged.

Marcus turned to Persephone. "Persephone," he began.

She shook her head. "No, Marcus, you don't need to apologize."

Marcus ignored her. "Persephone, I apologize for placing you in a situation in which your virtue might be questioned."

Persephone blushed and nodded.

"Is that acceptable?" Marcus said to Conall. There was an edge of exasperation in his voice. And anger.

Conall repeated Marcus' question to Gundabar. The German answered, gave a sharp nod of his head to Marcus, then turned his back on all of them and went over to the fire to get some supper.

"Well?" Marcus asked.

Conall hesitated.

Marcus sighed. "What did he say, Conall?"

Again Conall hesitated, then: "He said Romans often break their vows, and he would be watching to make sure you did not."

Marcus picked up his sword, jammed it into its sheath, and marched off into the woods.

The others returned to the fire.

A few moments later, Alexander sauntered into the clearing and dropped down beside Persephone. "What was all that yelling about?" he asked.

MEDIOLANUM, NORTHERN ITALY
LATE SEMPTEMBER A.D. 257

THE CITY OF MEDIOLANUM sat at the foot of the Alps in the centre of a vast fertile plain dedicated to agriculture. Vineyards vied with grains of every sort, flocks of sheep supported a thriving woollen industry, and in the nearby forests herds of swine grew fat on the fruits and nuts the trees produced. The city was also a cultural mecca, famous for its schools of philosophy and rhetoric and its theatre. The presence of the imperial mint, and the city's location at the nexus of all the roads in Northern Italy, made it significant for the emperor as well.

The Alamanni king, Chrocus, thought of Mediolanum as a consolation prize. Unlike Rome, it was undefended . . . or it was supposed to be. Chrocus was already in sight of the city when he learned that Gallienus' new cavalry was stationed there. Although Commander Aureolus had taken half its strength to Pannonia to help Gallienus' son, Valerianus the Younger, repel the Marcomanni, Chrocus found himself facing the other half supplemented by Gallienus' army, the army that was *supposed* to be in Hispania cutting Merovech and his Franks to pieces.

Chrocus was high with fever from the wound he had received at the Battle of Rome, and grieving over the death of his son, Altan. The Alamanni host had carried Altan with them on their long march north. His body lay on shields bound together and tied to javelins with leather cords. Chrocus had hoped to fill his son's burial mound with the gold and silver plundered from Mediolanum; now his only hope was to break through the enemy and take his son home, so his mother and sisters could grieve for him and lay his body to rest.

Unlike the Battle of Rome, the Battle of Mediolanum was long and bloody. The Alamanni host had no choice but to fight this time, as Gallienus' army stood between them and their homeland. For his part, Emperor Gallienus was in a rage—after unsuccessfully chasing the Franks across Gaul, he had finally managed to corner a barbarian army and was determined to make them pay.

And he had received reports about the Battle of Rome.

And its aftermath.

Chrocus was still drawing up his frontline when the Roman cavalry charged. The first sweep stopped short and released a barrage of arrows that dropped the enemy frontline before they could even draw their weapons. Before the Alamanni archers at the back of the host could return a volley, the cavalry had pulled back out of range and not a single arrow found a target. In that first barrage Chrocus took an arrow in the left arm, just above the festering wound from the Battle of Rome. The pain was so intense that he passed out and fell from his saddle. His chiefs picked him up and carried him from the field at the same moment that the Roman infantry attacked.

The legionaries hammered the Alamanni warriors with a ferocity that the Alamanni had never encountered before. Gallienus had promised a silver spear to any soldier who killed an Alamanni chief, and a gold spear to anyone who captured a chief and brought him to the emperor in chains. Alamanni chiefs throughout the host found themselves hunted down, and by the end of the third hour, all the chiefs had been killed or captured. Without its leaders, the host fell apart. Before the sun set, the battle was over.

Gallienus met with the chiefs to decide their fate. Victory had not improved his mood any. He lined the chiefs up and ordered them decimated in the true meaning of the word—every tenth man in line was butchered. The dead were then stripped of their armour and weapons and dragged away. The remaining chiefs were then lined up and decimated again. Then a third time.

The remaining chiefs, twelve including the unconscious Chrocus, were stripped of their armour and weapons and lined up a fourth time. Dirt and blood streaked their faces; their loose hair was wild; their leather shirts were torn and filthy and their shirt-tails dangled about their knees—they looked like naughty children standing before their father awaiting punishment. Gallienus ordered Chrocus revived. A creative centurion grabbed a bucket of night waste from a nearby tent and emptied it on Chrocus' face. The audience of Roman soldiers and officers laughed as Chrocus' sat up, sputtering, wiping the sewage from his face. "Get up," Gallienus ordered.

Slowly, painfully, Chrocus rolled onto his knees and pushed himself up.

"What am I to do with you?" Gallienus asked.

Chrocus stared at the emperor.

"I am tempted to slaughter the lot of you, then seek out your women and children and do the same to them."

Chrocus bowed his head, but made no response.

"Answer my questions, though, and you may live to embrace your wife and daughters again."

"I will answer," Chrocus said. His voice was raw; he shivered with fever.

"Who was in charge of the army at Rome?"

"Your praetorian praefect, Commander Festus."

Rage rippled through Gallienus' features.

"Who else was in this army?"

Chrocus looked up at the emperor. "Men," he said and shrugged. "Roman men—I'm not sure what you are asking."

"Not sure what I'm asking?" Gallienus snapped. "Were they clowns? Actors? Temple prostitutes? Who else was in the army?"

He nodded with understanding. "Many large men without armour but armed with clubs and spears and swords. Senators were there." He gave a bitter laugh. "Some were very old but excellent swordsmen. Praetorians. Young men with stout hearts. I'm surprised they did not field their women, too."

"And did you hear what this army shouted as you retreated?"

Chrocus nodded.

"Well? What did you hear?"

"They shouted, 'Festus for emperor.'"

Gallienus scowled. His hands tightened into fists. He turned to the tribune at his side. "Have this rabble escorted from the empire." He turned back to Chrocus. "If I ever see your face again, Chrocus, I will slice it off."

Chrocus bowed, turned, and stumbled away.

"Tribune Cecropius."

"Yes, Your Excellency."

He glared at the young tribune. "Fetch me Festus Macrinus. And while you're in Rome, inform the senators I am coming to spend the winter with them."

Cecropius face paled. "Yes, Your Excellency. Oh, and Your Excellency?"

"What is it?" Gallienus snapped.

"A man to see you, Your Excellency. One of the *Agentes in Rebus*."

"Send him to my tent," Gallienus ordered.

ANTIOCH, SYRIA
OCTOBER A.D. 257

THE PEOPLE OF ANTIOCH greeted Valerianus enthusiastically, and he blessed them with three days of games to celebrate the liberation of Syria from the Persian yoke. Scouts reported that the Persian king was still dug in on the border of Mesopotamia. That Shapur had tired of battle was too much to hope for. Valerianus concluded that Shapur was resting his army. And the grim corollary of that conclusion was that Shapur was planning to launch a new campaign in the spring that required his army at peak performance. Something *big*, in other words.

Valerianus had something big planned for the spring as well. The first phase of the persecution had reached its natural conclusion. Christian leaders across the empire were either in exile or in hiding. So far, the results of this persecution were different than Decius'. Under Decius, Christian leaders had raced to the altars to sacrifice. This time, very few of the leaders had recanted. In one of his letters Gallienus had pointed out that exile was not a harsh enough punishment to induce the Christians to deny the *Christos*. And the rank and file Christians? Instead of turning back to the old gods, they were actually rallying behind their exiled leaders. They saw them as heroes and even had a special name for them: confessors.

All that would change in the spring. Once the leaders were brought back and ordered to choose between life and death, they would choose life. And when wealthy Christians had their estates and monies confiscated, they would choose comfort over the *Christos*. After all, who in their right mind would choose to die for a dead Jewish carpenter of questionable parentage?

TENSIONS IN THE CLAN ESCALATED in the weeks following Gundabar's attack on Marcus. During the day it was easy for the two men to avoid each other, but at night when the Clan gathered around the campfire to pray, they had to endure each other's company. Persephone finally convinced Gundabar that Marcus had not "dishonoured" her. Unfortunately, Gundabar then got it into his head that Marcus *intended* to dishonour her at the first opportunity, as if Gundabar's original accusation had given him the idea! Try as she might, Persephone could not persuade Gundabar that Marcus' intentions were honourable, and eventually she stopped trying. Gundabar's obsession with keeping an eye on Marcus soon consumed all his spare time.

Winter fell without much warning in Germania. A warm day could suddenly drop to sub-zero temperatures; a sunny sky in the morning could cloud over and transform into a blizzard in the afternoon. One morning the Clan woke to find a thick layer of frost covering the ground. Alexander threw back his covers and shivered his way over to the fire, which had gone out during the night. His breath smoked as he got the fire lit again. Within an hour the sun turned the chill into a beautiful day, but the Clan wasn't fooled. They had had their warning.

Valens called a Clan meeting, and they gathered around the fire. By his calculations they were still seventy-five miles short of the Quadi village of Singone, where they had intended to spend the winter. Most of them thought they could make it—that they could beat winter to Singone. Valens was worried about Damarra. Her pregnancy was beginning to show, and he did not want to risk her or the babies with unnecessary travel. Perhaps, he suggested, they should dig in now? Use the mild weather to construct a few huts in which they could survive the winter. Prisca suggested they pray about it, much to Xerxes' delight, and so they joined hands and devoted the next half hour to seeking God's will. When they finished, they all got up and helped break camp. The unspoken consensus was that they should carry on, that the *Christos* would lead them where He wanted them to go.

A few hours later the Clan stumbled into an abandoned village. Most of the buildings were blackened shells that fell apart when touched. Ashes drifted on the breeze like grey snowflakes. There was no sign of human habitation—the village had been destroyed many years ago. They found the blackened skeleton of a horse and an ox, but no human remains. The inhabitants had fled the fire, or been dragged off as slaves.

In the centre of the village, one building still stood. It was a long, low structure made of logs and a rounded wattle roof. To judge by its size, it had once served as a meeting place for the entire village. A large skin—probably black bear—covered the entrance. They pushed it aside and entered the building. It was dark inside, but the darkness was pierced by hundreds of beams of light coming through the walls where new chinking was needed. Two long tables with chairs were pushed to one side. They were covered with dust. In the middle was a huge fire pit with a spit from which hung a large iron cauldron. Sleeping platforms lined the wall. At the back, divided from the living quarters by a sturdy fence, were several stalls for animals. Damarra threw out her hands and twirled around. "This is an answer to prayer," she said.

Instantly, the others saw it too and soon they were embracing and shouting with joy. Even Gundabar and Marcus. Although not with each other.

"It will need more chinking," Persephone pointed out.

"And firewood. Lots of firewood," Sukuta said. "Maybe I can find an axe somewhere," he added, then headed out the entrance to look. Cecht tagged along behind him.

"I'll check those stalls and see to horses," Conall said.

"We'll need to get some boughs in for those sleeping platforms," Damarra noted. "I think I saw some cedar just south of here."

Pretty soon everyone was at work.

At sunset, the temperature began to drop again, and by midnight it had started to snow. The guards threw lots and Gundabar and Alexander lost, so while the Clan was sleeping in its warm new home, Gundabar and Alexander were outside in the cold on guard duty. They stood together and chatted for a few minutes, and then they each headed off to start their rounds. Alexander followed the path north through the centre of the village to a small stream. The path then ran beside the stream for about half a mile before jogging off into the bush. There were no prints other than his own in the snow as he headed back to the village. He followed the path in the opposite direction. On this side of the village was another stream, wider than the first. A tree had been felled to serve as a bridge. He crossed the makeshift bridge, stopped, and stared into the darkness. The world was grey. Soft white flakes fell through a sky illuminated by a full moon. It was pretty. He decided that someday soon he would bring Persephone out here and kiss her . . . and maybe something more. Thinking of that brought a smile to his face.

Suddenly, he heard a branch snap and jerked his head to the right. Something had moved. In the trees. He saw a figure crouching in the drifting flakes. A human? Or an animal. It looked something like a wolf, and yet—

The crouching figure chuckled.

Alexander drew his sword. "Who are you?" he demanded. "Show yourself!"

The figure rose and withdrew into the trees.

Alexander waded through the snow after him. "Is that you, Gundabar?" he asked.

The figure chuckled again, then disappeared behind a tree.

Rage burned in Alexander's throat. This prankster had no idea who he was dealing with. He tightened his grip on the sword, then put on a sudden burst of speed, but when he jumped behind the tree, no one was there. For the first time he felt a tinge of fear. "What do you want?" he whispered.

The answer came from behind him, and the fear exploded in his chest. He had time to wonder how his adversary had gotten behind him, and then a familiar voice hissed in his ear, and he felt the cold touch of a blade slice into his exposed throat:

"My Persephone!"

TWENTY-SIX

MEDIOLANUM, NORTHERN ITALY
NOVEMBER A.D. 257

The atmosphere in Mediolanum during the first week of
November was festive. After annihilating the Alamanni
host, Gallienus had organized games to celebrate his victory. Wine flowed, at imperial expense, and the emperor himself
appeared at several dinner parties thrown by some of the city's
brightest luminaries. News arrived that the Franks had sacked the
city of Tarraco in Hispania, but even that disaster, so far away it
seemed almost unreal, could not dampen the city's spirits. Gallienus took up residence in one of the city's finest villas, and it was
there that Festus Macrinus found him when he arrived from
Rome.

Gallienus greeted him with an embrace, then called for wine
and food to be brought for his old friend. Festus regaled Gallienus
with stories of his adventures with Valerianus in their youth while
he ate. Gallienus listened politely and laughed in all the right
places, as he always did when Festus told these stories. At the end
of the meal, Gallienus suggested that they retire to the villa's library, which he had heard was one of the empire's finest. Festus
agreed.

The library was a massive room, octagonal in shape, with
rows of shelves that rose up three full storeys, each with a balcony
that could be accessed by a series of movable ladders. The shelves

held scrolls, piles of loose parchment, and books. Several desks were positioned throughout the library on the main floor. Windows high up on the walls provided ample light during the day. Two praetorian guards were waiting in the library, along with half a dozen of Gallienus' personal bodyguard. "Do you know these men?" Gallienus asked, pointing at the praetorians.

Festus looked them over. "No. But there are many praetorians, Your Excellency. I could not possibly know them all."

Gallienus nodded. He pointed to the largest of his own bodyguard. "This is Commander Julian," Gallienus said. "He is the commander of the imperial guard, and I trust him implicitly. Commander Julian, this is an old family friend, Festus Macrinus, commander of the Praetorian Guard."

Julian bowed his head to Festus. He was a tall, well-built man with brown hair and brown eyes. His jaw was large and square and jutted from his face. His breastplate bore the insignia of Gallienus' personal guard, a roaring lion.

"Let me show you how trustworthy the commander is," Gallienus said. He turned to Julian. "Please kill those two praetorians, Julian."

The praetorians gasped and reached for their swords, but Gallienus bodyguard surrounded them and removed the weapons, then forced the two guards to their knees.

Festus grey eyes narrowed. "What's going on here?" he asked.

Gallienus held up his hand for silence. Julian drew his sword, then removed their heads. He wiped his sword clean on a dead praetorian's tunic, then sheathed it and saluted Gallienus.

"You see," Gallienus said. "Completely trustworthy."

"Gallienus—"

"Unlike you, Festus."

"What? I—"

"You betrayed me!"

"I did no such—"

"Did you or did you not organize an army in the city of Rome without imperial permission?"

"I did, but—"

Gallienus banged his fist down on an alabaster table. "Yes or no!"

"Yes."

"Did you on a previous occasion place the Praetorian Guard at the senate's disposal?"

"Yes."

"Did you or did you not attempt to have me assassinated?"

"What! That's preposterous! How could you even think that?"

"Did you or did you not attempt to have me assassinated?"

Festus just stared at him.

"Julian!" Gallienus snapped. "Show him in."

Julian saluted, then marched out the door. A few moments later he returned with a man with black hair and a small black moustache. The man bowed to the emperor, then turned to face Festus.

"Do you know this man?" Gallienus asked Festus.

Festus looked him over, then shook his head. "No."

"His name is Tacitus. He is the Commander of the *Agentes in Rebus.*"

Festus nodded. "Of course! I didn't recognize him at first; it has been a long time."

Gallienus waved the remark aside. "I had some doubts about my assassin, Festus."

Suddenly, Festus frowned. "Doubts?"

"Yes—doubts. For the longest time, something about it bothered me. I couldn't put my finger on it, but I knew there was something . . . not quite right. And then it occurred to me. Strato's commander said he was a marksmen, that he could pierce the eye of a fleeing rabbit at seventy-five yards. Do you remember that?"

"Yes, I do. I was the one who told you. Strato was one of the best."

"Exactly. So how is it that a man who can pierce the eye of a running rabbit at seventy-five yards, cannot put an arrow through the heart of an almost stationary emperor twenty feet away?"

Festus' face blanched. Gallienus could see the man's mind desperately looking for an explanation.

"He missed intentionally, didn't he?"

Festus' mouth quivered.

"*You* set it up."

"I did not! I had nothing to do with it. I *saved* your life, remember? I was the one who shot him."

"Yes, you were, weren't you? And where did you get that bow and arrow?"

"I . . . happened to have—"

"How did you know you'd need it, Festus?"

"I—"

Gallienus turned to Tacitus. "Commander Tacitus, would you please explain what you discovered in the course of your investigation?"

Tacitus bowed to the emperor, then smiled at Festus. "I learned first of all that the assassin, Strato, was married and had five children."

Gallienus held up his hand. "You told me the man had no family, Festus."

"I . . . must have been mistaken."

"Odd," Tacitus said. "Strato adored his family, loved them dearly, talked about them endlessly. It was common knowledge. Next I learned that Strato was a gambler. A bad gambler. He had accrued substantial debts."

Again Gallienus held up his hand. "Does this sound familiar, Festus?"

"No."

Tacitus continued. "Strato's debtors gave him an ultimatum: pay your debts, or your family will be sold into slavery." Tacitus grinned at Festus. "Fortunately, a benefactor paid off Strato's debts at the last moment, saving his wife and children from a fate worse than death." Tacitus picked a piece of parchment up off the desk. "Here is the official document releasing Strato from his debts. His wife had it. It was signed by his benefactor."

Gallienus glared at Festus. "Would you read the signature please, Commander Tacitus?"

"The benefactor was . . . Festus Macrinus."

Gallienus snatched the document and threw it at Festus. "You *lied* to me!" he yelled.

"I—"

"You set it up and blamed the Christians. Why?"

"Because . . . you would not take a stand on the Christians. I . . . had to force your hand."

"You fool! I was already considering the Christian Problem!" Gallienus took a deep breath, then, "My father set this up, didn't he?"

"Absolutely not! It was my idea!"

"Why are you protecting him?"

"I am not protecting him."

Gallienus pushed his fists into his temples and screamed. "And then you made this . . . unholy alliance with the senate. How dare you join their little army!"

"We were trying to save Rome! For you!"

"For me? Were you thinking of me when your army was shouting, *Festus for emperor*?"

"I turned them down!"

"Because you knew I'd have a real army at your throat before the imperial crown settled on your head."

"You have to believe me, Your Excellency! I am loyal to you and your father."

Gallienus rushed forward and spit in Festus' face. "Believe you?" he screamed. "Believe that you are loyal? Is it loyalty you show me when you side with the senate? Is it loyalty you show me when you hire a man to shoot me in the back? Can you stand there and truly expect me to *believe* you? To *trust* you?" He turned to Julian. "I want this man in chains," he screamed.

Julian motioned to his men. Two of them came forward and grabbed Festus' arms. "Please, Gallienus," Festus pleaded. "I raised you as a son."

"And that is the only reason you will leave this room alive," Gallienus said. He grabbed Festus' cloak and ripped it off, then took his sword, snapped it across his knee, and tossed the pieces aside. "Remove his armour," he ordered. Two guards came forward and unhinged his breastplate, and let it drop to the floor. "Take him to the coast and put him on the first ship to Syria," he ordered, then he turned back to Festus. "My father can have you if he wants you. But know this: if you set foot in the West again while I rule, I will have your head."

"IS HE DEAD?" Valens asked.

They stood wrapped in their cloaks, staring down at Alexander. He lay face up in the snow, his eyes staring at the flakes falling gently from the night sky. A halo of blood surrounded his head. Gundabar looked up from where he knelt beside Alexander and nodded. "*Yeise*," he whispered.

Persephone and Prisca clutched each other and began to cry.

Gundabar stood up and raised the torch high above his head. "Someone here kill," he said.

Paulus laughed. "Someone *here*? Why not *you*, Gundabar? You had as much reason as any of us."

"No," Gundabar said. "Why I kill?"

Regulus answered: "Seemed to me that Alexander was interested in the pretty slave over there, and we all know how you feel about that."

Gundabar touched his ear and shook his head. Conall translated what Regulus had said. Gundabar scowled at Regulus. "No," he snapped. "No kill over Persephone."

Marcus scoffed. "I hate to say it, but Gundabar is right. If he was going to kill anyone over Persephone, it would have been me."

"*Yeise*," Gundabar said, and slapped Marcus on the shoulder. "No kill Marcus."

"I think we're all missing something," Valens said.

"And that is?" Marcus prompted.

"Maybe the murderer isn't one of us. Maybe there's somebody out there who doesn't appreciate the fact that we've just moved in here."

"That's true," Damarra said. Her teeth were chattering with the cold. "Maybe somebody else was living here. Or maybe we're being followed."

"No," Paulus said. "If we were being followed, one of us would have seen something by now. We've got, how many, eight guards on rotation?"

"Seven now," Sukuta pointed out.

"Seven guards, then. The point is, surely one of us would have spotted something by now."

"Unless they were good at not being seen," Sukuta said.

They fell silent. Valens and Damarra stared out into the grey darkness.

"What do we do with him?" Sukuta asked, pointing at the body.

"We'll take him back to the hall with us," Valens replied. "That way the wolves won't get him. We'll bury him in the morning. And from now on, nobody wanders off by themselves. And guards, when you're on duty, stay together instead of splitting up. If there is someone out there, we don't want to give him the opportunity to pick us off one at a time."

"And if it's one of us?" Marcus asked.

"If it's one of us . . . we'll . . . figure it out."

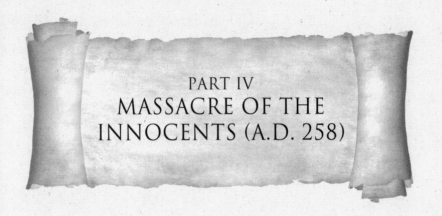

PART IV
MASSACRE OF THE INNOCENTS (A.D. 258)

"*Then Herod, when he saw that he was deceived by the wise men, was exceedingly angry; and he sent forth and put to death all the male children who were in Bethlehem and in all its districts, from two years old and under, according to the time which he had determined from the wise men.*"

MATTHEW 2:16 (NKJV)

"*The Tyrant dies and his rule is over; the Martyr dies and his rule begins.*"

SOREN KIERKEGAARD

TWENTY-SEVEN

QUADI TERRITORY, GERMANIA
MARCH A.D. 258

Prisca wiped Damarra's forehead with the cool cloth. "Doesn't that feel better now, my lady?" she said, her voice soft and soothing.

Damarra nodded at her. Her face was red from the exertion, but the pain had dulled, thanks to one of Persephone's herbal mixtures. Persephone was also beside her, holding her hand. "Almost, my lady," she said.

Sukuta and Paulus had constructed walls around her sleeping platform for this very moment. Valens was pacing back and forth just outside. "Are you all right, Damarra?" he called. There wasn't room inside for him too, and Damarra needed Prisca and Persephone right now.

"I'm fine, Valens," she said. "Take Ruth outside to play."

"Daddy," the little girl said. "Mommy says take me outside. Come on! We'll build a snowman."

Valens consented, and the two of them left. Damarra sighed out her exasperation. Were all men this difficult, or just Valens? She loved her husband dearly, but at times like this he was more a hindrance than a help. He had fretted over her all winter, and their living arrangements had only made it worse. All of them stuck together in one building day after day. There was no relief except when he went hunting or was on guard duty. Once this was over she was going to give him an ultimatum: either he stopped fretting over her like a broody hen whenever she was pregnant or no more children!

Another contraction, stronger than the last. She bit her lip and squeezed Persephone's hand. In a few moments the contraction faded. Prisca was right—not long now.

She smiled up at Persephone. The winter had been hardest on her. Alexander's murder remained unsolved, but almost every theory posited around revolved around Persephone. Paulus was convinced Gundabar had done it . . . because he was jealous of Alexander's attraction to Persephone. Gundabar thought Marcus was responsible . . . because he was jealous of Alexander's attraction to Persephone. Regulus theorized that Gundabar and Marcus had killed Alexander *together* . . . because they wanted to keep the battle for Persephone's heart between the two of them. In order to demonstrate the absurdity of all the accusations, Sukuta had blamed Prisca . . . because Persephone was getting all the attention. Damarra had even heard it whispered that Valens had murdered Alexander . . . because he secretly loved Persephone and wanted her all to himself. About the only person in the Clan who had not been blamed for Alexander's murder was Ruth.

Another contraction. She sucked in a breath and squeezed Persephone's hand so hard that the young girl winced. "Sorry," she said as the contraction eased off.

Persephone kissed her cheek gently. "It's alright," she whispered.

Damarra's heart soared. Persephone was such a sweet person, and she loved the *Christos* with such *passion*. She and Valens had already decided to free her when this was all over, and supply a dowry for her. Whomever she decided to marry would be blessed just to have her, but the dowry would ensure that she never wanted for anything as long as she lived. Persephone had confided her feelings for Gundabar to Damarra. Up until his fight with Marcus last fall, she had thought the two of them might eventually marry, perhaps even travel to his homeland and share their love of the *Christos* with the Suevi. Now, she was confused and uncertain. Gundabar had changed; his obsession with what Marcus *might* do had come between them . . . and it was almost as if he blamed *her* for the way Marcus felt about her . . . but didn't really feel about her, except in Gundabar's head.

"It's time, my lady," Prisca said. "When the next contraction comes, I want you to push."

Damarra nodded. She was glad the babies were coming. Winter was fading fast. Last week she had seen crocuses pushing up through the melting snow, and the songbirds were singing again. The Clan had gathered for a *Moot*, as Gundabar called meetings held to discuss anything that affected the entire Clan. Valens had called the *Moot* to set a departure date. They had decided to leave as soon as Damarra was able, which meant when she recovered from giving birth to the twins. After being cooped up in this hall all winter, she was eager to continue their journey. Every step brought the Clan closer to the *Thing*, closer to unravelling the mystery in which their lives had been wrapped for almost five years.

Damarra gasped. The pain started again . . . building . . . building, until her whole being, every thought, every muscle, every emotion, was screaming at her: *PUSH!*

"Now, my lady," Prisca told her.

VALERIANUS WAS PUTTING THE FINAL touches on the edict which would initiate the second phase of the persecution of the Christians, when a slave informed him of the arrival of Festus Macrinus. News of the Alamanni invasion of Italy had reached Valerianus, and he was surprised that Festus would leave his post in Rome. Even though Gallienus had defeated the Alamanni at the Battle of Mediolanum, it was crucial that Festus represent imperial interests and power in the capital. This was not the time to be visiting old friends in the Asian provinces.

Valerianus dismissed his scribes and slaves and ordered Festus shown in. He gazed out across the balcony to the Orontes river below. It was a beautiful and peaceful scene. His winter at Antioch had been a true blessing. He had commandeered this villa overlooking the Orontes and lived in pure luxury for the last five months. Stretching languidly, he turned on the dining couch so that he could see Festus when he entered. As emperor, this kind of luxury was his due, but the crisis facing the empire required great sacrifice, and he spent most of his time in military camps and on the battlefield. Still, an emperor did not live by battle alone. For the sake of the empire, he needed to relax and reinvigorate himself, thus his time here at this villa. Now he felt rested and refreshed and ready to face the trials that were in store for him this campaigning season.

The doors to his audience chamber swept open and three guards entered the room. One of them was Commander Julian, the man in charge of his son's bodyguard. The others he did not recognize, but they also wore the lion emblem on their breastplates that signified Gallienus' bodyguard. The fourth man was Festus Macrinus.

In chains.

Valerianus jumped up. "What is the meaning of this?" he bellowed.

Commander Julian saluted. "We are delivering this prisoner to you from the Emperor Gallienus."

Festus' silver head was bowed in shame.

"Release him," Valerianus ordered.

Julian saluted again, then gestured at the prisoner. One of his men produced a key and unlocked and removed the padlocks. The chains fell to the floor. Festus stepped out of them.

"Why was the Praetorian Praefect of Rome brought to us in chains?" Valerianus asked.

"It is best if Festus explains it himself," Julian said.

Valerianus flipped his hand in dismissal. Julian and his men saluted, picked up the chains, and then marched out of the room. When the doors banged shut behind them, Valerianus asked, "What happened?"

Festus looked up. Dirt and blood smeared his face. His tunic was ripped and stained and he stank like the hold of a slave ship. Tears welled in his grey eyes. "He found out about Strato," he said.

One of Valerianus' eyebrows lifted. "Does he know of our involvement?"

Festus shook his head. "No. I told him it was my idea, that you had nothing to do with it."

"And did he believe you?"

Festus hesitated. "He has no other choice. I would not betray you. I remember our oath."

Valerianus grinned. "Ah, yes. The oath." He thought for a moment, then, "Is there more?"

Festus nodded.

"Tell us."

Festus narrated the events leading up to the Battle of Rome and their aftermath. When he finished, Valerianus reclined on his dining couch. He drank a cup of wine, then poured another and drank it, too. At last he looked at his old friend and shook his head. "You old fool," he said.

Festus nodded.

"You almost ruined everything."

"No! You are emperor, the saviour of Rome. That has not changed!"

"Festus for emperor," Valerianus scoffed. "What were the fools thinking? Gallienus is right. The senate has prolonged this crisis with its endless plots and manipulations." He laughed. "We are the perfect example—a senatorial family that has manipulated its way onto the throne. Fortunately, the gods want us here, and we deserve this honour. But there are hundreds of other senators who believe they too deserve this honour, and they must be stopped. Forever. Whatever Gallienus decides to do to limit the power of the senate, he will have our support."

"And what of me, Your Excellency?"

"What *of* you?" Valerianus stared at his friend, pondering the options, then smiled. "You may yet be of some service, Festus. That is, if you are willing to serve your emperor?"

The old soldier in him woke up and he snapped to attention. "I will, Your Excellency."

"Will you serve the empire, Festus?"

"I will, Your Excellency."

Valerianus drew his dagger, and held it out to his friend. "Will you honour your vow, Festus?"

Festus did not hesitate. He took the dagger and bowed. "That has never changed, Your Excellency."

PRISCA WALKED OUTSIDE, into a bright, sunny day. Her eyes took a moment to adjust, after many hours in the hall's gloom. Valens and Gundabar were playing tag with Ruth. She cleared her throat, and Valens looked up. His face was a question mark. She grinned at him. "Come, my lord; your son awaits."

Joy shone on Valens face. He swept Ruth up into his arms. Gundabar slapped his back. "Did you hear, Ruth? You have a baby brother!"

She hugged him tight. "Let's see, Daddy!"

They hurried inside behind Prisca. The enclosure had been pushed aside. Damarra sat on the sleeping platform holding their baby in her arms. The baby was swaddled in tight, white cloth and was sound asleep. "A son, Valens," Damarra whispered.

Her face was radiant; she looked so beautiful that it stole his breath. He kissed her forehead, then gathered the baby into his arms. "Joshua," he cooed and touched the baby's nose.

"Joshua," Damarra repeated, tasting the name in her mouth. She smiled. "I like it."

"As for me and my house, we shall serve the Lord," Valens whispered over his son, then kissed his little cheek. "Joshua told the tribes of Israel that, and this Joshua," he held up his son, "shall pronounce it to our Clan and to the nations."

Gundabar had spread the news, and soon the rest of the Clan came to see the newest member. They took turns holding Joshua and praying over him and laughing over him, and then Sukuta asked the question that had not yet occurred to the others. "Wasn't there supposed to be two of them?"

Suddenly, every face fell in surprise. Prisca blinked, glanced down at her lady's abdomen, then up at Valens. "Only one, my lord. No twin."

Valens sat down on the sleeping platform beside Damarra. "That can't be right. Gundabar's prophecy said thirteen would leave for Germania. But we're only twelve. Are you sure there isn't another baby inside her?"

Prisca laughed, then covered her mouth. "No, my lord. Just the one."

Sukuta gasped. His eyes were brightened with whatever realization had just illuminated them.

"What is it?" Valens asked.

"Maybe you were right, my lord," Sukuta said.

"Right about what?"

"Maybe the person who murdered Alexander *isn't* one of us, at least not one of us here. Maybe he was murdered by someone who is following us, *has* been following us from the start—a *secret* Clan member. And maybe the murderer and the thirteenth member of the Clan are one in the same person?"

ROME
APRIL A.D. 258

GALLIENUS' STAY IN ROME that winter was a success by imperial standards. The senate had treated him like the emperor he was—showered him with compliments and gifts and promises of eternal loyalty. They had tossed him another bone—the senator "responsible" for the near-rebellion that had followed the Battle of Rome, as if one man alone were responsible for that debacle. They brought him Senator Sextus in chains and Gallienus had dutifully removed his head, thus playing the part they had expected him to play. As far as the senate was concerned, the status quo had been re-established. But they were wrong—the status quo had been one of the most destructive forces in the empire for centuries, and he would not permit it to continue. The senate did not realize it yet, but they would. Gallienus had drafted an edict and sent it to his father, explaining the new direction the empire must take and re-questing Valerianus' support. And Valerianus had complied. The dispatch from the East had arrived this morning, and in it was the edict, signed by Valerianus, thus making it official across the empire:

Henceforth senators were prohibited from serving as military commanders.

Why no one had thought of this simple solution before was inexplicable to Gallienus. There were two ways to deal with a vicious dog: kill it, or extract its teeth. The senate was the empire's vicious dog . . . at least, it was one of them. He could not very well exterminate the entire senatorial class, but with one, simple edict

319

he had removed its teeth. Permanently. Without access to military command, the senate no longer had access to the military. Without access to the military, the senate was all bark and no bite.

The dispatch from Valerianus had included several other documents as well. Festus Macrinus had sent a long and tearful admission of guilt punctuated with apologies. He took responsibility for the actions which led up to the senate's most recent foray into rebellion. He took responsibility for Strato's assassination attempt. *Complete* responsibility. Valerianus, he insisted, had played no part in the plot. Festus vowed it was true . . . before the gods, it was true.

He even sent his finger and signet ring as surety for his vow.

The sight of the bloodless finger and ring was in itself almost sufficient to persuade Gallienus that Festus was speaking the truth. But the letter from Valerianus, in which he described finding Festus Macrinus dead in his bath, was the proof that finally persuaded him of Festus' sincerity. His old mentor had slit his wrists and written a final message to the son he'd never had in his own blood on the wall:

Blood Vow

His vow. He had given his life for his vow.

Valerianus was innocent.

Gallienus smiled. Innocence was a matter of perspective. Festus' suicide did not convince Gallienus that his father was innocent, only that Festus *believed* his father was innocent. And despite all the subterfuge and machinations, Festus had helped him see the truth about the Christians. Like the senate, they were a vicious dog attacking the empire, with one difference: the Christian dog was rabid and the disease was spreading. And there was only one way to deal with a rabid dog.

Destroy it.

Gallienus removed the last document from the dispatch pouch. He saw the title of the edict and signed his name at the bottom. He did not need to read it; he trusted Valerianus to do the right thing. "Time to put the Christian dog out of its misery," Gallienus said to his scribes as he handed them the edict.

TWENTY-EIGHT

COTINI TERRITORY, GERMANIA
LATE APRIL A.D. 258

For the last month, the Clan had been travelling through the hill country that marked the eastern edge of Quadi territory and the smaller, more desolate territory that was the home of the neighbouring tribe, the Cotini. They had encountered the odd Quadi on their travels, hunters mostly, but a few Quadi merchants heading south to trade for luxury goods to sell to the tribes. They were a friendly, curious people, who asked lots of questions and believed that hospitality to strangers was a sacred duty . . . as long as those strangers were not Roman. None of the Quadi they met thought they were Roman. By now, the only Clan member who looked Roman was Persephone, with her olive skin. During the winter they had abandoned their cloth tunics for breaches and shirts and boots made out of deerskin, and the men had been many months without a barber and sported long hair and beards. The fact that they spoke Latin well did not bother the Quadi, whose trading ties with Rome necessitated learning the "enemy's" language.

Cotini territory looked similar to the eastern parts of Quadi territory, but it felt different. It seemed empty and quiet, as if nature was holding its breath and listening to them pass. The quiet was reverential, not sinister. It was the quiet of expectation. Something was coming; something was going to happen. They all felt it, and the silence infected them, and they became a whisper passing through the forest. A rumour.

That afternoon, the forest changed. Where before it had been a mix of oak and elm and aspen, suddenly the hardwoods transformed into tall, windswept pine. The trees grew closer and larger, the way became slower. Soon, although the sun rode high in the sky, the world beneath the canopy darkened. Even the trunks of the trees turned black. "Black woods," Gundabar whispered at one point, and then nobody spoke again for an hour.

At last they came to an opening in the trees, a clearing, but a clearing unlike any they had seen before. At ground level there was a wide, open area covered with a hundred generations of pine needles. It was soft and spongy to walk on. About ten feet up the circle of trees that defined the clearing all began to bend into it, so that at the height of thirty feet, the tops of the trees all touched, their branches twining together to form a natural wattle roof over the clearing. It was so thick that they could not see the sunlight, although the sun was still high in the sky. "Here," Gundabar said. "We camp here."

Although they normally travelled until just before dusk, no one argued. Camp was set up and a fire was started. Valens opened his bag to take out some diapers and swaddling cloth for Joshua. Just under the cloths he found a piece of parchment. He had not opened his pack since last night, just before he went to sleep; he was sure there had been no parchment there then. He took the parchment out and set down his bag, then opened the parchment. At the top was a message directed to him:

I thought this Certificate of Peace
might be of interest to you, seeing as
you know the recipient so well. Or
think you do . . .

From,
A friend

Beneath that was what he assumed was the original certificate, which he read with growing wrath:

*Know that we have granted peace to Marcus Gaius For-
tunatus, whose behaviour since the commission of his
crime is satisfactory; and we desire to make this known
to other episcopi also. We wish you to maintain peace
with the holy martyrs.*
    Lucian the Confessor Wrote This

He looked up from the letter, sought out Marcus. He was sitting by the fire, playing with Ruth.

"Ruth," Valens called. When she looked up at him, he said,
"Go to your mother."

"But I was playing with Uncle Marcus—"

"Go to your mother *now*," he snapped.

The little girl jerked back in fright. She had never heard her father yell like that. She looked around for her mother, who was
sitting on an log, breastfeeding Joshua, then ran over to her.
Damarra had heard his tone too, and was staring at him, mouth-
ing a question: "What's wrong?"

Valens marched over to Marcus, who was on his feet now, a
look of consternation on his face. "What is the meaning of this?"
Valens asked.

Marcus took the parchment, glanced at it, and his face faded
to a sickly white.

"You are *lapsi*," Valens spat and snatched the certificate back.

"I have been forgiven," Marcus whispered.

"Not by me, you haven't."

"That doesn't matter. What matters is the *Christos* has forgiven
me."

"You think so?" He bent down and grabbed Marcus' pack,
then shoved it at him. "Get out!"

Marcus took his pack and set it down. "I'm not going anywhere. The *Christos* asked me to come, remember?"

Rage trembled on Valens' face, but there was nothing he could
do. Marcus was absolutely right. The *Christos* had summoned him
to be part of the Clan, and just because Valens was the Clan
leader, he did not have the right to expel anyone. He spun around.
"Who put this in my pack?"

Clan faces stared back at him, shaking their heads.

"Someone wanted me to see this. Who?"

"What is it?" Sukuta asked.

"Marcus' Certificate of Peace."

Sukuta hurried over and took the document. When he'd finished reading it, he glanced at Marcus and shrugged. "I had no idea he was *lapsi*."

"Nor me," said Persephone.

The denials went round the Clan until it was Damarra's turn. She held Joshua up to her shoulder and started patting his tiny back. Ruth was peeking out at her father from behind Damarra's legs.

"You knew," Valens said.

"Yes."

"And you did not tell me."

"No. I did not."

"Why?"

"Because I knew this would happen."

"How long have you known?"

"He confided in me before we left."

"I do not suppose it was you who put this in my pack, then."

"Of course not!"

"And I'm supposed to believe you?"

"I have never lied to you."

"No, you only withheld the truth—that is just as dishonest."

Fire ignited in Damarra's blue eyes. "Stop now, my love, before you say something you will regret."

Valens' jaw worked furiously, the muscles bunching and unbunching. He wanted to strike out, but every avenue of release was closed to him. Finally, he yelled, "Who put this in my pack?"

"Perhaps it was the same person who killed Alexander, my lord," Sukuta suggested.

"To what end?"

"First, there was all the foolishness over Persephone. Then Alexander was murdered." Sukuta shook his head. "It's almost as if someone is trying to . . . stir us up, turn us against one another." He turned to Marcus. "I assume you didn't plant the certificate in Valens' bag yourself?"

Marcus answered with a bitter laugh.

"I thought not. Did you know it was missing?"

"Yes. I discovered it was missing the night before we left the Hermunduri village."

"What did you think happened to it?"

He shrugged. "At first I thought someone had stolen it." He gave another bitter laugh. "I had a nightmare that the thief would give it to Valens and he'd fly into a rage."

Valens snorted.

"But then nothing happened. The days turned into weeks and into months, and I finally decided that I *had* lost it. I mean, why would anyone take it and keep it all that time?"

"Exactly," Sukuta agreed. "And yet that's what happened. Someone stole it and kept it. For months. Then, when the time was right, they planted it in Valens' bag. So we have to ask ourselves, why is *now* the right time?"

"Because the enemy is trying to distract us," Damarra chimed in.

"Yes, but why?"

Damarra shook her head. "I'm sorry, Sukuta. You're right, but because you are not a follower of the *Christos*, you are missing a vital distinction."

"Which is?"

"The enemy that is trying to distract us is not human."

Sukuta's face scrunched into a question mark. "Not . . . human?"

"We are part of a spiritual battle here, a war between light and darkness, good and evil, the *Christos*—"

"And Satan," Persephone said.

"Yes, Satan. Satan is the enemy, and he is trying to destroy the Clan. He knows God has His hand on us. He does not know why, just as we do not yet know why, but he does not care. If God wants something, Satan will try to destroy it. It is the nature of the beast."

"So Satan is marching through Germania with us, my lady?" Sukuta asked. There was incredulity in his voice.

"He is, Sukuta. Oh, I have no doubt he is using a human to do his work, but it is Satan who is manipulating him. And we have allowed him to do it. We allowed him to use Persephone's beauty to distract us. We allowed him to use Alexander's murder to divide us. And now," she glanced at her husband, "Satan is using my husband's inability to forgive the *lapsi* to drive a wedge into the Clan that will destroy us."

"So now it is my fault, is it? I'm not the one who denied the *Christos*." He pointed at Marcus. "He is!"

"Do you think Marcus does not know that?"

"Of course he does."

"Then we do not need to remind him, my husband." She handed Joshua to Prisca, then went to Valens and embraced him. Then she looked up into his eyes and said, "If you cannot put aside your anger at the *lapsi*, then Satan has won."

Valens clenched his teeth. "You're right," he whispered.

She brought his head down and kissed his forehead. "Satan has been following the Clan, plaguing the Clan. We cannot allow it anymore."

He glanced at Marcus, then back at Damarra. "You're right," he said again. A little louder.

"Only the *Christos* may march with your Clan, *Sankt*," she said and smiled.

Suddenly, Valens threw his arms around her and hugged her to him. "Only the *Christos* may march with us," he cried.

He let her go, kissed her on the lips, then turned to the others. "It's the *Christos*! The *Christos* is the answer to Gundabar's riddle."

The others looked about, and one by one, the same light dawned in each of their eyes that was shining in Valens'. "It was never twins!" Valens exclaimed. "We were wrong. Joshua made twelve and the *Christos* is thirteen. He was with us all along. The Clan *was* complete when we entered Germania."

There was a shout of triumph from one of them—no one ever knew who—and then a light flashed above them, a brilliant illumination without shape or size that seemed contained beneath the wattled roof of the clearing and yet infinite. The entire Clan gasped in one breath as the light settled upon them, *infused* them, and for a breathtaking moment of pure ecstasy, the Clan and the Light became one, and Gundabar shouted in perfect Latin what they all knew in their hearts and souls: "The *Christos* is with us; the *Thing* has begun."

"WHAT'S GOING ON?" Paulus shouted.

"I'm blind," Regulus replied. "Is that you, Paulus?"

"Yes, it's me!"

"Can you see, Paulus?"

"No, I'm blind too! What happened?"

"There was a light," Regulus cried. He could hear the fear in his voice.

"Keep talking. I'll try to find you."

Regulus began reciting a poem he had learned as a youth, something by Horace. He could only remember the one line, so he repeated it over and over again: "It is sweet and right to die for one's country."

Finally, a hand touched him, and although he had been expecting it, he still jumped and let out a little squeak. They clutched at each other like frightened children. "What's going on?" Paulus asked again.

"There was a bright light."

"I saw it, too—"

"And then—"

"Blinded!"

"Yes, I'm blind. The light—"

"Blinded me!"

They panted together for a few moments, then Paulus called out, "Marcus!"

"Xerxes!" Regulus yelled.

"Gundabar?"

"Valens?"

"Anyone? Is anyone there?"

Silence. A bright, blinding silence.

"Where did they go?" Regulus asked.

Paulus was weeping. "It . . . can't end . . . this way," he sobbed.

Excerpt from the trial of Cyprianus of Carthage
before Proconsul Galerius Maximus

G.M   Are you Julian Cyprianus?

C.   I am.

G.M.   The most sacred Emperors have
         commanded you to conform to the
         Roman rites.

C.   I refuse.

G.M.   Take heed for yourself.

C.   Do as you are bid . . .

*Galerius, after briefly conferring with his judicial council,
with much reluctance pronounced the following sentence:*

"You have long lived an irreligious life, and have
drawn together a number of men bound by an
unlawful association, and professed yourself an
open enemy to the gods and the religion of Rome;
and the pious, most sacred and august Emperors,
Valerianus and Gallienus . . . have endeavoured in
vain to bring you back to conformity with their
religious observances;—whereas, therefore you have
been apprehended as principal and ringleader in
these infamous crimes . . . the authority of law shall
be ratified in your blood."

*He then read the sentence of the court from a written
tablet:*

"It is the sentence of this court that Julian Cyprianus
be executed with the sword."

C.   Thanks be to God.

MANLIUS ESTATE, THE OLD MASSALIA ROAD
EARLY MAY A.D. 258

MARCUS MANLIUS WAS SITTING in the front courtyard with his wife,
pouring over Plato's *Republic* for the fifth time. To Marcus it was a
masterpiece—a state run by philosophers! How divine would that
be! His wife, Acadia, was studying one of her lives of the *Christos*.
Probably the one by John; that was her favourite. He gazed lov-

ingly at his wife. She had just turned sixty, but in his eyes she looked as lovely as she had at fourteen, when they had married. Acadia was a wonderful person, loving, kind, compassionate; she had raised their children and imbued them with the same traits— even their two sons. All the children lived in the Massalia area and came home often for visits.

A slave came running into the courtyard—little Cilicia, Acadia's hairdresser. "Master," she said. "Soldiers are coming!"

Manlius let out a sigh. "Thank you, Cilicia. Come, Acadia; it's time to go."

Acadia stood up and kissed his cheek. "Sorry to put you through this again, my love," she said.

He laughed. "Nothing to be sorry about. You're worth the world to me. Now come along."

They hurried into the house, passing slaves who quickly got out of their way. They all knew what to do. At the end of the main hall was their bedroom. They entered, and then stopped before a smooth wall covered with a beautiful fresco—Zeus playing with the infant Hercules. He depressed Zeus' nose—the button was impossible to see unless you really looked for it—and a door sprung open at the bottom of the fresco. It was a short door, less than three feet high, and Acadia had to bend to enter. When she was inside, she wiggled her fingers in farewell, and he closed the door behind her. He hurried back through the villa and was sitting on his bench with the *Republic* in his hands when the soldiers entered the courtyard.

The tallest soldier was a centurion, one Manlius knew well. "Good evening, Centurion Clement."

The centurion bowed his head. He had a hard face and a crooked nose, which had been broken by a German war club in his youth. "We know Acadia is a Christian," he said. "The new edict demands that all Christians be rounded up. If they will not sacrifice to the gods, they are to be executed."

Manlius frowned. "So sad, Centurion. My wife is dead. I'm quite lost without her, you know."

The centurion smirked. "You told me she was dead when Decius started persecuting Christians."

"You're right. It was very sad. Tragic. There were large animals involved."

"But afterwards she was seen very much alive."

"A miracle, isn't it? Perhaps there's something to this *Christos* after all."

"But now you're saying that she's dead again?"

"Unfortunately."

"More large animals?"

"Strangely enough, yes."

Manlius smiled. The centurion smiled back.

"You don't mind if we look around, do you?" the centurion asked.

"Be my guest."

They disappeared into the house, and returned a few minutes later without Acadia. The centurion was carrying a basket covered with cloth. "Did you make out all right?" Manlius asked.

Clement pulled back the cloth to reveal freshly baked buns, just out of the oven. They were steaming. "Yes, she is still dead," he said.

Manlius stood up and shook the centurion's hand. "Stop by any time, Centurion Clement."

TWENTY-NINE

GOTH ENCAMPMENT, NORTH SHORE
OF THE BLACK SEA, EARLY MAY A.D. 258

Kniva woke in the middle of the night with the dream fresh in his mind. The grin stretching his features was invisible in the darkness; so was the shirt he had pulled off and tossed into a corner when he went to bed. He rose from his bed of skins, found his belt where he always kept it, and strapped it on. The shirt was unnecessary. The warm winds that drifted up off the Black Sea had melted the snows. The grass was already calf high. He imagined the feel of soft grass on his feet and grunted— forget the boots, too.

The guards on duty outside snapped to attention when he left the tent. He signalled them to be at ease and stretched out the kinks, then set off through the village of tents and huts his people had erected for the winter. All around him the Goth encampment slept. He heard snores and coughs as he picked his way toward the bay. The coughs reminded him of the empire. Sickness was rife there. Last summer in Asia Minor he had seen his first plague victims, and the ugliness of the horrible disease had plagued his dreams ever since: features swollen beyond recognition, snot and blood seeping from the nose, the rattle in the lungs that presaged the end. Worst of all was the necklace of death—the black bruises that encircled the neck and choked the life out of their victim. He had heard the disease appeared when the gods were unhappy. So far no plague had sickened his people. Perhaps The-God-With-The-Blood-In-His-Fists was protecting them?

The moon was high and bright, and the path to the bay was easy to follow. Down at the shore, he met the guards he had posted to protect the ships and nodded at their salutes as he passed. No one would steal his navy the way he had stolen it! The guard hut was lit up, and he entered to find Marrak and Clovis pouring over maps. They looked up and saluted; he waved them back to their work. For a long while he stood at the window, staring out at the ships floating on the serene waters. They had stumbled onto this bay by accident. The entrance to the bay was an inlet, a long, narrow neck that opened up into a wide, natural harbour that could easily accommodate three fleets. The bay ran parallel to the Black Sea, and the shoreline folded back towards the bay's opposite shore, creating the illusion of one continuous shoreline instead of two separate ones. From the Black Sea the entrance to the bay was almost invisible. It was the perfect hiding place for Kniva's navy, and though the Roman fleets searching for them had passed their position several times, they had not found them.

Clovis banged the table with his fist and sank into a chair. "Hopeless," he said. "Cappadocia, Pontus, Bithynia, Asia, all the provinces of Asia Minor are out of reach now. That many ships, they'll spot us the moment we get close."

Kniva clasped his hands behind his back. The muscles of his arms were taut. "You're right, Clovis. It is hopeless," he agreed.

Marrak dropped into a chair beside Clovis. "What use is a fleet if we can't sail it without being caught?"

Kniva finally turned around; he was grinning.

Marrak and Clovis glanced at each other, then at their king. "You have news," Marrak said.

"Good news."

"I gathered that."

Kniva laughed. "A dream."

Clovis stood up. "The-God-With-The-Blood-In-His-Fists?"

"Yes."

"He can get us into Asia Minor."

"He could, but we have another target." Kniva put his fist on the map. "We are raiding here instead: Greece and Macedonia. We are plundering temples; there is much gold in their temples."

Clovis and Marrak studied the shoreline of their new target.

"Do you know how many fleets are assigned to protect Greece and Macedonia?" Kniva asked.

Marrak shook his head.

"At least one," Clovis said.

"None," Kniva told them.

Both Clovis and Marrak looked surprised.

"Greece and Macedonia are not frontier provinces, therefore their shores do not need protection—according to Roman wisdom. And how many legions are waiting for us in Greece and Macedonia?" Kniva asked.

"Two," Marrak guessed.

Clovis nodded. "That sounds right, about two."

"None," Kniva told them.

"That cannot be!" Marrak cried in amazement.

"Greece and Macedonia are not frontier provinces, therefore their borders do not need protection—"

"According to Roman wisdom," Marrak finished.

"No fleets, no legions," Kniva said. "They will hand their riches over the moment we appear."

Marrak glanced at the map again. "Greece and Asia Minor are neighbours," Marrak pointed out.

"Yes, they are separated only by a narrow body of water," Kniva said.

"When the enemy learns of our attack on Greece and Macedonia, he will send ships and troops to intercept us."

"Valerianus has all his ships invested in protecting the shoreline of Asia Minor, where he expects us to strike again. So, yes, when he discovers we have outwitted him yet again, he will send ships and troops, but by the time he arrives, we will be gone."

"You expect to pillage both provinces that quickly?"

"No, I expect to pillage them long enough to draw Valerianus' attention, but to withdraw before he shows up."

"Why?" Marrak asked.

"Because I love the look on Valerianus' face when we slip through his fingers."

Marrak and Clovis laughed.

"But the real reason is because we *will* be pillaging Asia Minor again."

Clovis scratched his head. "This sounds like another one of those cat and mouse games The-God-With-The-Blood-In-His-Fists loves to play."

"Yes," Kniva said. "So that is what we shall do—Greece and Macedonia to begin our horde, then Asia Minor to finish it. With one stop in between."

"One stop in between? Where?"

"More riches. But not for us."

"If not for us, then for whom?" asked Clovis.

"A gift for our foe," Kniva replied. "Treasure for Valerianus' horde."

"WELL, SEARCH *AGAIN*!" Dionysius shouted.

Ulf threw up his hands in exasperation. "I told you—the trail ends here. They walked into this clearing, and they never walked out. I have gone over every inch of it—footprints in, none out. It's as if something . . . snatched them away, a dragon, a harpy, something with wings."

"Then where is their equipment?"

Ulf threw up his hands again. "I don't know. But look, you can see where their fire was. The logs are scorched, but never finished burning."

Dionysius sat down on a log. "If we do not find them, Valerianus will have our heads."

Ulf shook his head. "Not mine! I'm not going back."

Dionysius had his dagger out and under Ulf's chin before he could take another breath. "The penalty for desertion is death," he reminded the Saxon.

Ulf stared at Dionysius with wide eyes. "A joke, commander. Just a joke."

Dionysius put away his dagger and sat down again. "You," he said, pointing at two of the soldiers he had requisitioned from the barracks in Massalia, "Matthias and Gregorius. One hundred yards out, establish a perimeter. Keep your eyes and ears open.

We'll spend the night here, then head out in the morning."

The two soldiers saluted and rambled off. Ulf went to check the clearing again.

Dionysius pulled his long hair back into a tail and tied it off with a leather strip. None of them looked like soldiers anymore. Like the Clan, they had adopted German clothing, breaches and shirts sewn from the skins of the deer they had lived on during the winter. Dionysius hated the clothes. They stank of sweat and improper curing, but he supposed it was better than freezing to death. The winter had challenged their survival skills—they had not found an abandoned building to live in, and they were too far from the frontier to seek out Roman hospitality. Instead they had spent the winter in a cave a few miles south of the Clan. Seven men in a tiny cave! It was surprising that any of them had survived the winter.

And now this. Dionysius picked up a pinecone and whipped it at the Clan's last fireplace in the centre of the clearing. He could rant and rave at Ulf and the others all he wanted, but that would not help him find the Clan. Where could they have gone? A week they'd been searching, and they kept ending up here, at this clearing. He laughed. In the empire, the saying was, "All roads lead to Rome." Out here, it was, "All trails lead to this clearing."

Tomorrow, they would move on. The Clan had been travelling east more or less, so he'd proceed under the assumption that they were still travelling east, and head that way himself. Maybe he'd pick up their trail again a little further on. It was the best he could do. He just hoped he found the Clan soon. Much further east and Germania became Sarmatia, and Sarmatia went on forever, just one vast, endless plain full of strange tribes with strange habits. He'd heard about one tribe way off in the east that had slanted eyes and pointed heads and lived on horseback. Not a tribe he wanted to run into out here.

South was the only other option. South would take them to Asia Minor or the Black Sea or Persia's back door. If only he knew what their destination was, where this "*Thing*" was supposed to be.

Ulf skulked back over and sat down beside him on the log. "Nothing," he said. Dionysius pulled a hunk of dried venison from his pack and handed it to Ulf. It was as close to an apology as Dionysius would come, and Ulf knew it. "Thanks," he said, and bit into the tough, leathery meat.

"When this is all over, we'll go to one of those fancy places Tacitus likes, eh?" he slapped Ulf on the back.

"Yeah. Lots of fruit."

"And sweet breads."

"And a gallon of milk."

"No, a gallon of wine."

Ulf laughed. "A gallon of each."

Dionysius bit a chunk of his dried meat and swore. "Just as long as venison isn't on the menu."

CEMETERY OF PRAETEXTATUS
ROME, EARLY MAY

EPISCOPUS SIXTUS WAS ELDERLY, but still spry. *A Christian has to be spry to stay alive these days*, was one of his wife's favourite aphorisms, and so far it had kept him alive and serving the *Christos* long after many of his colleagues had gained the glorious crown of martyrdom. Unlike many other *episcopi*, like poor, dear Cyprianus down in Carthage, he and his deacons had escaped the round-up of Christian leaders that Gallienus' first edict of persecution had produced last year. The soldiers had come looking, but Sixtus had sprinted away, and so he had had the privilege of remaining with his flock, instead of guiding them from exile. Gallienus' first edict had also forbidden them to congregate, but that was ridiculous! Forbidding Christians to meet and worship the *Christos* was like forbidding people to breathe!

Some of his flock had begged him not to come this morning. But how could they worship without their shepherd? They said it was too dangerous, but it was dangerous for them, too! It was not right for him to hide away just because he was the *episcopus*. When the emperors had targeted only Christian leaders, that was one thing. But now, with this new edict, when every Christian was in mortal danger, he had no more right to hide than his flock. And if his flock insisted on meeting, so be it. He would share their danger.

They had gathered for worship in the catacombs of Praetextatus because it was a private cemetery that was not under surveillance, as the other cemeteries were. He chuckled to himself. It was probably the last cemetery in Rome that didn't have a permanent guard watching it. Imagine that! All those Roman soldiers guarding the dead! How absurd!

His deacons led him to a chair that the faithful had set up for him. So kind! He was spry, but he was also elderly and tired easily. The chair was not overly comfortable—it was a wooden monstrosity with a hard seat, but he would not complain.

The worship service began. Psalms were sung, and there were readings from the *Scripturae*. And prayer! Oh, Lord *Christos*, there was so much to pray for, so many to pray for. He remembered the blessed Cyprianus of Carthage, who had earned a martyr's crown. And word had come that Novatianus had also died for the *Christos*. No more would Cyprianus and Novatianus argue about the fate of the *lapsi*—now they were standing together before the *Christos*, tossing their crowns at his pierced feet.

There was a sudden commotion at the back of the chamber, and Sixtus opened his eyes and looked up. Roman soldiers were marching into the stone hall! How had they found this place? It was a secret, known only to the faithful!

Sixtus sighed as two burly soldiers grabbed him by his thin arms. "Not secret anymore," he whispered, and then the two soldiers picked him up and slammed him into the chair. The wind went out of him. A rib snapped, and the pain made him gasp.

Another soldier approached him, bigger even than the two who had hurled him into the chair. He was a centurion. "You are sentenced to death," he said and drew his sword.

Sixtus managed to laugh. "What, no trial?"

The centurion smiled. His teeth were very white, like two rows of grave markers bleached by the sun. "Meeting in cemeteries is punishable by death. No trial necessary," he said.

And swung.

THE IMPERIAL PALACE
ROME, EARLY MAY

EMPRESS NINA ARRIVED IN ROME unannounced the night before Gallienus was scheduled to leave for the frontier. Before the Battle of Mediolanum and the subsequent revelations about the treachery of Festus Macrinus, Gallienus had planned to winter at home with Nina and their two youngest children. Instead he had spent the winter in Rome with the senate. Neither he nor the senate appreciated this forced cohabitation.

Days of bickering and half-hearted compromises that Gallienus laughed down alternated with evenings of sumptuous banquets where every guest wore a mask of civility over a heart of rage, a cycle that turned the city of Rome into a prison that neither side could escape. In the end, Gallienus won the game—having an army camped outside the city as an incentive was like using loaded dice in a game of *tali*—and a new era dawned in the history of the Roman senate: the era of obsolescence. The senate entered it kicking and screaming, and it would hold on to the vestiges of power until its nails were ripped to the quick, but the long ride to oblivion had begun, and the senate hated Gallienus because of it.

The feeling was mutual. Gallienus confided in the new commander of the Praetorian Guard—an equestrian, *not* a senator— that he had fantasized about inviting all the senators in the empire to the *Curia Julia*, and then setting it on fire. Now that spring had returned, he wanted to escape Rome as soon as possible. Facing an army of howling barbarians was infinitely more entertaining than the prospect of yet another dreary dinner party with the senate.

Nina was escorted into the imperial bed chamber by two members of his personal bodyguard. He looked up from his desk by the window, and the unexpected sight of her beautiful face drove every thought about the senate from his head. He jumped up and raced to her (as quickly as decorum would allow an emperor to race), and swept her into his arms as his guards closed the doors behind them. She held him tightly, and he heard the hitch in her breath and released her. "Nina, what's wrong?"

The tears that he had heard in her breath spilled from her

brown eyes. "Oh, Gallienus, my love," she said. "It's Valerianus. He's dead."

My father, dead? That was his first thought. And on its heels came emotions that surprised him. Relief. And then a hint of something else; not exactly joy, but close to it. Was it . . . satisfaction? Smugness? But as fast as those thoughts and emotions came, they fled, because the sorrow on Nina's face was too deep for his father to have evoked. Suddenly, the truth pierced him like a javelin through the heart.

Valerianus the Younger. His son, Valerianus.

Nina fell into his arms and he crushed her to his chest. She began to weep, and he was pummelled by guilt: she had borne this sorrow by herself all the way from their estate in Etruria. She had needed her husband and he had been in Rome fighting with the senate. For the first time since he had accepted the responsibility of the imperial office, he truly regretted it. In that moment while his wife wept in his arms, he wished he could go back to that fateful day in his father's tent outside of Narnia and refuse to share the empire with him. "Was it the plague?" he asked.

She looked up at him and shook her head. "A hunting accident," she said.

"What? What do you mean?"

He was hunting boar with General Ingenuus. They had the creature cornered and it charged. It . . . it gored our son," she sobbed.

General Ingenuus. *Senator* Ingenuus. "What proof is there?" he asked.

She looked confused. "Proof? What do you mean, proof?"

"Who saw this hunting accident?"

"Ingenuus did."

"Who else?"

"I . . . I don't know. He sent a letter."

"Give it to me."

"It's in one of my bags."

They sent slaves to fetch her luggage. She found the letter and gave it to Gallienus. He took it to his desk at the window where the light was best and read it. When he finished, he put down, glared at it for a moment, then slammed his fist on the desk.

"What is it, Gallienus?" Nina asked.

"Treason and betrayal," he snarled. "Ingenuus was the sole witness; they cremated Valerianus' body. There is no way to corroborate his story or prove it a lie."

"You do not trust him? He is by your own admission a fine general."

"And a senator, one of the last generation of senators to have a military command, because of legislation that I drafted. This is the senate's reply to that edit—a rebellion led by Senator Ingenuus. A usurper who will take the throne and hand the senate back its power."

"But Gallienus, there is no mention of rebellion in his letter. There is great sorrow and regret, feelings you should be experiencing right now, but there is no rebellion."

"You do not know how to read between senatorial lines, my love. Trust me, their next step will be open rebellion."

She shook her head. "I do believe our son died for a reason, but not that."

"What then?"

She hesitated, turned away, then hurried over to the desk and took his hand. "The *Christos*, Gallienus; He is responsible."

"The *Christos*?"

"Yes! Can you not see it? Every step you take against the Christians results in tragedy for us. Look at what the barbarians have done."

"Ridiculous, Nina! The barbarians were attacking us before the persecution began."

"Yes, they were, but not like this. The Franks, Gallienus! Have you ever encountered a barbarian invader that organized and powerful? And the Alamanni! Look at the damage they did in Rhaetia and Germania Superior. And they entered Italy; they marched to within sight of Rome—the Germans have *never* done that before. This is a new thing, and it is because of what we are doing to the Christians."

Gallienus hesitated. He had not thought of it that way—the Franks and Alamanni, they *were* different than anything he had experienced up to that point. And despite his defeat of the Alamanni at Mediolanum, Romans everywhere were horrified by

their intrusion into Italy, to the gates of Rome herself—it was tantamount to the raping of virgins. Unthinkable. Impossible. "No, I
cannot believe it," he finally said.

"And what of the plague? Thousands have died in this city
alone. And the earthquakes? Thousands more dead." She stood
up, her hands balled into fists. "And now your son, Gallienus.
How much warning do you need?"

"Coincidence, nothing more."

She closed her eyes and sighed deeply, then: "There is a story
in the Jewish holy books about a man named Moses—"

"I know the story."

"Yahweh, the God of the Hebrews, sent Moses to Pharaoh to
demand that Pharaoh let his people go."

"And Pharaoh refused," Gallienus observed.

"Yes, Pharaoh refused. So Yahweh sent plagues to convince
him. Do you remember that?"

"Yes, lice, frogs, boils, locusts, etcetera."

"And Pharaoh *still* refused. Yahweh showed his power nine
times, and nine times Pharaoh refused."

"Your point, Nina?"

"My point is the tenth plague: the firstborn sons of Egypt, including the Pharaoh's firstborn." She looked into his eyes and ran
her hand through his hair. "The God of the Christians has taken
our firstborn, my love."

"No."

"The *Christos* is calling out to you."

"No."

"He is saying, *Let my people go*."

"I am not some weak Egyptian Pharaoh."

"And if you do not listen, He will destroy us."

"Stop it, Nina!"

"First your father—"

"Enough, Nina!"

"Then you—"

"I will not warn you again."

"Then the empire."

He slapped her across the face.

Her eyes burned with accusation.

"I'm . . . sorry, Nina."

She nodded, touched the cheek he had slapped. Then turned and left the room.

And Rome.

THIRTY

Someone was crying for help. He heard desperation . . . fear . . . anger . . . emotions that did not belong in him anymore, emotions that had no place in the *Thing*. And that was how he knew it was over. He was back, they were all back, and an overwhelming sense of sadness and loss engulfed him; the weight of the physical world attached itself to his body once again, and there were trees and pine needles and Clan members standing about in rapt silence, while the crying voice—voices—begged for help. He felt himself "touch down," as if he had been floating, and with that sensation the real world became real again. "Paulus, Regulus," he called. "We're here."

"We can't see—"

"We're blind—"

"Help us!"

Sukuta moved toward the blubbering guards, who had not been with them at the *Thing*, and yet had obviously experienced something out of the ordinary. Sukuta's face was shining, his black skin as bright as a new day. He reached Paulus and Regulus and grabbed them under the arms to pick them up. Instantly, their vision returned, and they both cried out the Ethiopian's name and embraced him. Sukuta held them in his big arms for a moment, then let them go and returned to the Clan, which was gathering around the circle of stones they had set up in the middle of the clearing. The fire was still burning.

"Sukuta, Prisca?" Valens said.

They knew it was a question and they both nodded yes. "I didn't believe," Sukuta said, amazed by his former scepticism. "I thought you were all addled in the brain. But you were right. The *Christos* is God. He did die for our sins. He is the Saviour. And He was . . . beautiful. It was love . . . made physical, made real . . . love personified, the poets would say." His mouth hung open, as if he had more to say, then he shook his head and snapped it shut.

Prisca looked around the circle. "I just never thought of it," she admitted. "Until Xerxes, I didn't think of it at all; even when I listened to you and Damarra, begging your pardon, my lord *Sankt.*"

Valens laughed. "That hardly seems important anymore, does it? Owners and slaves, rich and poor—all meaningless."

"I am a Christian and a slave, my lord, and I am happy with my lot; I find joy in serving." She gently touched Damarra's cheek, then kissed Ruth, who was sleeping in her mother's arms. "And bringing God's children into this world."

"I will buy her freedom," Xerxes said.

"Not until Damarra has had all thirteen of the children she's planning to have," Valens said.

Damarra slapped his hand, then hugged his arm.

"Then I shall be your slave, too, and Prisca and I will be together. In this life and in the next."

Prisca grinned as Xerxes kissed her plump cheek.

Conall rubbed his boy's head. "How long were we . . . gone?" he asked.

"It seemed like a moment," Marcus replied.

"Like an eternity," Damarra said.

"A day, a week, a year," Sukuta shrugged, "I don't think it matters when you're with the *Christos*. Time is . . . *not*," he explained.

Valens turned to Paulus and Regulus, who were standing at the edge of the clearing, staring at them. "And what did you see?" he asked.

Paulus shook his head. "Nothing. We were blind. It was the two of us together in nothing. We called for you and you did not answer. Nothing else."

"We still do not know our destination," Gundabar said.

The others looked at him, amazed. He was speaking perfect Latin, after all this time. He grinned at them, then turned to Marcus. "I'm so sorry," he said. "I was wrong about you; can you forgive me?"

The two embraced, then slapped each other's backs.

"I know where we are to go next," Valens said.

The others looked at him, but it was Gundabar who spoke. "You truly are Chief now."

"He is *Sankt*," Damarra said. There was pride in her voice.

"Did you learn what *Sankt* means?" Persephone asked.

Damarra nodded. "Yes, that was given to me during the *Thing. Sankt* is a Chief who is also a Holy Man," she explained. "Moses was *Sankt*; Joshua was *Sankt*; David was *Sankt*. And for this Clan, Valens is *Sankt*."

The weight of the world settled even more firmly on his shoulders. "I don't feel like a *Sankt*," Valens said. "Moses, Joshua, David—those are daunting shoes to fill."

"They were all men, like you," Damarra said. "Just men. And even though they were leaders chosen by God, they made mistakes. God does not expect you to be perfect, my love." She kissed him. "He expects you to be *Sankt*. And you must lead us where we must go."

"Why me?"

Damarra laughed. "You were all at the *Thing*. Did the *Christos* tell any of you where we are to go next?"

One by one, the other Clan members shook their heads.

"That is why it's you, my love. Because the *Christos* told you— that was what was given to you during the *Thing*."

Valens nodded. "My map," he said. "Where is my map?"

Marcus brought it to him and unrolled it. "This is our final destination," he said, pointing at the eastern edge of the map. "But first we go here, about two hundred fifty miles." He nodded, and Marcus rolled the map up again. "We leave at dawn," he said.

Just before he dismissed the Clan, Conall raised his hand. "I was given something at the *Thing*, too," he said.

"What was it?" Sukuta asked.

"I was told to share it only with *Sankt*," he replied.

The others moved off to the edge of the clearing, out of ear-shot. "What is it, Conall?" Valens asked.

"There is a traitor in our midst," Conall replied.

THE NEXT MORNING, the Clan left at first light. Now that their destination was clear, their pace quickened. They had no idea why they were to go where the *Christos* wanted them to go, but the very fact that He had directed them was enough. They were eager to get there and discover what came next. They shared their memories of the *Thing* as they rode and walked. Conall reminded them of the definition of a *Thing* he had provided that first day: a council of warriors under a king, the leader of the clans. It had meant so little then, just words, but now they understood. From large Sukuta to baby Joshua, they were warriors privileged to attend a council—"*A-zem-bly*," Gundabar reminded them, laughing at his former flawed Latin—under a King, the leader of the clans, the true King of kings: the *Christos*.

Damarra was walking with Persephone, the two of them giggling like little girls with a secret . . . that wasn't actually a secret. Like the others, the *Christos* had given Persephone something during the *Thing*. In her case, it was a vision of the future, a vision she shared with Damarra and no one else. The two friends had their arms linked together as they walked. "When do you go?" Damarra asked her.

Persephone shook her head. "The *Christos* did not say."

Damarra glanced over at Gundabar, who was singing a Psalm as he walked. "He is very handsome," she whispered to Persephone, which started them giggling again. Gundabar heard, and looked at them inquisitively, which made them laugh harder. He shrugged and went back to his song.

"Yes, he is. And he's gentle and sweet . . . when he's not punching Marcus."

More laughter.

"Are you going to tell him?" Damarra asked.

"No, I'll let it happen all on its own."

"Will you invite us to the wedding?"

"I will need your permission, my lady!"

"No, you are free to do as you wish." She grinned. "Free to be a servant of the *Christos*."

"Thank you, my lady . . . Damarra."

Damarra squeezed her arm. "I love you, Persephone. You have been my best friend, and always will be. I will miss you when you go, but the *Christos* has work for the two of you."

"Yes, missionaries to the Suevi—I can hardly wait."

They chatted for a while longer, then Damarra left Persephone to her exciting expectations and went to her husband. She had noticed he had been walking alone all morning. He had not sung or laughed with the others. His mood was sombre. Sad, she thought, and wondered how any of them could be sad after the *Thing*. She slipped up beside him and took his hand. He looked at her and smiled, and that was when she knew something was truly wrong. "What is it, *Sankt*?" she whispered.

He looked away; his eyes were wet. "It is nothing, Damarra. Nothing I can share."

"The weight of leadership lies heavy on your shoulders," she said. "I read that once, I can't remember where. But when I look at you, that's what I see."

"The *Christos* gave something to each of us, Damarra; to some, a gift, to others, a duty. And my duty is—" He left the words unspoken, and Damarra felt it was wrong of her to ask.

She laid her head against his shoulder. "If there is anything I can do, my love," she said.

He smiled at her, the sad smile again. "Pray for me, Damarra," he said.

"THE GOTHS HAVE INVADED GREECE," General Eutropus announced.

Valerianus rose from his dining couch and screamed at the heavens. When he finally stopped, he glared at Eutropus. "How?" he asked.

"They must have slipped through the Bosphorus at night, Your Excellency. No one at Byzantium saw a thing."

"An entire fleet sails through the Bosphorus and nobody sees it? How is that possible?"

"There is worse, Your Excellency. Athens has been sacked."

Valerianus could scarcely believe what he was hearing. Athens sacked? Athens was the cultural father-in-law of Rome. It was a city of philosophers, artists, and true devotees to the gods. Such a disaster coming on the heels of the Alamanni invasion of Italy was devastating and an insult to the Valerian dynasty. The whole Roman world must be wondering if the Valerians had lost the blessing of the gods. How is it that these barbarians knew just where to attack to make the most impact?

"Send word to the *Classis Syriaca* to meet you in Ephesus. The fleet will take you and half the army to Greece. Find and destroy Kniva. I don't care how you do it. Just do it."

Eutropus bowed. "One more item, Your Excellency."

Valerianus' hands clenched into fists. "Good news for a change, General."

"No, Your Excellency."

Valerianus resisted the urge to release another scream. "Report."

"A soldier was found dead this morning, Your Excellency. There was a ring of black bruises around his neck."

A shiver crawled up Valerianus' back. "Fetch me the priests," he ordered and dismissed Eutropus.

The general left and Valerianus dropped onto his dining couch again. He would wait three more days to start the march to Mesopotamia. He must sacrifice to the gods. All of them. Continually. If it took every goat in Asia Minor, it did not matter. They must present their plea to the gods, regain their trust and assistance. For some reason the gods had deserted him—everything was going wrong. But he could win them back again. They would keep the plague at bay; they would destroy the Goths; they would lead him to his destiny, to that day foretold when he would stand in all his glory in the throne room at Ctesiphon. "Your time is short, Shapur," he whispered. "The gods are coming for you on the tip of my sword."

THE RHINE-DANUBE FRONTIER had exploded. Except for the Ala-manni, who were still recovering from the Battle of Mediolanum, and the Franks, who were happily turning Hispania into a waste-land, it seemed that every tribe in Germania had decided to try their luck against Rome. From the moment the snow melted, Gal-lienus' generals were at war up and down the Rhine, repulsing one invader after another. His cavalry at Mediolanum was doing the same work along the Danube frontier in the provinces of Noricum and Upper Pannonia. But Gallienus' eyes were on Lower Pannonia, where his general, Ingenuus, had proven him right. Af-ter the murder of Gallienus' son, Valerianus the Younger, In-genuus had sent a letter declaring his innocence; Gallienus had ordered him to prove his innocence by coming to Rome and com-mitting suicide in the throne room. Ingenuus' response? The le-gions of Lower Pannonia had declared him emperor. A usurper. A *senatorial* usurper.

Gallienus had held games in Rome to honour his son's mem-ory, and now the time for mourning had ended. His army was ready, and so was he. "Vengeance is mine," he told his generals at their last meeting before they marched on Pannonia. "I want In-genuus kneeling at my feet before the winter winds blow down from Germania." His strategy was simple. General Aureolus, the commander of his cavalry, would meet them on the border be-tween the two Pannonias; together they would sweep Ingenuus and his soldiers into the Danube.

On his way north, Gallienus stopped to see Nina. His mourn-ing was finished; hers was not. He apologized to her again—in all the years of their marriage, he had never lifted a hand against her, he reminded her. She accepted his apology again, but he saw the truth in her eyes. That one slap had driven a wedge into their mar-riage. How deep the wedge went, he could not tell. He knew only that he must not drive it deeper. A wedge had only one function— to divide. It must either be extracted or allowed to fulfill its func-tion. And for Gallienus, life without Nina was not an option.

"WHAT OF YOU, XERXES?" Prisca asked. "What were you given at the *Thing*?"

"Yes, tell us." Marcus said. He had been walking with them most of the day, swapping stories about life in the military as a Christian.

Xerxes took Prisca's hand. "Persia, my love. If you ever get the chance to see it, you will never wish to leave."

"It sounds wonderful!"

"The *Christos* asked me to return to Persia and share his message there. I am honoured, but it is a difficult task."

"Difficult?"

"Yes, for a man alone. Now a man with a wife! Ahh, that would make the task much more enjoyable." He winked at Prisca. "I understand that a wife makes *everything* much more enjoyable."

"Do you have anyone in mind?" she asked playfully.

"Hmm. There are many women who would jump at the opportunity to marry a handsome Persian such as myself. But there is one slave I am rather fond of."

Prisca tittered at him.

"I was serious when I offered to purchase you from *Sankt*."

"And I was serious when I said I was content to be a Christian slave."

Xerxes rolled his eyes at her, then turned to Marcus. "You have not said yet what you were given at the *Thing*, Marcus."

Suddenly Marcus' eyes shone like twin stars. "He asked if I loved Him enough to stand for Him in the face of persecution. And I told Him I did and I would, and He said it might come to that."

"It might?" Xerxes said.

"Yes. Not that it would happen, but that it *might* happen. He wants us to face that challenge, Xerxes, even if we never face the reality of it. I denied Him once; I will not deny him again. I am prepared to give my life for the *Christos*. I know it is true, and so does He. He told me He knew I would stand for Him now." A tear slipped down Marcus' cheek. "That was my gift—He trusts me again. He knows my heart is true and loyal. My guilt is gone. Completely, utterly gone. Never again will Satan be able to torment me with it."

"That *is* a great gift," Xerxes said.

"It is," Prisca agreed. "But of all the gifts the *Christos* gave, my favourite was the gift He gave to the children."

Marcus and Xerxes smiled at the memory.

"To see Cecht and Ruth sitting with the King of kings." She shivered, joy sparkling in her eyes. "He held Joshua in his arms the entire time. I wept when I saw that."

They had come to a stream, wide but shallow. They took off their boots and waded across. On the far side, they could see light shining through the trees. "Probably a clearing," Gundabar said. He glanced up at the sky. They could not see the sun for the canopy, but the light was brightest in the west. "It might be a good place to set up camp for the night, *Sankt*."

Valens nodded, and they led their horses through the trees, into the clearing. To their surprise, the clearing was already occupied. A fire flickered in a ring of rocks. Horses stood to one side, enjoying the grass that covered the ground. Valens counted seven men. One was cooking over the fire, several were stretched out on bedrolls, napping. The rest were sitting around the campfire waiting for their food to cook. They were obviously Germans, although which tribe was impossible to tell. They wore skins, as the Clan did, and their hair and beards were long and unkempt. One of the men rose from his seat by the fire. Massive. One of the biggest men Valens had ever seen, probably just short of seven feet and made of solid muscle from shoulders to calves. As he walked towards them, he looked imposing and dangerous . . . until he grinned and lifted his hand. Valens watched in amazement as the man's hand engulfed his. "Welcome," he said in a deep voice. He spoke Latin; to judge from that single word, he had no accent. No German accent. Despite his appearance, the man was Roman. "Welcome all of you to our fire," he said. "My name is Dionysius."

THIRTY-ONE

Shapur and his commanders stood around a long table, finalizing their plans for the invasion of Roman Mesopotamia. His generals were arguing strategy, using the map on the table for reference. Shapur was scarcely aware of their raised voices. He was studying the map, his black eyes roaming east to west, taking in the entire world, from India to the western Roman province of Hispania, where the Franks had just looted the city of Tarraco. His father, Adashir, had been a master of the game *Chatrang*, and had taught his son to love the game as well. *Chatrang* was a war game, played on a board with sixty-four squares alternating black and white. Each side had a Shah, a Councillor, two War Elephants, two Horses, two Chariots, and eight infantry soldiers called pawns. His father had once told him that every warrior should study the game, because it trained the mind to think strategically, to plan ahead, to prepare for any eventuality.

When Shapur looked at the map, he saw a *Chatrang* board. He had wintered on the Mesopotamian border to signal his next move to Valerianus—as though to say, "I will invade here"—knowing that Kniva would also make a move in the spring. The result? Double the pressure on Valerianus to make one of the three moves available to him. One, attack Kniva—that had been his move last year, and it had failed. Two, attack Shapur—which would allow Kniva a free hand in his pillaging, thus further alienating his already unhappy subjects. Or three, divide his forces and attack both Kniva and Shapur. Shapur had been counting on option three, and Valerianus had not disappointed him. One of his generals was in pursuit of Kniva with half the army; Valerianus and his half were marching toward Mesopotamia. Thanks to Kniva, Shapur had some thirty thousand less soldiers to worry about. "We invade Roman Mesopotamia," Shapur announced.

His generals ceased arguing and bowed to his decision.

DIONYSIUS AND HIS COMPANIONS turned out to be traders, returning home after visiting the Quadi and the Daci. "We have fewer problems if we look German," Dionysius explained, pointing at his hair. He scratched his beard. "Although, I have to confess I can't wait to get home and shave this thing off my face."

"I know what you mean," Valens said.

The Clan shared dinner with them and caught up on the news from back home, although the traders had been in Germania almost as long as they had, it turned out. One of the men, a Saxon named Ulf, asked them where they were heading and Valens answered with a vague "east" and provided no more information. Later in the evening, as they sat around the campfire under a starry sky, the Clan began to talk about the *Christos*. Dionysius, who was obviously the leader of the trading venture, did not seem surprised to discover that, except for Regulus, they were all Christians. He asked them if they had fled to the safety of the Germanian wilderness to avoid the persecution.

"No," Marcus explained. "The *Christos* wanted us out here."

"For what?"

He looked at Valens, who nodded. "We attended a council meeting of sorts. Do you know what a *Thing* is?"

Ulf spoke up. "A council of warriors."

"Yes. We attended a *Thing* with the *Christos*."

Dionysius laughed. "Are you serious?"

"Very."

"Where was this . . . *Thing*?"

"A day's journey west of here. In a clearing where all the trees bend in to form a roof."

Dionysius blinked. "I know that clearing. We spent a week there."

"A whole week? Why?" Valens said.

Dionysius hesitated, then: "Some of us came down with a fever. We rested till we were well again."

"When did you leave the clearing?"

"Yesterday."

"We left it this morning," Valens said.

"That's not possible," Dionysius said.

"And yet, it's true."

Dionysius stood up. "My men and I are tired. It is time we slept. We . . . are still recovering from the fever."

Valens got up. "Certainly. Good night then." He shook Dionysius' hand.

Marcus got up as Dionysius and his men wandered over to the far side of the clearing to bed down. "What do you think of that, *Sankt*?" Marcus asked.

"I think we are being lied to," Valens replied.

"I think you're right."

GALERIUS MAXIMUS WAS LOOKING forward to a quiet dinner and then bed. As Proconsul of Africa Proconsularis, he had spent the last few months addressing the Christian Problem, and he was fed up with it. Just when he thought he'd dealt with the last Christian, the soldiers would find more. Or worse, the Christians would come running into his chambers and demand to be martyred. From what he'd heard, Christian leaders frowned on members of their sect throwing their lives away like that—being martyred was one thing; turning yourself in and insisting that the judge martyr you was a different thing altogether—but then, most of the Christian leaders were dead themselves. He had personally dispatched Cyprianus and his . . . what did they call them? . . . presbyters? Whatever it was, he had personally dispatched them. Unfortunately, things had gotten worse instead of better. He longed for the days of Decius, when most Christians had preferred sacrificing to the gods over death.

With a deep sigh, he left his chambers and went outside into the African heat. He had come to Utica, twenty-five miles from Carthage, to judge a special case. Soldiers had stumbled into a secret Christian meeting place and arrested three hundred Christians. Three hundred! In one place! It surprised him that there were more than three hundred Christians in the entire empire, let alone one place!

Now that they had been found, it was his job to deal with them.

The prospect of spending several weeks in Utica hearing the testimony of three hundred Christians had chilled him to the bone. Fortunately, he had had an inspiration—surely a gift from the gods. It would save time and expense and aggravation for everyone involved. With a yawn, he shuffled over to the area where the work crews were—he hoped—finishing up. When he arrived, he glanced over the edge of the pit, then smiled—it was ready. "Bring them out," he told the centurion.

They had set up a chair and table for him under the shade of a fig tree. He sat down and signalled a slave over to fan him. The heat here was oppressive, but in a few months his tenure in Africa would be over. Maybe he'd ask for an assignment up in Britannia, where there was rain and snow and it was cool most of time.

The sound of marching signalled the arrival of the Christians. Galerius stood up as they approached. Quick was the word; no dallying. The soldiers gathered the Christians in the space between him and the pit. Over to his left was a brazier and incense. The Christians were murmuring, glancing at the pit, then back at him. He saw understanding in some eyes, horror in others, but determination in all. This was going to be quick after all. "You are Christians?" he asked.

There was a great yell in response. Maybe that was not the best approach. He cleared his throat and started again. "To my left is a brazier and incense. Anybody who offers a pinch of incense to the gods may leave. Behind you is a pit of quicklime. Quicklime disintegrates human flesh on contact. Anybody who will *not* offer a pinch of incense to the gods will be thrown into the quicklime." He cleared his throat again. "Please step forward if you are willing to offer incense to the gods. You have one minute."

He waited, counting the seconds under his breath, tapping his foot restlessly. When he reached sixty, he looked up. All three hundred Christians were huddled together in a tight group staring back at him. "Centurion, if you please," he ordered.

He turned away, wondering what his staff was preparing for supper tonight. The screams followed him back inside, but the smell that greeted his nostrils made him forget all about the Christians.

Roast duck.

AN URGENT VOICE WHISPERED in the darkness: "Dionysius!"

Dionysius grinned. He had been lying awake, waiting for that voice. He rolled over and got up. A shadow in the trees beckoned him on. When they were thirty yards from the campsite, they stopped. Dionysius could not make out the man's features in the darkness, but he knew who it was now. Tacitus liked to play games. Before starting this assignment, he had told Dionysius that the inside man would be one of the *Agentes*, but he would not say whom. All he *would* say is that Dionysius would recognize the man when he saw him. And he had. The moment the Clan walked into the clearing.

"Well," Dionysius said. "Fancy meeting you here."

"I have information for you," he whispered.

"Are we still playing that game?"

"Until they reach their destination, yes."

"Are you sure they don't suspect who you are?"

Laughter: "They haven't got a clue."

"I could arrest them now," Dionysius said. "Make for the Danube."

"The Clan will save you the trouble."

"They're going to the Danube?"

"Better."

"You know where they're going?"

"Uh-huh. Valens showed us on the map."

"We'll travel with you," Dionysius suggested.

"That's unwise. I think they already suspect you are not who you claim to be. They'll figure out if we don't split up."

"Then we'll go back to following you."

"That won't work either."

"Why not?"

"Because where we're going, you can't follow."

NO GOTHS IN GREECE. No Goths in Macedon. Valerianus will have my head.

General Eutropus stood on the deck of his flagship, the Minerva, staring up at the city of Athens. Even from the harbour the damage was obvious. The Goths had entered, pillaged, destroyed, then moved on, leaving nothing but rumour in their wake. This was a sign that they could no longer ignore. The time when posting legions along the frontier was a good defensive policy was gone. Too many times the barbarians had broken through that defence and plundered cities that had no protection. Athens had no walls and look what had happened to her. Rome had no walls either. The Alamanni had been repulsed. Next time, Rome might not be so lucky.

And where would Kniva strike next? If he sailed down around the southern tip of Greece, he could be in Italy in a few days and do to Rome what he had done to Athens. Would he do that? Or would he go home? Where would he go?

Kniva's ships were full of Greek booty, and it was only June. He could sail home, empty his holds, celebrate yet another victory, then sail off for another round of plundering before winter set in. Yes, if he were Kniva, that's what he'd do.

Eutropus summoned the ship's navigator. "Set sail for the Bosphorus," he ordered. "We're heading to the Black Sea. I think Kniva is making for home."

THE NEXT MORNING, Dionysius and his men said farewell and headed south, toward the Danube. The Clan continued east, through mountainous terrain. That day they entered Daci territory, but the Daci were raiding the empire like most of the other tribes, and they met no one. By mid-June the Clan had reached the eastern portion of Carpi territory and had entered the lowlands that sloped down to the Black Sea and their destination. Their spirits were high as they travelled, buoyed by memories of the *Thing* and their union with the *Christos*. Only Valens was quiet, not speaking unless spoken to. The others left him alone—he was *Sankt* and his duties were heavy—but Damarra, who knew him best, knew that it was more than just his role as Clan leader that troubled him.

Something was tormenting him.

Sometimes she caught him staring at her, and there was pain in his eyes. Sometimes he would hold his children in his arms and gaze at their faces and tell them how much he loved them. Once she woke in the middle of the night and saw him slipping off into the woods. She followed him to a small stream, a few hundred yards from camp. She thought he was kneeling to wash in the cold water until he cried out. He was praying, and the sound of his anguish made her nauseous with fear. But instead of running to him, she turned and crept away, because whatever he was suffering was between him and God, and she had no right to pry or interfere.

The next night as they lay together in the darkness, he kissed her forehead and whispered, "I love you, Damarra; I always will."

She kissed him back, and suddenly knew that she *had* to pry, she *had* to interfere. "Talk to me, Valens. *Please*. You're scaring me."

There was no response. She had the strangest notion that he was listening to the silence. After a minute, he let out a long, jagged breath. He was on the edge of tears. Finally, he spoke: "I learned much at the *Thing*, Damarra. More than I have told."

"I know."

"The time has come for me to tell. Some of it."

"To me?"

"Yes, to you." He cleared his throat. "Will you trust me, Damarra?"

"You are *Sankt*, and you are my Valens. Of course I will trust you."

His laughter was joyless. "Yes, I am your Valens and I am the Clan's *Sankt* . . . and sometimes those two parts of me do not agree."

"I can see that happening."

"Two days from now the first part of our journey will end. Part of the Clan must go on but . . . part of the Clan must stay behind."

Fear whispered at her heart. Was he going to send her away? Was that it? Leave her behind while he continued on alone? She would not allow it. Never. "I understand," she said, but the firmness of her voice said something different: *I disagree.*

"Gundabar and Persephone will not be coming with us. Their part in this is done."

She felt surprise . . . and sorrow. Losing Persephone was heartbreaking.

"And . . . they will be keeping . . . Ruth and Joshua with them."

Damarra snapped upright. "What!" she exclaimed.

Clan members groaned in their sleep.

She held her tongue, waiting for the camp to settle again. In the growing silence she heard weeping—it was Valens. "I'm sorry," he cried. "It must be."

"Why?"

"Because . . . it is not safe for them to continue with us."

She breathed a sigh of relief. Of course. Whatever was coming . . . the *Christos* was going to spare their Ruth and little Joshua. And Gundabar and Persephone. She took her husband into her arms. "I understand," she said. "This is a blessing disguised as a curse. The *Christos* is keeping our children safe."

"I'm sorry," he sobbed. "Valens wants them to stay, but *Sankt* knows they must go."

She kissed him, then lay back down and let him weep in her arms. "We must listen to *Sankt*," she whispered.

FOUR HUNDRED GOATS LATER, the gods were appeased, and the Roman army was marching the Divine Valerianus to his destiny. The energy of divinity empowered him; he felt it in the very core of his being. If he were to step off the highest tower in Ctesiphon, he would float to the ground unharmed. If his army were to run out of food, he could turn the stones under their feet into bread. The whole world lay prostrate before him. He was Valerianus the

Great.

Or would be when Shapur was crushed.

He rode a pure white stallion named Zeus, a gift from the citizens of Antioch to their saviour. Gazing out over his army, pride soared in his chest. Romans. The greatest people on earth, the greatest nation of all time. And they were at his command. Over to his left, an infantry soldier stumbled and fell. His helmet flew off as he hit the earth in a cloud of dust. His neck was swollen and black. Even as he breathed his last, his fingers clawed at his throat, trying to open it and let the air into his wet lungs. Another victim of the plague. Ten so far today and it was only mid-morning, and how many had died since they left Antioch? He had lost count. When they stopped tonight, he would ask a tribune for an update. But a few dead plague victims was no cause for concern. His army was large and strong and the battle was near. Rome's soldiers were the best in the world—they would not let a little thing like plague keep them from victory.

OVER THE LAST HILL they saw the sea, stretching out into the horizon like a sheet of black glass. At last they had arrived. Valens tried to remember when they had first entered Germania. It had been just after the start of the persecution, sometime in June. And here it was, June again or early July. A year! A year of their lives. A year of changes he could scarcely comprehend. But soon it would all be over. *Take this cup from me, Lord*, he prayed.

Below them was a village of huts and tents. There were people everywhere. A group of children was playing a game with an inflated pig bladder. Women were washing clothes, carrying water, chatting with neighbours. Four men were building a large hall, not unlike the hall in the abandoned village where they had spent the winter. A ship was entering the harbour, a *trireme*. Others were following it. As they headed down the hillside into the village, the harbour filled with ships, all making their way toward shore. "Roman ships," Marcus noted. "But the men on them don't look Roman."

People waved at them as they walked through the rows of tents toward the first ship, which was pulling up beside a long dock made of huge logs lashed together with ropes. Gundabar said something to a group of men who were watching them pass, and the men began to laugh. "Do they speak Suevi?" Persephone asked him.

"Close enough," he replied.

As the *trireme* slid to a stop, a man jumped off, onto the dock. He strode toward the Clan, his face beaming with pleasure. "The-God-With-The-Blood-In-His-Fists say you here when I return," he said in broken Latin. He grabbed Valens by the shoulders. "And you here. I Kniva, King of Goths."

Valens grinned up at the Goth King. His face was split into two halves by the scar that ran up his nose and forehead to his hairline. His face was hard, like a statue chiselled out of granite, but his eyes were full of mirth. Valens liked him immediately, and, despite his reputation, he trusted him. "I am *Sankt*, and this—" Valens gestured to his wife.

Kniva released Valens and hugged Damarra. "Damarra, yes? You are beautiful, like rumours say."

Damarra blushed. "You've heard of me?"

Kniva laughed; it was deep and loud and infectious. The Goths who had disembarked behind him began laughing, too. "Some say you Valerianus' Bane; some say I Decius' Bane! We both bad for emperors, eh?"

"Yes," she whispered.

He raised her chin, studied her face. "Valerianus pay ransom for you. Much, much ransom."

Marcus's sword found the hollow of the Goth's throat. Kniva laughed harder. "No, Roman," he said, pushing the sword aside. "No ransom Damarra. The-God-With-The-Blood-In-His-Fists say take *Sankt* and Damarra east. I take east."

Marcus sheathed his sword. "My apologies, King Kniva."

"We go?" Kniva asked, pointing at his ship.

Valens nodded, "A few moments, please," he whispered.

"Yes," Kniva said. He ordered his men to start loading the horses and baggage.

Valens turned around. This was the moment he had been dreading; *one* of the moments, anyway. One by one he looked at each Clan member, then he took a deep breath and announced:

"Some of you must stay behind."

Voices rose in protest. "You cannot split up the Clan," Conall objected.

"I cannot, I *would* not. But the *Christos* wishes it."

That silenced the objections.

Conall glanced at Paulus and Regulus. "Then who will stay?" he asked.

"You and Cecht."

Conall opened his mouth to object, then nodded and bowed his head. He put his arm around his son's shoulders and drew him close.

Valens turned to Gundabar next. The German gave a start of surprise. "Me? Stay?"

Valens nodded. "And Persephone. The Christos has other plans for the two of you."

Persephone and Gundabar smiled at each other.

"And I . . . have a favour to ask of you."

"Yes," Gundabar said. "Whatever *Sankt* asks, I will do."

"Me as well, my lord," Persephone added. "Anything."

Ruth was holding Damarra's hand. Valens knelt down and took her into his arms. "I love you, Daddy," the little girl whispered in his ear.

His heart snapped. Tears threatened in his eyes, but he would not let them flow. He had to be strong for Ruth. "I love you too, Ruth," he said. "Uncle Gundabar and Aunt Persephone . . . need you to go with them."

The little girl's blue eyes grew big. "They need me?"

"Uh-huh. You and Joshua."

She grinned. "Where are we going?"

"That will be up to Uncle Gundabar."

"Okay, Daddy." She leaned over and kissed his cheek. "I'll miss you and Mommy."

"I'll miss you too, sweetheart," he whispered. He took her into his arms again, so she would not see the tears he could not hold back any longer.

Damarra kissed Joshua on the nose, then handed the sleeping baby to Persephone. Her eyes were shiny with tears. "Goodbye, Persephone," she said and they embraced.

"Goodbye, Damarra." Persephone began to weep.

Damarra cupped her cheek. "Not forever. Never forever."

Persephone smiled. "Dearest friend," she whispered. "You will always be in my prayers."

Damarra went to Gundabar. "Take good care of them," she said.

"You have my word as follower of the *Christos*," he replied. He embraced her, then kissed both her cheeks.

Finally, she knelt down and took Ruth in her arms. "I love you, sweet girl."

"I love you too, Mommy."

"Be a good girl for Aunt Persephone and Uncle Gundabar, Ruth."

"Yes, Mommy."

"And remember, I love you."

"You just told me that, Mommy."

Damarra laughed. She stood up and gave her daughter's hand to Persephone, then took her husband's arm and with the rest of the Clan followed Kniva on board the *trireme*.

Gundabar and Persephone and the children watched from shore as the *trireme* pushed off from the dock and headed back out to sea. "We'll wait here a month," Gundabar yelled after them.

Valens waved, then stood on deck with his wife and watched as their children vanished in the distance. "We'll see them again," Damarra said and hugged him.

Valens just nodded. He was *Sankt* and *Sankt* knew things the others did not. And he was sure that he would never see his children again.

THIRTY-TWO

Once the ship cleared the harbour, the Goths unfurled the sails and caught the wind. The Clan gathered at the prow to pray while Regulus and Paulus sat nearby, watching the sailors work. They prayed for God's will; they prayed for each crew member on the ship, and on the ships that were following in their wake, and they prayed for Kniva.

Mostly they prayed for *Sankt*.

Once everything was secure, Kniva joined them at the prow. Two warriors appeared from below decks with bread and cheese and mugs of yeasty beer for Kniva and his guests. Kniva laughed and slapped backs and made the odd risqué remark, sometimes about Damarra, whom he jokingly asked to be his queen if she ever tired of "the Roman." Valens found he liked the Goth king more with each passing league. It was hard to believe that this big, friendly barbarian was the man responsible for the downfall of Decius. And the downfall of Decius' successor, Emperor Gallus, who had allowed Kniva to return to Germania unpunished *and* with all his plunder and thus had won the enmity of Roman soldiers across the empire. Valens grinned. From the sound of Kniva's most recent excursions, he was doing his part to end Valerianus' reign as well.

Unfortunately, not soon enough for *Sankt*.

Kniva spent much of the journey with the Clan. He asked

them what they knew about The-God-With-The-Blood-In-His-Fists, and they told him about the *Christos*, when He had lived, His life, His death, His resurrection. Valens and Damarra told him what had happened to them during the reign of the Emperor Decius, how they had earned Valerianus' wrath and his vow to destroy them and his attempt to crucify Valens. They told him about the *Christos* forming the Clan, and their journey through Germania to the *Thing*. They attempted to describe the *Thing*, but they did not have the words to do it justice, and Damarra told Kniva that the words probably did not exist, not in the mortal realm. Finally, they told him about the gifts and the tasks the *Christos* had given them, and how Kniva was now part of that quest.

When they finished, Kniva sat and stared at them with his big hands resting on his knees. Valens knew the Goth believed everything they had told him; there was wonderment in his eyes and excitement, but no doubt. Finally, he stood up. "This *Christos* . . . is God of war?"

"He is that," said Valens.

"And . . . God of . . . love?"

"That, too," said Damarra.

"God of . . . all things?"

"Yes," Valens said. "He is the Creator. He is First and Last. He is all the universe and yet can fit in your heart."

Kniva nodded. "How you . . ." he laced his fingers together, "join him?"

They explained it. When they were done, Kniva grunted, then went off to help his crew.

"Do you think he understands?" Damarra asked.

"Probably better than most people," Valens replied.

AS HIS ARMY APPROACHED the border of Mesopotamia, Valerianus learned that Shapur had invaded the province from the south, just as he had suspected he would. A hot sun raged in a stark blue sky and all around him men sweated as they marched through the dust. They were close now, a week, no more. Based on current reconnaissance, Shapur's destination was the city of Edessa. He might beat the Persian there; he might not. But even if the Persian had begun a siege of the city, the sight of Valerianus at the head of an army would scare him off.

News of the fall of Athens had reached Valerianus the previous week. A true tragedy. The day he heard, he ordered an early halt. The priests set up an altar, and he sacrificed a bull in honour of the fallen city, a gift to insure Athena's protection as the city named in her honour was rebuilt. The next day he declared a day of rest, much to his army's delight. He sponsored athletic competitions—horse and foot races, swordplay, javelin toss, wrestling—and donated prizes for the winners—golden cups, gold and silver spears, and for the soldier with the most wins, a sword with a jewel-encrusted hilt in a leather scabbard adorned with gold and silver filigree.

The soldier who won the grand prize, a centurion from Carthage named Lucius Adonis Patricius, died of the plague two days later.

His prize sword vanished.

KNIVA'S *TRIREME* SAILED ALONG the rugged Pontic shoreline. High cliffs alternated with gorges where rivers gushed into the sea. Here and there were narrow valleys that cut through the low coastal mountains, providing access to the interior. Finally, when Valens signalled, Kniva ordered the sails lowered and the anchor dropped. He stood beside Valens gazing up at the cliffs. The water was so deep that they were only a few feet from shore. Beside them was a gorge with a small stream. "Here?" he said. "*Sankt* sure?"

"Yes, Your Excellency, this valley just west of Trapezus. This is where we must disembark." Valens held up a piece of folded parchment—a letter he had written during the crossing. "And you'll deliver this?" he asked.

"Yes," Kniva said, taking the letter. "Send messenger today, right?

"Thank you."

Kniva had planks brought out and laid down as a bridge between ship and shore. The Goths walked off the Clan's horses and provisions. The Clan followed. Kniva came ashore to say goodbye. He picked Damarra up and gave her a bear hug, then set her down. "You stay? Be Goth Queen?" he teased. She stood on her tiptoes and kissed him. "Tempting, but I'll stay with the Roman," she replied.

He gave a great laugh, then embraced Valens. "*Sankt* be safe, eh? I pray *Christos* watch you."

Valens shook his hand. "I'll pray for you too, friend."

Kniva slapped his back. "Kniva friend with Roman! Hah!"

He said farewell to the rest of the Clan, then boarded his ship and ordered the planks pulled in. He inhaled the salt air. "No Roman ships. The-God-With-The-Blood-In-His-Fists hide us from enemy. How far Trapezus?"

"Three miles, Your Excellency," Valens replied.

Kniva grinned. "Goths here. We visit. Find messenger. Pillage."

The Clan waved as Kniva and his fleet headed back out to sea, then they prepared their packs and readied the horses. The gorge was narrow, but there was room to ride and they made good time through the mountains. By the end of the second day, they were into the southern plains and for the first time since they'd started the journey, the landscape allowed them to put the horses through their paces. On the next day they crossed into Armenia. The western end of the province was a wedge separating Pontus from Mesopotamia. It was while riding across this flat, open country that Marcus noticed that they were being followed. "Horsemen. Seven of them, *Sankt*."

Valens didn't look back. "I know. They've been following us a long time."

"How long?"

Valens slowed his horse to a walk. "Over a year now."

"Pardon me?"

Valens called a halt. It was mid-afternoon, but he ordered camp set up, then he gathered the Clan around the fire. Regulus and Paulus were heading off to keep watch but Valens called them back. "We need you here, too," he told them.

The two guards glanced at each other, then came back and squatted down.

For the longest time Valens stared into the fire, saying nothing. At last he looked up. "There are seven men following us on horseback," he said.

Sukuta jumped up, his sword already in his hand. "Where?"

"A few miles back. They stopped when we stopped. They've been following us since we entered Germania."

"Are you serious?" Sukuta asked.

"Who are they?" asked Marcus.

"Valerianus' men. He's had people watching us since he became emperor."

"How do we lose them?" Marcus asked.

"We don't lose them; we let them catch us."

Complete, uncomprehending silence.

"We have a traitor in our midst," Valens said.

There were gasps and denials, but Valens shook his head. "It's true. The *Christos* told Conall, and Conall told me."

"Why did you not say anything?" Sukuta asked.

"Because it was not time."

"And now it is?"

"Now it is."

"Well who is it?" Sukuta asked.

Valens turned to Regulus and Paulus. "Which one of you wants to answer Sukuta's question?"

Regulus jumped up. "I'm no spy."

"I know," Valens said and stared at Paulus.

Paulus got up. "How long have you known?" he asked. He took a brand out of the fire, then began waving it to signal the men following them. Marcus lunged at him, but Valens grabbed his arm and pulled him back.

"For certain? Not until Conall told me. But I suspected before that. When you killed Alexander."

Paulus laughed. "Yes, I'm afraid I let my passions get away from me there. Alexander was pitting Marcus against Gundabar so he could steal Persephone. Quite a devious plan; I admit I admired him for it. But when he told me he would take Persephone by force if necessary, I had to stop him. That is no way to treat such a beautiful young woman."

"So you killed Alexander to . . ."

"To protect her honour, of course. Gundabar had the right idea there, not that he deserved Persephone either."

"Yet you didn't kill him."

"Kill Gundabar and run off with Persephone? I'm may not be the wise and wealthy Julius Valens," he sneered, "but I'm not a fool! Why should I traipse through the wilds of Germania with Persephone when I could wait until this mess was over and claim her as my prize? Besides, sometimes love must give way to duty. Surely you understand that?"

"And what exactly is your duty?"

"Valerianus wanted someone on the inside to keep you under close surveillance. He left the decision to me, so I chose . . . me!" He laughed. "I fell in love with Persephone the first time I saw her, which was the night I killed your friend, Commander Paulus, by the way. This was the perfect opportunity to be near her."

Valens mouth dropped open. "*You*? You killed Paulus?"

"Indeed," he gave a sarcastic bow. "Commander Tacitus of the *Agentes-in-Rebus* at your service. I delivered the message from the Divine Valerianus, plunged it right through your friend's heart. I chose the name Paulus in memory of your dear friend. Thought it was a nice touch."

Marcus drew his sword, but again Valens pulled him back. "And was it you that stole Marcus' Certificate of Peace?"

"That was me. Stole it and planted it in your pack."

"Why?

"Keep your enemy on edge, confused, divided—one of the basic tenets of warfare.

Marcus put his sword away. The sound of hooves was audible now. Tacitus glanced over his shoulder. His accomplices were galloping across the plain toward them. "Less than five minutes," Valens said.

"Pardon me?"

"Your men. They'll be here in less than five minutes." Valens stood up.

"Where are you going?" Tacitus snapped. He drew his sword.

Valens turned his back on Tacitus and addressed the remnants of the Clan. "Our journey is almost over. Damarra and I are being sent to witness to Valerianus, and then I . . . I am to suffer for the

Christos. The Christos did not tell me what would happen to the rest of you, but any who wish to leave may do so now. Take the horses and food. There's money in my pack to help you on your way. There is no shame in leaving."

Marcus stood up. "I will stay with you, *Sankt*."

"As will I," Sukuta said.

"And me," said Xerxes.

"Us, you mean," said Prisca.

Regulus went and stood beside Marcus. "I've seen many strange things since you bought me, Lord *Sankt*. I may not be a follower of the *Christos*, but you have been a good master, and I will see this through to the end."

Valens squeezed Regulus shoulder. "You are a good man, Regulus."

Valens turned back to Tacitus. "And you, Tacitus, this is your chance to change your life. Something happened to you and Regulus in that clearing, something not of this world."

Tacitus shook his head. "Nothing happened," he snapped. "We were temporarily blind—that's all. It meant nothing."

Valens stepped toward him. "Are you sure?"

Tacitus lifted his sword and pointed at Valens' face. "Just stay where you are and shut your mouth!"

"The *Christos* will forgive you if you ask him. Salvation is a precious gift."

Tacitus laughed. "Salvation? The Divine Valerianus offers salvation—he has given me wealth and status, all I have ever dreamed of. He is god enough for me. I do not need your *Christos*."

"Please," Damarra said. "Listen to him, Tacitus. It is not too late."

"Ah," Tacitus moaned, "the beautiful Damarra. Perhaps Valerianus will give you to me as a plaything?"

Valens scowled at him.

Tacitus laughed. "Oh-ho! What would your *Christos* think if he saw that look on your face?" Suddenly, Tacitus grabbed Damarra's wrist and dragged her into his arms.

Valens lunged at him. His fist caught Tacitus' chin, and he went down in a shower of dust. Tacitus rolled over and jumped to his feet, snarling. "I will *kill* you for that," he yelled.

Marcus drew his sword and jumped in between them. He turned Tacitus' thrust, then struck him across the chin with the hilt of his sword, knocking him down again. He lay there dazed, shaking his head.

Dionysius and his men rode into the encampment. With a glance Dionysius sized up the situation and jumped from his horse, his sword already out and levelled at Marcus. "Drop your sword," he barked.

Valens grinned. "Marcus, a merchant is telling you to drop your sword."

Dionysius laughed. "Very well. In the name of Emperor Valerianus, drop your sword. All of you. Remove your weapons."

Valens drew his sword and dropped it at Dionysius' feet. He nodded at the others. One by one they put their swords and knives at the big man's feet.

"By the gods, I'll *kill* you," Tacitus screamed and jumped up. He swept his sword off the ground, but Dionysius grabbed his wrist and squeezed it until the sword fell from his hand. "That will be up to the emperor," Dionysius reminded him.

Tacitus held his wrist to his chest and cursed the big Greek. "You broke it," he yelled.

"It's fine. I just saved your life."

Tacitus spit at his feet. "How do you figure that?"

"Valerianus will want to question them. Kill any of them now, and I guarantee he'll have your head."

Valens laughed. "Let me guess—Dionysius was the one who beat you up and left you in the ditch for us to find."

Tacitus' anger suddenly melted into laughter. "That was good, wasn't it? You never suspected a thing. Poor hurt Paulus. Had to lay there and let pretty Persephone take care of him—a real trial."

"That's enough, Tacitus," Dionysius said.

Tacitus smirked. "I'll find Gundabar and Persephone when this is over. And when I do, I'll gut him and your children, and your *Christos* won't be able to stop me."

"Enough!" Dionysius yelled. He turned to his men. "Tie them up. I want to get started."

"You don't need to tie us."

"Why not?" Dionysius asked.

"We want to go to Valerianus."

Dionysius looked confused. "You . . . *want* to go?"

"The *Christos* is sending us to him."

"And why would the *Christos* send you to Emperor Valerianus?"

"To tell Valerianus about the *Christos*."

Dionysius' mouth gaped open. "You're going to try and convert Emperor Valerianus. To Christianity?" he asked.

"Yes," Valens said.

"You're insane."

Valens shrugged. "Possibly . . . but we're going to do it nonetheless."

Dionysius dropped his sword back into its sheath. "All right," he said. "Let's go."

Tacitus went to his horse. "Where is the Divine Valerianus?" he asked.

"Not sure." Dionysius thought for a moment. "We'll head for the nearest garrison town; they'll know."

Valens climbed up on his horse. "Edessa," he said.

"What about Edessa?" Dionysius asked.

"That's where Valerianus is. That's where we were heading."

"And how would you know where Valerianus is?"

Valens smiled at him. "The *Christos* told me."

Dionysius laughed. "You expect me to go to Edessa because your god told you Valerianus was there?"

Tacitus mounted his horse. "The Divine Valerianus is at Edessa," he said.

"How do *you* know?" Dionysius asked.

"Because the *Christos* told Valens."

Valens laughed. "Watch yourself, Tacitus, or soon they'll be hanging a placard around *your* neck that says *Christianus Sum*!"

"Shut up!" Tacitus spat.

THIRTY-THREE

EDESSA, MESOPOTAMIA
JULY A.D. 258

The scouts returned with news before noon: Edessa was under siege. Shapur and his Persians had arrived two days before and encircled the city. There was no way in or out. The Shahanshah's engineers were constructing siege towers and *ballistae* in preparation for the initial assault on Edessa's high walls.

Valerianus raised his voice in thanksgiving to the gods. He would arrive in time. Edessa was under attack. Even now its citizens were offering sacrifices, pleading with the gods to send them a saviour who would drive the enemy back to Persia. A quick march through the midday heat and their saviour would be with them, and Shapur would learn the consequences of evoking the wrath of a Roman emperor.

A standard bearer suddenly went down and did not rise again. Another soldier snatched the standard from his dead hands and fell into line. Pride surged through Valerianus—his men knew what to do and did it without the need for constant orders. Another man lurched and fell over sideways. There was a choked scream as an officer's horse trod on the man's chest, but from the black ring of bruises around the man's neck, being trampled by a horse was a mercy. What was the official count now? A centurion had told him this morning: 4,582 plague deaths. Yes, that was it. A tragedy, but defeating Shapur was more important, and there were plenty of soldiers left to achieve that goal.

Just before they arrived at Edessa, the gods sent Valerianus an omen, proof of imminent victory. It had been months since he had thought of his daughter and her husband. His duties as emperor had consumed all his time and thought. But the sight of a small white-haired rider approaching from the north burst open the memories that duty had bottled up, and they poured into his consciousness, mixed with the latent bitterness and anger, and rekindled his thirst for vengeance. How long had it been since he'd received a report from Dionysius or Tacitus? Last fall, Dionysius had sent a message from Quintiana, a remote town on the Danube frontier, reporting that Damarra and Valens were wandering around Germania of all places. He had left them under the watchful eyes of Dionysius, but since then he had heard nothing. And nothing from Tacitus, either. Gallienus had introduced Festus Macrinus to a man claiming to be Tacitus and was not. Thinking that this False Tacitus was somehow tied to one of Valerianus' schemes, he had not corrected Gallienus. But if Tacitus was not in Rome, where was he?

The white-haired rider was closer now, and a thrill of expectation quivered in Valerianus' shoulders. He halted his horse. The rider was small enough to be a woman and . . . by the gods, it was her! Damarra! And the man riding beside her was Valens! Valerianus began to laugh. A passing officer gave him a sidelong glance, then spurred his horse on. Valerianus turned and waited. His soul lifted praises to the gods. A gift! A sign! At last, victory! At last he could pick up where the arrival of Aemilianus had forced him to leave off. Unfinished business. How he *hated* it! But now Aemilianus was dead, and Valens and Damarra were back in his hands. The world had come full circle . . . only this time he was the most powerful man in the world. No one could stop him from finishing the business he, Valens, and Damarra had begun seven years ago.

His daughter and her husband were travelling with others. One of them, the big man who made the large horse he rode look like a small pony, had to be Dionysius, although, apart from his size, he looked nothing like the commander of his bodyguard. He raised his hand in salute as he came to a halt to Valerianus' left.

"Emperor Valerianus," he said. "I have prisoners to present, Your Excellency." He turned as the others stopped. Dionysius' men formed a circle around the Clan members. "This is Marcus Gaius Fortunatus, Roman general and your son's aide."

"We have met before," Valerianus said. "You are a fine general."

Marcus bowed. "Thank you, Your Excellency."

"And a Christian, we understand."

"I am a servant of the *Christos*," Marcus admitted.

Valerianus smiled. "Perhaps we can change that."

"I doubt it, Your Excellency."

"We shall see."

"This is Xerxes," Dionysius said, pointing to the Persian. "He is a Persian officer, a member of the Cataphracts."

"An honour," Valerianus said.

"A Christian," Xerxes said, pointing at himself.

"We understand Shapur permits Christians to worship freely in his realm."

"That is correct, Your Excellency."

"But you are on Roman soil now."

"Not for much longer, Your Excellency."

The Clan laughed.

Valerianus scowled at the Persian, then pointed at the black man. "Sukuta, a slave," Dionysius said.

"Would you like your freedom?" Valerianus asked.

"I pray to the *Christos* daily for that," Sukuta replied.

More laughter from the Clan; red rose in Valerianus' cheeks.

"And these others?" Valerianus asked.

"If I may, most Divine Valerianus," Tacitus said.

Valerianus smiled. "We wondered what had become of you, Tacitus."

"You ordered me to select a spy to watch Valens and Damarra, Your Excellency. It seemed too important a task to assign to just anyone, so I selected myself."

"And who assumed the role of Tacitus at Rome?"

"My aide, Martial, Your Excellency. The nature of my work is such that few people know my face. The Divine Gallienus had never met me, so it was a simple thing to convince him Martial was me." Tacitus bowed. "Forgive me for deceiving your son, Divine One."

Valerianus gestured for him to continue.

"As you know, they call themselves the Clan," Tacitus explained. "They were led by a Suevi warrior to a clearing in Germania for a meeting with the *Christos*, which they claim took place."

A passing soldier gave a wet cough. Even from a distance the rattle in his lungs was audible. "They claim?" Valerianus prompted.

"Neither I nor the other guard, the slave Regulus over there, saw anything."

"That's because we were blinded by a great light," Regulus said.

"Are you a Christian?" Valerianus asked Regulus.

Regulus shook his head. "No, Your Excellency. But I'm starting to think I should be."

"A poor choice, we assure you." Valerianus turned back to Tacitus. "Continue, Commander," he ordered.

An officer gave a muffled cry and toppled from his horse. A nearby soldier bent to check him, then grabbed the horse's reins and marched on.

"After this meeting, we journeyed to a Goth encampment on the shores of the Black Sea."

"Kniva's encampment?" Valerianus asked.

"Yes."

"Could you find it again?"

"Easily, Your Excellency."

"Wonderful. You shall be rewarded richly for this, Commander Tacitus."

"As always, I am your servant," Tacitus said. His eyes shone with expectation. "Kniva claimed that a god whom the Goths call The-God-With-The-Blood-In-His-Fists directed him to take the Clan to the province of Pontus, just west of Trapezus."

"Tacitus gave us this information while we were still in Germania, Your Excellency," Dionysius added. "We were thus able to ride to Tomis and commandeer a ship to take us to Trapezus. We arrived several days before the Clan did, and were waiting for them when they landed."

Tacitus continued. "A few of the Clan members stayed behind with the Goths—the Suevi warrior and a slave named Persephone, Conall—Valens' Master of Horses—and Conall's son, as well as Ruth and Joshua, your daughter's children."

Valerianus looked very pleased. "Children!" he cried and clapped his hands. "Damarra, our daughter—are we a grandfather?"

Damarra did not answer.

"We wish they were here; we would so love to meet them."

"We thought we'd save them the butchery," Valens said.

Valens gave a cynical gasp. "Our own grandchildren? Do you really think we are that cruel?"

"Yes, I do," Valens said.

"Alas, you're probably right. But when this is over, we can send someone after them, bring them to their grandfather."

"I would be honoured, Most Divine Valerianus," Tacitus offered.

"Thank you, Tacitus. Now, as to this Clan, is that all?"

"The woman beside the Persian is Prisca, a slave. And the other two," Tacitus grinned, "I believe need no introduction."

"Well then, let us be on our way and see what delights await us at Edessa," Valerianus ordered.

SHAPUR WAS WAITING FOR THEM when they arrived at Edessa a few hours later. His siege engines were built but unused, waiting in the rear to be called into action. The Persian troops around the city were dug in behind defensive fortifications, waiting like the siege towers. In the middle of the open and otherwise empty plain west of the city, a solitary rider sat atop an armoured horse, an emissary from the Shapur, waiting to speak to Valerianus.

Valerianus ordered his army to make camp, and assigned Dionysius and Tacitus and their men to guard the prisoners. All the Clan and Regulus were bound hand and feet and taken to the emperor's tent to await his pleasure. Valerianus and two of his generals, as well as a unit of the imperial guard, proceeded to the field to speak with Shapur's emissary. He was a tall, dark-skinned man dressed in red silk pants and tunic. On his head was an armoured cap; at his side was a jewelled scabbard and sword. He introduced himself as Camishr, the Shapur's Field Marshall—or Spahbod, as he gave his title—and the Shahanshah's chief peace negotiator. Valerianus grinned when he heard that—so Shapur wanted to talk terms already. Just the sight of Valerianus' army was enough to frighten Shapur into suing for peace. This was going to be easier and quicker than Valerianus had hoped. "Greetings, Spahbod Camishr," Valerianus said. "What news do you bring from your master?"

Camishr grinned. His front teeth, top and bottom, were made of gold. "We have received news that you are holding one of our citizens," Camishr replied in excellent Latin. "Commander Xerxes of the Shahanshah's cavalry."

"That is correct."

"The Shahanshah demands his immediate release."

Valerianus' lips pursed together. Perhaps Shapur was trying to save face by demanding his man back. If he complied, it might quicken the negotiations. He really had no use for Xerxes, and at this point his only offense was Christianity, which Valerianus could tolerate in a foreigner. "And what does the Shahanshah offer in return?" Valerianus asked.

Camishr continued as if he had not heard the question. "The Shahanshah also demands the release of the slave Regulus and the other Clan members: the slaves Prisca and Sukuta, General Marcus Gaius Fortunatus, the lady Damarra, and Lord Valens."

"What!" Valerianus roared.

"The Shahanshah has offered sanctuary to Lord Valens and Lady Damarra, and they are thus under his protection. They were on their way to the Shahanshah's realm when they were intercepted by your soldiers. If any harm comes to any Clan member, the Emperor Valerianus and his army will be destroyed."

"Tell that Persian pig Shapur—"

"You have until dawn to meet the mighty Shapur's demands," Camishr added, then without another word turned his horse and galloped away.

Valerianus watched him go, seething, a mere breath away from launching an immediate attack . . . but his men needed rest after their long march, and he had guests tonight. He turned to speak to his general, then stopped. Perspiration dotted General Quintus' forehead. His breath rattled in his chest. Black bruises were beginning to appear under his jaw. He had seemed fine when they rode out here, a little hoarse, but otherwise fine. "You look . . . unwell," Valerianus commented.

General Quintus' eyes were glazed with fever as he looked up at his emperor and wheezed, "Give Shapur want he wants. Let the Christians go."

Before Valerianus could order the man beheaded for daring to suggest such a thing, Quintus toppled from his horse.

PANNONIA
JULY A.D. 258

"IT IS AS IF SOMEONE ORDERED every tribe in Germania to attack us," Aureolus observed.

Gallienus looked sidelong at the commander of his cavalry. They had just repelled a Juthungi raiding party, only to learn that the Quadi had crossed the Danube . . . for the second time that year. And he still had not dealt with his son's murderer, Ingenuus, who now called himself Emperor. "Changes are being made, Commander," Gallienus replied. "You and your cavalry are part of that. The empire has just come to the realization that stationing all its legions on the frontiers is no longer a sufficient defence. We need a secondary line of defence—legions posted further back to finish off invaders that make it past the frontier legions. And walls, Aureolus. The fall of Athens is poignant proof that all our cities need walls, not just those on the frontiers. Changes like that take time. And they take money."

Aureolus entire face smirked. "Money the Christians *kindly* provide."

Gallienus scowled and turned away.

"Forgive me, Your Excellency," Aureolus said. "My comment was . . . inappropriate."

"But true," Gallienus sighed. "Walls built with the mortar of Christian blood, soldiers born from the womb of Christian death."

He laughed. "I wonder if they appreciate the irony."

Gallienus fell silent. For the first time in many months he thought of his friend Marcus and his sister Damarra. They had disappeared shortly after the start of the first phase of the persecution. Why, he did not know—he had offered them protection, no one would dare touch them, and yet for some reason they had chosen to flee to . . . where? Where were they this minute? Were they even alive? He shivered and pushed their images from his thoughts.

They rode on across the gently rolling Pannonian hills. Clouds of black smoke billowed up out of the horizon, the first sign of the Quadi intruders. They had pillaged a town, then torched it. *Emperor* Ingenuus was attacking from the east and having little success; Gallienus was pressing from the west. The Quadi roamed in between, a gift from whatever gods Ingenuus worshipped—if not for the Quadi, Gallienus' hands would be wrapped around Ingenuus' throat. "The Empress Nina believes the *Christos* is sending the barbarians to punish us," he said. He had not meant to confide in Aureolus; it had just happened.

Aureolus clicked his tongue and his horse veered to the right. "I had not considered that," he said. "Perhaps she is right?"

Now that he had started, he decided to continue. He respected Aureolus. The man had risen from poverty to one of the most powerful positions in the empire. As far as Gallienus was concerned, the emperor's Master of Horses was more important even than the commander of the Praetorian Guard. It would take some time for the Roman world to grasp that, but for Gallienus it was already true—especially since Festus' betrayal had demonstrated the need to curb the Praetorian Guard. "She feels the earthquakes, the plague, the attacks on our frontiers, the death of our son, all are warnings from the *Christos*."

"Warning us of what?"

"Of worse to come if we do not stop persecuting his followers."

"Hmm. When you put it that way, it does seem . . . possible." Aureolus rubbed his chin. "What do you feel, Your Excellency?"

"We feel . . . we should wait to see what happens next."

THIRTY-FOUR

That night the emperor and his officers celebrated their impending victory over Shapur. They feasted on wild boar stuffed with pigeon and drank amphorae of wine. The officers toasted the gods and the Divine Valerianus who had deigned to join mere mortals and make their humble celebrations complete. The augurs worked ceaselessly, slaughtering one animal after another, and the future was the same in every bowel, victory for the Romans. And when one of the augurs suddenly dropped dead of the plague, his colleagues took it as a gift from the gods and opened him up to read the future in his steaming organs.

Victory.

After the feast, after the drinking, after the assurance of the gods that tomorrow Shapur would feel the yoke of Roman domination settle permanently on his shoulders, Valerianus ordered the entertainment to begin. The Clan members were untied and led out of Valerianus' tent to the feast which had been set up under the eastern stars. The imperial astrologers had consulted those same stars on Valerianus' behalf, and they had told the same story as the augur's innards: Valerianus' future was magnificent, his star ascendant, his glory brighter than any star in the night sky, brighter even than the moon, brighter even than the sun.

Officers and the local magistrates of Edessa lay on dining couches arranged on rugs rolled out on the sand. Dionysius and

Tacitus were guests as well. They had spent the afternoon cutting and shaving and looked like Romans once again. The whole area was lit by torches and a blazing bonfire that turned night into day. Across the plain, the cooking fires of the Persians twinkled, and one of the generals proclaimed that even in their fires the Persians could not match the glory of Rome. During the gales of laughter that greeted the general's quip, Valerianus rose and raised his cup, then drained it and held it out. A slave scurried over and filled it for him again, then withdrew. "Greetings, daughter," Valerianus said with a magnificent bow.

Suddenly, the night was silent.

The beautiful woman with white hair bowed her head. "Father," she said.

"And our son-in-law."

"Valerianus," Valens said. "I had hoped never to have the pleasure again."

The guests snickered. Even Valerianus laughed.

"Yes, why is it you are here?" Valerianus asked. "By all reports you could easily have avoided capture. You could be enjoying snake or spider or whatever it is that passes for a delicacy at Shapur's table."

"The *Christos* sent me."

"The *Christos* sent you to us? Why?"

"He wishes to offer you salvation, Valerianus—one last time. It is not too late, even for you. Believe on the *Christos* that you might be saved."

"You came to . . . convert us?" he asked.

Low laughter met the question. Valerianus' objections to Christianity were a matter of record. The absurdity of Valens' goal escaped no one.

"I was sent for that reason."

"Please then, tell your god we refuse."

"He knows."

"Is that the only reason you came, then?"

"Yes."

"And now, we should let you go?"

"You should, but you won't."

"And why do you say that?" He turned to his guests. "Am I

not magnanimous?"

he asked them.

"Most assuredly," one of his generals shouted, and there was a round of applause.

"You see?" he said to Valens. "Why would you doubt that I will let you go?"

"The *Christos* told me . . . that I was to suffer for Him."

"Did he?"

"He did."

"Hmmm. We'll come back to that, shall we?" He looked at Marcus. "General Marcus."

Marcus stepped forward and saluted.

"You are a Christian?"

"I am."

"You know that the punishment for professing Christianity is death?"

"I do."

"You are willing to face that punishment?"

Marcus smiled. He *beamed*. "Oh, yes, Your Excellency."

Valerianus studied him for a moment, then nodded. "Yes, I can see you *are* willing."

"I would die for the *Christos*, Your Excellency. He told me I must be ready to die for Him, and I am." Marcus dropped to his knees and raised his hands. "Before you all, I confess the name of Jesus the *Christos*, King of Heaven, King of Glory. I will never deny the *Christos*. Not iron, nor fire, nor water, nor mutilation, nor torture, nor bribe—nothing, *nothing* can persuade me to deny Him. My loyalty is absolute and—"

"Yes, yes," Valerianus waved him to silence, "don't go on so. Guards, bind this man and take him back to our tent. We will save him as a gift for our son."

Two guards came forward and grabbed Marcus by the arms. "All glory to the *Christos*!" he shouted as they dragged him away.

"Mind you, gag him," Valerianus shouted after them. He shook his head and looked at Sukuta. "You see how merciful I can be, slave?" he asked.

"I see a fool with too much power," Sukuta replied and bowed his head and added, "Your Excellency."

The Clan laughed.

A guard struck Sukuta's head with the hilt of his sword and Sukuta went down. Two guards grabbed his arms and dragged him to his feet. Rage burned in Valerianus' eyes as he turned to his guests. "How shall we destroy this one?" he asked.

"Throw him in the fire," someone yelled out.

"Drown him!"

"The sword! Cut him to pieces!"

"Quicklime! Proconsul Galerius did that in Africa! Very effective!"

Tacitus seconded that.

Valerianus turned to Valens. "And what do you think should be done with this slave?" he asked.

"I think you should let him go."

Valerianus nodded. "Very well, we shall let him go."

The guards holding his arms released him. Sukuta rubbed the back of his head where he'd been struck. Valerianus raised his hand. "We shall let him go if Valens will deny the *Christos*."

More snickering from the guests.

"Do not deny the *Christos* for me, *Sankt*," Sukuta said.

Valerianus went to Sukuta and slapped him across the face. "Silence, slave."

Valens bowed his head and mumbled a prayer.

"Ah! No praying unless it is to us," Valerianus warned him.

Valens opened his eyes. "Do you *really* believe you are a god?" he asked.

"We know we are."

"If I run you through with a sword, will you not bleed?"

"When Pilate nailed your *Christos* to a tree, did he not bleed?" Valerianus laughed. "Bleeding does not negate divinity, Valens; your own god teaches you that."

"You are no god," Valens said.

Valerianus turned to his guests. "Who are we?" he asked.

"The Divine Valerianus," Tacitus exclaimed.

"A god!" replied others.

"And who is the *Christos*?" he asked his guests.

"A carpenter!"

"A Jew!"

"A fool!"

"A criminal!"

"God Himself," cried Valens.

"The Creator," said Xerxes.

"Emmanuel," Damarra proclaimed.

"You see, Valens?" Valerianus said. "By our count, your god loses, and the god Valerianus wins. So god now offers you a choice: bow down before us and proclaim our divinity, and we, in our infinite mercy, shall let Sukuta go."

"Never," Valens said.

"Will you deny the *Christos*?" Valerianus asked.

"The only god I will deny this night is you," Valens replied.

Valerianus turned to the guard holding Sukuta's left arm. "Your sword, please."

The guard handed the emperor his sword.

Valerianus held it to Sukuta's chest: "Last chance, Valens?"

"I am sorry, Sukuta," Valens whispered.

"I am not," Sukuta told him. "I did not want to return from the *Thing*, but the *Christos* sent me back. He said I would be with Him again soon and I am ready." He looked Valerianus in the eye and grinned: "I am ready."

"Go to him, then," Valerianus said and thrust the sword through Sukuta's chest. The slave groaned once, then crumpled.

"Take him away," Valerianus ordered. The guards dragged him off into the night.

Valerianus took the sword to Prisca and wiped it clean on her leather shirt. The little slave whimpered with fright. "Fear not, slave," Valerianus said. "I am done playing games." He turned to Valens. "I attempted to crucify you once."

"I am ready," Valens said.

"Ah yes, the great Confessor Valens. Isn't that what the Christians call you? Holy Confessor? Blessed One? *Sankt*? Never a concern for his own life. That has always been true, hasn't it?"

"I don't know what you mean."

"I mean that you never feared death. Your own death, that is. Think back, my friend. You risked everything for honour, remember? You accepted Emperor Philip's request to serve as Praefect of Rome, even though you knew it might cost you your life."

"That is true."

"You risked your life for love, remember? You and me and the *tali* dice for the hand of the fair Damarra?"

"Yes."

"You risked your life for Rome. You risked it for the Christians. And then, at the end of the game, you risked it for the *Christos*. You let Commander Croatus drive nails through your wrists. Because you are a man willing to risk your own life."

"What is your point, Your Excellency?"

"Our point?" Valerianus went to Damarra and rested the blade of the sword on her shoulder. "Our point is that you will risk your own life, but we do not believe you will risk another's."

Valens glared at him.

"Oh, there are some lives you would risk. Sukuta, obviously. Marcus, most assuredly. Prisca, Xerxes, and Regulus over there. You would risk their lives, I'm sure." He leaned down and kissed Damarra on the cheek. "But not her life, Valens. We do not believe you would risk hers."

"I am willing to die for the *Christos*," Damarra said. She turned to Valens. "Be strong, my love."

Valens grinned. "The *Christos* said I would be the one to suffer. And I am ready."

"You fool!" Valerianus laughed. Do you not see? The *Christos* knows you almost as well as we do. He knows that you would die for him. That is not a challenge, that is not *suffering*, not for *you*, not for the brave, heroic Julius Valens. We are not Christian, but we believe you misunderstood your god, Valens. When he said you would suffer, he meant you would have to watch the person you love most in this world suffer. Watch her scream in agony as the blade bites into her pretty flesh, as her bones snap, as her beautiful face is burned beyond recognition. That is suffering for you, Valens." He slid the sword across Damarra's shoulder. The edge nicked her neck, and blood swelled from the cut and slid down her chest.

"Be strong, my love," Damarra whispered.

"You see, Valens? Even our dear, sweet daughter knows that she is your weakness. If there is one thing in this world for which you would deny the *Christos*, it is Damarra. If you must choose between the *Christos* and Damarra's life, you will choose her life. Am I right?"

"I will not deny the *Christos*," Valens said, but his voice trembled.

Valerianus lifted his cup and drained it, then tossed it aside. "We have a gift for you, daughter."

"Do you feel no love for me?" Damarra asked.

He smiled. "None."

"Do you hate me?"

He smiled again. "Very much. And you? Do you feel love for us?"

"No," she confessed.

"And do you hate us?"

"No."

Valerianus placed the blade of the sword on her other shoulder and nicked her neck on that side. Blood swelled from the cut. He dipped his finger into her blood, then raised his finger to his mouth and licked it clean. "Do you hate us now?" he asked again.

She reached up with a trembling hand and touched his face. His eyes widened with surprise. "I feel . . . pity for you, Father. And sorrow. I know you can love. You loved Mariniana once."

Rage contorted his face. "How *dare* you mention her name in my presence."

"Gallienus doesn't know why you sent her away."

"He does! She was unfaithful to me; I told him that."

"Infidelity, Father? No, it was more than that . . . and I *know* what it was."

"How could you? She died before you were even born."

"I met her, Valerianus. At the *Thing*."

"What? What is this . . . *Thing*."

"A council, an assembly of warriors and chiefs under a king. We of the Clan are warriors, *Sankt* is our Chief, and we gathered under the one true king, the *Christos*. But we were not the only warriors at the *Thing*. There were many warriors, many chiefs, for when a servant of the *Christos* dies, they are admitted to the *Thing*, which never ends."

"And what does this insanity have to do with my Mariniana?"

"She was *there*, Father. At the *Thing*. Your wife, Mariniana, was a Christian, wasn't she? That was why you sent her into exile."

The blood drained from Valerianus' face. "You can't know that," he whispered. "Nobody knows that."

"And that is why you hate the Christians, why you've dedicated your life to destroying us, exterminating us. Because your wife gave her heart to the *Christos*, and you cannot be second in anyone's heart."

"She betrayed me for a dead carpenter," Valerianus screamed and struck Damarra with his fist, knocking her to the ground. He lifted his head and screeched at the bloated full moon, lost to the hatred and bitterness and bloodlust that had risen wraith-like from the deep pit of his soul. Senators and soldiers jumped to their feet for a better view as Valerianus began to kick his daughter. His screams echoed through the night. Somewhere in the darkness a war elephant trumpeted in response.

Valens ripped free of the guards and threw himself on top of Damarra. One kick broke Valens' nose. Another kick to the face and he was spitting out teeth. And then, as if some lever deep inside the emperor had been flipped, he stopped kicking, stopped screaming, stopped moving, even stopped breathing. He stood like a statue, his silk toga covered with his daughter's blood, and stared off into the night.

Groaning, Valens rolled off Damarra, then helped her up. "Are you all right?" he whispered. The pain was bad; his whole face was throbbing.

"Yes," she replied. One of her cheeks was bruised. A kick had opened a gash on her shoulder that was bleeding.

They struggled to their feet. The guards glanced at each other, then at their emperor, uncertain what to do.

Suddenly, Valerianus' face animated again. "Seize them!" he ordered.

Guards grabbed their arms and held them upright. Valerianus glanced at Valens' swollen, bloody face, and then gave a moan of mock concern. "Let us make you more comfortable," he said. He ordered a seat for the senator and a few moments later two slaves appeared with a large wooden chair with thick arms and a high back. The guards pushed Valens into the chair, then tied his arms and legs in place. When Valens was secure, Valerianus turned to Damarra. "We have a gift for you, Daughter," he said and snapped his fingers. A slave appeared with a placard, which he slipped over Damarra's neck. The sign read *Christianus Sum* in red letters.

Damarra read the words and smiled at her father. "Thank you," she said. "I shall wear it proudly."

Valerianus gave her a curt bow, then turned back to Valens. "Now, where were we before we were so rudely interrupted? Ah yes, you were telling us that you would never deny the *Christos*." Without looking, he struck Damarra a blow to the stomach. She collapsed forward, gasping for breath.

"Leave her alone!" Valens yelled.

"Do not . . . deny . . . the *Christos*," Damarra gasped.

The guards dragged her upright and Valerianus struck her again. Again she doubled over. "*Do* deny the *Christos*," Valerianus advised with a grin.

Tears streamed down Valens' face. His arms bulged as he tried to break free of the ropes, the chair rocked with his effort.

"Bring out the rest of my daughter's gift," the emperor commanded.

Two slaves dragged in a long timber and laid it on the ground. They hurried away and returned a few moments later with another timber, half the size of the first, which they laid across the first timber, about two feet from the top.

A cross.

Valens saw it and his face paled. "No," he whispered. His eyes flitted to the emperor. "Please, I beg you—not that."

Valerianus smiled at him. "We've had many years to think about this, Valens. We tried to crucify you and instead turned you into a Christian hero. But what would have happened, we asked ourselves, if we had started with Damarra instead? Would you be a hero today? We think not. We think you would not even be a Christian today."

"I will never deny the *Christos*," Valens whispered. Tears were streaming down his swollen face.

"Let us find out." Valerianus gestured at the cross. The guards holding Damarra walked her to it. She shook off their hands.

"Don't deny Him," she told Valens as she laid down on top of the cross.

Valens wailed with grief and doubled his efforts to escape the ropes. One of the chair legs cracked.

Xerxes and Prisca held hands and began to pray.

A soldier appeared stripped to the waist. His arms were large and muscular. He carried a mallet and spikes in his hands. "Commander Linus, this is a dear old friend of ours from Rome, Senator Julius Valens."

Linus greeted Valens with a nod. His face was expressionless.

"I'll give you anything!" Valens cried.

"Deny the Christos," Valerianus said and ordered Linus to proceed.

Linus stretched Damarra's arm out, then knelt on her hand and set the tip of the spike on her wrist.

"All my riches, all my wealth—yours."

Valerianus laughed. "I have those by law. Deny the *Christos*."

Linus lifted the mallet and struck. Damarra screamed in agony; blood squirted from her wrist. Linus struck again, and the spike was through, the tip dimpling the wood.

"Stop!" Valens screamed.

Valerianus held up his hand. Linus paused, the mallet poised to strike a third time. "What is it?" Valerianus asked.

"I will bow down to you. I will lay prostrate before you and eat the dirt under your feet. I will call you mighty emperor; I will be a loyal subject. A slave! I will be your slave. Anything you want."

Valerianus nodded his head. "All wonderful promises, which we will hold you to. But right now we want you to deny the *Christos*."

"No!" Damarra cried. Agony trembled in her voice.

"Deny the *Christos*," Valerianus demanded.

Valens hesitated. He looked at Damarra, he looked at Valerianus, his mouth opened . . .

And then a flaming arrow sailed out of the night and pierced Linus through the heart.

THIRTY-FIVE

The mallet and spikes dropped from Linus' hand, and he crumpled on top of Damarra. Fires leapt up all around them and night turned to day. Elephants trumpeted. Dying soldiers screamed. The Persians had launched a surprise night attack, and Roman soldiers were pouring out of the encampment into the plain to meet the enemy.

Valerianus drew his sword. "My horse," he cried. He spun around to the guards. "Get them into my tent. We'll finish this later."

The guards pulled Linus off Damarra and hauled her up on her feet. One of them grabbed the spike and yanked it out. Damarra screamed and fainted. The guard tossed the spike aside, then they dragged her away. Two guards untied Valens and dragged him around to the front of the tent, then tossed him inside. The guards ordered them to stay put and left. A few moments later, Xerxes and Prisca were thrown inside as well. The sounds of battle were everywhere, as if the emperor's tent were surrounded. Elephants roared; trampled soldiers screamed in agony. Metal clashed, men died, and the battle went on.

Valens crawled over to Damarra and took her into his arms. "I'm sorry," he cried. Tears dropped from his eyes onto her shirt as he rocked her back and forth. Suddenly, Marcus was beside him, examining her wrist. Xerxes and Prisca had untied him.

"She'll be fine," he said. He saw one of the emperor's togas, grabbed it, and ripped strips from it, then used them to bind her wound.

Damarra began to groan and her eyes fluttered open. Valens crushed her to his chest. "I'm sorry, I'm so sorry."

She touched his cheek, then kissed it. "It's alright," she whispered. "You were strong for the *Christos*. We both were." She looked around at the other Clan members, standing and kneeling around her. "We were all strong for the *Christos*."

"No, I wasn't strong," Valens wailed. He turned to Marcus. "I'm so sorry," he said. "I despised you because you were *lapsi*. I was so wrong. Forgive me."

Marcus embraced him. "It's alright, Valens. The *Christos* gave me the chance to stand for Him again, and this time I did!"

"It's not alright," Valens whispered. He looked at each of them, his eyes wide with anguish. "Don't you see? I was weak. I . . . I was about to give in and . . . and deny the *Christos*."

"No," Damarra said, "you would *never* do that. I *know* you."

"I *would*! I could not stand by and watch Valerianus crucify you. I couldn't do it. Thank God that arrow killed Linus. Thank God, thank God, thank God! A few seconds later and the words would have been out of my mouth."

Damarra embraced him. "Oh, my darling," she said. "The *Christos* will understand. Confess to him. He'll deal with it for you."

Nodding, Valens buried his head in her shoulder and wept.

AS THE BATTLE RAGED AROUND THEM, the Clan prayed and sang psalms. They thanked the *Christos* for this brief reprieve and asked for strength for *Sankt* when Valerianus returned to torture them again. All night Damarra and Valens held each other, all night she whispered assurances in his ear, all night he listened and wept. Toward dawn, the sound of battle lessened, and with the sun came silence. They ceased their prayers and singing to listen. Nothing stirred outside. Even the normal sounds of a military camp were absent. "Guard?" Marcus called out. The other Clan members jumped at the sound of his voice.

No response.

"Is anyone there?"

No response.

Marcus got up, took a deep breath, then stuck his head out the flap. A moment later he hurried back. "There's no one there," he said, amazed. "No guards. Nobody."

Suddenly, they heard footsteps. One person, alone. The tent flap opened and a voice ordered them outside. They went out into the bright morning sunshine, and their hearts leapt with joy. The soldier telling them to follow him was Persian. "Shapur won?" Damarra whispered incredulously.

The Persian heard her and laughed. "The Shahanshah is victorious," he said. "Now the Mighty One wishes to speak with you."

They walked slowly through the Roman camp. Cooking fires still burned here and there, and all the tents waited in neat rows, but the camp was empty. Not a single soldier was in sight. "Where is everybody?" Marcus asked.

"Dead or prisoners," the Persian replied.

The Persian led them out onto the battlefield. Dead and dying men were everywhere, some Persians, but most were Romans, and many of those were plague victims. By the time the battle had begun, over half of Valerianus' army had been infected. Soldiers had dropped dead drawing their swords; officers had tumbled from their horses without any help from Persian weaponry. More men died from wounds inflicted by plague than by the swords of the enemy.

At the far end of the battlefield, Shapur waited with his entourage to greet them. He was dressed in his royal finery. His hair and beard curled just so, his silk clothes flowing about him like colourful waves. The crown on his head was tall and regal. Xerxes bowed before him and touched his forehead to the ground, then stood. "I bring you friends from the West, Mighty Shahanshah," he said, gesturing to Valens and Damarra.

Shapur opened his arms and embraced them both, then beamed as they bowed as Xerxes had done. "Welcome, friends," he exclaimed. "May you know peace and prosperity under our benevolent rule."

"We are your loyal servants," Valens said and bowed again.

Shapur glanced at Damarra and frowned. "Your hand is injured," he said. "We shall summon the physicians."

Damarra bowed. "Thank you, Your Excellency."

"But first, we wish you to see something." Shapur clapped, and from behind him came two guards dragging Emperor Valerianus between them. The emperor was in chains. "We believe you know this fool," Shapur said to Damarra.

Damarra gaped at Valerianus, unable to believe what she was seeing.

Shapur laughed. "So end all who dare challenge Shahanshah Shapur." He swept his hand to the left, where a long line of prisoners were already beginning the long march back to Ctesiphon and slavery. She recognized Tacitus and Dionysius; the two of them were chained together.

The Persian host raised a mighty cheer which continued for five minutes. At last Shapur raised his hands for silence. "They tell us this has never happened before. Never has an emperor of Rome been captured and thrown into chains and dragged off as a prisoner to a foreign land."

"No," Valens said. "No emperor has suffered such a fate."

"Ah, the mighty Shapur leads the way in this as well," he said. "When we return to Ctesiphon, we shall have the story of our victory engraved on rock for all to read. History shall remember Shapur as the Shahanshah who defeated a Roman emperor."

"It is truly a great victory, O Mighty One," Valens agreed.

"I demand you release me," Valerianus yelled. His eyes were black with rage, but with that rage was fear.

Shapur laughed. "We hear it is said in the streets of Rome that one Roman soldier is worth ten Persians." He held his hands out and shook his head. "That equation does not seem correct to us!"

More cheers.

"Release me, now," Valerianus demanded. "This is no way to treat an emperor. I would never have treated you this way."

"Of course," Shapur said. "Guards, release him."

The guards let him go and the weight of the chains dragged him to his knees.

"Much better," said Shapur, then he called for his horse. A groom brought the animal to him. The horse's saddle was studded with gems and the beast was covered with a blanket of iron plates. "Now, Emperor of Rome: on your hands and knees."

"What!" Valerianus roared.

"We wish to mount our horse. We will use the Roman emperor as a footstool. Down on your hands and knees."

"I will do no such thing."

A guard struck Valerianus in the back of the head. "How dare you!" Valerianus screamed. "I am Valerianus the Great; I am god, and I say this is not the end. One day I will stand in glory in your throne room, Shapur! It has been foretold!"

Shapur grinned at him. "Prophecy is sometimes fickle, Emperor Valerianus." He nodded, and the guard struck Valerianus in the kidneys with the flat of his sword. With a gasp, Valerianus fell forward onto his hands. Shapur stepped on his back and mounted his horse. Picking up the reins, he turned to the Clan. "You are free. You may return to your home if you wish. If you come to Ctesiphon with us, you will live as kings. The choice is yours." He pointed at Valerianus and said to the guards, "Bring him. I wish to dismount at my tent."

Shapur spurred his horse and rode away. The guards dragged Valerianus to his feet. He glared at Damarra and Valens. "This is not over," he hissed.

"I think it is," Valens said. "I think this time you are finished."

"I will be back and I will destroy you," Valerianus vowed.

Damarra stepped up beside her husband. "Do not think of this as failure, Father; think of it as a chance for redemption. Your last chance. You can go into captivity and let your schemes and plans eat what remains of your soul away, or you can start again. Turn to the *Christos* in your hour of need; He will be there for you. All you have to do is ask."

"A god does not need a carpenter's help," he spat and the guards dragged him away.

EPILOGUE

PANNONIA
AUGUST A.D. 258

G allienus rode his horse off the battlefield, so weary that he could barely stay in the saddle. The usurper Ingenuus was dead. When he saw that the battle was lost, he fell upon his sword in despair: better to die by his own hand then suffer Gallienus' wrath. Gallienus glanced back. A sea of corpses as far as the eye could see—and all of them Roman. The Germans were pouring over the Rhine, the Persians were flooding Mesopotamia, and here he was killing Romans.

He continued back to his camp, wondering what to do next. This morning he had received news from Illyricum: his general, Regalianus, had just been declared emperor by his troops. And so while Ingenuus' blood had not yet cooled, another usurper had risen to take his place. Gallienus sighed with weariness. When would this cycle end?

He thought of Nina at home in Italy. What would she say about this development? He knew. He could hear her voice ringing once again in his ears: *Every step you take against the Christians results in tragedy for us.*

She believed the *Christos* was behind the trials the empire was facing. And maybe she was right.

Let my people go . . .

He came to his tent and dismounted. Inside, a dispatch from

the East was waiting on his desk. "More bad news," he whispered.

And he was right.

The Battle of Edessa. A Persian victory. And Valerianus a captive at Ctesiphon. He put the document down, rubbed his eyes, then picked it up and read it again. Still devastating. The dispatch pouch also contained a letter. From Valerianus—details of the battle (from his perspective), an account of the march to Ctesiphon, his mistreatment by Shapur.

First your father . . .

Demands that Gallienus ransom his colleague or launch a campaign against Shapur and free him.

. . . then you . . .

He set the letter down. A ransom. Millions of *denarii* for what? To free the man who had killed his mother? So he could continue losing soldiers and butchering the innocent?

. . . then the empire . . .

No. No more. It had to stop here and now.

Let my people go . . .

Nina was right.

Gallienus summoned his scribes, and before night fell over Pannonia, he drafted a new edict and sent it out to the Roman world. And then he went to bed and slept better than he had in many, many years.

The Toleration Edict of Gallienus

"The emperor Caesar Publius Licinius Gallienus Pius Felix Augustus to Dionysius and Pinnas and Demetrius and the other [episcopi]. I have given my order that the benefit of my bounty should be published throughout all the world, to the intent that the places of [Christian] worship should be [returned to their rightful owners], and . . . also that none may [persecute] you."

CTESIPHON, PERSIA
A.D. 260

THE EMBASSY FROM ROME waited three weeks to see the Shahan-shah Shapur. On their arrival, they were escorted to an elegant palace on the banks of the Tigris River. As was customary with Shapur, the diplomats were treated with respect and even doted upon. The finest wines were available and sumptuous delicacies the likes of which none of the ambassadors had ever tasted. Daily they were entertained by acrobats, gymnasts, dancing girls, and magicians; their hosts provided everything the ambassadors requested. The head ambassador, Marcus Gaius Fortunatus, later told his friend and emperor, Gallienus, that the Persians had treated them so well that he had been tempted to stay in Ctesiphon permanently.

At the end of three weeks, the embassy was granted an audience with the Shahanshah. They were admitted to the throne room through two massive doors covered with gold plating and studded with gems. Inside, the walls were made of gold on which craftsmen had etched images of the glories of Shapur's reign. One whole wall, directly behind the throne, was dedicated to the Battle of Edessa. The final act depicted Shapur mounting his horse by stepping on Valerianus' back.

Shapur's throne was carved out of alabaster and inset with ivory and pearl and a thousand rubies and emeralds. The floor about the throne was silver and gold, engraved with more images of Shapur's victories. At his feet lay a tiger from India. About its neck was a diamond collar. It purred as the ambassadors approached, watching them with its green eyes. Shapur rose and they bent down before him. "Rise, friends," he said, and the ambassadors stood up. Marcus approached with a chest. "A gift from the Emperor Gallienus," he said. Slaves came forward, took the chest, and opened it. Shapur looked inside and smiled. It was filled with gold coins and jewels.

"Beautiful," he said, then snapped his fingers and two slaves appeared with a bigger chest and handed it to Marcus. Not even in the giving of gifts would Shapur allow a Roman emperor to best him. "And now, you wish to see Valerianus?" he asked.

Marcus bowed his head. "If it pleases you, O Mighty Shapur."

Shapur lifted his hand and gestured at a curtain beside his throne. The curtain pulled back to reveal Valerianus. He wore a crown of gold and silver upon his head and was dressed in his imperial finery: a purple toga and crimson cape. Shapur laughed. "Beautiful, is he not? The prophets of Rome promised he would stand in glory in my throne room one day, and so he does!"

"May I approach him?" Marcus asked.

Shapur nodded.

Marcus climbed the stairs to Shapur's throne, then entered the display on the right. He studied Valerianus with a critical eye. The emperor held a sword in his hand, which pointed at Shapur's throne. Obviously Shapur's idea of a joke. He reached out and touched Valerianus face. The skin felt cold, unreal, and the eyes glittered in a way that was vaguely . . . disturbing. The artist had somehow captured Valerianus' madness. "How did you accomplish this?" Marcus asked, impressed despite the nausea churning in his stomach.

Shapur joined him and explained. "The skin was flayed from his body in one piece, then preserved and stuffed with manure. Very lifelike, we believe."

"Yes, Your Excellency." What else could he say? It was a horrific reminder of a cruel man who had suffered a fate not even he had deserved.

"The eyes are gems," Shapur said. "Carved and coloured to look like human eyes." Shapur gestured to the rest of the embassy, which was waiting below. Every face was locked in the same grimace of horror. Marcus bowed and returned to his colleagues. "You will take news of this to Gallienus," Shapur ordered.

"Yes, Your Excellency."

Shapur grinned. "If he wishes to join his father, all he need do is come. The mighty arm of Persia will oblige him."

"Yes, Your Excellency."

"We believe that Rome has learned a valuable lesson, Ambassador Marcus."

Marcus hoped it was true. But lessons had a way of fading with time, and what this generation had learned at the cost of so much blood, the next generation might forget. The Christians had

peace. For now.
But for how long?

AFTERWORD

Emperor Gallienus had the dubious honour of ruling the Roman Empire during the darkest days of the Third Century Crisis. Warfare was endemic. Several major and countless minor invasions on the Northern Frontier effectively redrew the map of the Western Empire, and after Valerianus' catastrophic defeat at the Battle of Edessa, Gallienus also had to contend with rebellions and invasions in the East. During his fifteen year reign, no less than eighteen usurpers rose to challenge his rule, a record he could happily have done without. It is a wonder his sword ever saw the inside of its sheath.

Criticism of Gallienus is often unjust and fails to take into account his accomplishments. That he stayed in power for fifteen years during the worst of the Third Century Crisis is in itself a miracle, especially when we remember that his predecessor, Aemilianus, reigned only three months. His attempt to exclude the senate from military command eventually helped his successors to reinvigorate the Empire, and his in-depth defensive policies saw fruition when cities—such as Rome in the 270s—built walls to protect themselves from the ever-increasing barbarian menace. And finally, and perhaps most significantly, Gallienus' creation of a standalone cavalry unit was a method of warfare later adopted by the barbarian tribes which eventually inherited the Western Empire. In other words, Gallienus' innovation was actually the forerunner of that oft-celebrated figure that dominated the Middle Ages: the mounted knight.

Many of Gallienus' enemies would not respond to brute force. The sword was useless against pestilence, famine, and rampant inflation, and only slightly more effective at weeding out citizens who complained about such ills. And then there were the Christians. Men like Decius, Valerianus, and Gallienus were "social scientists" conducting a brutal experiment designed to answer one question: can we solve the Christian Problem with violence alone?

The answer they discovered: Almost.

The Decian Persecution created a new group of Christians— the *lapsi,* those who denied the Christ rather than face death. The resulting controversy split the Church into three factions:

- Those who believed the *lapsi* could be forgiven after a lengthy period of penance (e.g. Cyprianus of Carthage).
- Novatianists, who subscribed to Novatianus of Rome's credo, "Once lapsed, always damned."
- The Confessors, who were considered special friends of the Christ and thus able to grant forgiveness to the *lapsi* in His name.

I have attempted to give readers a taste of this controversy without burdening them with excessive detail. Anyone interested in examining the controversy more thoroughly can find the extant works of both Cyprianus and Novatianus translated.[1] The horrific tale of the Martyrs of Utica—three hundred Christians thrown into quicklime—recounted in Chapter Thirty-One, is a fictionalization of an actual event.[2] See the *Oxford Dictionary of Popes* for the martyrdom of Sixtus II of Rome (Chapter Twenty-Nine).[3] The ini-

---

[1] Roberts, Alexander and Donaldson, James. eds. *Fathers of the Third Century: Hippolytus, Cyprian, Caius, Novatian, Appendix.* Vol. 5 in Ante-Nicene Fathers. (Peabody: Hendrickson Publishers Inc., 2004).

[2] Frend, W.H.C. *Martyrdom and Persecution in the Early Church* (New York, 1967), p. 321.

[3] Kelly, J.N.D. *The Oxford Dictionary of Popes* (Oxford, 1986), p. 21.

tial trial and exile of Cyprianus of Carthage (Chapter Nineteen), and his final trial and sentencing (Chapter Twenty-Eight), are available in Stevenson's excellent sourcebook of primary documents.[4] Gallienus' Edict of Toleration (Epilogue), which brought the Valerian Persecution to an end, has not survived, but there is extant a copy of a letter which Gallienus sent to the Egyptian bishops, which reiterates the terms of the edict.[5] Marcus' Certificate of Peace (Chapter Thirteen) is an actual Certificate of Peace,[6] with Marcus' name inserted.

The *Agentes in Rebus* which are mentioned in *Christianus Sum* and *What Rough Beast* did not actually exist until later in the third century A.D. In the mid-third century, the *Frumentarii* performed many of the duties later entrusted to the *Agentes* (and were generally hated and feared because of it). I chose to use *Agentes in Rebus* instead of *Frumentarii* because the term *Agentes* suggests an agent or "secret agent," with all its connotations to the modern reader.

The fate of Emperor Valerianus is uncertain. He was defeated by Shapur at the Battle of Edessa and taken prisoner. Sassanid carvings still exist which show Valerianus standing contritely before a mounted Shapur. That he was forced to act as Shapur's footstool, and that he was subsequently executed, flayed, and stuffed with manure or straw (or both!) is a story related by Edward Gibbon in his monumental *The Decline and Fall of the Roman Empire*.[7]

The use of "chemical warfare" at Dura-Europos was postulated by Simon James, an archaeologist from Leicester University in Great Britain, based on chemical analyses of the excavations under the walls.[8]

Finally, let me apologize to readers for taking certain chronological liberties in *What Rough Beast*. To begin with, many of the

---

[4] Stevenson, J. ed. *A New Eusebius: Documents Illustrative of the History of the Church to A.D. 337* (London, 1983), pp. 260-262.

[5] Ibid. p. 267.

[6] Ibid. p. 231.

[7] Gibbon, Edward. *The Decline and Fall of the Roman Empire* (New York, 2003), p. 161.

[8] As reported by Tanya Syed, BBC News, Monday 19 January 2009 (http://news.bbc.co.uk/2/hi/science/nature/7837826.stm).

dates are disputed by historians. Was the Battle of Edessa in A.D. 259 or 260? Did Ingenuus' rebellion predate the Battle of Edessa? Or was it a result of Valerianus' capture? Because of these controversies, and because of concerns that *What Rough Beast* might become overlong, I decided to place the final events depicted in the novel in A.D. 258, rather than 259 or 260. The actual events of 258 were "more of the same": the same two emperors running up against the same enemies they had faced the previous two years. Nothing was to be gained by putting the reader through yet another year of chaos—the point, I hope, had already been made. To any diehards out there who don't appreciate "chronology tampering," all I can say is that it happens more often than you think! And one more thing: I take full responsibility for any errors or omissions.

GLOSSARY

Agentes in Rebus:	literally "doers of things," the *Agentes in Rebus* were the Roman equivalent of the Secret Service (from which the term "agent" is derived) and was organized in the third century.
Amicula Christi:	"dear friend of the Christ;" a term of endearment used for martyrs and confessors.
antoninianus: (pl. *ni)	a large silver coin originally worth two *denarii*; by the time of Gallienus, it was little more than a bronze coin with a silver wash.
atrium:	the open central court about which Roman houses were built.
augur:	a Roman priest who read the future in the entrails of animals and the flight of birds.
augury:	a ceremony performed by augurs to interpret the future.
aureus (pl. *ei):	a gold coin originally worth twenty-five *denarii*; by A.D. 324, it was worth over four thousand *denarii* due to inflation.
ballista (pl. *ae):	a siege weapon which used a torsion spring to shoot large darts or stones.
cataphracts:	heavy armoured cavalry used especially by the Sassanids.

chatrang:	a Persian game that was a forerunner to modern chess.
Christianus Sum:	the battle cry of martyrs and confessors, literally, "I am a Christian!"
cingulum militare:	a military belt worn by Roman soldiers which protected the groin and held the sword sheath.
classis:	a Roman fleet, as in *Classis Syriaca* (the Syrian Fleet).
Curia Julia:	the senate house in the Roman Forum.
damnatio memoriae:	literally "damnation of memory"; a curse which resulted in the removal of a person's name from public records.
denarius (pl. *rii):	the base Roman coin, eventually replaced by the *antoninianus*.
Dies Solis:	literally "the Day of the Sun." or Sunday, as we call it.
ecclesia (pl. *ae):	a church. Originally, any group or gathering of Christians; in the third century A.D. it came to signify the actual church building as well.
Elysium:	or Elysian Fields. In Roman mythology, the place in the Underworld where heroes and good people spent eternity.
episcopus (pl. *pi):	a bishop.
foederatus (pl. *ti):	federates; Roman allies.
garum:	a fermented sauce made from fish guts that was a staple in Roman cooking.
gyse:	the Anglo-Saxon word for "yes."
ides:	the fifteenth or thirteenth day of a Roman month, depending on the month.
IXΘYE:	the Greek word "fish" used as an acrostic by early Christians; each letter represented the first letter in the words "*Iesous Christos Theou Huios Soter*" (Jesus the Christ, God's Son and Saviour).
kalends:	the first day of the Roman month.
lapsus (pl. *si):	a Christian who denied Christ rather than face martyrdom. The Church recognized degrees

of *lapsi*. Thus a *Libellaticus* only obtained a false certificate of sacrifice and was not considered as sinful as a *Sacrificatus*, who actually sacrificed to the gods.

libellus (pl. *li):	a certificate, as in a Certificate of Sacrifice or a Certificate of Peace.
liburna (pl. *ae):	refers to a smaller Roman warship, or warships in general.
limes:	a boundary, as in between properties or between peoples (i.e., the frontier).
Limes Germanicus:	an extensive system of frontier forts and watchtowers that protected the Roman provinces of Germania Inferior, Germania Superior, and Rhaetia from the tribes of Germania proper.
lorica (pl. *ae):	or *lorica musculata*; armour worn by high ranking Roman officers which simulated a muscular human torso.
Magister Equitum:	Master of Horses. One of the highest ranking military officials in the Roman world in the fourth and fifth centuries A.D.
meta:	the turning post at each end of the centre median (the spina) about which chariots raced in the Circus Maximus (and other circuses).
moot:	a gathering or meeting (Anglo-Saxon).
mot:	see "moot."
mulsum:	wine sweetened with honey.
onager:	a type of catapult used as a siege engine by the Romans.
peristylium:	an open courtyard and garden inside a Roman house.
quinquereme:	literally means a "five-oared" Roman warship; the actual set up is a matter of debate.
River Styx:	in Roman mythology, the river which separates the Underworld from the world of the living.
sesterces:	small silver coins originally worth one-

quarter of a denarius; they disappeared in the third century A.D., usually melted down for their silver content to make other coins.

Shahanshah: literally King of kings, the title appropriated by the rulers of the Sassanid Dynasty in Persia.

sippe: a Germanic word that designated an extended family or "clan."

Spahbod: a Sassanid military rank; second in command after the Shahanshah; a Field Marshall.

spina: the raised centre median about which chariot races were run.

stola: the long gown traditionally worn by Roman women of. *tablinum*: a room set off from the atrium and used as an office.

Thing: an assembly of warriors; variations on this term were found in many ancient Germanic languages.

triclinium: a Roman dining room.

trireme: literally "three-oared;" the exact design of this Roman ship is a matter of conjecture.

via: the Roman word for "road," as in *Via Aurelia* (the Aurelian Road).

weregild: literally "man price," a weregild was the estimated worth of a man or woman based on their status. Generally it was used to avoid blood feuds: the payment of a fine based on a murdered person's "worth" rather than exacting a death for a death. It was also used as punishment for other crimes, such as rape.

witan: a king's council of noblemen (Anglo-Saxon).